DEATH OF AN UNSIGNED BAND

Tim Thornton was born in northern England in
the early seventies. So far, he's been a member of
nine unsigned bands and two signed bands,
neither of whom acquired their record deals
during his tenure. *Death of an Unsigned Band* is
his second novel.

TIM THORNTON

Death of an Unsigned Band

VINTAGE BOOKS
London

Published by Vintage 2011

2 4 6 8 10 9 7 5 3 1

First published in Great Britain in 2010 by Jonathan Cape

Vintage
Random House, 20 Vauxhall Bridge Road,
London SW1V 2SA

www.vintage-books.co.uk

Addresses for companies within The Random House Group Limited
can be found at: www.randomhouse.co.uk/offices.htm

The Random House Group Limited Reg. No. 954009

A CIP catalogue record for this book
is available from the British Library

ISBN 9780099531876

The Random House Group Limited supports The Forest
Stewardship Council® (FSC®), the leading international forest
certification organisation. All our titles that are printed on
Greenpeace approved FSC® certified paper carry the FSC®
logo. Our paper procurement policy can be found at
www.randomhouse.co.uk/environment

MIX
Paper from
responsible sources
FSC® C016897

Printed and bound in Great Britain by
CPI Bookmarque, Croydon, CR0 4TD

FT
Pbk

To my two Cs, with love

A Brief History

Russell Groom (b.1973) spent his early childhood in Kuching, Malaysia, where his father managed various projects for a British construction company. The family returned to the UK in 1979 and settled in Bracknell. Russell did not respond well to the relocation, channelling much of his frustration into self-mastering first the guitar and later the piano.

In 1988, Russell met Jake Wilcox at school. Raised in nearby Camberley, Jake (b.1972) had been singing and playing various instruments since the age of four. Together he and Russell formed first a heavy-metal group called Nerveswill, then the indie band Plainly Amy, who achieved minor success in 1991 when their demo cassette, *Demo*, was played on BBC Radio 1's *Steve Wright in the Afternoon* show. Russell and Jake parted company acrimoniously in 1992 and did not work together again for six years.

Russell continued to play rhythm guitar in outfits of varying genre through the nineties while following a modern languages degree at the University of East Anglia, from which he graduated in 1995. After a brief period in Japan, he returned to the Greater London area in 1996 with a plan to form a new group, playing exclusively Russell Groom compositions. Auditions for members commenced and continued into 1997, eventually unearthing drummer Ashley 'Ash' Williams and bassist Karen Frost.

Ash (b.1975) had lived in the Birmingham area all his life before the offer of a job in a London call centre brought him to Brentford in 1996. Having drummed mainly for progressive rock bands, he was intrigued by the inclusion of Queen in an otherwise standard list of indie influences (Pulp, Radiohead, Manic Street Preachers, etc.) within Russell's *Rhythm* magazine advertisement, and duly responded.

Karen (b.1977) grew up in Uxbridge. At sixteen she gained a place at the Italia Conti theatre arts school in west London, but dropped out after four months. She spent the next three years playing bass for all-girl country group The Braxton Hicks, before spotting Russell's advertisement in *Loot*.

For the remainder of 1997 the newly formed three-piece continued to search for a singer while working on Russell's songs, playing a few unsatisfying gigs with Russell and Karen sharing lead-vocal duties. It wasn't until the spring of 1998 that a promising audition was conducted while Russell himself was out of the country; he returned from the trip to find the male vocalist who had impressed Ash and Karen was none other than Jake Wilcox, trying his hand at singing again after a lengthy break. After some persuasion, Russell agreed to allow his estranged former musical partner to join the group.

The line-up thus complete, the band swiftly recorded a demo tape, *Four Songs*, enthusiastically received by an experienced rock manager and two A & R departments. This interest, however, soon waned. Unperturbed, the band have been consistently active for the past three years, appearing all over the UK and completing a further four demos, *Demo* (1998), *The Yellow Cassette* and *Hook-laden* (both 1999), and *Demo* (2000), finally releasing a self-financed EP, *EP*, in January of this year.

Part One

'There are times when you wake up the morning after a gig, and your head's pounding, your back's aching, your ears are ringing, your pocket's burning with the seven whole pounds you got paid the previous night, and the thought does cross your mind – what the fuck am I *doing*? But I usually manage to hoick myself out of bed, throw the curtains open, light a ciggy, make some tea. Put one of our CDs on, whack it up loud, gaze into the mirror and tell myself it's gonna happen. Leave the bad thought there, under the duvet. Bash on to fight another day. So yeah, there's a kind of invincibility there.'

KAREN

Putney

In later years, when Russell Groom looks back over his career, he'll probably remember this moment and laugh. He'll view the whole sorry scene from whichever lofty vantage he's managed to reach – relaxing on the balcony of his river-view South Bank apartment perhaps, or maybe in the perfectly rustic garden of his ample but inoffensive house in the Cotswolds. He'll take a freshly squeezed organic mouthful from a pristine highball glass and recall the horrific embarrassment, the cringe, the series of emotionless hugs, the forced smile and stomach-curdling sight of those mindlessly happy and all-too-familiar faces grinning with alcohol-fuelled glee as they holler out those ubiquitous words, while with each wretched repeat Russell's helpless despair crescendoes as he watches the man previously eye-marked as Damo Tocks from Eluxor Records shuffle out of the room, never to return.

One blissful morning in the long hot summer of his success Russell will gaze across his roof terrace at the Colosseum or the Basilica du Sacré-Coeur, sip espresso from a spotless little white cup and cheerfully brush away the memory of this latest abortive evening like the insignificant foot soldier it'll have become within the grand tale of *How It All Happened*. He'll shake his head and marvel that even the most excruciating of events can simply vanish amid the dripping wealth of the greater story, with all its majestic strokes of luck and exhilarating injections of sheer brilliance. But, for now – right now as he stands on the dirty, three-foot-high stage in this smelly back room of a pub in Putney, uselessly swinging his bottle-green Telecaster as the last of the whoops thankfully die out – Russell Groom looks absolutely mortified.

Mercifully (or, depending on your point of view, agonisingly) the rest of the gig has been pretty good. The changeover was smoother than usual: Ash refused to share a drum kit and was able to place his pre-constructed set-up straight onto the stage without the customary palaver, the synth's connections behaved themselves, Jake appeared at the show with the proper cables for once and didn't vanish to the toilet thirty seconds before the band were due onstage. The choice of material – a well-rehearsed sprint through the best tracks from their recent demos and debut EP, along with two of Russell's more impressive new compositions ('Testing Ground' and 'Ghost of Pop') – has made for a lean and energetic set, denying Jake the chance to launch into any of his notoriously embarrassing freestyle outros. Even the regular audience (Karen's mates, Ash's colleagues from work, Jake's 'crew' – including, as usual, at least three members of his immediate family) are managing a pretty good impersonation of a knowingly hip in-crowd, helped by the addition of six animated, groovy-looking new female co-workers of Karen's from the bar at the Wimbledon Imperial. All in all, the uninitiated observer could easily believe they've stumbled across an exciting new gem of a band with a fervent, rapidly multiplying gaggle of fans.

Until the penultimate song.

KAREN: Every unsigned band knows what a fucking nightmare it is getting an A & R man down to a gig. It's a joke, a cliché. When they eventually bother to show up, you're so fucked off with the whole thing you can't actually be arsed to play them the best gig they've ever seen. There's a big part of me that always feels like, I dunno, insulting them, twatting them or throwing beer all over them.

ASH: Yeah – which is why you always end up flirting your tits off with them.

KAREN: Exactly, it's the next best thing (*laughs*).

RUSSELL: I think you're less inclined to behave like that if you're the one who's made most of the effort to get them down.

JAKE (*wearily*): Oh, fucking 'ere we go.

So how do you feel when they turn up, Russell?

RUSSELL: Relief. At first. Then nervous. Like you're at the top of a mountain, standing on a precipice. (*The others snigger, Russell remains straight-faced.*) If you step one way, you remain up there, balanced, but unsteady. Step the other way and you fall. Right to the very bottom.

JAKE (*beaming*): Like Jenga!

RUSSELL: Oh, for the love of –

JAKE: That's *exactly* like playing Jenga.

ASH: Yeah . . . know what you mean, man.

9

KAREN: Me too. You've got one chance to impress them, having chased the fuckers for the previous month –

RUSSELL: Try *four* months.

KAREN: Whatever . . . and if you fail . . .

JAKE: The whole bloody thing comes crashing down!

Is that really what it's like, Russell?

RUSSELL (*shrugs*): If you must.

It's reasonable to presume marshalling the audience through a chorus of 'Happy Birthday' to a bandmate near the climax of the most strategically important gig they've had in months was probably Jake's idea. Keeping up even the most rudimentary of appearances in front of music industry players has reportedly never sat particularly high on Jake's list of priorities (legend has it he once concluded a well-attended but drunken Water Rats performance with the words 'wank you very much, all the breast'), but at the present time one suspects Jake's agenda to be split into two equal parts: 1, to not let one's musical career get in the way of having as good a time as possible, and 2, to irritate Russell as much as possible. Happily, Jake can often kill both birds with the same stone.

Minutes after leaving the stage, he is typically unrepentant about his behaviour.

'I wanted everyone to sing "Happy Birthday" to the miserable cunt!' he barks, swigging from a can of Carling. 'He's been in such a fuckin' awful mood, I thought it would cheer him up. He probably thought everyone forgot.'

It seems unlikely Russell would care about his birthday, given the prospect of a keenly interested, prominent A & R man.

'Well, he *should* care. The guy's in severe danger of losing sight of reality right now. I mean, so what? The A & R man walked out. He probably had another gig to go to. You can't tell me "Happy Birthday" ruined everything. If he was impressed, he'd *still* be impressed. If he wasn't, he can fuck off anyway.'

Outside the pub, packing the band's equipment into the back of his estate car with heightened geometric accuracy as a result of tonight's debacle, Russell remains unconsoled by Jake's logic.

'Oh, how *convenient* for Jake to believe that. He clearly didn't see the expression on the man's face.'

Which was?

'A *smirk*. A knowing, pitying, all-dismissing smirk. The spell – completely broken. By a bunch of provincial halfwits, watching a few of their friends play at being musicians on a Thursday evening. Oh, what a jolly time we're all having. Oh, and now everyone's singing the birthday song to the rhythm guitarist, the slightly moody one who doesn't drink, but who apparently writes *all the songs*! What a clever fellow. Oh, and look, here comes my ninth pint of beer.'

Russell angrily slams Ash's cymbal case into a perfectly sized gap between a guitar amp and the bass drum, then pauses.

'But I saw him,' he says, wistfully. 'I saw him during "Testing Ground". He looked *astonished*. That bit when the synth does the sub-bass and the drums build up, then it kicks into the chorus? I could see it in his eyes. "This could be a hit." And now it's all gone.'

But surely, a hit is a hit. Why would a slightly mistimed bit of private celebration alter that?

'You don't understand. It's all about the bigger picture. The kind of band who'd sing the birthday song during a career performance might also spend their entire advance on cocaine, or get drunk before a Jools Holland appearance, or wimp out of a lengthy American tour, or make a slapdash follow-up to a Mercury Prize-winning album. These small things *matter.*'

Now seems a bad time to suggest Russell might be getting a little ahead of himself, or that he is in fact describing how 90 per cent of successful rock groups are expected to behave anyway. For what it's worth, there's hardly a soul present who found the show anything other than a triumph. Jake's followers, including his camcorder-wielding father, are uniformly ecstatic, occupying a large, loud corner of the pub where they compare highlights and ply Jake with booze. Karen is praised by a tableful of devoted friends, while Ash drinks on the pavement outside with a similarly enthusiastic gaggle of associates, including Clem and Miki from *Zinehead*, a respected, near-professional quarterly fanzine which regularly features and champions the band.

'Best one yet, I reckon,' claims Clem. Miki nods vigorously.

'Naah,' Ash smilingly protests, sucking on a roll-up. (Most of Ash's sentences begin with either 'naah' or 'yeah', the extent of vowel lengthening generally a good indicator for how drunk or stoned he is.) 'You guys *always* say that.'

'Always mean it, too,' Clem retorts. 'Not our fault you get better every time, is it?'

Miki, a small, jet-black-haired photographer from Tokyo with a camera almost bigger than she is, waves the June 2001 issue of their publication and points at the cover: this most recent one boasting snotty new London quartet The Libertines and Brighton hopefuls The Soft Parade.

'I would like to see you guys right here in September,' she gushes.

'Yeah? On the front page?'

'Uh-huh. All we've gotta do is get it past Marko.'

'Which'll be easier said than done,' Clem interjects. 'He's trying to avoid putting unsigned bands on the front these days.'

'Ah,' Ash frowns. 'Usual shite.'

'But anyhow,' Clem continues, 'you ain't gonna be in the bloody mag at all if you don't get that new EP done.'

'Yeeah,' Ash says. 'Could have a bit of trouble with that one.'

Ash refers to a bitter stalemate over the method of recording this feted new product. With the conspicuous exception of *The Yellow Cassette* (universally deemed an expensive disaster), all the band's recorded output has so far been presided over by Morgan, an enigmatic university friend of Russell's, who – while of debatable artistic talent – possesses a unique attraction in the form of his readily available and absurdly overstocked home studio. Aside from a seldom-seen cut of any sales profits, Morgan offers use of his services and equipment free of charge on the proviso that, as producer, he is allowed as free a creative rein as any band member; he is emphatically not 'just an engineer'. Although the resulting sonic experiments and finishing touches are not without merit, any poor reception the recordings receive is invariably blamed on 'Morgan's mixes'. Consequently Jake has decided to put his foot down this time and insist they work somewhere, and with someone, else: a rather flimsy resolution considering Jake's chronic inability to contribute cash for anything (unlike his bandmates, Jake has no job, and handouts from his well-off parents have recently dwindled). Karen and Ash are happy to go with the flow; Russell, while ironically the member best equipped to meet the costs of a commercial recording studio, is staunchly committed to the Morgan solution. Plans for the new EP, then, remain firmly locked in the box marked 'no one has a bloody clue what's going on with it'.

And now, as if by magic, Morgan himself ambles outside, jingling his car keys, smiling his inscrutable smile.

'Enjoy the gig, Morg?' asks Clem.

'Couldn't hear the drums,' Morgan remarks in his Lancashire brogue, mooching straight off towards his Volvo.

'He couldn't hear the *drums*?' whispers Clem. 'Was that sarcasm?'

'Yeeahh . . .' ponders Ash. 'Probably not.'

Karen appears, clutching the remnants of a pint, looking distracted. She crosses the pavement and walks out slightly into the road, squinting down the little side street running along the left-hand side of the pub. As usual, most of the assembled male eyes follow Karen's path and await her next move.

'Y'all right, Kaz?' Ash enquires.

Karen puts her index finger to her lips and beckons him over.

'Wha's goin' on?'

'Who's *that*?' she hisses, pointing down the side street.

Russell's car can be seen, wedged into the small bay by the pub's back entrance. Unlike the obsessive, hyperactive packing of earlier, Russell is now calmly leaning against his hatchback door chatting to a newcomer: a medium-height, raven-haired bloke in a light blue shirt and chunky jeans who occasionally sips from a bottle of Beck's.

'Who *is* that?' Karen repeats.

'Nah, never seen him before,' Ash replies.

'He looks . . . different.'

'Different?'

'You know what I mean. Different to the usual crowd. And he's drinking *bottled beer*.'

Ash sniggers.

'All right,' Karen shrugs, 'I know I shouldn't read too much into it, but no one drinks bottled beer at the Half Moon, specially when seeing us.'

'Yeeah . . . maybe he wasn't seeing us.'

Karen continues peering down the street. His interest in the matter concluded, Ash returns to the pavement.

'What was all that about?' Clem asks.

'Dunno,' grunts Ash. 'Bird shit.'

Karen hasn't moved.

'And why's Russ *talking* to him?'

Ash chuckles disparagingly. 'For God's sake, girl.'

'No, but d'you know what I mean, Ash? Russ never speaks to *anyone* when he's packing his car or there'll be, like, some major catastrophe when he gets to the lock-up, the bass amp won't squeeze in next to the synth, or . . . I dunno. Miki, sweetheart, can I nick a cigarette off you?'

Miki hands her one.

'Ta. But also,' she continues, lighting up, 'Russ was in, like, one of his total fucking pits of mental arse before, cos of "Happy Birthday", and –'

'I don't blame him,' admits Clem, the only onlooker so far to share Russell's view. 'What were you guys thinking?'

'Oh, who gives a fuck,' Karen snaps. 'That A & R guy probably thought we were shit anyway. But like I was saying, Russ was in a *foul* mood, so . . . sod it, I'm gonna find out who that guy is.'

She plonks her empty glass on the windowsill and marches back into the pub – busier now, following the end of the final band's set. She waves at a couple of friends queuing by the bar and hurries into the back room, now the standard post-gig scene of equipment being hoicked off the stage, groups of chatting punters gradually moving towards the exit and a drummer sweatily dismantling a kit. Karen makes a beeline for the fire escape and strides out into the yard, but Russell is alone again, lovingly wrapping a blanket around the case of his precious Telecaster before lightly nudging it into the designated slot between the synth and Ash's stand bag. At the sight of Karen he jumps (brother caught stroking hair of sister's Barbie doll) then makes a rather poor attempt at a natural smile.

'Ah, um . . . OK! Ready for your amp now, Karen.'

'Who was that, Russ?'

'What?'

'You heard me,' she glares.

'Who . . . the guy before? Oh, no one. Friend of a friend.'

'Liar.'

'No, honestly. Uh . . . your amp, if you don't mind. Rehearsal room closing soon.'

Karen gives Russell a long, suspicious stare, then saunters back into the gig room.

Back in the pub, Jake has been accosted by a cheery bloke with dungarees and ginger dreadlocks.

'Hello, mate, I'm Ginger,' he announces, in a thick Cardiff accent.

'I can tell that!' hoots Jake.

'Promising tonight. Who you managed by?'

'Managed by?' Jake grins. 'You're having a laugh, aren't you?'

'Erm . . . no, serious.'

'We're managed by no one and everyone, my friend. We're a rudderless ship. A floating vessel in a sea of whatever. Russell tries to manage us sometimes, we all ignore him. Why? D'you know someone who'd be up for it?'

'Um, yes. *I* would, see.'

'Oh yeah? You got contacts? What's your name?'

'Umm . . . Ginger,' he repeats.

'Oh, Ginger's your *actual name*! Hahahahaa!'

Ginger frowns.

'So, come on,' Jake blethers, 'who d'you know? Some record companies? Booking agents? Publishing?'

'Well,' Ginger says gently, 'first things first, eh? I'm thinkin' . . . for a start you ought to be playin' better venues than this one. Places that are more on the right circuit, y'see? I know a few things happenin' up Shoreditch way . . .'

'Shoreditch? That's east London, innit?'

'Tha's right,' Ginger nods, handing Jake a couple of flyers. 'There's some great nights starting up at the Vibe Bar and downstairs at the Strongroom . . . plus we've got a slot down the road there at the Rhythm Factory . . .'

'Oh, we don't really like all those trendy wankholes,' Jake replies, taking a cursory glance at the slips of paper. 'We like doing venues like this one, cos then it's easy for us and all our mates to get the last train home . . . Fuck me, would you look at the rack on that . . .'

Jake breaks off as one of Karen's new colleagues, a very pretty, slightly gothic-looking Mediterranean with a lip piercing, carries a couple of pints from the bar. By the time Jake turns back, Ginger has escaped.

Meanwhile, Karen has dispatched all her gear and is back outside receiving a critique from her female work friends, around whom Ash keenly hovers. Sadly the news is not all good, as the girls explain in their friendly but frank European manner.

'Some of the songs I like,' comments one, 'but some? Not so good.'

'Ah, right,' Karen nods diplomatically.

'Most of them too commercial for me,' says another. 'I no like that rocky-pop thing. Is like that band, how are they called? Starsailor.'

'You thought we sounded like Starsailor?'

'A little.'

'Christ.'

'I quite enjoy,' shrugs the young lady whose attributes Jake was previously admiring. 'Some of the good ones sound a little Dandy Warhols, y'know? But what it is with singer's hair? Long and greasy.'

'Tell me about it,' Karen agrees.

'But you,' offers a pixie-like creature with red eye make-up, 'you are good bass player.' The others eagerly nod their accord. 'You great onstage.'

'And the guitarist,' adds another, 'he perform well to the crowd.'

'Oh, yes,' enthuses the pixie, 'and he's –'

'*Gorgeous!*' they all chant, then giggle hysterically.

'More fans for Russell, eh?' smiles Ash, seizing his moment to join the circle. 'How does he do it?'

'Yep, that sounds like Russell,' summarises Clem. 'Fit as fuck, but dull as dishwater.'

'Oh, no!' Miki objects. 'That's not fair. He's . . . reserved.'

'I would not be reserved with him,' naughtily grins one of Karen's colleagues.

'Well, try chatting him up at work,' Karen suggests, to a series of blank looks. 'Didn't you know? He works at the Imperial too.'

'He does?' asks the pixie. 'I have not seen him.'

'Yep,' Karen nods. 'Not on the bars, though. He's a kind of

maintenance man during the gigs. Runs around with a radio, sorting stuff out –'

'Cleaning up vomit,' Ash adds, to a chorus of disgust.

'He does other things too,' Karen reassures the girls. 'Occasionally. Ahp, talk of the devil . . .'

Russell's car has zoomed into view from the little side street and now waits to turn onto the main road. Karen turns to Ash.

'Has he said goodbye to you?'

'Nah, he hasn't, actually.'

'Oi! Groom!' yells Karen, starting towards the vehicle.

One of Ash's larger drums is strapped in its usual place in the passenger seat, over which Russell peers as he checks for oncoming traffic. Spotting his approaching bass player, Russell floors it and lurches rightwards into the street, missing – by a hair-raising margin – a passing 22 bus that blasts its horn as it thunders by. Although Russell is halfway to Putney Bridge by the time anyone puts the realisation into words, Bottled Beer Man is clearly visible, squashed into the back of the car.

Karen and Ash are amazed, although by somewhat different things.

'Naah . . . no idea how he did it,' Ash mutters, in the vague direction of Miki and Clem. 'He's gotta be some kind of bloody contortionist, and he'll have all my cymbal stands up his arse . . .'

'I just don't get it,' moans Karen, to no one in particular. 'I mean, what the hell can he be up to? Creeping around like this, hiding a bloke in the back of his fucking car . . .'

Miki the photographer puts two and two together, and makes five.

'Is he . . . gay?' she blinks.

'Nah, bollocks,' Ash declares confidently, to a baffled shrug from Karen. 'No way. Not Russ.'

Jake's lanky frame comes barging out of the pub, clutching a tumbler of whisky.

'Anyone seen that shirtlifter?'

Karen and Ash fill Jake in on the recent episode. Karen, it now transpires, was in fact approached by Russell's mystery acquaintance as she retrieved her equipment from the gig room.

'He's got this . . . hair,' she describes. 'Hair that flops. The sort Ash tries to do but can't now his recession's started, bless his cottons.'

'Yeeahh, thanks for that, Kaz,' Ash grumbles, ruffling his nondescript, thinning brown mop.

'No offence, sweetheart,' Karen smiles. 'But this guy, well, it's kind of Alex James meets Chris Cornell. Looked pretty fit from a distance. Anyway, I'm coiling my leads and bagging my shit when he comes up, smiles in a sort of . . . ugh, quite creepy way, and says, "Great show." Quite posh voice. "Great sheeoah." Not so fit up close. Bit of stubble. One of those faces like he's been frowning too long . . . perhaps too much coke. So I said, "Really?" He says, "Yah . . . rough around the edges, but promising."'

'Rough around the edges,' Jake growls. 'I'll give him rough around his fuckin' edges.'

'Anyway,' Karen continues, 'I was about to ask who he was, when he says, really posh and a bit patronising, "Eeoahh, you must need help with your bass amp."'

Jake and Ash chuckle into their drinks.

'Which went down great, as you can tell. I didn't answer, I just squatted down and picked the fucking thing up, carried it straight out to Russ's car. Can't bear that shit. Reminds me of the first six months when you guys were still being cocks.'

'We were being polite!' Jake protests.

'Oh, yeah? Like when you insisted on giving me that shoulder massage in Hounslow, and after two minutes you were practic-ally milking me? Sleazy bastard. So anyway, I missed out asking the dude anything else . . . He'd fucked off by the time I came back for the bass.'

'Who did Russ say he was?' Ash asks.

'Friend of a friend.'

'Bullshit,' Jake remarks. 'Russ hasn't got any friends.'

'Right,' Karen agrees – then, perhaps remembering Morgan, 'well, certainly none that have other friends.'

'Karen reckons Russ picked him up,' Ash comments.

'No, Ash, I did *not* say that.'

'What,' Jake blinks, 'picked him up, as in gay?'

'Yeah,' Ash confirms, to a thump on the arm from Karen.

'I never said that, did I? Dickbrain. All I'm saying is . . . I just don't understand what he's playing at.'

'Well,' Jake states firmly, 'whatever it is, it's not a gay thing. Trust me, I've known him for –'

'Yes, yes, you've known him for years and years. So what's your explanation?'

'Dunno. Must be something else. Russell's a lot of things, but he ain't queer.'

'You just called him a shirtlifter,' Ash points out.

'Oh, I call him that, but I don't *mean* it, do I? I just mean he's a bit . . . y'know. Gay. But not *actually* gay.'

Clem, who *is* in fact 'actually' gay, feigns amused fascination at Jake's conversational cul-de-sac.

'Oh, come on,' Jake blusters, 'you know what I mean, fella. He's not *your* sort. He's just . . . oh, whatever. Has anyone picked up the money?'

The truth about Russell's behaviour remains, for the time being, shrouded in mystery. Talk moves onto other things, Clem and Miki depart ('It's way past bedtime for *my* sort,' Clem informs Jake a little acidly), Karen's friends dissipate. A finally-quite-drunk Ash is preparing to leave when an equally trolleyed female co-worker of his exits the pub with her boyfriend, shrieking with laughter as she spies Ash.

'Ahh! There you are, my little pop star!'

She throws her arms around him and plants a sloppy kiss on his cheek.

'Ooh, your band are so good, can't believe I'm gonna be working in the same office as a pop star! You'd best be nice to me, or I'll sell my story to the *Sun* when you get famous! Hahahaa!'

Ash rolls his eyes and glances apologetically at the boyfriend.

'You'd better gimme your autograph now,' she bleats, 'it'll be worth something when you're on *Top of the Pops*! Hahahahaaa!!'

The boyfriend smiles benignly and leads his drunker half away to a waiting car. Ash and Karen look at each other with tired eyes and reach a silent, unanimous decision that the evening is over.

What do you think gets a band signed?
  (*Silence.*)
  Are you of the opinion that it's mostly luck — right place, right time — or that talent will eventually out?
JAKE: Luck.
RUSSELL (*quietly*): No.
KAREN: Mixture of the two, definitely.
Ash?
ASH: Yeah . . . mixture. I mean . . . you can have all the luck

in the world, you can get . . . I dunno . . . bloody Bono accidentally showing up at your gig, but you've gotta impress him once he gets there.

KAREN: Yep.

JAKE: But I think it's one of them which creates the other.

RUSSELL (*irritably*): Sorry?

JAKE: You get the luck first – like, your mate knows the head of EMI or some important bastard personally, so he comes to see you play, then he sits you down and says what you've gotta do to impress the fuckers . . .

(*General hum of disagreement.*)

RUSSELL: You *know* it doesn't work like that.

JAKE: Oh, yeah? What about the Famous Dad rule?

RUSSELL: But even a band with the most famous fathers in the world still need to have talent . . . I mean, look at Bonham . . .

JAKE: That's a bollocks example.

KAREN: I still say it's a mixture. Like, sixty–forty.

JAKE: Which is which?

KAREN: Sixty is talent, forty is luck.

JAKE: Other way round.

ASH: Naah.

JAKE: I'd say even less than that. Thirty–eighty.

RUSSELL: Which makes a hundred and ten.

JAKE: Whatever.

What about you, Russell? What do you think gets a band signed?

RUSSELL (*sighs heavily*): Something that's uniquely attractive to a prospective record company. (*The others roll their eyes and make fake snoring sounds, which Russell ignores.*) But of course, getting signed is only half the battle. Not even half, actually.

ASH: A quarter.

JAKE: Two-ninths!

RUSSELL: Far too much emphasis is placed upon getting signed. We're all guilty of it. Me particularly, I think. (*The others nod frantically.*) But what's really important is . . . being good.

JAKE: Stop using such technical language, Russell.

So, what makes a band 'good'?

KAREN: The songs.

ASH: Rhythm section.

JAKE: The singer!

Russell?

RUSSELL: Well, inevitably, it's all of those things. But I think discipline has a lot to do with it. And analysis. Examining each bit of the music you play, and wondering how – between the four of you, or five, or three – you can make it as good as it can possibly be. (*Sees Karen miming a yawn and changes tack.*) Of course, spontaneity can be great. Sometimes you play something for the first time and it's perfect. Which is why we should record our rehearsals. We used to do that –

ASH: Yeah, but I had to sell my machine.

RUSSELL: And Morgan refuses to come and record us practise after that last argument.

KAREN: We could use my MiniDisc.

JAKE: The quality's total toilet, though.

KAREN: I'm sure it'd be good enough for us to –

RUSSELL: Anyhow, anyhow. We digress. The point is, you look at any of the great contemporary bands today, and there's a kind of . . . minimalist discipline to them, which makes their music that much more exciting. And a lack of ego. Doves, for example. Each of them as happy playing one instrument as another. Simply doesn't matter that Jimi Goodwin sings one song, plays drums on another, guitar on another . . . if that's what the song requires. And Radiohead are the masters of that, of course. Look at Ed

O'Brien – what dignity, what selflessness, what concentration. He strums the taut strings above the nut of his guitar for the entire length of 'Lucky' – a *huge* song – because that's all that's required.

JAKE: Boring.

RUSSELL: Not boring.

JAKE: I like a bit more showmanship. It's fine to be all discipliney in the studio (*Russell emits a derisive shout of laughter*) . . . but live, that's when the shackles should come off. Look at Muse.

RUSSELL (*winces*): Oh God . . .

JAKE: Stunning. The bloke's a one-man entertainment machine. I dunno how he does what he does – all I know is I've tried and failed.

ASH: Yeeah . . . luckily.

RUSSELL: The thing that destroys me about Muse is that their first album had these unbelievable moments. Pure power, dynamics, delicacy . . . little touches they stick in there to delight the listener . . . like the closing section of 'Cave' . . . and then live, they just bulldoze over the whole lot.

JAKE: Bollocks.

RUSSELL: You can see them trying, but that guy Bellamy just can't resist a good –

KAREN: Wank.

JAKE: Aw, I thought you liked 'em, Kaz?

KAREN: I do, I was just completing Russell's sentence for him.

RUSSELL: It's just so sad to see the bass player – who I think is brilliant, incidentally – looking almost embarrassed by his own singer.

JAKE: He's not gonna be embarrassed by his bank balance though, is he?

RUSSELL: No, but how long's it all going to last? The new album's pretty rubbish, I can't see them surviving beyond –

JAKE: What a crock of arse.

But even if they don't last beyond this record, that's still a fairly decent ride: a successful first album, massive support tours, success in France, and now a top-three showing in the UK with this album. Clearly they have something going for them.

RUSSELL: Clearly, but I think they need to be careful.

JAKE: I'm sure they'd really appreciate your advice, Russ. Why don't you offer your services as a consultant?

RUSSELL: And The White Stripes are another one.

KAREN: For fuck's sake, is this just gonna be a rundown of the bands Russell hates and Jake loves from now on?

All right, let's look at the whole thing another way. Why do you think you're not signed yet?

(More silence.)

Jake, why are you giggling?

JAKE: Because I love watching Russ trying to come up with answers to questions like this.

Why?

JAKE: It's all he ever thinks about. You may as well ask him to summarise his entire life.

RUSSELL: You're wrong, actually, Jake. I wasn't thinking of an answer at all. I was trying to remember whether I'd triple-locked the equipment cage. (*The other three collapse into hysterics.*) Is anyone else going to answer the question?

JAKE: No, please – after you.

RUSSELL: Well . . . I . . . (*Looks very uncomfortable.*) . . . Oh, someone else have a go, for goodness' sake.

KAREN: You know . . . we *did* almost get signed once.

It's been mentioned, yes. By Deceptive?

KAREN: Deceptive, yeah.

ASH: In the first six months.

JAKE: Ha. The Six-Month Rule.

Which is?

JAKE (*takes a deep breath*): Everything good that's ever going to happen to an unsigned band happens in the first six months. After that, you might as well fucking give up. (*The faces of Karen and Ash adopt a faintly amused 'so what the hell do you think we're still here for?' expression; Russell simply looks away.*) It sounds stupid, but to be honest – it's amazing. I've basically been in four bands in my life, give or take, and the Six-Month Rule has applied to every single one of the fuckers.

KAREN: Same for the rest of us.

What happened in your case, Karen?

KAREN: Well, in The Braxton Hicks we got taken on by a management company after about three weeks. They came to a gig by chance, whatever. We did a few tours, they got us onto this summer season thing on the south coast, we did Glastonbury –

RUSSELL: You didn't do Glastonbury.

KAREN: We did fucking Glastonbury!

JAKE: Doing one of those shit bandstands in the Green Fields is *not* 'doing Glastonbury'.

KAREN: What the fuck would you call it, then? As far as I'm concerned, we did Glastonbury.

ASH: Yeeah . . . quite right, Kaz.

JAKE (*mimicking*): Yeeaahh, quoite roight, Kezz.

KAREN: Oh, fuck off, the lot of you. Anyway, a few record companies saw us, told us all to lose weight, we refused, the management dropped us. Six months, almost to the fucking day. Then we spent the next three years wondering why the phone had stopped ringing.

RUSSELL (*very reluctantly*): It really is amazing how accurate it is. Radio play, publishing interest, festivals, tours – no matter how much you've got going on, if you don't seal it up within the first six months, it never ends up happening.

Why do you think that is?

RUSSELL: Failure to progress . . . then expired shelf life, I suppose.

JAKE: The length of an A & R bloke's attention span.

RUSSELL: I imagine if you immediately hit an interested party with a brand-new demo, say, one week after they said they liked the first one, things might be different . . .

JAKE: But who's got the bloody time or money to do that?

RUSSELL: Well, in our case we didn't really need the money . . .

JAKE: Yes, we did.

RUSSELL: We didn't, we had Morgan.

JAKE: Yeah, but that's the thing, I think Morgan's mixes were probably one of the reasons why they didn't –

RUSSELL (*coldly*): Jake, as I've told you time and time again, Morgan's production is perfectly fine –

JAKE: Yeah, compressed beyond all fuck and overloaded with twiddly shit.

RUSSELL (*angrily*): Well, this is just one of those many areas where you and I differ, Jake.

KAREN (*in 'mum' voice*): Come on, you two. Not in front of the journalist.

JAKE (*under his breath*): Well, he can fucking –

KAREN: So anyway, this is why we keep changing our band name (*laughs*).

To escape fate?

KAREN: Yeah.

Is it working?

RUSSELL: In the sense that the record company receptionists don't hang up the phone instantly, yes. But otherwise . . . as you can see, we're not exactly overwhelmed with suitors.

So what's the plan?

(*Russell screws his face up for a few seconds – for once the others are silent as they wait for his response.*)

RUSSELL (*shrugs*): We keep going. Until it happens.

Soho

Russell's trusty Volkswagen Passat creeps along Old Compton Street, mingles unsteadily with Soho's diverse midnight pedestrians and navigates a cautious left turn onto Dean Street, where it finally parks. Josh is the first to emerge, hurriedly lighting a cigarette, rubbing the part of his inner thigh pranged by Ash's hi-hat stand when Russell braked suddenly on the Wandsworth one-way system. He loiters outside the Groucho, peering into the darkened club to see if he can spot any notables, while Russell fusses with his rucksack and debates whether to hide his road atlas under one of the car seats (the band's equipment has been safely stashed en route in their rehearsal-room lock-up). Finally Josh leads Russell back towards one of Old Compton Street's all-night cafés.

'Full of queens, this gaff,' Josh volunteers, 'but they do the best late-night turkey sandwich this side of the Brooklyn Bridge. You eating anything?'

'No, just a coffee, black,' Russell replies, fiddling nervously with his mobile phone.

Josh, it seems, is a man who places much emphasis on the setting of a conversation. Hurtling around south-west London in a cumbersome ten-year-old green estate vehicle is clearly no place for a Big Chat either about himself or the band he's just seen, so when the pair settle down at one of the buzzing café's metal tables – Josh chain-smoking, contemplating his cappuccino and presently ignoring his sandwich, Russell already halfway through his coffee and considering a second one – they're pretty much starting from scratch. Josh furnishes Russell with the essentials, all delivered in his grating blend of designer street talk and posh public-school patois: he's the only child of a record producer ('Lenny Chigwell . . . dropped a lot of chunes in the seventies and eighties . . . some arranging and pre-prod for Brotherhood of Man . . . co-prodded some of the early Sheena Easton stuff . . . was Beverley Craven's first manager'), his parents split up when he was six so he divided his time between his upper-class mother ('she's one of Lord Elmuir's nieces . . . spent a lot of my kidhood at his pad near Cheltenham . . . got wanked off by one of the maids in the pantry when I was nine, that kinda thing') and his father in Sussex ('Dad had this studio so I was the classic grown-up-around-rock'n'roll nipper . . . my earliest memory was sitting at a drum kit with Pete from Smokie . . . got taught my first bar chord by Ian Wilson from Sad Café . . . used to call Hazel O'Connor "Auntie Hazel", and so on'), eventually finishing up at a boarding school near Bristol where he embarked on the standard teenage procession of bands, girls and academic failures. His twenties so far seem to have spoken the language of the trustafarian: living off parental handouts, mainly in a (reportedly modest) Chelsea flat, singing and guitaring for more bands — all of whom felt the productional touch of Daddy Chigwell, some signed ('The Eclectic . . . we were one of the last few groups to be discovered by Jonathan King before he became a paedo'), a few more dropped ('Hypotenuse . . . we died in the great cull of '97, pretty much the worst year for any guitar group to be trying to make it') — avoiding the twin pitfalls of real employment or home-minded females ('Got engaged in '98, managed to bounce at the last minute,' he grins conspiratorially), until this year when an ultimatum of sorts was issued by his grandfather.

'The old boy took me aside and ordered me to do something with my life, basically . . . he's my old man's dad so he's got this really strong working-class vibe going on, unlike mum's side of the fam whose idea of hard work is giving the servants a bollocking and pouring another brandy. So the deal is, I've got to get my arse in gear before he croaks.'

Russell makes a few awkwardly sympathetic noises at this, finishes the last of his coffee and launches into his own life story, but Josh's attention wanders after a few sentences, he lights another cigarette and curtly cuts to what is clearly his main agenda.

'Russell, mate, I don't know you too well but I can tell you're a wholesome dude. I'm not gonna shit you about. I need a break, and I need a bunch of coolios to break it with. Right now, you and your crew are on a B-road to Shitsworth in the London Borough of Nowhere. But together, we can get a first-class ticket to Fame Central.'

It's hard to tell whether Russell's ensuing gape is the result of sheer disbelief at Josh's vernacular, or whether he simply hasn't the foggiest idea what he's being told. Either way, he keeps quiet. A large group of loud, scantily dressed men descend on the table behind; Josh leans forward and lowers his voice.

'I hooked up with this manager at the end of '99, name of Barry, he's Jack the Lad and as vulgar as *Viz* but he's got contacts spilling out his anus. We tried to get some people together once or twice via the usual shit, *Maker* an' ting, but man, it was just too woesome. Decided it was better to jump in someone else's cab, so to speak – with a few little tweaks. Cos the big problem I've got – truth – is I've never been much of a song-writer. Whereas you, my friend, are a *bad* songwriter.'

Russell spots the faux-urban spin which makes this a compliment, but only just.

'Thank you.'

'No tragic, chap. The works have gotta be hung properly, no question, but the strokes are there. And that bass player? What a piece, man.'

'Karen.'

'That's the name. It speaks volumes. It's gonna do you lots of favours, dude. Like I told you when you were packing the gear, I only caught you doing your thing because I clocked it and followed her into the gig room – blown *away* when I realised she was playing. She's got gravity. She looks like a young Chrissie Hynde, but far, *far* fitter. Chrissie Hynde meets Jennifer Love Hewitt, and, fuck, if that ain't a rock'n'roll wet dream I don't know what is. You've done well to hang on to her, man, she could bounce higher *easy*.'

Russell shifts in his seat, visibly unsure of where all this is heading. Perhaps simply for something to say, he returns to the cause of his earlier discontent.

'Sorry about the birthday thing.'

Josh laughs. 'Oh, *mate*, there's your trouble, right there! It ain't what you do, it's the way that you do it. As Toto Coelo once sang.'

'Bananarama,' Russell quietly corrects.

'Same difference,' Josh shrugs. 'What I'm saying is, you can drop any shit you like onstage, with the right delivery. But in tonight's case, the damage was already done before the singing even started.'

Russell nods vigorously. 'I know. You're right. It was horrendous. Jake sounds like a bingo caller when he announces things like that to the crowd.'

(Jake's preamble was: 'Thursday is the new Friday, boys and girls, and we've got a treat from you now cos over here – Mister Russell Groom, rhythm guitarist from hell, songwriter from heaven, he turned twenty-fucking-eight today! So right now I want every single one of you, the Camberley massive, the Bagshot booze-boys, the Four Horseshoes of the apocalypse, the Wimbledon posse, the Green Man has-beens, all of you's gotta give the Groomster the biggest fuck-off Half Moon-style "Happy Birthday" Putney's ever seen, starting right now, well, right after I've handed the man himself this can of Red Bull, as he's not a drinker, old Russ, Christ knows what he does with his disposable income, but let's not worry about that, so here we go, altogether now, one, two, three . . .')

'Oh God, I almost died. You know, we had Damo Tocks from Eluxor there tonight – *Damo Tocks!*' – Josh displays indifference at this supposedly impressive name – 'and he walked *straight* out the room, right then. Ruined everything for him. And up until that moment, he was sold – I *swear.*'

Josh shakes his head sadly at this final proclamation.

'Russ, chap. Sorry to break it to you. I didn't mean before the singing of "Happy Birthday". I meant before the singing *period.*'

'Period?'

'The singing, dude. Full stop.'

Russell collects himself and knee-jerks his way into a fit of diplomacy, throughout which Josh smiles quietly and stirs his cappuccino.

'Yes – yes. You've got a point. Of *course* you've got a point. But he's . . . ah, he's surprisingly good value, Jake. He's a complete and utter nuisance, don't get me wrong, but what he lacks in finesse, he makes up for in . . . oh . . . fun factor, I suppose. He's always laughing, being laughed at, making jokes, being joked about. Never a dull moment.'

'Fun factor?' deadpans Josh. 'What – you mean, lighting his own farts, water bucket over the rehearsal-room door, that sort of fun, yeah?'

'Um . . .'

'I bet he says "ex-squeeze me" and "step into my orifice". Comedy gold.'

'Well, he –'

'If there was a musical equivalent of making a photocopy of his arse, Jake would have nailed it.'

Either Russell is inwardly quaking at Josh's accuracy, or truly feels the need to defend his abused collaborator.

'Honestly, no . . . it's weird, there was a rehearsal recently which Jake couldn't make. We got a lot more work done, but something was noticeably lacking. There was no . . . spirit, I suppose. And his voice . . . it's *so* powerful. Honestly, I've never encountered anything like it. He hardly needs a mic. Come along to this acoustic show we're doing next week in Holland Park – he probably won't even *use* a mic. This great big sound just comes cannoning out of his mouth. Oh, and he's great for networking. I'm hopeless at it. I suppose not drinking doesn't exactly endear me to people, but really . . . put Jake in any situation, any party, never mind the level of, er . . . *importance* of the people present, and within five minutes everyone there knows who he is.'

'For better or for worse.'

'Oh, for better! . . . I suppose. Well . . .'

'That wasn't a question.'

Russell sighs, defeated.

'Listen, I know Jake can initially come across as a little, um, challenging . . . perhaps even objectionable. But trust me. There's heaps of good stuff to be tapped into. He just has so . . . *much* personality.'

Josh has stopped smiling and now leans back on his metal chair, frowning as Russell clutches the remains of his straws.

'With a little coaxing from someone who knows what they're talking about, Jake would . . .'

And here Russell finally runs out of optimism.

'What?' he cries, prompting a curious glance from the table of blokes behind. 'Why're you shaking your head at me like that?'

Josh leans in again.

'He's a *disaster* onstage.'

Josh injects a little Bristol twang into the word so it rhymes with 'alabaster' and 'canasta' – somehow making the verdict more damning and absolute. In case Russell hasn't got the message, Josh repeats himself.

'A dis-*ass*-ter. He's gotta go.'

Having passed this epic judgement, Josh takes a huge bite of his turkey sandwich, leaving Russell to survey the wreckage. After ten seconds or so, Russell blankly rises and orders himself another coffee.

★　★　★

Russell must have been fairly surprised when he discovered you and Ash had auditioned Jake, six years after their fallout.

KAREN: Oh God – it was only the funniest thing I've ever seen. For Russ I s'pose it was like one of those times when your mate bumps into your ex, and you'd forgotten they even existed, and it's that sort of horrid realisation – 'oh, *shit* – they're still out there somewhere!' Russell almost shook with the shock. He was literally terrified.

And Jake had absolutely no idea that it was Russell's band?

KAREN: Well, no, but I still reckon it was just Jake being an airhead. He claims we never mentioned our guitarist's name was Russell, but we definitely showed him a picture – this shitty promo shot we got done of the three of us. But then Russell looked completely different back when Jake knew him before. I've seen photos, it's true. Russ was doing the whole grunge thing – tartan shirts, very long hair and bloody awful glasses. Now he's got contacts and looks like a fucking catalogue man, so Jake didn't know who the hell the guy in the photo was.

But Russell clicked?

KAREN: Yeah, instantly. Before we even mentioned Jake's name (*laughs*).

He'd been on holiday?

KAREN: Yeah, him and Morgan went on a 'songwriting holiday', somewhere in bloody France. And you can imagine how much fun *that* was – 'Russ, lad, pass us the fookin' Camembert. What was that chord again?' 'Morgan, I've told you time and time before, I do not take *lait* in my *café*. E diminished minor seventh.' Anyway, Jake phones up on the very day Russell left, says he saw the ad in *Melody Maker* a month ago but only just found the time to call. (*Rolls her eyes.*) Huh, yeah . . . we shoulda listened to *that* alarm bell. So me and Ash have been instructed by Russ not to 'let the grass grow under our feet', and all his usual bullshit, so we just thought, why not? Be proactive. We arranged an audition, Jake rocks up . . . and man, you've got to understand, we've been auditioning fucking singers for almost a year by this point, and we've seen the biggest bunch of tossers and weirdos you can possibly . . . (*screws up her face at the recollection*) . . . oh God, some who can't even sing a note . . . actually, *most* who can't even sing a note . . . people who turn up drunk, stoned, ill . . . one guy on crutches who shows up with a load of dog shit on his trousers . . . and, of course, people who fucking instantly start coming on to me. Then some at the complete other end of the scale, who are *too* good – there was this one guy, who was like this fifty-year-old Belgian opera singer, a really freaky long red beard, amazing voice, but dude, what do you think this *is*? A fucking Lloyd Webber musical? Then he corners Russ in the men's toilets afterwards, asks if he wants to 'come over sometime' (*laughs*). And then just before Jake got in touch, there was this bloke Matt . . . oh, it still breaks my heart . . . *such* a nice guy, he was really cool on the phone, sounded like one of us, y'know? Suggests that we all meet in a pub beforehand – me and Ash are like, 'wahey!' So we have a pint, and he's honestly the nicest guy you can think of, likes all the same music as us, cool-looking, even Russ likes him, all good. So he goes to the loo just before we leave to start the audition, and there's Ash, Russ and me having this kind of excited group hug at the pub table, all just repeating '*please* be a good singer, *please* be a good singer' over and over . . . and then of course we get to the rehearsal room and he's fucking shit. Worse than shit. He can't even *speak* into the microphone, let alone sing . . . his voice just vanished! But we think he's such a nice bloke that the audition turns into this kind of crazy singing lesson, with the three of us sitting around him, the PA switched off and everything, going – 'Matt, repeat after me, laa . . . laaaa . . . *Kaaarma police* . . . no, Matt, like this . . . *kaaaa* . . . like laaa, yeah? *Kaaarma police, arrest this maaaan* . . . maaa? M–m–m–maaa?' Jesus, it was fucking absurd. So it all ends up back in the pub, the three of us consoling him, telling him to go for some proper singing lessons. After that we're, like, *totally* crestfallen. As you can imagine. And then . . . Jake.

Did you like him immediately?

KAREN: Yeah, but don't get me wrong, I knew he'd be a handful. For one thing, he shows up with this girl he was seeing at the time, and he just says – 'Aw, she'll be all right, she's just gonna sit over there in the corner and read her magazine' – which she did, for the next *four hours*. Bit weird. And then he kept taking calls on his mobile, and nipping out for long trips to the loo – which he still does. Christ knows what he does in there. But otherwise he was a hoot. It felt like we were auditioning a character from *The Fast Show*. He kept saying all these little things about the songs, like – 'Aw, I like that one, *very* alternative, I must say' and – '*What* a chorus! *What* a hook! Listen to that, eh? Brilliant! You could hang an entire wardrobe on that!' And he had this thing of yelling 'INDIE POP!' at the top of his voice, for no reason at all. And – 'Ooh, they're *smashing*, those pumpkins!' – which he still says from time to time. I mean, he looked like shit, he had these frightful baggy black jeans on, and a *huge* Kula Shaker T-shirt, and a backwards baseball cap, and his hair was even longer then, almost down to his arse, but . . . I dunno. Something about him made me think it would work. His voice was great. He can be very ambitious – it seems to have tailed off recently, but at the beginning he was so focused he was almost aggressive. It was all, '*Why* won't you fucking sign us?!' Which, as you can imagine, Russell found *most* inappropriate (*laughs*). But Jake's incredibly gregarious – he basically gives you no choice, you've *got* to like him, or life becomes quite unbearable. (*Sighs*.) Of course, that's where Russell's found himself right now.

In the time it's taken Russell to neck his second coffee, Josh's hypothesis has effortlessly progressed from outsider's frank observation to full-scale conspiracy. Russell's eyes appear to be alive with audacious possibilities and Soho-strength caffeine, but his responses are weighed down by hefty inbuilt scruples, which Josh is ruthlessly batting away.

'Russ, chap. Step away from the vehicle for a second. Imagine I'm The Man. I'm an A & R cock from some biggie, and I'm there, at your gig. I see your band. So? The songs have their moments, the earworms are there, coupla hits – at the very least they're all workable. A decent producer like my old man would bash 'em into shape with brevity, dude. Then the band. The rhythm guitarist – well, mate, you're a good-looking cat.'

'Thank you,' Russell replies, cringing slightly.

'Respect. And your lambchops – exemplary, man. The bassist, OK, so we've covered that particular ground *déjà*. She's gonna shift ten thousand units to a herd of wanking schoolboys on the strength of her arse alone. Drummer – yep, it's adequate, a few little adjustments aside in the stylistic department. Bleached hair I thought would work for some reason – cuts back on the ol' monk progression. So, all boiled down, an industry dick like me's gonna be into it for def. Ain't much I need to fuck around with. On a purely mathematical level, that's gonna save me five Gs. Your singer, on the other hand, would still suck

Kelly Jones's nutsack after five *hundred* Gs. Ain't no getting away from it, chap. So what am I gonna do? Curtains. Fuck him off. He's dead. Jake's gone. There is no Jake.'

A dramatic pause. During which Russell draws breath to speak, but doesn't quite make it.

'Russ, man, I know. I *know.* You're a band. Solid, solid as a rock. We're in this together. All for one, one for all. Blood on blood, 'til kingdom come. And all that toss. But seriously. How much d'you wannit?'

Russell's reactions have diminished to little more than a few defeated blinks, the latest of which Josh accepts as a reply to his question.

'Because I'm telling you now, chief, I could get this thing *goin' awn* within weeks.'

Now Russell screws up his face, as if experiencing a painful bout of wind.

'Er . . . when you say "going on", you mean . . .'

'Signed, my brother. Contractually committed. The holy dotted grail.'

Russell is having an unusually hard time keeping up. Even his movements have become slow and difficult. He glares over at the café's counter and for a moment appears to be considering one of the cakes, but at last returns to face Josh, who clearly isn't remotely fazed by his companion's befuddlement.

'Russ, dude. The industry is wide open like a fucking sore. The whole sorry pack of 'em are still looking for the new Radiohead. And if they ain't looking for the new 'Head, they're looking for the new Coldplay. And if it ain't the new 'Play, it's the new Doves. Or even the new Muse. Fuck, man, some of the pricks are already looking for the new Libertines. And what's all that giving us in return? Not a lot, my friend. The most dreary heap of undeveloped wank available. My Vitriol? My anus. Starsailor? Give me strength, and while you're at it, gimme my Waterboys albums back. The Manics are dead, long live King Adora – but they probably fucking won't. Ed Harcourt? Holy shit. The Mull fucking Historical Society – what the fuck is *that*? Thank Christ for the Super Furries, but even they ain't selling much. Idlewild, The Beta Band – they're taking a very long time to be an overnight success, I must say. Toploader can fuck off. Elbow, well, it's reasonable, but they're hardly gonna set the world on fire, are they? Man, at a time when even the fucking Ash album gets to number one, no wonder everyone's ejaculating over The Strokes and Gorillaz. The time is *now*, Russ. And I can *so* put you there, chap. I got six – no, seven A & R twats literally emailing Barry every day, asking what's occurring. Not only that, my 'rentals know one or two *major* fucking arseholes who owe 'em favours. Dad can give us all the studio time we need, he can polish it up himself . . . get it *singing*. Then we send in Barry to fucking tear 'em apart. Done. Deal on the table.'

He leans back and pops the last crumb of sandwich into his mouth, before delivering the punchline.

'But not . . . I repeat . . . *not* with Jake.'

The crowd on the table behind shriek at something in the corner of the room; a closer look reveals it to be a small, motionless black mouse which one of the staff starts prodding with a broom handle. Josh continues.

'Russ, whatever your rationalisation, man – however you care to cook it – Jake may as well be striding around wearing a sandwich board saying "Music industry? Don't fucking touch us with a bargepole." Although, to be fair, that'd probably be better than what he actually *was* wearing [with sincerity none too prominent on the menu, Jake tonight sported an extra-large white T-shirt, boldly bearing the legend "WORKING CLASS HERO"]. But dude, at the end of the day, Jake smells. The guy smells *bad*.'

And now, finally exhausted by Josh's lingo and decimation of all things Jake, Russell lays both fists heavily on the table and at last starts to return some of Josh's serves.

'OK . . . look. This is all very well. You calmly appear and tell me all this stuff . . . which I can see the logic in, don't get me wrong . . . but like it or not, Jake happens to be a quarter of the band you heard tonight. He's as inseparable from what you heard as any of us. We've worked long and hard to sound as good as we did this evening – and I don't just mean blindly practising, I'm talking about every intricate detail you can think of: making sure the other instruments don't clash with Jake's register, writing and arranging the songs specifically for Jake's range, even adjusting the lyrics for his personality. To take Jake out of the equation now would send us flying backwards!'

'Then you guys ain't ever gonna get anywhere,' Josh replies, giving a tiny but endlessly dismissive shrug. 'And deep down, Russ – you *know* it.'

'Plus,' Russell continues, for the moment undeterred, 'do you *realise* what an utter nightmare it is, trying to find a singer? Have you any *idea* how long I searched before Jake turned up? Two years!'

It's Josh's turn to blink in disbelief. After about ten seconds, he leans in close across the table and murmurs, 'Erm . . . Russ?'

'Yes?'

'*Where's . . . your . . . head . . . at?!*'

Josh yells this, playfully tapping Russell's head with his fist. 'My head?' splutters Russell.

'Dude. Basement Jaxx?'

Russell looks blank.

'Oh Christ, never mind. Russ, man, what have you been *thinking* for the whole entire length of this chat? I'm talking about *me*!'

'You?'

'Rus-*sull*! For fuck's sake! Being a teetotaller certainly ain't done your brain much good, has it? I'm talking about me, Russ. *Me*. Replacing Jake. As your vocalist.'

Josh exhales and glances around the café.

'Man, I wish this joint sold beers.'

Josh's desire for a beer soon gets the better of him, and one quick phone call later he is heading further into Soho where a friend presides over a late-night drinking hole. Naturally Russell is neither invited on, nor remotely interested in this expedition, and now wordlessly steers his Passat back towards Colliers Wood, the only clue to his frantic frame of mind being the speed at which he heads down the standard thirty-miles-per-hour London streets. Halfway along Albert Embankment he reaches a cool seventy-five, then decelerates dramatically at the sight of a police car joining the road a couple of hundred yards ahead.

'Wow,' he comments. 'Time to get a grip, perhaps.'

Thoughts running wild?

'Yeah,' he nods, and for a few minutes is unable to elaborate further. Then, just past Vauxhall station:

'OK, so let's examine what we have here. Allegedly – everything I've ever wanted, on a plate, for the taking.'

He slows down for some red lights.

'But at a price.'

And does the price seem worth it?

'Sort of. But it's not just Jake though, is it? It's *him*.'

Josh?

'Correct. Let's face it, he's pretty obnoxious. Speaks like a moron. Too slick, too good-looking. Karen will probably . . . you know. Plus, it's likely he's just as unacquainted with reality as Jake is.'

But even if Jake and Josh are equally, albeit differently, offensive, it comes down to a choice between succeeding with one, or not succeeding with the other. A no-brainer?

Russell makes a face. 'More complicated than that.'

The lights turn green and he lurches off.

'Getting rid of band members is . . . tricky. It takes ages, for one thing. The right moment, the right reasons, the right place to do the deed. Also . . .'

A night bus pulls out, forcing Russell to swerve into the middle of the road.

'. . . I meant what I said to Josh, about Jake being a quarter of the band, but I wasn't only talking musically. Odd things happen when you lose personnel. The social chemistry changes. What might seem like a good idea sometimes makes things worse. I know this, I've seen it happen. Other members don't hit it off as well as they used to. Arguments start. The unit ceases to function effectively.'

Would you describe it as a model of an effective working partnership at present?

'Oh, we argue and get on each other's nerves, but we *function*.'

A bunch of partying student types chaotically traverse a zebra crossing. Russell waits in silence, making little effort to hide his disdain when the straggler of the group drops his full can of lager and spends ten or so drunken seconds trying to pick it up.

'Karen and Ash will never agree to it,' Russell mutters, pulling off again.

Morally or theoretically?

'Karen only morally, I'm fairly sure. She knows Jake is slowing us down. She *must* do.'

Ash?

'Both, probably. He and Jake have got this . . . connection. Dope smoking, and so on. Not sure Ash will like having no one to slip out for a joint with. Unless Josh . . .'

He trails off for a minute. Nearing Stockwell Tube he stops at more red lights and instinctively buzzes his window shut.

'And Ash is one of those people . . . you know, anything for a quiet life.'

Lights change.

'Plus, we've no idea whether Josh is actually any good or not! He might be rubbish.'

True.

'Oh, hang on . . . actually . . .'

Remembering that this is a concern which can be answered here and now, Russell extracts a disc (one of Josh's near misses, it is presumed) from his combats' leg pocket and prods it into the CD player. Unremarkable indie rock fills the car – distinguished by a strident baritone lead vocal: a less doomy Ian Curtis, Dave Gahan if singing for a guitar band. Russell drives on impassively as what passes for a second chorus gives way to a perfunctory instrumental break, but when the vocalist pulls off an impressive octave leap in the final swingaround Russell shrugs as if to say: 'Well, that's that one answered, then' – and unceremoniously ejects the disc.

The question of Josh's vocal proficiency is never raised again.

Russell remains lost in thought as Stockwell becomes Clapham becomes Balham, by which time his speedometer starts to nudge the higher fifties once more.

'But *something*'s got to happen,' he volunteers suddenly, slowing the car to a less conspicuous forty. 'We're dying like this. It's funny, I've spent most of the last ten years thinking the key to this whole business is to work hard, use your talents accurately and maybe benefit from, oh, just a little bit of good luck to speed you on your way. But recently I've come to realise . . . all that's probably naive nonsense. It's absurd to assume that some oh-whoops-I-just-happened-to-be-watching Mr Big will instantly sign us for huge amounts of cash, just the way we are now. Something has to *alter* before that. Something large.'

Another set of red lights.

'You see, I've started to think that unsigned bands never actually become signed bands at all. It's like expecting a wood-louse to turn into a butterfly. Being an unsigned band isn't a temporary period. An unsigned band is just another type of band.'

Not quite sure I'm with you.

'Think of any successful British rock group – Radiohead, Coldplay, Muse. None of these were ever unsigned bands. Oh, sure, they were *without a record deal* for a brief period at the start of their careers, but that's just a historical detail. In reality, they were "signed" the moment they formed . . . from the second Yorke met Greenwood, Martin met Buckland, and Bellamy met . . . [He drifts off, the names of the other Muse members escaping him.] Did you ever see these bands first on at the Water Rats on a Tuesday? No. Did you ever hear their demo on an unsigned radio contest? You did not. Did they ever play an open-mic night called "Talent Spotter", or "Undiscovered Talent", or anything else involving that word? Don't be silly. They didn't *do* things like that.'

Without having detailed biographies for any of the three bands immediately to hand, questioning this point seems futile.

'Meanwhile, in a thousand damp and foul-smelling rehearsal rooms from Inverness to Penzance, banging out derivative ideas on cheap instruments in preparation for fortnightly perform-ances at equally obnoxious pub venues, a million unsigned bands are waiting for their lottery numbers to come up. But are you ever going to see these poor so-and-sos on the cover of *NME*? Of course not. They're doomed. They might as well give up now.'

And with that, Russell is quiet again. As his big car continues to trundle south he occasionally mouths a few things to himself, at one point breaking into light laughter. Tooting is finally turning into Colliers Wood before the cause of this laughter is revealed.

'I had a conversation with Badly Drawn Boy once. He told me that if the clock hadn't started to tick by the time I was twenty-eight it never would.'

Although never articulated, it's plain that Russell now believes – in the final minutes of his twenty-eighth birthday – Josh has handed him a ticking clock.

West Kensington

What sort of an image would you like to present to your audience?

JAKE: Image? (*Shrugs.*) Good songs, played properly, by people who look like they're having a laugh. Simple as that.

What about you personally?

JAKE: Me?

As frontman.

JAKE: Never really think about it.

So there isn't some kind of conceptual aim you have in mind, however vague?

(*Silence.*)

An influence?

JAKE: I've got plenty of influences.

For example?

JAKE: Who are my influences? (*Grins, then looks slightly affronted.*) There's loads of 'em.

Come on.

JAKE: Well . . . Vedder, naturally. (*Long pause.*) Mercury. Albarn. Suggs from Madness. Axl Rose. Kate Bush. (*Looks up and frowns – then loudly, almost crossly:*) Y'see, this is why I don't like questions like this, cos you always get laughed at. Kate Bush, as it happens, is the inspiration for most of the movement I do onstage. Y'know when I'm kind of crouching at the front? That's Bush. When the guitar ain't in the way, obviously.

Any others?

JAKE: Oh, loads . . . Daltrey . . . Bon Scott . . . Cobain, Kiedis, Gallagher, Ashcroft, Thom Yorke . . . Bradfield . . . Bruce Dickinson. And then some you might not notice, Simon Le Bon, Morten Harket, Hadley . . . big fan of Michael Hutchence, of course . . . Sting – you know when I'm doing that swaying-to-and-fro thing, and then leaning back from the mic? That's Sting. Um . . . Macca, Lennon . . .'

Quite a selection. Are there any you concentrate on in particular?

JAKE: No, not really . . . I guess it all blends, bit of everything, makes it more fun to watch . . .

Don't you think that might be a little confusing for your audience?

JAKE: Aw, God, that sounds like a bloody Russell comment. He's *always* spouting that kinda shit, Russ – 'ooh, we've got to think about our audience', and 'ooh, we've got our niche market to consider' – like it's some fucking job!

And it's not?

JAKE: Oh, well, *yeah* . . . in a *way*, but not like *that* sort of job where you have to constantly think about what you do, and plan shit, and . . . I dunno, log everything on a fucking database. I always say to Russ, *when* we've got some record company or management company *paying* me to think like that, then I'll start doing it, but not before.

Russell would probably argue that such a company won't be showing interest until you start to think like that.

JAKE: Yeah, you're absolutely right, he probably would. But what does he know? Has he been signed before? No. It's the blind leading the blind. And at the end of the day, none of us know whether all this is gonna lead anywhere, so we might as well have some fun and please ourselves getting nowhere, and then if we *do* end up succeeding, it'll be a bonus. I mean, if you can't please yourself, then who the fuck can you please?

Usually they try to avoid each other for a few days after a 'big gig', but the next evening has previously been earmarked for a band meeting.

'Russell does this every so often,' Karen explains, lighting a cigarette as she waits for the others to appear. 'It's supposed to be a kind of gig post-mortem thing, but we all secretly know we're gonna get a bollocking. Whenever Russell's got something controversial to say, he arranges an actual meeting rather than just discussing stuff at rehearsals like we normally do – so if one of us storms out, we haven't wasted a rehearsal. It's also always in a place like this [she gestures around the nondescript, steadily filling West Kensington pub] – equally easy for everyone to get to, but connected to none of us. Neutral territory, as he calls it.'

Karen takes a sip of her cranberry juice (she avoids alcohol for the early part of these meetings, 'just in case things get hectic later on') and leans in across the table.

'All carefully planned,' she stage-whispers, 'to the point of nausea.'

Jake is the next to arrive, the lure of a pint perhaps assisting his timekeeping. He grabs his drink and flops down on the sofa next to Karen, pulling his Primal Scream T-shirt around his slightly distended belly, the presence of which Karen acknowledges with a hearty slap.

'Putting on a few beer pounds, Wilcox!'

'Aw, it's the summer,' Jake protests. 'Makes me drink more.'

'You say that in the winter too.'

They cheerfully compare notes on last night's gig and anticipate Russell's arrival.

'Eleven minutes late,' forecasts Jake, 'and he'll want to move somewhere with upright chairs.'

In fact Russell is only eight minutes late ('Someone pulled the emergency cord at Parsons Green! How come you both got here on time?'), but as predicted he squints at the spot Karen has chosen and glances around the pub for alternatives.

'I'm not moving a fucking inch, Groom,' Karen asserts. 'Before you say *anything*.'

Russell mumbles something and mooches off to order his customary lime and soda. A minute later, an incredibly sweaty Ash barges into the pub.

'Quick!' Jake shouts, pointing in Russell's direction. 'He hasn't paid yet!'

This game – getting the teetotal songwriter to buy Karen, Jake or Ash an alcoholic drink – is part of the Russell Olympics, bringing fleeting minutes of amusement to otherwise fun-free band situations; further Olympic fixtures include 'accidentally' putting lots of milk and sugar in Russell's coffee, giving him the wrong change and – most high-scoring of all – hiding his car. Jake once succeeded in moving it from a perfectly straightforward street space to a nearby NCP car park while Russell was on the loo; extra points were awarded as the car park had been locked for the night by the time Russell located it.

Ash grins and hurries over to the bar, greeting his waiting band captain with a suspiciously enthusiastic double handshake. Even from this distance, Russell's discomfort is all too visible as he deliberates whether or not to add Ash's pint to his own trivially priced order, bumping up the total cost by about 800 per cent. Karen and Jake watch excitedly for the triumphant moment Ash points out his desired drink's draught pump – but no. Russell mutters some sort of excuse, Ash gives a shrug and an awkward smile, then Russell grabs his glass of weak, green iced liquid and marches back towards base.

'Denied!' gasps Jake.

'OK,' mutters Karen. 'We are *definitely* in for a bollocking.'

Russell seems to occupy a strange place within the group's structure, serving as both universal object of mockery and the main creative engine room. Do these contrasting roles make working with him difficult?

KAREN: Not really. The three of us totally know that if we get anywhere, it'll be cos of Russ. We take the piss and stuff, but when push comes to shove, everyone knows that Russell knows best.

Even Jake?

KAREN: Oh, God yeah. One of the reasons Jake winds up Russ so much is cos he knows full well Russell is streets ahead of him and it drives Jake fucking bonkers. But . . . well, a lot of Jake's issues with Russ come from a different place. They've got such a lot of history, it's . . . complicated. Also, I think Jake's the only person who can get away with saying certain things to Russ, so sometimes he just says them because he *can*.

But there's also a respect there?

KAREN: Oh, God yeah. They'd be *lost* without each other.

Russell sometimes gives a different impression.

KAREN (*lights a cigarette, thinking hard*): The thing you've got to remember is . . . they're both of them at their wits' end trying to get somewhere in this stupid industry. It comes out in very different ways – Jake's bored out of his mind so he just fucks about, Russell's frustrated beyond belief so he disappears even further up his own arse, and the pair of 'em end up wanting to murder each other. But they're totally besotted with each other really. Particularly Jake with Russ . . . you should hear him after he's had a pill, banging on about what a genius Russ is.

And what do you *think of Russell yourself?*

KAREN: How do you mean?

On a personal level.

KAREN: Oh . . . well, put it this way, if I wasn't in a band with him, I wouldn't . . . I mean . . . he *is* bloody odd. The not-drinking thing alone is enough for me to think he's a weirdo.

Why doesn't he drink?

KAREN: Ha. Good question. He claims he's intolerant, that one little drop will make him keel over or fucking projectile vomit everywhere, but . . . I dunno. I saw him sneak a bit of champagne at my sister's wedding a couple of years ago and nothing disastrous happened. I reckon it's more to do with control. He *needs* to be in complete control.

He seems to have picked rather a strange career for a teetotaller.

KAREN: Tell me about it! To be honest, the amount of times I've just wanted to force a glass of wine down his throat so he fucking chills out for a while . . . it'd probably do him a lot of good, y'know? Also, he drinks his coffee by the gallon and that makes him even worse. Oh, but . . . he's a classic bloke, really. He's got quite a sense of humour, once you find it. And he means well. He was very nice to me when I had a bad break-up a year or so ago. And I'll say one thing – he *never* patronises me, as a woman. Ash and Jake have both said crap over the years, like – 'Oh, you must need a hand carrying that', or 'do you want me to come with you, cos you're a bird?' And so on. Plus all the dirty shit you hear them say about other women . . . I just don't need it. But to Russ, I'm an equal.

Has he ever been interested in you?

KAREN (*almost spits out her drink with laughter*): Russ?! Hahaha! Nah. *Never.* Not at all. I never even catch him staring at my tits like the others do. Christ knows what he *is* interested in, but it ain't me. Ash probably (*laughs*).

And you him?

KAREN: Euurrgh! *Don't!* Oh, the thought of it . . .

But he is *quite an attractive man . . .*

KAREN: Oh, no-no, don't get me wrong, he's bloody good-looking! I know *dozens* of people who fancy Russ. But they're too shit-scared to go anywhere near him, he's so . . . well, he seems so self-absorbed. But, fuck no, he's *far* too clean-cut for me. His hair, oh my God, fucking Action Man. And he hardly needs to shave. I'm just not into that pretty-boy thing.

Russell's 'bollocking' comes in four flavours: general lethargy, the Morgan recording situation, the 'birthday song' incident and Jake. Bearing in mind the meeting was arranged about a week ago, one wonders how differently it would have gone had Josh not ridden in on his white horse last night: similar content, perhaps, but certainly Josh's appearance has given a formidable boost to Russell's confidence.

'If you ask me, I think you're all scared. Scared of getting somewhere, scared of being bailed out of your comfortable, unexciting, unthreatening little lives. To you this is all a game, isn't it? A bit of fun, and something to reassure yourselves that you haven't admitted defeat just yet – that you're still keeping your hand in, keeping that old teenage rock'n'roll dream alive. But wait! Oh no! Here comes someone important, someone who could really turn things around for us! Someone from the *actual music industry*, rather than this pretend world we've built around ourselves. Panic! Help! He might actually take us seriously! Better do something quick to mess it all up! Quick – let's get everyone in the venue to sing the birthday song to Russell, so we look nothing more than a part-time, amateur covers band in a Surrey pub on a Sunday afternoon. That'll get rid of him! It's like when dogs chase birds because they know the birds will fly away. But sometimes the birds don't fly away! They stand their ground, and what happens? The stupid dog hasn't got a clue what to do, so it lollops back in the opposite direction. And that's what this is like for you, isn't it? If the birds stay still, you're scared. Scared of the moment when someone says, OK, here's a hundred thousand pounds. Jack in your jobs, go and make an album, and while you're at it, here's a tour bus.'

Jake, apparently unaffected by Russell's tirade, grins broadly and nudges Ash in the ribs.

'A hundred grand, eh? Wow. I know exactly what *I'd* buy –'

'No, you *wouldn't*, Jake! God, how many times do I have to explain this? If we got a hundred grand as an advance, it's not some kind of prize money! It's not the lottery! It's not a reward for being in unsigned bands for ten years, either! It's *wages*! This is a *job*! Don't you get it? That's what you *live off*! And after all the lawyer and manager stuff has come out of it, it actually isn't that much!'

Karen finally finds her tongue.

'All right, Russell. Don't fucking patronise us. We know what an advance is.'

'Then why do I have to put up with this incessant refrain of "Ooh, what would I buy with my record company money? A PlayStation? A car? A boat? A flat?"'

'Oh Christ, it's called *fun*, Russell!' Karen snaps. 'Indulging in a little fantasy! Why's everything so bloody black or white with you? We all know we wouldn't buy any of those things if we really got signed, but right now, who cares? It's just a laugh. Relieves the fucking *mind-numbing* boredom of . . . all this . . .'

'If you're so bored with "all this",' Russell moans, 'then why don't you get off your —'

'Arse?' Jake suggests.

'Yup — and *do* something about it? When was the last time you guys booked a gig? When was the last time you . . .'

And so it continues.

While almost everything Russell says is logical, well constructed and not without passion, he presents his arguments with such teacher-like pickiness and unremitting force that the others' reactions — silence followed by a few catty, expletive-filled retorts — are wholly understandable. His attack on Jake particularly seems futile and, at times, unnecessarily personal.

'You refused the original plan of getting posters and flyers printed, because you apparently had no money to contribute. So you offered to do them all at your dad's office, which we all agreed was a decent compromise. But they never materialised. When I reminded you last Friday, you calmly announced that you no longer had the time. Then I happen to scroll further down that forwarded email from Mark Higgins, and I learn that you were out on a Camden pub crawl *all day* last Saturday!'

'It was Higgsy's birthday.'

'I'm sure it was! But don't you see? Something doesn't add up. You say you've no money – but how much did you spend that day on the pub crawl? You say you've no time – but how long were you out drinking? Six, seven hours? More?'

'Nine.'

'Nine! Exactly! And what do you do with the rest of your time? Why didn't you get it done earlier that week?'

'Had better things to do,' Jake murmurs.

'There are *always* better things to do, aren't there? And yet you're quite happy to moan to all and sundry that we aren't getting anywhere, that we're being "ignored", or "wronged", or even "dissed" by the industry, or however you care to phrase it, and all in this sickening, woe-is-me, the-world-owes-me-a-living tone of voice, when, really, I think it's *you* who's already given up –'

'No . . .'

'– and really, you're only still doing this because you know, the very *second* you announce you're quitting, your parents will start charging you rent and you'll have to get a job.'

Jake winces and rubs his cheek.

'That's bullshit, man.'

'No, it's not. I've heard you admit it. Your dad's supporting you now because, to an extent, he wants to vicariously experience any musical success you achieve. But if you give up? He'll order you *straight* out the door to get a job.'

'Russy, you haven't got a clue what my dad –'

'Your dad's a businessman, he's not stupid. That's *precisely* what will happen. Well, if you think you're fooling anyone, you can think again. It's pathetic. And what about getting that box of CDs to Fopp? How long ago did you say you'd do that? How many times have I . . .'

And so on. At one point Jake is so besieged that he retires to the bar for a calming Jack Daniel's by himself. Karen flies at Russell.

'Why the fuck are you doing this?'

'Doing what?' Russell blinks.

'Do you honestly think this is going to achieve anything?'

'Well, I –'

'Because it isn't. You're just making everything worse.'

'Hang on, *I'm* not the one –'

'No, Russell. You're never the one. Nothing you ever do is wrong, is it?'

'Look, I'm just trying to –'

'I know what you're trying to do, but it isn't working. You'll never change him, so stop trying!'

'Well, in that case –'

'What?' Karen asks. 'In that case, what?'

Russell looks away. 'Nothing.'

In terms of actual outcomes, only two things are really achieved by this evening's scrap. The first is an unsteady compromise regarding the recording situation: they will use Morgan again but without his creative input, so he will therefore be offered a modest flat fee for use of his equipment and engineering skills.

'He won't like it,' Russell warns, 'but I'll see what I can do.'

The second thing is the kind of brilliant result which the usually passive Ash produces from time to time, often in the direst of circumstances (rather like the frequently recalled occasion when, minutes before a live radio session on BBC Southern Counties, the electrics on Karen's bass packed up and Ash miraculously produced a soldering iron from inside his bass drum). Today, the good tidings are seemingly only mentioned at all because everyone – a few drinks down and finally in the mood for properly fighting back – is having a massive go at Russell. This procession of long-term grievances and disappointments is led by Jake but features sizeable contributions from Karen and, most unusually, Ash – specifically: that Russell has become intolerably cold, anal, the drive for his musical career having superseded everything else (Karen: 'We used to occasionally go to gigs together! When was the last time that happened?'); that he has a nasty habit of barking orders at people (this the most universally acknowledged point – Ash: 'That time at the King's Head when the whole gig was running late and I stayed onstage after the line check instead of coming off so we could do the "grand entrance"? Mate, you shouted at me like I was some fucking kid at a borstal, I nearly jumped off that stage and decked you'); that he has developed as much of an obsession with time as Jake has with money (Jake: 'I try to chat to you after rehearsals sometimes, but you're always dashing straight off – "oooh, I haven't got the *time*, I've got too much to *dooo*"'); that he never answers his phone (Karen: 'What's the point of having a mobile if you're never gonna answer the bloody thing?'); and finally (perhaps the most alarming for Russell) – that his prowess as a lyricist has taken a turn for the worse.

'You're starting to really crap out on your verses,' Jake reveals. 'I mean, "Ghost of Pop" – great tune, but what's with the words? It's like you're so desperate to finish off a song that . . . well, I've got a funny feeling you're just going through the motions.'

Russell glares at Jake. 'Which motions in particular?'

'Well, quite a few of the lines . . . All right, verse one – "*I've had my life and I've seen it all, I've had the rise and I've had the fall, The heartbreak hotel and the brick in the wall*" – OK, that's all fine, but then – "*And now it's time for me to follow the call*"? What's that all about? He needs to go to the toilet?'

'No,' Russell protests, ignoring giggles from Karen and Ash's corner. 'It's because –'

'Anyway,' Jake continues, 'that's the first bit . . . then basically it's the last line of every verse. It's like you run out of ideas – "*I am the melody on the street, I am the voice behind the beat, I am the cause of their defeat*" – actually, that line's a little shoddy too, but then – "*I am the wind beneath the dancing feet*"? What's happened there? Someone left the back door of the nightclub open and there's a bit of a draught?'

'Listen, if you're so good at –'

'And then the last verse is all a bit shodsworth . . . it's like the ending to one of those shit poems we had to recite at primary school – "*Next time you turn the radio on*" – very stock, I must say, like bloody "My Old Man's a Dustman" – [sings loudly] "*Next time you see a dustman, a-lookin' all pale and sad-aahh . . .*"'

Russell's face is an increasingly dangerous thunderstorm.

'But then,' Jake concludes, '"*You'll hear my whisper in every song, If they think it's original they'd be wrong*" – how in cock's name am I meant to make the word "original" scan comfortably with that rhythm? It's so awkward.'

'All right, genius, if you're so brilliant at writing lyrics, why don't you have a go?'

'What,' Jake gapes, 'you mean you'd actually let someone else write something in one of *your songs*?'

'On this one occasion, yes,' Russell nods.

'OK, then! You're on!'

'Seeing as I'm clearly unable to provide convincing lyrics for it.'

'Aw, don't act all bloody wounded now.'

'No, no – obviously my songwriting ability has completely deserted me overnight.'

'Fuck's sake, Russell,' growls Karen. 'It's only the first time anyone's criticised anything you've done. Deal with it.'

In the moment of silence which follows – as Russell processes his new-found role of slightly-less-than-perfect songsmith – Ash grins at the assembled and readies his trump card.

'*I* know something that'll cheer you up, Russ.'

'A free evening class in lyric-writing?' Jake deadpans.

'Well,' Ash begins, lighting a strategic roll-up, 'I was, er . . . having a chat with my dealer Welpo last night. Remember I told you guys he was part of that clubbing collective who sometimes put on club nights at the Dogstar in Brixton?'

'It's not at the forefront of my memory, no,' Russell mutters.

'Yeeah, well . . . they've got a connection to this other collective, more of a rave collective, all based in this little town in the West Country somewhere, can't remember the name. Anyway, they've been doing, like, a DJ exchange . . . DJs from London go down there and do a set at one of their rave parties, vice versa, that kinda thing . . . and a lot of the time it's for trade, like, they'll keep 'em in booze and drugs, maybe just pay their travel, and . . . well, a lot of the time they hitch up and down, but –'

Karen loudly plonks her empty glass on the table. 'This is sounding really promising, Ash.'

'Naah, honestly, hang in there! It gets better. So they've been planning for years to do a kind of joint all-dayer festival thing, with DJs and bands and all that, and Welpo's always said that if it happened, he'd get us to play. And now – turns out it's happening! So Welpo asked me last night if we could play, and I . . . er . . . I said yes!'

Russell looks blankly at Ash for a few seconds.

'You said yes?'

'Yeah!'

'To what . . . exactly?'

'To the show! It's like a festival all-dayer, and cos it's gonna be big, and cos the two collectives are doing it jointly, they're calling it the Big Joint.'

'Ahh, fella!' Jake chuckles. 'That sounds like my kinda gig!'

'Hang on!' Russell snaps. 'Where's this all taking place?'

'Yeeah, well . . . that's the quite good bit. Cos it worked out being easier and cheaper than doing it up here, they're doing it at this big estate in the West Country . . . like an old stately home kinda thing . . .'

'You fucking little wizard,' smiles Jake, clinking Ash's pint glass with his own.

'So,' Russell asks, summoning all his patience, 'Ash . . . the obvious question is . . .'

'Oh, sorry! Yeeah. Bank holiday weekend. On the Sunday, I think.'

'*August* bank holiday? As in, next Sunday?'

'Uh . . . yeeah, guess so!' chuckles Ash. 'Good, huh?'

'And you've waited this whole evening to let us know?'

'Yeeah, well . . . we were talking about other stuff, I didn't want it to get in the way.'

'Ash, you're a real piece of work,' Karen laughs.

'Classic,' Jake agrees. 'Oblivion, here we come . . .'

Russell still looks like a man in need of immediate root canal surgery.

'Sorry, Ash . . . this is great and everything, but there's just a few things we need to know about this event! Like, are we getting paid? Are travel expenses included? Do they provide accommodation?'

'Always the fucking details,' Jake growls under his breath.

'Yeeah,' Ash replies. 'I, erm . . . I think they mentioned some of that, yeeah.'

'No, but seriously!' Russell insists. 'We need to know!'

'Chill, Russ,' Ash smiles. 'I'll give 'im a call later – find out what the dilly is.'

Ash's ramshackle announcement has the welcome effect of finishing the meeting with a relatively happy bang. Jake celebrates by buying himself a large Courvoisier, but then glumly discovers Ash is off to meet a friend for a late curry in Hammersmith, and Karen is heading straight home for an early night. Faced with the unthinkable prospect of Russell as a cognac companion, Jake knocks back eight quid's worth of liquor in one and informs Ash of a sudden craving for chicken jalfrezi.

RUSSELL: Jake has no recollection of how he and I originally met. 'Aw, it's hilarious,' he'll tell people, 'we've known each other *sooo* long, neither of us have a clue how we *pacifically* got together. Lost in the *midsts* of time, it is . . . simply doesn't matter how we met any more . . .' And then that wretched *Spinal Tap* quote gets its daily airing – 'We're closer than brothers.' Although of course it's all rubbish, I remember *precisely* how we met, but I pretend I don't, partly so Jake appears less of a thicko, but mainly as it would burst Jake's bubble if I owned up now. It's also a rather dull story. I was hopeless at biology, and I got moved down into Jake's biology set. I showed up in his class one day. He was late, I was sitting in his seat. 'That's my seat, Groom,' he said. I suppose around school he'd seen me as this rather punchable little goody-two-shoes. So he elbowed me out of his chair and I budged up, and (*winces*) . . . oh God, it's so utterly clichéd . . . a plectrum fell out of my pencil case.

(*Takes a deep breath.*)

Jake's world lurches on its axis. 'What the eff are you doing with a *plectrum*, Groom?' And so on. The penny dropped that I actually played guitar and his behaviour changed dramatically, like I'd gained that extra strand of DNA which finally made me human. He instantly started talking about AC/DC. Asked me whether I liked them. I said yes – well, what else could I have said? 'No, I actually prefer Prince and Depeche Mode, and I'm currently learning the rhythm guitar parts to the entire It Bites album'? Conversation over – back to punchable little wimp again. You see, I already knew he was an idiot, but you've got to remember there was no one else at school who played. Literally. God knows what we were living in, the middle of some total musical drought or something, this must have been what . . . 1987, '88. So we start to play. Hooked up in the common room, or round at his house, or mine. And suddenly, against all possible odds, we gel. Musically, we become a team. We actually improve one another. He brings me out of my rigid shell, I tone down some of his natural flamboyance, rein him in a bit, give him some time structure. And his singing voice was there from the start . . . confident, powerful. But as soon as we stop playing – nightmare. He steals my guitar strings. He never has a capo. I give him mine, he loses it. He shows up at practice without a lead, borrows mine, breaks it. He gets me to lend him money, I never see it again. He starts to drink, smoke. Which obviously I've no time for. Is late for *everything*. Never stops talking to me during biology . . . I fail my GCSE. But there's no one else to play with . . . *no one*.

Raynes Park 1

It doesn't take an especially comprehensive study of Russell Groom's life to realise that, besides doggedly hacking away at his ambition of being a widely respected, supremely tasteful, altruistic but satisfactorily wealthy songwriter and musician, there's not a lot going on. He rehearses, alone and with the band. He writes songs. He dreams up designs for flyers, fiddles around with the band's minimalist website, maintains the mailing list. He sleeps four or five hours a night on a mattress on the floor of a small self-contained bedsit on the third floor in a large house in Colliers Wood, the other inhabitants of which he usually ignores. He listens to the radio, scours the music press, creates (on carefully shaded and formatted Excel spread-sheets) extensive 'music industry domination' work plans, which he then meticulously follows to telephone, fax and email the offices of record companies, promoters, booking agents, managers, publishers and anyone else he can think of. He has even gone so far as tacking photographs of some of these figures onto the large map of London which traverses his wall, with multicoloured map pins indicating their office locations. Occasionally he cycles over to Morgan's house in Raynes Park where they work on commercial pop songs (another long-held goal is to sell one of these to the likes of Kylie Minogue or Ronan Keating), chop up backing vocal parts and argue relentlessly about types of reverb. He works five evenings a week at the Wimbledon Imperial, a job appealing to Russell's indestructible sense of economy in that it ticks four boxes at once, simultaneously providing the social life (small talk with some of the distantly admiring female bar staff as he hurries past with a mop or an industrial-sized loo roll), exercise (racing all over the four-floor, two-thousand capacity rock venue keeps him supple and free from any excess bodily baggage), live musical entertainment (once he's completed whichever current task it is – sweeping up litter outside the building, restocking the dressing-room fridges, taking a wheelchair user to the toilet – there's little more to do than stand around watching the show) and modest income he requires. A fifth box – direct benefit to his own musical career – remains unticked, but tantalisingly presents itself every so often when a support band cancels; the Imperial's venue manager has standing instructions to mention the immediate availability of Russell's band on these occasions. Promoters and headliners have so far managed to resist.

And that, for Russell, is pretty much it. Certainly any activity that doesn't directly serve his musical ascension is regarded as frivolous and uncalled for; he takes time and care over his clean-cut looks and selection of 'vintage original' jeans and long-sleeved T-shirts, but solely in the context of how the combination will appear onstage and in promo shots, rather than any romantic interest his appearance may or may not generate. Food is approached with the expected blend of economy and functionality, his meagre menu chosen with only the stipulation that he can eat meals with one hand, 'so I can read at the same time' (he's currently halfway through Camus' *The Fall*). Pasta, then, is top of his shopping list – a regular accompaniment being tomato ketchup and value-range sausages, which he buys in bulk and keeps in his cabinet freezer. Alcohol, as we have seen, is avoided entirely – although the reason for this depends greatly on who you ask.

Russell's one indulgence, if it can be termed as such, is coffee. It wouldn't be an unseemly exaggeration to say Russell is to caffeine what Oliver Reed was to alcohol. He takes it strictly black, with no sugar, but there the lack of variety ends: espresso, filter, cafetière (top-of-the-range equipment for all of which Russell owns and keeps well hidden from the soiling hands of his housemates or – heaven forbid – bandmates), Colombian, organic Nicaraguan, Fairtrade Ethiopian, iced, Turkish. Even instant doesn't disgust him – although, paradoxically, he eschews higher-quality lines which 'pretend' to be real coffee, instead favouring cheaper brands such as Nescafé Original, 'so then it's a separate drink in its own right, like in Israel'.

But the coffee bean and the indie band do not a whole life make, as someone might have said. So in some ways, having a sizeable dilemma to contemplate provides Russell with a welcome diversion to his usual routine. Today, a pleasant Saturday, he has biked over to Morgan's, the long way round, up the hill and through Wimbledon Village: Russell's 'thinking' route, he explains, but which this morning has failed to untangle the uneasy Jake situation.

'Impossible,' he laments, padlocking his bike to some railings. 'Just as I told you – an obstacle at every turn. I planned on speaking to Karen and Ash last night, but then Ash comes out with his festival news and . . . well, ruins everything.'

Refreshing, though, to look forward to a booking arranged by someone other than himself?

'Ha,' he says, with a subtle but unmistakable sneer. 'We'll just see what happens with *that*.'

He pushes open the door to the caff beneath Morgan's flat. As Morgan has bothered to supply his home with neither coffee, tea nor kettle, Russell must equip himself before each visit.

'A black coffee to take away, please,' he instructs the male teenager behind the counter.

'Milk?'

'No, thanks,' Russell replies, adding quietly, 'The clue was in the word black.'

The caff's proprietoress, possibly the teenager's mother, bustles out from the kitchen and glares at Russell.

'You can tell your friend to turn that racket down,' she snaps. 'I can't hear my bloody radio!'

'Uh, will do,' Russell nods, eyeing the caff's ceiling, which indeed reverberates to a pounding rhythm.

Russell pays for his coffee and mounts the threadbare staircase to Morgan's. The muffled but already deafening din soon reveals itself to be 'State of Independence' by Donna Summer. 'One of Morgan's favourites,' Russell explains. 'He plays it every morning to check his equipment's working OK.' (Other choices apparently include Sparks' 'This Town Ain't Big Enough for Both of Us', Joe Jackson's 'Steppin' Out' and 'Fading Like a Flower (Every Time You Leave)' by Roxette – 'Flawless pop,' reckons Morgan.)

The volume increases to tooth-loosening as Russell unlocks the door at the top and steps into what could be mistaken for a music shop after an attack by vandals. Here, in what once might have been a small, pleasantly bright lounge, dozens of ripped cardboard boxes litter the profoundly unhoovered floor, as do endless bits of shattered polystyrene packaging and dust-covered appliances of a wide-ranging vintage and working order: a few DAT machines, an eight-track, a Betamax video player, a regular hi-fi cassette deck, a couple of record decks, a doorless, unplugged fridge containing a couple of books and a child's xylophone, an old tabletop Space Invaders game, an electric fan and at least three ghetto blasters (a fourth is later spotted behind an empty water cooler). Then – takeaway containers, empty sandwich packets and an overflowing bin liner full of soft drink bottles and cans, half a drum kit surrounded by microphones, a couple of dirty sheets randomly draped about, one supported by some black gaffer tape, another hanging from a pair of dilapidated cymbal stands, a thick, black loom of cables snaking past various guitars, keyboards, assorted fruit-shaped shakeable percussion items – a banana, an orange, an apple (another, resembling a potato, turns out to actually *be* a potato) – effects pedals, Jiffy bags and hand-painted electronic boxes of uncertain provenance and purpose. In the far corner of all this wreckage, every inch the disapproving elder, squats a photocopier-sized reel-to-reel tape machine – although even this majestic contraption is besmirched by a half-eaten slice of pizza.

The main room is adjoined by three others – a small bath-room (in which another microphone on a stand can be seen), a room perhaps originally destined to be a kitchen judging by the presence of a sink, but which is now dominated by shelf after wonky shelf of CDs, magazines, sheet music and boxes of master tape, and a third room, in which Donna Summer continues to throb behind the closed door. Russell coughs, sneezes, pulls open one of the windows, distastefully removes the pizza from the reel-to-reel, and then cautiously nudges the door. And here, within a Santa's grotto of multicoloured cables and twinkling lights, sits Morgan, his eyes shut in apparent ecstasy, reclining in a *Mastermind*-style leather chair as the sonic assault continues. Banks of effects units and other studio wizardry tower on both sides of the small room, and in the centre, a vintage mixing desk so large that a trench has been crudely carved out of the three surrounding walls to accommodate it. A flat-screen computer monitor presides over the scene, on which Donna Summer's soundwaves leap and dive – but these graphics haven't a hope of representing how hospitalisingly loud the music is. The source of the sound is a pair of giant speakers, unsteadily hung from the ceiling with a chain which wouldn't look out of place on a fishing trawler. Hilariously, Morgan himself is protected from the unholy din by a stout pair of industrial ear-defenders.

Russell edges his way round to the studio computer and deftly guides the mouse to the on-screen pause button. With a rush of sudden silence, Summer is finally over.

'Morg,' Russell says quietly.

'Fuuck!' Morgan screams, jumping up from his chair and whipping off his earmuffs. 'Don't bloody *do* that, cockhead.'

Morgan (which is his surname; 'No one knows his first name,' says Russell) is a slight, jumper-wearing thirty-year-old with large eighties specs and a metal digital watch. He originally hails from Clitheroe, Lancashire, and carries the flat vowels to prove it. He played keyboards in one of Russell's many bands at university, but soon left to pursue a sound technology course in London. His home studio was conceived as a moneymaking – or at the very least, breaking-even – concern, but has long since become little more than an itching post for his all-consuming addiction to *gear*. Where Morgan finds the money to pay for it all (rumours have ranged from some sort of car-crash compensation to frightening amounts of credit) remains a mystery, as does the question of where in the flat he actually sleeps ('It's quite possible he simply *doesn't*,' Russell muses).

Once Morgan has calmed down, he sticks on a featureless, electronic instrumental track at low volume and starts to fiddle with stuff while Russell perches on a wooden stool in the doorway.

'Had a band meeting last night,' Russell begins.

'My envy knows no bounds.'

'Yeah, well . . . it was a little tricky, actually . . . the idea was to have a go at them, and it ended up being the other way round . . .'

Morgan flicks on the power switch of a hefty-looking compressor, which starts glowing expensively. 'While you're sat there telling me all this gripping stuff, you might make yerself useful and tidy some of them cables in that box.'

Russell grabs a handful and dutifully starts untangling.

'So,' Russell continues, 'they kept saying all these completely unreasonable things, like – I'm anal, I'm cold, obsessed, that I order people around, that my lyrics are going downhill –'

'What were the completely unreasonable things, then?'

Russell sniggers and rolls his eyes.

'What yer laffing for?' deadpans Morgan.

'Look, I'm in no mood for your alleged humour. Anyway,

I didn't come here to talk about that. They've decided they want to pay you . . . to engineer the next recording.'

'Why?'

'Because they only want you to engineer it.'

'Fair enough. Where you gonna do it?'

Russell is slightly taken aback at how well Morgan has swallowed this bombshell.

'Er . . . well . . . here.'

'You'll have to pay for the studio time as well, then. Who you gonna get to mix it?'

'Erm . . . well, you. But instructed by them.'

'What d'you keep bloody sayin' "them" for? Have you left the band, then?'

'Of course not,' Russell winces. 'I'm saying "them" to illustrate that I don't agree with the decision.'

Morgan shrugs. 'Fine. I'll work out a rate and let you know.'

Russell frowns, concentrating for a moment on a particularly stubborn cable knot.

'Erm . . . well, we were thinking of offering you, um . . . a hundred per day?'

'Plus the studio.'

Russell blinks. 'Including the studio.'

'Yeah, and the fookin' rest. You know how much a commercial studio with this level of gear would cost?'

'Yes, but Morg, it's *not* a commercial studio, is it? It's a dirty, cramped shambles in a flat above a greasy spoon in Raynes Park with no kettle, no loo paper and nothing to sit on. You may have the same equipment as the Townhouse but that doesn't mean –'

'I'll not be charging the same as fookin' Townhouse, though, will I? But your lot, they –'

'I know, I know . . . they need to learn the value of what you've been giving them.'

Morgan grumpily fiddles and Russell silently untangles for a few more minutes.

'I met someone the other night,' Russell volunteers suddenly.

'Someone special?'

'Not like that, moron. A guy came to the Half Moon. Singer, guitarist. Been signed before, dropped a couple of times. Recognised that Jake was the problem, suggested replacing him. Son of a record producer. He seemed –'

'Name?'

'I'm sorry?'

'Name,' Morgan repeats, conjuring a laptop from somewhere. 'Of the producer.'

'Um . . . Chigwell. Lenny Chigwell.'

'Ah yes – seminal.'

'Really?'

'Fool,' Morgan smirks, typing in the name.

'Anyway . . . it seemed like he had contacts. Has a manager. Liked the music – the songs. Said that if he came on board, he could turn things around within months.'

'Oh yeah? And how's he gonna do that, then?'

'Um . . . well, apparently, these industry people are actually waiting for him to present them with something.'

'After being dropped a couple of times?'

'For financial reasons, though. And he says his folks have –'

'Here y'are,' Morgan interrupts. 'Lenny Chigwell. "Contact Lenny Chigwell for more information."'

'What is it?' Russell asks, trying unsuccessfully to peer over Morgan's shoulder at the laptop screen.

'Some residential studio in Sussex.'

'Oh, yeah – his dad owns a studio.'

'Owns or runs?'

'Dunno. Both?'

'That's the only mention of him on the Web,' Morgan scoffs.

'Well, I guess the stuff he produced wouldn't feature much on the Internet anyway . . .'

'What's his lad called?'

'. . . it was all in the seventies and . . . sorry, what?'

'The lad. What's he called.'

'Josh.'

Morgan bangs in the name and narrows his eyes, scanning the entries.

'Erm . . . duh-de-duh-de-duh . . . blah, blah, "with guest vocals from Josh Chigwell" . . . some dance record.'

'He's a pretty good singer, actually. Anything else?'

'A tax attorney in Pittsburgh.'

'Yeah,' Russell nods. 'That's him.'

'Doesn't exactly sound like the whole world is awaiting his next musical note, does it?'

Russell grabs the final lead from the box. 'He was pretty spot on about Jake.'

No response from Morgan, who is scribbling something in a notebook. Russell exhales, then tries another angle.

'What would you say if I told you we were giving Jake the push?'

Morgan continues scribbling for a moment, then rips out the piece of paper and hands it to Russell.

'I'd say you'd have to find someone new to argue with . . . There y'are – daily rate for me and use of everything in't studio. If that's too dear, the rate underneath is without the Neumanns. Given that your lot wouldn't know a Neumann microphone if it banged on their door and tried to sell 'em double glazing, I'd go for the one below.'

Russell glances at the quote, then looks back up.

'What d'you mean, I'd have to find someone new to argue with?'

'Without Jake, it'd just be so much cotton wool. I know you, Groom. You'd not function without a struggle of some kind.'

Russell exhales crossly and leaps up.

'You know, that's a myth,' he says, pacing around the larger room. 'It's totally untrue that I *enjoy* arguing. Honestly, I don't! I'd much rather people just agreed with me from the start.'

Morgan chuckles and shakes his head.

'Right, are we gonna do anything worthwhile or are you just going to irritate me all day?'

Russell sighs again and returns to his stool.

When you collaborate with Russell's band, do you keep a potential music-industry audience in mind, or do you simply try to produce the best possible piece of work?

MORGAN: Neither. I just try and make summat listenable quickly so they bugger off and leave me alone as soon as possible.

But seriously.

(Silence.)

Do you think they've got a good chance of making it?

MORGAN: What's that, these days?

Well . . .

MORGAN: If you're asking whether I think they're likely to be offered a record contract, then yeah, possibly, who knows? Isn't much of an accolade, is it? It's also probably the worst thing that could happen to them. They'll get squashed, minced, ripped apart by some clueless dickhead with pound signs in his eyes.

What would be your advice then?

MORGAN: Their problem isn't that they're unsigned. It's that they're all daft. They've already got all the tools they need to be successful – it's all there, on the Web. They could sell their music, publicise themselves, even play virtual gigs if they wanted to. Who needs a record company? They should do it on their own. You just look – in two or three years everyone'll be at it. People'll be having top-forty hits without releasing a record. Russell and that lot should get in there first, blaze a trail. But they never will, partly cos bloody four of 'em can never agree on anything, but mainly cos they're all blinded by this juvenile concept of 'getting signed'.

What do you think of them yourself, as a band?

MORGAN (*looks desperately uninterested*): They're all right. There's a lot of faff, though. I wish they'd ditch the guitars. And the drums.

What, be more of an electronic band?

MORGAN: Nah, the synth can go too. Just keep the bass.

That sounds rather radical.

(*Silence.*)

And how about on a personal level?

MORGAN (*deadpan*): Can't abide 'em. Bane of me life.

Even Russell?

MORGAN: Especially Russell.

Wandsworth 1

To spend an evening with the band at their Wandsworth rehearsal studio, although interesting and occasionally very amusing, is to be filled with the uneasy sensation that you should no longer be there; that, in fact, everyone really ought to have left ages ago. Each member, even Russell, glances at their watch or mobile phone every five minutes. We are constantly reminded, usually by Karen, of how much rehearsal time is left, ostensibly in a constructive way, but it's not hard to guess what's really going through her mind when she brightly announces, 'Only forty minutes left, better crack on!' Faces light up when someone decides it's time for a coffee break, or a cigarette, or even to visit the loo. There are lots of weary sighs, furtive eye-rollings, the occasional angry glare and numerous instances when one of them (most frequently Jake) simply can't be bothered to apply any real thought, let alone passion, to a song they've played a hundred times. Lyrics are forgotten, drum-fills are fluffed, musical flourishes are lacklustre. Even the prospect of Ash's upcoming West Country festival slot isn't enough to shake everyone out of their malaise. Of course, any successful band is obliged to play all their songs several hundred – even thousand – times, but the energy from the audience's reaction must sufficiently recharge the passion and enthusiasm battery night after night, at least until that particular tour is over. But for Russell, Jake, Karen and Ash, their already near-empty battery is leaking all over the grimy rehearsal-room carpet, making their every movement leaden and lethargic. A couple of attempts are made (by Russell, unsurprisingly) to tweak arrangements and so inject a bit of new life into a given song, but it's always in the context of that timeless preoccupation: 'This is *exactly* the sort of thing a record company would go for.'

Still, there are a couple of moments when one sees a flash of glory. Midway through the session when Jake and Ash pop to the off-licence, Russell tries out the catchy Who-esque synth motif of a brand-new song and is enthusiastically joined by Karen on the guitar. Soon Jake returns and picks up Karen's bass; finally Ash begins pounding his drums. For five brief minutes, the four of them become a radically different group of people, rocking out, repeating the main riff again and again, grinning like lunatics at each other: directionless, but who cares when it sounds this good? Then, abruptly, Jake puts down the bass, cracks open a beer and announces, 'That was great, Russ. We should have a go at that one sometime. Fancy skinning up a number, Kaz?'

Such is Jake's attention span that it's debatable whether anything of any use is achieved by tonight's practice, aside from some superficial oiling of joints. They're certainly able to perform nothing they couldn't have performed before. Russell hides his exasperation well, but his trips to the coffee machine become so frequent that there's a suspicion he's really exited to vent his rage. Again, there are fleeting glimpses of his and Jake's former working relationship – they join forces to argue vehemently with Raz the rehearsal-room boss when he barges in at one point, accusing them of short-changing him on the rent money – but in the main, we witness little short of an irritation offensive on Russell from Jake, and no episode exemplifies this more accurately than The Pudding Incident.

Mainly to fit with Ash's work schedule, they almost always rehearse from seven until eleven, thus encircling most people's dinner time. Ash has established the routine of ordering himself a ham-and-cheese toastie from the studio café when he first arrives, which he then swiftly scoffs while setting up his kit. Karen normally appears with a home-packed sandwich of some sort. Russell never seems to eat anything, although he can occasionally be seen munching an apple or a cereal bar. For Jake, who is unlikely to have eaten more than a piece of toast all day, this functional opportunity to refuel is afforded all the enthusiasm one might reserve for a slap-up birthday binge; he is, by some distance, the café's most cherished customer.

'Ah-haa! Jakey!' cries the café's charming Brazilian cook as the man himself enters.

'Chocolate salty chef, how the devil are you!' beams Jake, slapping the chef's raised hand. 'What's happening with tonight's banquet, my friend?'

'Jake, I gotta lovely chicken curry for you this evening – is quite Thai, I think, some dried apricots and fresh mango –'

'Ooh, man, you're spoiling me.' He spots a middle-aged

heavy-metal band on a nearby table who are halfway through the very dish. 'How is it, guys?'

'Legendary,' one of them judges.

As popular as Jake is in the café, the reception he usually receives when he enters the band's room carrying his starter (tonight, an order of cheese-slathered garlic bread and a large packet of crisps) is tepid. His guitar and amp typically remain in the band's lock-up until he's finished his first course; whether he then immediately goes to retrieve his equipment depends on the progress of his main dish. This evening, the chef is cheerily proffering the mountainous plate of curry as Jake reopens the heavy studio door.

'Ah-haa! Jakey-oh!'

'Bang on time, you culinary hero,' smiles Jake, carrying his food back inside and settling himself on the sofa. 'Wow. This is a meal fit for a fucking king.'

The dish is consumed at a leisurely pace, after which Jake reclines on the couch for a moment, patting his expanded belly. Incredibly, although it is now nearing twenty to eight and the rest of the band have been ready to begin playing for over a quarter of an hour, this is not the end of Jake's dinner. When he returns from the lock-up with his equipment, he loudly states an intention to finish his feast with a portion of chocolate brownie and ice cream.

'Fuck's sake, Jakey,' moans Ash. 'Are we gonna get going soon, or what?'

'Sorry – I just *have* to have something sweet to round it off.'

'Get a fucking KitKat or something then, you cock,' suggests Karen.

'Aw, it's just that chef does it so well,' Jake grumbles, plugging in his guitar tuner pedal and kicking the switch a couple of times. 'Shit, my pedal's dead. Russ, have you . . . ?'

Before he's even finished speaking, a silent, stony-faced Russell has extracted a battery from his rucksack and tossed it over.

'Cheers, Russy, my man,' Jake smiles, catching the battery and snapping it in while singing, '*Russy, Russy, Russy with his bag of spares . . .*' – to the tune of *Jamie and the Magic Torch*.

A couple of minutes later Jake's guitar is tuned and his mic positioned. Ash nods hopefully at his three bandmates, ready to click-start the intro to 'Smaller Weaker', a gig favourite and their standard rehearsal warm-up song. But no.

'Right,' announces Jake. 'All ready.'

'Yup,' concurs Russell. 'Go for it, Ash.'

'So I'm gonna run and quickly order my pudding.'

Karen and Ash hurl general abuse in Jake's direction as he once again unstraps his guitar. Russell takes a deep breath and looks away, one of his guitar effects units apparently requiring immediate attention, but a little vein in his forehead has started to bulge ('the Jake vein', as Ash calls it).

A minute later Jake is back, and a breezy rendition of the song is at last completed. Towards the end of Russell's closing arpeggio, banging on the door can be heard.

'Hey, hey, Jakey! Your *sobremesa* is here!'

The bowl is placed on top of Jake's amp, and for the next twenty interminable minutes Jake works his way through the gigantic sweet portion. But rather than availing himself of a few quick bites in between songs, Jake appears to be timing his mouthfuls with great care: the central synth build-up in 'Testing Ground', which isn't particularly long, thus rendering him unable to sing half the chorus; the crucial point in

'Warning', when his lead guitar riff counts in the middle eight; during the driving, harmonised third verse of 'On the Radio', so stranding Russell and Karen's backing vocals without a main melody; the entire outro of 'River Song', where Russell's synth pattern makes absolutely no sense without Jake's accompanying chords – and so on. After the fifth song an amount of dessert ample for a small family remains in the dish, at which point Russell – although it must be tempting to simply grab the bowl and hurl it at the PA system – removes it from Jake's amp and places it carefully on the arm of the sofa.

'Right, Jake – I've got an idea. We'll have a little five-minute break, so why don't you sit there, finish your meal and then we can carry on, OK?'

'No-no, it's all right . . . there's too much to finish all in one go, plus it's *soo* nice, I was making it last . . .'

'Well,' replies Russell, with remarkable restraint, 'it'd be better if you just left it there and finished it in a little while, so we can get through the songs properly.'

Jake mumbles something and the rehearsal continues, but sadly the pudding's repositioning has only made things worse. Jake still insists on sporadic, ill-timed titbits, but he must now traipse across the room to the sofa each time, taking him directly past the spot where Russell is stationed. During a couple of quieter songs, attempted in anticipation of the band's acoustic show tomorrow night, Jake takes extra-large mouthfuls and makes loud, exaggerated chewing sounds on his way back to the microphone. Russell shuts his eyes each time Jake passes, but the vein in his forehead is now throbbing furiously. Karen and Ash, clearly familiar with the impending doom of such a situation, keep quiet.

Still a quarter of his helping to go, Jake wipes a moustache of ice cream from his top lip and suggests running through

'Krystal Palace', a metronomic, keyboard-led track with a powerful rock explosion in the final minute ('It'll be great at the festival,' he enthuses). As Russell tucks his guitar behind his back and readies the synth for the intro, Jake – unnoticed and for no apparent reason – balances his bowl precariously on the very edge of the sofa's arm. He then innocently returns to his mic, and the song proceeds.

Three minutes pass, and a false sense of security has been thoroughly conjured. Jake has refreshed his singing and playing with passion and enthusiasm, Russell and Karen's eyes are closed in concentration. The emotional crescendo of the third chorus works its magic, Ash gradually intensifying his beat then skilfully reining in his cymbals in readiness for the huge dynamic shift. Thrilled to be finally playing a truly impressive piece of music, Russell and Karen spontaneously leap into the air as Ash's three thunderous smacks on the snare, kick and floor tom herald the ferocious, pounding pay-off. We could be at Brixton Academy, supporting (and upstaging) Placebo; or bringing a career-defining set to a close before the beautifully setting Glastonbury sun; or, most poignantly, at the Wimbledon Imperial (as former colleagues still serve drinks and mop up vomit), on the final night of a sell-out tour as the debut album turns platinum.

But – once again – no.

The sudden, sheer volume of the music sends Jake's pudding bowl, replete with liquefied ice cream and soggy bits of brownie, spinning to the floor, splattering white and brown mush all over Russell's wah-wah pedal. Jake whips off his guitar (producing a vicious blast of feedback) and hurries over to the scene of the calamity. The music falls apart as Jake kneels down, rescues the capsized bowl and starts ineptly mopping up the mess – with one of the sofa's cushions.

Russell, his face now a study in unrestrained malevolence, stamps on all his guitar pedals, slams his Telecaster as violently as he can allow himself into the guitar stand, strides over to Jake's amp, snaps the power off (the feedback squeaks its last) – and lets rip.

'What on *earth* do you think you're *doing*?'

'I'm mopping up my pudding,' Jake replies calmly. 'The ice cream'll stain the carpet.'

'You *know* what I'm talking about, Jake!'

'Well, what would you prefer me to do, Russell – leave it on the floor so Raz can have another go at us?'

'I'm talking about *all* of it, you imbecile! This entire pudding performance!'

Jake scrapes up the last of the gunk and empties the bowl into the bin.

'Well, frankly, Russell, it was your idea to move the bowl, it was perfectly happy on my amp –'

'Oh, don't you *dare* start blaming –'

'It was! I've no idea why you moved it over to the arm, what a daft place to balance a bowl –'

'Jake, I am *not* prepared to –'

'I'm quite pissed off, to be honest, Russell. That was a quarter of my pudding you wasted . . .'

Back and forth this goes. By the time the argument runs out of juice, with Jake attempting to extract 75p from Russell in lieu of his lost dessert, Karen and Ash have silently left the room and are presumably doing something more worthwhile, like having a cup of tea, or wandering around in the car park collecting gravel.

RUSSELL: The thing which drives me potty about Jake – of all the many, many things that could potentially send me gurgling, frothing and gnashing my teeth in the direction of the nearest secure mental unit – is that he's actually very intelligent. I know this. I've had plenty of conversations with him over the years wherein he's been lucid, thought-provoking and thoroughly engaging. He's surprisingly well read. We once had a long discussion about Miller's *Death of a Salesman* – it was in the car home from a battle-of-the-bands in Coventry, if memory serves – and he pointed out some details even I hadn't noticed. He can play the violin. He actually speaks passable German. He's an incredibly good people-person – much better than me. In the early days, when we were speaking to Deceptive and the management company, he handled all the communication and was quite articulate and convincing. You've never seen him speaking to his mother – for some reason she's never allowed to come to gigs, or maybe she can't face them, and who could blame her – but his persona changes hugely when he's talking to her. Even his accent changes a bit. They discuss films, books, music from shows . . . and she asks far more salient questions about the band's progress than practically anyone else. I haven't been round there in a few years but it was never, 'Duh, how's the band going?' – instead always something more considered, like whether we'd found any good new venues to play, what festivals we'd lined up . . . she once asked me whether I'd thought about working with a professional songwriter, to see where the collaboration took us . . . that sort of thing. I think she had something to do with music in the sixties, so she kind of knows her stuff. Anyway, to see Jake behave so differently on a day-to-day level is just utterly maddening.

Why do you think Jake hides this side of himself?

RUSSELL (*treading carefully*): I think that, subconsciously, Jake has decided he's . . . *not* going to be a rock star. Inwardly, he's already admitted defeat. His oft-repeated dream of being 'the most famous person to come out of Surrey since Paul Weller' is dead. And I think that scares the living daylights out of him. Because eventually . . . he'll have to become normal. His parents will stop sponsoring him, and he'll have to get some grim job in Camberley. And to all his friends back home, having for years been the slightly quirky one who sings and plays in a band, he'll be a failure. Even worse, a failure who doesn't fit in. Someone with concerns other than the football scores, or what drinks in the local nightclub are on two-for-one . . . but with no one to discuss them with. Someone who thinks about chord progressions and recording techniques when listening to music, rather than just roaring out the words to the chorus. OK, I'm not saying Camberley contains no one with an ounce of intelligence, but – for want of a far, far more appropriate word – the slightly more *intellectual* side of Jake isn't going to be much use down at the Four Horseshoes on a Friday night. So – again, subconsciously, as I'm certain Jake wouldn't have the slightest idea what I was talking about if I presented this theory to him – by downplaying his more refined side, Jake is really . . . preparing himself for normality.

That sounds like quite a complicated process. Are you sure?

RUSSELL: Positive. I've actually seen him do it. I went to a party last year at Sarah Nuttall's house, who was Jake's girl-friend at the time. Usual scenario, everyone else is drunk, I'm sober, so I notice things. I was in the kitchen talking to a few people – Ash, Karen and some friend of hers who was talking about Pedro Almodóvar. She'd seen *All About My Mother* that week. Now, I know for a fact Jake had seen that film with Sarah the previous year, and enjoyed it – he told me so on the way to Southampton when we played the Joiners down there.

So, we're all chatting away, and Jake walks into the kitchen, catches the drift of the conversation, actually draws breath to speak, it looked like it was going to be something positive . . . then Big Paul, one of the so-called 'booze brothers' from Bagshot, comes in to get a bottle from the fridge, Jake's eyes dart over to him, they clock each other, Jake turns back to us and says, in his desperately annoying, double-strength Estuary voice – 'Aw, I hate all those foreign films, full of queers and too bloody arty, and I can't stand reading subtitles . . . you look down at your popcorn and bang, that's half a scene gone!' Big Paul laughed and responded with something equally clanging and vacuous and the two of them left the room.

Perhaps that's just insecurity.

RUSSELL: Yes, but he's only been this bad recently. I can actually put a date on it. Last May . . . Monday the fifteenth, when we'd finished *Demo*. The CDs came back from Key Production and we sent out the usual email to the mailing list asking who wanted to buy copies. When we did this for *Hook-Laden* the previous year Jake returned home to something like sixty emails in his inbox, all saying 'yes'. With *Demo*, I think there were eight.

Eight?

RUSSELL: Eight. And three of those were from Karen's mum who kept thinking the email hadn't sent properly. (*Looks down for a moment, then sips coffee.*) I mean, to an extent, I can understand it – if you've got a friend in an unsigned band you're going to be constantly hassled to go to gigs, to buy this demo, buy that T-shirt . . . the novelty's bound to wear off after a while, especially if you can't perceive any tangible progress up the ladder. For that reason alone I've always avoided friends' opinions as a measure of whether you're on the right track or not. So my view was – OK, that's a shame, but let's move on, write better songs, play better gigs, record better demos, concentrate on impressing the industry. Whereas Jake's reaction was to instantly lose all enthusiasm and focus, and start behaving like a fool.

So how does that make you feel?

RUSSELL: Well, it's unbearable. But funnily enough, I've got more sympathy for the actual reasons behind it than you might imagine.

Really?

RUSSELL: Look at it this way – Jake's just a salesman. That's what he *does*. His dad's a salesman, albeit a very successful one. Jake did Business Studies at, oh, that pretend university in Basingstoke, and he *understands* the concept of selling. So, whether he's singing onstage or sweet-talking an A & R man, at base level he's simply selling a product. (*Pauses, sips coffee.*) And it's not working. In Jake's mind, the product is not selling. Now – if a conventional salesman was selling a certain brand of, I don't know . . . mayonnaise, and no one bought it, after a while the salesman would just give up. So that's Jake. But I don't think like a salesman. I'm the guy in the kitchen, making the mayonnaise. My brain says: let's improve it. Keep on making better mayonnaise. Until no one can refuse it.

You're an artist.

RUSSELL (*looks uneasy at the word*): Um . . . yes, I suppose. I'm not saying Jake's view is any less valid. I'm simply explaining his behaviour. He's a salesman who's lost faith in his product, and needs to move on to something else . . .

But he isn't moving on to something else.

RUSSELL: No, he's not, and that's . . . that's where the analogy falls down. Because selling mayonnaise – the act itself – I imagine is only enjoyable if you succeed in selling it. Unless you're a bit strange. But playing in a band, for most musicians, is *intrinsically* enjoyable, whether anyone's listening or not. So Jake just carries on, irrespective of whether anyone buys it. And you do see glimpses of his old drive – don't get me wrong, it's still inside him somewhere. It mainly comes out when he's arguing with me. Or when someone denigrates us. We got a bad review last month in a local paper and Jake was *incandescent* with rage – baying for the writer's blood. But generally, his fire's gone out. You hear him telling people all the time: 'Who knows whether we're ever going to make it? We might as well just have a laugh getting nowhere.'

What about at the rehearsal? There didn't seem to be much laughter going on there.

RUSSELL: Oh, Jake enjoys . . . other things about the band. The friendship. The drinking. Going for a spliff with Ash. The occasional bursts of thrilling music.

The fun of driving the rhythm guitarist insane.

RUSSELL (*in a very small voice*): He has that quality.

Holland Park

Russell is halfway to Holland Park when Josh phones. His responses are short, quiet, worried.

'Yes, tonight . . . Eight thirty . . . Yup . . . Oh, sevenish . . . Oh! how come? . . . Erm . . . yes, I suppose so, but . . . Who will I say you are? . . . No, I haven't mentioned anything to anyone yet . . . Well, because I haven't . . . I know, but . . . Sure, but you have to realise how sensitive all this is . . . True, but . . . Barry too? . . . Ah . . . No-no, that'll be fine, but please tell him not to say anything, you understand . . . Yup, a pair of managers, OK . . . See you then . . .'

He puts his phone back in his pocket and glances furtively around the Tube train. Then he takes it out again and hits one of his speed dials.

'Karen, it's Russell . . . Fine, you? . . . No, you're not late, I'm not even there myself yet, but . . . Listen, forgot to tell you this the other night, but . . .'

The venue for tonight's acoustic gig is the dingy cellar bar of a pleasant but decidedly un-rock'n'roll pub on a smart residential street near the Holland Park roundabout. Despite the unlikely surroundings, the evening in question, Acoustic Payback, has developed something approaching prestige on the London gig circuit. Hosted by one Rapacia Davis, an early-eighties C-list It girl who claims to be close friends, and occasionally much more, with a large selection of music-industry shakers (Simon Moran, Andy Ross, Vince Power, etc.), it is also a favourite early-evening haunt with the A & R chaps at EMI's nearby headquarters in Kensington: they often swing by for a free drink on their way to other shows around town. Consequently, Rapacia's weekly Tuesday nights boast a better selection of bands than they probably deserve – a record company will sometimes send along a new signing to cut their acoustic teeth, for example – and Russell has accordingly deemed a monthly slot essential for his own troupe. What neither Russell nor Rapacia fully realise is that Acoustic Payback has also managed to become something of an industry-wide joke, partly because of Rapacia's hopeless elder brother Gordon – the de facto doorman and sound engineer – who is invariably moody, rude and drunk to the point of high comedy, but due as well to poor Rapacia herself, who at thirty-eight cuts a rather sad, borderline-rotund shadow of her younger, more fragrant presence: chain-smoking, white-wine chugging and air-kissing in a style suggesting the delusion that her funny little acoustic bash is actually a high-end jazz club on the French Riviera. It's not unusual for the evening's closing entertainment to be a drunken argument between Rapacia and Gordon as they stagger about packing the PA system away ('Like an old deaf couple fighting over the CD player,' as Jake quipped).

Russell is the last to arrive ('The indicator was wrong at Earls Court! I got on the wrong train') and is soon at the business end of a brisk grilling from Karen. All the band have received Russell's rather nervous phone call, and the consensus is that it's a little bizarre – two guys from a management company coming to see them play and have a chat beforehand, and Russell is behaving like they're being visited by the fraud squad. Nor is it like Russell to 'forget' to tell them something of this significance.

'Don't give me your innocent-little-boy bollocks, Groom,' she glares. 'I *know* there's something else going on.'

'Honestly, I've no idea what you're talking about,' Russell replies, extracting his acoustic guitar from its case.

Luckily, further questioning is soon curtailed by the arrival of Gordon, who is on his usual splendid form.

'Right,' he growls, 'there's five bands this evening so I don't want any of your shit. I'm soundchecking one drum kit and that's the lot, and if you think I'm changing the levels and EQs for every single vocalist, you can think again.'

Ash produces a pair of bongos from his duffel bag and holds them up for Gordon's approval.

'You can mic them up yourself. I've got other things to do.'

The band shuffle around, arranging the small corner stage for themselves as Gordon concentrates on the first of his 'other things to do': predictably enough, uncorking a bottle of red.

'Gordon,' asks Russell gingerly, 'where are the DI boxes?'

'Christ! There's always something, isn't there?'

Karen looks up from tuning her bass.

'Tell you what, Gord – how about we all just go home again and spend the evening watching telly?'

An adequate soundcheck is nonetheless managed, towards the end of which Josh (to Russell's slight alarm) descends the stairs and seats himself at one of the tables. As the band strike the final chord, he rises and approaches the stage.

'That was sweet, guys,' he says, clapping. 'Josh Chigwell. Saw your show last week. Fan-*tass*-tic.'

He shakes each of them by the hand – with the conspicuous exception of Karen, whose hand he kisses. She is having none of it.

'Urgh, get over it, you cheesy fucker!'

Russell wastes no time in taking Josh upstairs for a private word while the others finish removing their gear from the stage.

'It's him, innit?' Ash hisses.

'What, the posh knob from the other night?' Jake blinks.

'Yeah,' Karen nods. 'That's him.'

'Manager, then?'

'Apparently,' Karen shrugs, stashing her bass case in the corner of the room.

Gordon looks up angrily from his copy of the *Metro* newspaper, which has been spread across the diminutive mixing desk since midway through the soundcheck.

'Right, you can take the coffee morning upstairs now. I've got another four acts to get through. You think I want to compete with you lot gossiping away? I don't think so.'

'Wow – yeah, Gord,' comments Jake, feigning shock, 'you've got your work cut out, eh? And all the other acts are here, on time, all of 'em clamouring to soundcheck first!'

'Yah,' snaps Gordon, turning back to his paper.

'Can we get you anything to make your evening easier? Bag of crisps? Plate of nachos? Another vat of wine?'

'Less of your cheek, arsehole,' Gordon murmurs. 'Or I'll make you sound like Leonard Cohen with a hangover.'

'Go ahead,' Jake retorts, mounting the stairs. 'Might brighten things up a bit.'

Barry is the kind of man one knows will be unpleasant before he's even got out of his car. The band, plus Josh, are sitting around a table outside the pub when the blue Volkswagen Beetle screeches round the corner and tries to insert itself into a minuscule nearby gap between a motorbike and a Range Rover, next to a postbox. A perfectly good space can be seen fifty yards further up the street, but this would not be Barry's style. The little car wiggles noisily back and forth for a minute or so before Barry's head appears out of the sun roof and beckons to Josh for assistance. Josh lights a cigarette and remains seated.

'You've got about four millimetres between you and the bike,' he shouts, 'and about half a foot in front.'

The Beetle lurches forward too enthusiastically and knocks into the Range Rover's rear bumper. The alarm shrieks.

'Too much,' sighs Josh.

'Fuck it, Josh. Get up off your arse and help me properly.'

Josh takes a long drag on his cigarette, flicks his hair back and ambles over. Half a minute later Barry's car is as parked as it's going to get and the Rover's alarm has mercifully stopped, the silence broken only by Barry's car door clanking loudly against the side of the postbox as he attempts to get out. Josh chuckles, so do the band.

'Aw, very fucking funny.'

And so, finally, here is Barry. Medium height, stocky build – he possesses an awkward body that looks fat without actually being particularly fat – and short, mud-coloured hair. He wears a yellow Ben Sherman shirt and a permanent scowl which brings to mind Thom Yorke's quote about his own father: 'the sort of face that people want to hit'. To say Barry is of indeterminate age sounds a bit feeble but it's true: he really could be anything from twenty-five to fifty. He greets each member of the band without much warmth; unsurprisingly, the most is reserved for Karen, the least for Jake. Then he ventures inside the pub and returns a few minutes later with a bottle of Sol, lime wedge and all, from which he periodically sips while texting someone.

'How'd the showcase go?' Josh asks him.

'Mad,' sighs Barry, not looking up. 'It was fuckin' packed. We had to turn people away.'

'Oh yes?'

'Yeah. The rehearsal-room guy came and had a word with us . . . said it'd start being a fire risk . . . we had to ask a few blokes to leave cos McGee showed up halfway through and they wouldn't let him in . . . seriously, mate, it was one in, one out . . .'

'Who was there?'

'The usual, Lawrence, Stephen, Andy . . . then some guys from Parlophone, four – no, five guys from Parlophone . . . Infectious . . . Universal . . . a crowd from Sony and some guys from New York, Geffen . . . Universal Japan . . . Warner Chappell . . . Harvey Goldsmith poked his head in . . .'

It's interesting to watch the expressions on the band members' faces as Barry reels off this dubious list. Russell is obviously listening intently but tries to remain poker-faced, an illusion scuppered by the frantic fingering of his coffee cup. Jake looks both amazed and affronted, as if he's on the point of asking,

'Well, why didn't you bloody bring some of them along here, then?' Karen is busy with some scissors and a Black Rebel Motorcycle Club T-shirt she's converting into a vest top, but keeps looking over at Russell, perhaps gauging how impressed she's allowed to look. Only Ash seems unmoved, entirely absorbed by the sports section of his newspaper; Barry might as well be discussing his tax return.

Meanwhile, the list is getting sillier.

'. . . John Peel came in for a bit . . . Lamacq . . . Power . . . a bloke from BMG . . . Panda . . . coupla guys from Eluxor –'

'Eluxor?' Jake interjects. 'We got seen by someone from Eluxor.'

Barry briefly raises his head from his text message.

'Did ya?'

'Yeah, Damo Tocks. Came last week.'

'Tocksy's gone now,' Barry smiles nastily. 'Gone off travelling for a coupla years.'

Then the list resumes, as does the text.

As the next hour progresses, a few things become abundantly clear. One is that Barry doesn't excel in the art of making his stories even slightly entertaining, much less believable. The sheer, hundredweight quantity of supposedly notable names he drops, whether genuine or not, is enough to make anyone scoff, and everything he says – be it discussing the 'madness' of a current bidding war for one of his other bands, or wondering aloud whether he's in danger of getting a parking ticket – is delivered in the same monotonous, world-weary tone, soon sending his assembled listeners into a dense fog of boredom. As the band begin to think about returning downstairs to see the first act of the evening, Barry embarks on the tale of a recent 'mad' (and highly unlikely) episode when Noel Gallagher sent out a car in the dead of night to bring Barry up to

Manchester to discuss amplifier endorsement deals, but by now it's plain that only Russell is still really listening.

'I didn't think Noel Gallagher lived in Manchester any more,' Russell offers.

'Oh, he's still got a place up there,' grunts Barry – adding, for no detectable reason, 'Johnny Marr was there too.'

A second trait of Barry's takes longer to sink in, but is potentially more disquieting, and will be discussed at great length in the days to come: as far as the band can make out, he doesn't appear to actually like any music *at all*. In none of his ramblings does he mention the quality, or even the basic features, of the musical sound produced by his various charges (currently three, by Russell's count), and certainly any admiration for popular contemporary acts is expressed solely through reference to their sales figures, or the shrewdness of their recording and/or publishing deals, rather than the catchiness of their songs or richness of their albums. In any case, most bands he mentions he seems to detest. When regaling the assembled with the tale of his greatest (in financial terms, at least) success – an erratic-sounding mob by the name of Fat Cynic, for whom he brokered a £1.5 million publishing deal but who never ended up releasing a record – this facet becomes all the more blatant.

'They were shit,' he remarks. 'Crap songs, crap live, and couldn't organise their way out of a fuckin' bag of glue. They weren't even pleasant to be with. One of them had, I dunno, fuckin' . . . whassat thing when you keep swearing?'

'Cocaine?' Josh suggests.

'Nah, you plonker . . .'

'Tourette's,' Russell obliges.

'Thassit . . . he was a fuckin' nightmare . . . but they had this one track called "Fare Evader", exactly the sorta thing they were all looking for in '97, kinda "Firestarter" mixed with that Chumbawamba one. Fuck, it was rancid. But they went for it. Mad.'

Despite all this, or perhaps because of it, Barry appears to have convinced everyone that his managerial connections and capabilities are formidable, and the short-term result as show-time approaches is that they're all a little nervous. Jake, already nearing the end of his third pint, deals with this in his own unique way.

'We had a manager once,' he tells a barely interested Barry. 'Me and Russ. Back in the day.'

'Which day would that be?' Josh asks.

'Early nineties. We had two groups, same members – a metal band that was really good, and an indie lot that were shocking.'

'Other way round, in fact,' Russell quietly points out.

'Anyway, we had this really wet indie song called "Clockwork Apologies" – *totally* gay, but Steve Wright played it on Radio 1. Then this manager reared his head. Called Paul something, weren't he, Russ? Took us on. The cunt did nothing for four months. Not a thing. Never arranged a rehearsal, never bought us any equipment, never sorted out a recording session, never gave us any money for anything, hardly gave us *any* advice apart from saying our clothes were shit and that we needed to write a single. Useless! Then had the fucking nerve to tell us he couldn't do anything for us until we had something worth selling to a record company. We said, well, we've been sat around doing nothing for four months, waiting for you to manage us – how can we get anywhere when we've been waiting for *you* to do something? Dickhead.'

The look of contempt Barry gives Jake would coax most people into silence. Jake, however, is not most people.

'Why bother, that's what I say. Why bother having a manager, unless they're going to *do* something. Know what I'm saying? I mean – you boys, for example. What would *you* do for *us*, if you took us on tomorrow?'

But this question never gets answered, for at that moment Rapacia – dyed-blonde hair still wet from the shower, Turin Brakes T-shirt and an almost offensively expensive-looking handbag – comes flouncing round the corner. The band look up and ready themselves to greet her, but she ignores them completely and throws her arms around Barry.

'Barry, you bad boy,' she drawls in her deep, posh smoker's voice. 'What brings you here?'

'Hi Raps, sweetheart,' he grins, rising. 'What are you drinking?'

And that is that. The pair of them amble into the pub, and Barry isn't heard from again until after the show.

RUSSELL: Being in a band is mainly an exercise in constantly repeating yourself. I've lost count of the amount of times I've had to explain the role of manager to Jake and the others. They're not there to book your rehearsals, make the tea, wipe your bottom. Why would they be? This was actually one of the reasons – one of the many, many reasons – that Jake and I fell out in the first place. A manager, of course, is only there to do the things a band *cannot* do – negotiation, networking, planning, budgeting and so on. But this always gets overlooked. Again, no one else in the band sees the bigger picture – another perpetually repeated phrase. Also demanding constant repetition is the more mundane stuff – what date and time a gig is, how much a rehearsal costs, how much petrol money they need to give me, why we're doing a particular task at a particular time. It gets so bad I've even thought about writing a little handbook, and maybe giving out printed memos, but then everyone would just say I was even more of a control freak. Which I don't necessarily agree that I am.

Why do you think they forget these things?

RUSSELL (*sighs*): I'm afraid it's probably booze.

That must irritate you.

RUSSELL: Well, I try not to let it. I'd go mad otherwise. Instead I try to turn it to my advantage. Being sober obviously means I have a unique viewpoint on events – what occurs, in what order it happens, who does what, who says what, and when. It comes in useful occasionally – handy with settling arguments. Although (*laughs wearily*) . . . the arguments are usually with me, so then the control-freak tag gets wheeled out again. Round and round we go.

Because there reaches a point in certain evenings – most evenings – when all of them are drunk, I've developed a sort of grading system for myself so I know each of their precise levels of intoxication. It helps me to know what I can expect of them conversationally and physically. There's Level 1, the pre-kicking-in phase, when they're essentially still normal. Jake and Ash rarely remain at this level for more than about three seconds. Level 2, slightly tipsy, just about bearable – basic functions still unaffected, misunderstandings not much more likely than usual. Then Level 3. On the one hand this level is the most fun – inhibitions have gone, everyone's quite cheerful and affectionate. The very few times in my life when I find myself wishing I could have a drink, I'm always thinking of this level. The snag, though, is that they start to *forget* they've had a few, and they get careless, so if they're helping me pack the gear they quite often drop something. Ash fell down the stairs at the Barfly when he was at Level 3. He was carrying the synth. Broke the oscillator. *Very* annoying.

Equally, they might get careless in conversation – a friendly debate could become a rather messy argument at this level, because they don't believe that they're drunk. Then Level 4 – the worst all round. Useless physically and conversationally. Unable to understand anything rational. Laughing hysterically at things which aren't funny. Repeating themselves over and over, totally forgetting what they said five minutes ago. Mostly in a perpetual bad mood. Sadly, this is the predominant level these days. Not sure why. Then, ironically, at Level 5 things get better again. I think it's because by now they're so acutely aware that they're drunk, they make the extra effort. Having Jake help me pack the car at this level is an absolute breeze – I almost wish he was like that all the time. Karen is very good at collecting money from the promoter when she's like this. Insists on counting everything three times – she once caught Sound Republic short-changing us by fifteen quid. Then finally, Level 6 – comatose, passed out, totally gone. The one advantage to this state is that they can't mess anything up. Unless, of course, they vomit – which Ash did once, down the back of Jake's amp.

So who is the best in the band at holding their drink?

RUSSELL (*without hesitation*): Karen. In fact, I'll say this – and you can appreciate, this is pretty high praise coming from me – *if* I was able to drink, which thankfully I'm not, Karen would be the sort of drinking companion I'd prefer. She's virtually indistinguishable from how she is normally. Which, of course, begs the question – why bother in the first place?

A little queue forms at the top of the cellar stairs as eight thirty approaches, although it soon transpires that this has more to do with Gordon's dexterity on the door than the popularity of any of the evening's acts. Halfway down, Josh has found himself waiting behind a bespectacled bloke in a Marks & Spencer's jumper. Perhaps driven by some pleasant childhood memory, Josh taps him on the shoulder.

'Nice jumper, dude,' he says.

'Eh?' frowns Morgan.

'Yah. Remember being given it for Christmas in the late eighties. Classic.'

Morgan looks away. 'Cock-end,' he mutters under his breath.

Downstairs, the current band, a rather sickening girl and boy duo, bring their final song home with a particularly painful close harmony. The small audience claps politely as Rapacia leaps onto the stage, pointing a toothsome smile towards the paltry stage lights.

'Oh, so marvellous. Wonderful songs there from Thruxton Higgett, let's hear it for them one more time!'

In a dark corner of the room, Karen nearly spits out her drink.

'What the fuck?' she splutters. 'What did she say they were called?'

'Hinge and Bracket, something?' Ash suggests.

'Thruxton Higgett,' says Russell. 'That's both of their surnames.'

'The girl's quite fit,' Jake observes.

'Dream on, loser,' Karen replies.

Innocuous incidental music strikes up (Air's *Moon Safari* – 'Either Gordon's favourite CD or the only one he owns,' comments Karen), the band plug in their gear and, after a rambling introduction from Rapacia, they get started ('Next, some old friends of Acoustic Payback returning for their fourth – no, fifth? – visit . . . we've got Jake on vocals, Russell and Carol on guitar, and then Adam's there at the back on those . . . *cheeky* little bongo drums . . . a four-piece in every sense of the word . . . four instruments, four minds, four spirits, four souls . . .'). The set largely consists of new stuff – Russell's new ballad 'Laurie Lee' is played for the first time, Jake reading the words off the back of a business card – and even features one of Karen's compositions, a currently wordless collection of chords entitled 'Thameslink', on which Jake merely shakes a tambourine and flings his hair about (for acoustic gigs Jake relaxes into the single role of vocalist, his prowess on the acoustic guitar deemed insufficient). But 'Smaller Weaker' gets its usual airing, as, for the second time, does 'Ghost of Pop' – during which both of the gig's noteworthy moments occur.

By this number, the sound quality has taken a major dive. The reason for this isn't clear – Thruxton Higgett sounded reasonable and Gordon hasn't looked at the mixing desk for the last fifty minutes, let alone touched it – but there is definitely some sort of problem. Karen's bass is distorted, Russell's guitar tinny and Jake's vocals practically inaudible. Realising this, Jake ostentatiously tosses the microphone aside halfway through the intro, and for the rest of the song – and indeed, the gig – sings unamplified. Puzzlingly, he is louder than he was before.

A by-product of this sudden clarity is that the words he is singing can now be heard. This is unfortunate. In a rare attack of industry, Jake – and it's difficult to believe this is a coincidence, though it probably is – has in the last twenty-four hours delivered on his promise of rewriting the offending sections of 'Ghost of Pop', and now proudly belts out his new lyrics for everybody, including the rest of the band, to hear for the first time. 'And now it's time for me to follow the call' has become 'The Lennon John and McCartney Paul' – while verse two's 'improvement' abandons any notion of sticking to even the song's most basic theme: 'I am the cause of their defeat, I am the wind under the dancing feet' is now 'I am enough to make you weep, Or sit through a film with Meryl Streep.'

Jake's deadpan delivery extracts a few chuckles from those nearest the stage, but a quick glance at Josh and Barry – the former staring intently at Karen, the latter impatiently tapping a cigarette on the table – reveals nothing. Ash grins hugely behind his bongos and Karen keeps a commendably straight face, but the member giving the most away is Russell himself, who attempts to convert a sizeable knee-jerk cringe into one of those passionate expressions of lyrical empathy traditionally reserved for R & B backing vocalists. On Russell this looks absurd and the muted giggles become hearty guffaws.

Finally, Jake's new third verse – formerly Russell's rather glib wrap-up – plunges the gig helplessly into the realms of bad improvisational comedy and small-hours stoner humour: '*Next time you turn your girlfriend on, And get your hand inside her thong, Take a quick hit from the bong, It'll help to make your willy long.*' Warming to his new role of musical comedian, Jake throws out his own howlingly earnest expression, which Russell, apparently unaware of the audience's earlier reaction, complements with a second heartfelt pout of his own. A further untimely patter of laughter rents the air and Barry abruptly exits the room, talking loudly on his mobile.

RUSSELL: Lyrics are actually a pain in the neck. I don't enjoy writing them at all. Remembering you have to write lyrics for a new tune is like discovering you have chewing gum on the bottom of your shoe.

Don't the lyrics ever come first?

RUSSELL: Hardly ever. Sometimes the titles come first, like 'M3' and 'Krystal Palace' – and 'Ghost of Pop', in fact. But I normally go straight to the music, and leave writing the lyrics 'til the very end.

How important are lyrics?

RUSSELL: To a band like us, not very. We're music-driven. Some bands are clearly lyric-driven – The Smiths, The Divine Comedy, R.E.M. perhaps. But most, I'm convinced, write lyrics simply because they're obliged to. With this band I always think as long as a lyric has a theme of some description and a singable chorus, the music will do the rest. Words should never, ever distract people from the music. Which is one of the reasons I never let Jake write lyrics, as he can't resist making them 'funny'.

Of course, 'Ghost of Pop' is just meant to be a straightforward song about musical plagiarism. Admittedly, not one of my finest lyrics – Jake was right, I *was* in a rush – but it *had* a theme, a theme which could have been improved upon. But Jake's just turned it into nonsense.

Don't you think that's the whole point?

RUSSELL: What, you think he's making a statement about my lyrical themes by turning them into drivel?

It's possible.

RUSSELL: Or do you think he's just blithely trying to irritate me? (*Sips coffee and thinks for a few seconds.*)

Hmm. Maybe.

The remainder of the acts judged not worth bothering with, the party gravitates back upstairs to the pub, where Barry offsets the usual 'whose round is it anyway?' debate by buying everyone a drink. He does not, however, ask anyone what they want, and soon Russell is staring unhappily at a frothing pint of premium-strength lager. Jake is delighted.

'Don't worry, Russ, I'll have yours for you,' he chuckles, tossing Russell a fifty-pence piece. 'Here, buy yourself a Vimto.'

'Don't ya drink?' Barry asks.

'No,' pronounces Russell, 'I do not.'

'Ya should've told me, you silly bleeder.'

Eventually band and companions gather round a large table in the corner, where the conversation naturally turns to the performance.

'I hate acoustic gigs,' Jake comments. 'Simple as that. Dunno why we do them.'

'You *know* why we do them,' Russell sighs.

'Sorry,' Jake shrugs. 'Must've forgotten.'

Karen displays vague enthusiasm for the benefit of Josh and Barry.

'I think they're useful,' she explains, 'for, like, trying out new stuff in front of an audience that isn't . . . um . . .'

'Yeah, go on . . . say it,' grins Ash, sipping his beer.

'. . . important,' she finishes, to a bellow of laughter from Barry.

'That's not it,' Russell frowns.

'But I'm never really sure we're at our best acoustically?' Karen continues.

'Yeeah,' Ash agrees. 'Especially when one of us decides to turn a song into a *Two Ronnies* sketch.'

'That was the best bit,' Barry mutters, once again mid-text.

'Oh yeah?' Jake asks, hopefully. 'Did you think so?'

Barry ignores him.

'Oh, acoustic gigs have their uses,' offers Josh. 'But none of you looked totally comfortable up there, to be straight.'

'We weren't,' Karen confirms. 'I fucking hate playing that acoustic, it crushes my tits.'

'I'm sure you could get one of those guitar dudes to modify it for you.'

'Ha!' Jake hoots. 'Imagine that. They could cut the perfect shape out of the wood –'

'Yeah, yeah, get over it, smutty arsehole,' Karen scowls.

Morgan approaches the table and silently hands Russell a CD. Ash smiles at him amiably, Karen and Jake look down into their drinks.

'Eleven tomorrow?' Russell asks.

'If you like,' Morgan shrugs, jingling his car keys and wandering off again.

Josh waits until Morgan is out of earshot.

'Who *is* that cat?'

All four members answer simultaneously.

'Our producer.' (Russell)

'Our engineer.' (Karen)

'Morgan.' (Ash)

'No one.' (Jake)

Josh laughs. 'You punks should get your story straight.'

'He produced the EP that I gave you,' Russell states, firmly.

'Producing would be stretching the definition,' Jake grumbles.

'Well, whoever the kid is, he's rocking some *bad* threads.'

'So what did you think of the EP?' Karen enquires.

'Nice,' Josh replies, glancing at Barry, who nods without looking up from his phone.

The discussion proceeds in this awkward, jerky manner for a few more minutes, before Jake, presumably bored, decides to break the deadlock.

'So, I'm just curious – when you manager types come to a gig like this, what are you looking out for?'

'All sorts of things,' Josh improvises. 'The performance, how you work together, how you look . . .'

'Whether we can hear a single,' Barry says.

If this was intended to rile Jake, it works.

'Aw, fuck! That's it!' he trumpets. 'A single. That's all anyone's interested in! A finished product. Seems that no one wants to do any bloody work in this industry.'

'Why should we?' smiles Barry.

'Why should you? Why *should* you?'

'Easy, fella,' Ash mumbles, nervously tugging Jake's arm.

'See,' Jake continues, 'what I don't understand is why you lot can't look at something like our gig tonight, and see the shape of things to come. Why can't you look at a band like ours, and think – OK, there's a good song, there's a decent vocalist, there's a – sorry, Karen – fit female bassist . . . with a bit of work this lot'll be great!'

'But why the fuck should we?' Barry repeats, shaking his head and continuing to prod his phone.

Jake looks so beside himself, there momentarily appears to be several of him. Josh intervenes.

'Jake, what Barry is *trying* to say – if he wasn't working on his entry for the world's longest ever text message – is why should an A & R cat, or a manager dude, *choose* to put their own cash and time into an unfinished band, when they could easily find a crew who don't need any sweat at all? Those bands are out there, somewhere, and they're the ones getting signed.'

'So you're saying we're unfinished.'

'Yes,' Barry states flatly, finally resting his phone on the table and looking Jake straight in the eye. 'We are.'

'What about our songs?' Russell asks miserably.

'Songs,' Barry sneers, 'are *not* the fuckin' be-all and end-all. A band with good songs is like a girl with a pretty face. Basically, it's a good start. But she's got to have the tits and arse to back it up.'

'Oh, *please*!' Karen cries.

'Sorry, babe, it ain't pleasant, but hear me out. It ain't no use a bird having a sweet boat race but then a body like an ice-cream van. Same with a band. They can have Jagger and fuckin' Richards' greatest hits up their sleeve, but it ain't no good if they look like fuckin' *Blue Peter* presenters and drink lemonade. If a band's got swagger, they're gonna rock. The songs can come later. Look at it like sex, OK? Hearing a band's songs is like kissing 'em. But the kids want to be fucking 'em too.'

'Cover the face and fuck the base,' Ash mutters, absently. Karen thumps him.

'*Ash!*'

'Tough, but true,' Josh nods sagely.

'Right, thassit,' Karen spits. 'You lot can fucking fry.'

She stomps off to the bar. Russell dives back in.

'Hold on, guys. This is contrary to everything we've ever been told. "Work on your songs" has been the recurrent phrase of the past three *years*. No one's ever told us to work on our . . . erm . . . swagger.'

'How could they?' Barry shrugs.

'Russ, man, it's not something that can be learnt,' Josh suggests. 'It all comes from the doing . . . not the learning. You gotta get yourself fucked up, crash some stages, gig 'til it hurts. Wake up at two in the afternoon in an Aberdeen crack den with the tour manager honking the horn outside. Walk it like you talk it, peeps.'

'Yeah,' Barry continues, 'but there are some other more fuckin' real things you can do before all that. Buy yourself some fuckin' clothes, think about your appearance. Get a real producer. [Jake flashes a smug smile in Russell's direction at this.] Make some proper fuckin' recordings. Think about your stagecraft. Get a sound engineer who understands your sound and doesn't make a complete tit of you, like that fuckin' prick tonight. Think about lighting, get some visuals going.'

'Well, yes,' Russell begins, 'we have talked about doing all those things, but –'

'Don't talk about it – do it,' Barry snaps. 'That's the trouble with unsigned bands. They're always talking about stuff, never actually doing it.'

This comment is met with such fury, Russell and Jake are temporarily robbed of all speech. Ash, however, seizes a rare chance.

'Oi, that's a bit fuckin' unfair!'

'Is it?' Barry replies.

'Well, yeah, it is! I mean . . . we *would* be doing all those things if –'

'If?'

'*If we were fucking signed*!' Jake yells, so loudly that the rest of the pub turn round to look, including Karen, who is quietly sipping a spirit of some sort by the bar.

'But that's just it, innit, mate?' leers Barry, with a nasty smile. 'You'll never *be* signed. You're an unsigned band. You're a fuckin' *deeply* unsigned band. You look like an unsigned band. You sound like an unsigned band. You think like an unsigned band. You *talk* like an unsigned band. Why on God's fuckin' green earth would any record company want an unsigned band on its roster? It ain't gonna happen, pal.'

Visibly summoning all the self-control he possesses, Jake silently rises from his seat and staggers off towards Karen.

'Harsh, Bazza,' Josh tells him.

'Whatever,' Barry replies, picking up his phone again. 'Dunno why we're talking to that cunt anyway.'

Josh glances apologetically at Russell, then Russell glances worriedly at Ash – who blinks at them both for a second, then frowns and also slips away to the bar.

'Fuckin'ell,' laughs Barry, spreading out around the table a bit. 'You forget to put your fuckin' deodorant on today, Josh?'

On the face of it, you seem slightly less ambitious than the others. Are you?

ASH: Yeah, I s'pose so.

Personally, what would your ideal situation be in, say, two years' time?

ASH: Well . . . doing music, really. I'm not terribly bothered how, or to what level. I suppose the others have got more . . . grand ideas, you could say. Jake wants to be up there, on the big stage, commanding the big crowds – famous, havin' it. Karen wants to live the life. Russ wants Thom Yorke, or whoever, to see him in a restaurant and think – that's Russell Groom, and he writes bloody amazing songs. But me, I dunno. I just don't wanna be working in a call centre.

Does the others' constant obsession with these big dreams ever bother you?

ASH: Yeah, sometimes. I mean, to an extent I get it, y'know . . . reach for the sky and all that. Set out with the goal of only playing the Barfly and you'll probably end up . . . y'know. Playing the Barfly. But set out to play Wembley Arena and . . .

You still end up playing the Barfly?

ASH (*laughs*): Yeah, maybe . . . something like that. But I dunno. Those lot can get a bit hysterical. Karen's pretty level-headed, but Jake and Russ – Christ. Sometimes you do feel like banging their heads together.

Who's the worst, in your opinion?

ASH: Well . . . I agree with most of what Russell says, but that doesn't stop him from being a bit annoying. I think he gets so wound up that he forgets what it's all about.

And what is it all about?

ASH: Well . . . music, basically. The love of music. Bit cheesy, but there you go. Music is why all of us started this whole thing. Sometimes, with Russ, you get the impression that . . . I dunno, it could be *anything* he's trying to do. Stockbroking. Selling paint. Even being a scientist or something. He'd approach it all with the same . . . intenseness. No compromise.

So he's just obsessed with succeeding at something?

ASH: Yeah, kinda. Whereas . . . I dunno. Not trying to say my reasons are more . . . y'know . . . genuine. But I just love music, I think I'm an OK drummer, and I'd like to be paid a bit for doing it. I think that's the least I can ask from life. I don't want to be a millionaire, or famous, or anything. I just fuckin' . . . (*Goes a bit misty-eyed.*) Oh Christ. Music. I adore the stuff. It's ridiculous. I was on my own in the flat the other night, must've been elevenish, I'd had a beer or two and for some reason I started playin' all my vinyl. Zeppelin, Purple, Floyd, Sabbath, that kinda thing. Sparked up a number, just zoned out. 'Fore I knew it, it was five thirty in the morning. Hadn't even noticed. Sleeves all over the floor. Amazing.

It's hard to imagine Russell having a night like that.

ASH: Yeeah . . .

And what about Jake?

ASH (*looks a bit wary*): What about him?

Do you think Jake's capable of zoning out, forgetting everything, all for the love of music?

ASH: Depends how numbered he is (*chuckles*). But . . . hmm. I dunno. Jake . . . I do love the old fucker, but . . . mm. He's tricky.

Barnes

Jake officially resides with his parents in Camberley, but the combination of his late-night cannabis schedule and the various activities of the band means he can often spend up to five nights per week on assorted London floors. Sometimes this will be at Ash's shared digs in Brentford, occasionally with Karen in Southfields (less so since he bedded Karen's flatmate Rachel), and never – for fairly obvious reasons – with Russell. The place he most frequently settles for, and the roof under which he has awoken this Wednesday morning, is the shared Mortlake flat of his ex-girlfriend, Sarah. Today being Sarah's day off, the ex-partners are enjoying an alfresco brunch at a smart café on Barnes High Street, where a hung-over Jake is an ill-fitting presence in his cut-off shorts and faded Green Day T-shirt.

'Ahh . . . sweet, sweet breakfast,' he exclaims, chomping into a tuna melt.

'My eggs aren't cooked properly,' Sarah grumbles.

'Tell 'em.'

She squints around for the waitress, who is nowhere to be seen. After a minute or so Sarah shrugs and carries her plate back into the café.

'We split up in February,' Jake explains, spooning sugar into his tea, 'but she's still not over it, the poor girl. I think me coming round from time to time makes it slightly easier for her, y'know?'

Sarah, also originally from Camberley, is a mature student at nearby Roehampton's teacher training college.

'That was one of the reasons we split,' Jake continues. 'Obviously, me being a musician, late nights are the order of the day . . . but she doesn't want me crashing around in the middle of the night when she has to get up early and teach a classroom full of kiddies, does she?'

Then he leans across the table and lowers his voice.

'Also,' he winks, 'there are certain advantages to being in a rock band, you know what I'm saying . . . I didn't wanna mess the girl around . . .'

Jake grins cheekily and leans back in his chair, as a black Mercedes halts a few metres up the street. An attractive, wealthy-looking older woman in a beige suit steps out, flamboyantly frees her dark, glossy hair from a gold clip and slams the car door. Noticing that Jake is staring, she glares distastefully as she passes.

'Fuckin'ell,' Jake comments, moments later. 'That's one for the wank bank.'

Sarah returns and their discussion continues – about, predictably enough, last night and Barry.

'I dunno what you're panicking about,' Sarah reasons. 'If

Karen and Ash both thought he was an arsehole then Russell can just piss off.'

'Yeah . . . but they might think he's an arsehole who can *do* things.'

'Well, you just flippin' well *leave*, then.'

Jake frowns at her.

'How could I? They'd be fucked.'

Sarah's plate returns with her recooked eggs and the pair munch away. The conversation proceeds as only those between exes can: familiar, effortless, uninhibited, but prone to fiery revisits from old arguments at any given moment. One such battle rears its head when the bill arrives and Jake casually mentions that he has no money.

'No problem,' Sarah replies, matter-of-factly. 'Cash machine up the street.'

'No,' Jake clarifies. 'I mean, I have *no money*. Overdraft limit reached.'

'You're kidding me. You suggest coming out for brunch, knowing full well you can't pay?'

'I still have to *eat*, Sarah.'

'Oh, you're such a child! We could've cooked at home! Blimey, you never change, do you?'

'Aw, come on . . . just sub me 'til my dad sorts me out at the end of the week, I'll treat you next time, promise . . .'

'Heard that one before,' Sarah growls, tossing her debit card onto the little white plate as Jake's phone starts to ring. He snaps it up.

'Chris! . . . Yeah, bro . . . Barnes . . . No, *Barnes*, as in where horses sleep . . . Oh, having a spot of brunch with the lovely Sarah . . . [Sarah rolls her eyes and turns away.] Yeah, mate, lah-di-fucking-dah . . . OK, tell me . . . You *have*? . . . Fantastic, my brother . . .

ow up at the next rehearsal, get there early, Russ is
inutes late like he always is, and obviously it was
else's fault, like it *always* is . . . so I show the letter to
guys in the band — who were also already at screaming
Russ — and we all just left. Took all the gear. Went
. And that was it. End of the band.

you were pleased to be reunited with him.

, well, y'know . . . time knocks the edges off, doesn't
really seemed to have changed, like Ash and Kaz had
him, or something. He came out to the pub — just
le! Very unusual. We went to gigs together — Suede,
ovin' Criminals . . . even Fat Boy bloody Slim. And
Glastonbury — can you imagine that? And he was
gh! I mean, a sober Glasto can't be that much fun,
to it! Had his little schedule of bands, buggered off
lace with his rucksack . . . I even saw him with a
oint, but turns out he was actually holding Ash's
d he (*giggles*) . . . he kept repeating this one phrase,
with the quality of the coffee here!' — he repeated
ny of the other shite we were all spouting, and he
t one! Became a kind of catchphrase in the end
Russell, and he's really *jolly* impressed with the
offee here . . .'

ncast.)

ged?

ame . . . intense again.

why?

stopped moving forwards. And he blamed me.

Aw, mate, you've *totally* come through for us this time . . . Three
quid each? You sure they're good? . . . Ah, mate rate . . . OK, ha
ha, I trust you . . . Yeah, put me down for twenty . . . Yeah, and
a half of green, it's gonna be a big weekend . . . I'll see you tonight,
my friend . . .'

Jake hangs up and immediately starts dialling someone else.
Sarah glares at him.

'Jake . . . *who* . . .?'

'Uh?' says Jake innocently, his phone pressed to his ear.

'How are you going to pay Chris, your *dealer*' — Sarah says
this word extra loudly, so some of the smart diners turn to
look — 'when you can't afford to pay for your bloody *meal*?'

'Shhh!' Jake spits. ' . . . Ashley! . . . Hey, drummer boy, I've got
some corking news for *you* . . .'

Sarah coughs with disgust and starts gathering up her things.

' . . . three quid each, mate, and all the fucking green you
can shove up your transom . . .'

Jake's expression flattens slightly.

'Oh. OK . . . No worries . . . Yeah, call me back . . . Uh,
bye . . .'

He looks at his phone for a second.

'Hmm,' he murmurs, dialling a second number. 'Don't sound
too grateful, will you . . .'

Sarah looks up from the debit-card slip she is signing, and
leers.

'Oh, whassamatter? Didn't he have the time to talk to you?'

'Yeah, yeah, whatever . . . Hey, hey, Kazza! . . . Got some
grand news, babe — Chris the Fizz has provided . . . Uh? . . .
Oh, bollocks, what *is* it with you guys? Ash just said the same
thing . . . Eh? Whassat? . . . Yeah, OK, call me straight back,
bye . . .'

Jake lays his phone down on the table and blinks at Sarah.

'They were in the same place,' he frowns.

Sarah shakes her head, barely interested.

'Same music playing in the background,' Jake continues.

'So?'

'Why would they be in the same place?'

'Why not?'

'It's Wednesday. Ash is at work. Why would Karen be there?'

'Having lunch together?'

'Why would Karen go all the way to Brentford to have lunch?'

'How would I know?'

Jake picks up his phone and dials again. 'No, no . . . I bet that . . .'

'Maybe it was the radio,' Sarah shrugs. 'Lots of places play the same radio –'

'Voicemail!' Jake shouts.

'Shut up, will you?' Sarah hisses, rising to leave. 'Come on, people are trying to eat.'

'Russell's phone went to voicemail,' Jake splutters. 'They're having a *meeting*.'

'Jake . . .'

A look of horror crosses Jake's rapidly paling face. 'About me!'

'Oh, Jake, just bloody chill out, will you? . . . Come on, let's go . . .'

'No, no, you don't understand . . . I know the way Russell works . . . they can't meet tonight, him and Kaz've got work . . . they can't meet tomorrow night, we're rehearsing . . . so they have to meet today . . . neutral territory . . . Jesus fuck, they're booting me out!'

'Oh, come *on*, Jake . . . they v

'It's Barry . . . it's that fuckir cunt . . .'

More diners glare in their di Evidently all too familiar with spells, Sarah sits again and qui a nearby pub. Soon, a still jit leave, all the while scorning t and Josh.

'Sneering, ugly little arsev di-dah cockface . . . the pa swear . . .'

'Well, why not get the one,' Sarah advises, helping him away from the table.

'Fucking right,' Jake a 'Can't believe it. Can't out. After all these year

Sarah trots after him,

'Please God, let it b

Why did you and Rus

JAKE: Oh gawd. N

A painful memory

JAKE: Well . . . th prick. Absolutely u it's so long ago – words he says to not fucking true me out. By wri and everything.

Wimbledon 1

Karen is late. With the tenuous reasoning that she was 'already in west London', she decided to cheer herself up after her lunch with Ash and Russell by making a quick trip to Portobello Road ('I needed some new boots,' she explains, brandishing a large paper shopping bag, 'which is most of my recording money gone now, but I figured – the band'll probably be over by this time next week, so why worry?'). Then she got held up in the rush hour on the way back to Wimbledon. Now nearing six thirty-five (as a 'Bar Leader' she is expected at the Imperial by six), she still risks running to the cafe next door for a cheese roll. Russell is already in there, waiting for his caffeine fix before the rigours of the evening. Karen spots him from the outside and hesitates by the door, but Russell waves. Karen enters and expressionlessly saunters up to the counter.

'Hi,' Russell says.

'Yeah,' replies Karen, folding her arms and looking away as she waits to be served.

The female server holds up Russell's coffee. 'Milk?'

'No.' Russell risks a nervous laugh in Karen's direction. 'The clue was in the word black,' he whispers.

'Not in the mood, Russ.'

They wait in awkward silence for half a minute as the sound of Dido drifts from the cafe's stereo. Russell's walkie-talkie, clipped to his combat shorts, crackles loudly with some near-indecipherable drinks-related broadcast.

'Need to check those IDs tonight,' Russell smiles.

Karen glares at him. 'You what?'

'Overrun with teenie metallers.'

'Oh. Right.'

Russell's attempt at small talk refers to the juvenile fans of the evening's main act, Alien Ant Farm – in the UK for a Reading Festival slot this weekend, and currently omnipresent on Radio 1 with their inconsequential reading of Michael Jackson's 'Smooth Criminal'.

'A cheese roll and a bottle of water,' Karen says to the server, after Russell is handed his cup.

'See you later, then,' Russell yelps.

'Uh-huh.'

Russell gets halfway out the door, then:

'Karen, I –'

'Russell, I *don't* want to talk about it.'

He frowns at her. 'I was just going to tell you the Bar-fly has offered us a cancellation. Tuesday week, the fourth.'

Karen says nothing.

'I said yes,' Russell concludes, flouncing off.

'He said yes,' she repeats, watching him go. 'Well, he can play the bloody thing by himself.'

Karen pays for her snack and hurries up the street to the venue. The next fifteen minutes are given over to various pre-show activities, the routine nature of which seems to cheer her up: signing in with security, racing through the stale corridors and discovering with distaste that her evening is to be spent on the ground-floor bar, and not her usual station ('Level one,' she says, 'the cool one, where the industry hang out . . . along with all the liggers, of course'). She makes sure to apologise for her lateness at the same time as swapping her purple shirt for the obligatory black 'STAFF' top ('Bloody tubes were a *nightmare*,' she smiles sweetly to Howard, the forty-something bars manager, who doesn't look like he's about to reprimand her), then she summons up a surplus of alcopops and soft drinks from the cellar, dispatches a junior to get the ice (Karen originally set out to fetch it herself, but saw Russell changing a light bulb at the other end of the corridor and turned back), stops briefly to check the support act (a rather shouty British rapper) completing his customary five-minute soundcheck, and finally, just before doors-open, she grabs a quick cigarette outside one of the fire exits, where her previous gloom returns. She exhales, staring up the little alleyway at the animated queue of pubescent punters as they prepare for the great dash to the front of the auditorium. Then, without warning, she retches.

'Shit,' she coughs. 'This is ridiculous.'

She gathers herself as a tanned chap with jet-black hair, Iron Maiden T-shirt and facial jewellery passes, flashing a laminate at the security guy by the venue's back door.

'The gulf between the dream and reality,' Karen comments suddenly. 'The dream – fifty metres that way,' she points, 'with a triple A, dressing room, fridge full of beer, and someone line-checking my bass. Reality — out here, dry-hurling, about to serve a hundred bottles of J_2O to a bunch of fucking children.'

She takes a hefty drag, and all but spits out the smoke at the line of fans.

'The dream — that lot, queuing up for *us*. Reality — wondering whether to replace one tosser with another.'

She thinks for a moment, then grimaces.

'Christ, I feel shit.'

Nerves?

'Nerves, worries, fucking . . . fear. Ugh, I hate it. My mind's always been stronger than my stomach, y'see. Dunno why.'

The fire door opens and Russell appears. He pours a bucket-ful of something unspeakable down a nearby drain, then vanishes again. Karen growls.

'The fucking thing is, y'see — he's right. As fucking usual. Russell-who-is-never-wrong is absolutely, *nauseatingly* fucking right. Jake is hopeless. Worse than hopeless, he's . . . unusable. That's the thing. Un . . . fucking . . . whatever. Unmarketable. If he was just hopeless — just shit — it'd be OK. Nah, not OK. Easier. But, ugh. Fuck me. Bloody Jake. Poor bloody Jake. Stupid fucking Jake. What a prick. Why can't he just . . . be *all right*?'

Perhaps it's —

'And the thing that *really* pisses me off is that we have to settle for some nauseating little twat just because he's got a famous dad and a horrible pit bull of a manager.'

Do you *have* to?

'Oh . . . no, of course we don't *have* to . . . but . . . let's face it. This is the last gasp. The last-fucking-ditch effort. It sounds awful, but . . . I'm gonna be twenty-five next year. The girl from JJ72 is twenty-one *now*, and they had a top-twenty album *last* year. If we got signed tomorrow, I'd probably be twenty-fucking-six by the time an album came out. Russell would be almost thirty. That's *old*.'

Hardly.

'In this industry, yes.'

So . . . you're convinced, then?

She takes a last drag and tosses the cigarette into the drain.

'Urgh,' she moans, clutching her stomach. 'I don't fucking know. It's one thing thinking, another thing doing.'

What about Ash?

'Oh . . . who *ever* knows what Ash is really thinking.'

Russell may have a clearer view of Ash's opinion. Later, his pre-show chores completed, he is finishing another coffee in the little maintenance room where all his equipment is kept: mop and broom, spare fuses and light bulbs, bin bags, paint and various cleaning substances, plus the red plastic lettering used to emblazon the current headliner's name on the front of the venue ('The best part of the job,' Russell enthuses, carefully amassing a quantity of characters to announce Friday's appearance by the reformed Electric Light Orchestra). Such is the Victorian layout of the Imperial that although Russell's bolt-hole can only be reached via a small door on the far side of the auditorium's second level, it shares a wall with the biggest of the three dressing rooms ('I heard The Cranberries having a massive argument when they played here last year,' he confides). Once again, the gulf between the dream and reality is yawningly huge and achingly slight.

So what, then, about Ash?

'Ha,' Russell snaps, locating a third letter C in one of the storage containers. 'He reacted just as I thought he would. They both did, actually.'

Sighing agreement?

'More or less, in Karen's case. Ash is less convinced. Either way, they want no part in the actual dirty work. Of course. But the thing is, they're both angry.'

With what?

'Me. For suggesting it. Because it's put them both in an awkward position.'

He arranges the letters he has found so far, smiling quietly at the therapeutic order of the task. ' L CTRIC LI T ORC STR ' is soon spelt out on the wooden board he uses for the purpose.

'Usual nonsense,' he says, suddenly. 'As if it won't be awkward for me too! But I at least realise it's an awkward position that might actually get us somewhere. You want to bake a cake, et cetera. Not that I'll ever be thanked, mind you.'

He finds an A and drops it into its place.

'And they both loathe Barry.'

Understandably, perhaps.

'Perhaps. But I think a good manager probably needs to be rather loathsome.'

Russell's radio crackles and a gruff voice says his name, summoning his presence to the foyer where a scattering of gig flyers requires immediate tidying.

So how has the situation been left?

'We all agreed to make a final decision after the weekend.'

Why wait for five days?

'No particular reason,' Russell admits. 'But some major soul-searching, I guess.'

He pauses for a moment – then:

'Also . . . we still want to play the festival gig.'

He dashes off, looking suitably guilty.

For Karen, the rest of the evening passes pitifully slowly.

With most of the audience below the age of eighteen, there isn't much to do beyond pour a few Cokes, check some IDs, hand over umpteen free glasses of tap water and the very occasional pint. That, of course, plus witnessing with distaste the nu-metal being served up to a thousand or so moshing children by virtue of a successful *cover version*, and wrestling with the moral turmoil of the Jake Situation ('I feel like I'm about to chuck a boyfriend,' she grumbles, midway through her sixth cigarette break).

Only one thing unexpectedly lifts her spirits. Towards ten thirty (normally the curfew on week nights), a pair of guys approach the bar and order a couple of lagers. Only when Karen has finished pouring does it become clear how drunk one of the guys is. His companion is far from sober, but is at least capable of standing up straight. 'Six pounds forty,' Karen tells them, then watches with diminishing patience as the drunker of the two, regrettably the financier of this transaction, searches hopelessly for his money, his messy hair escaping from its ponytail and his eyes almost popping out of his skull with inebriation. He staggers around, checking pocket after pocket for the presence of hard currency: front jeans, back jeans, secret pouch, in both chest pockets of his filthy tartan shirt, then even in his bloody socks ('I almost told them not to bother at that point,' Karen confesses later). His friend vainly makes a few suggestions ('Is it tucked into your travelcard wallet?' 'In your mobile-phone case?' 'Stuffed in your pants?') as the hunt continues. After about five minutes the soberer one looks up, smiles a big, boyish smile and rolls his eyes.

'Funny old world, innit?'

Charmed by this unexpectedly fitting summation, Karen

grins back at him, cheekily helps herself to a large gulp, hands over the pints and tells both blokes to sod off.

'Something clicked in me, right then,' she recalls, wiping down the bar as the last of the sweat-drenched punters file out of the venue. 'I know it sounds weird, but I saw Jake in that guy. It's precisely the kind of thing Jake would've said. And I thought – Jake's a cock, a big, lovable twat with a glint in his eye and a voice that could deafen a cow. He's annoying as fuck, for sure, and Russell's never going to fully get along with him, but maybe – just maybe – someone in this stupid fucking industry is going to spot something great in Jake. Christ, if Shaun bloody Ryder and . . . God, that moron from the Pogues can do it, then surely *someone* out there is going to take a chance on Jake.'

She throws the bar towel into the sink, opens up the till, then pauses.

'And how can we say which one of us is stopping the band from getting somewhere? How do *we* know? Did Van Halen ever think David Lee Roth was gonna stop them from getting signed by being a bit too bonkers? No. They didn't. So how the hell are we to know that *Jake* is the spanner in the works? Maybe it's me. Maybe it's Ash. Christ on a bike, maybe it's bloody *Russell*. Shock-fucking-horror.'

So?

'So – we go back in there. We tell Russell to shove it up his arse, we tell that posh prick and his Rottweiler to piss off, then we *demand* that Russ and Jake have a summit meeting, just the two of them – and they have it all out. Russell raises everything that fucks him off about Jake, and Jake tells Russell everything that pisses him off about *him*. The things they can change, they change. The things they can't, they bloody well *live with*. And then we stop all this cocking about and just go for it.'

Her new mission statement devised, Karen cashes up, calmly writes off a few pints of beer as wastage, changes out of her work top, says goodnight to her colleagues, signs out with security, ignores a text message from Russell ('*Fancy a post-mortem coffee?*') and strides off in search of a bus.

Only then does she spot Josh, standing on the other side of the road, next to a black cab with the meter running. She gasps a little, then keeps her eyes straight and completes her short march to the bus stop.

After thirty seconds or so, Josh ambles across the street. For some reason he is dressed in a sharp dark suit, no tie but an immaculate dress shirt, and his hair has been partly slicked back, the remainder flopping appropriately.

'Karen.'

She looks up at him with weary eyes.

'Been to a wedding?' she mumbles.

'Something like that,' Josh grins. 'Fancy a drink?'

Karen pauses.

'I'll pay,' he adds.

Karen waits a few seconds, then nods. 'Yeah, all right.'

Josh smiles and crosses back to the waiting taxi.

'Whatever,' Karen sighs, following. 'Buy me a drink and I'm just a hopeless tart.'

JAKE: Karen? She's the real deal. Without a doubt, she's the most rock'n'roll of all of us. She lives the dream, man.

ASH: Yeah. She can drink both of us under the table.

JAKE: Oh, fucking hell, can she ever. God, d'you remember that one night . . . ?

ASH: Yeah . . . Borderline.

JAKE: That's right. Tequila shots. Oh, my sainted underpants. She's had about nine or ten, after, what? Must've been six or seven pints each –

ASH: Easily.

JAKE: – and she's leaping about on the dance floor, ordering more drinks, having perfectly intelligible conversations with people . . . but him and me, we're rolling about all over the place, then Ash pukes in the loo, I manage to stagger upstairs to get some air, then it all goes horribly wrong and I end up pulling my cacks down and taking a shit in an alleyway.

ASH: I fell asleep on the night bus, woke up at bloody Heathrow . . .

JAKE: And I lost my wallet, had to make a reverse-charge phone call to Sarah even though we'd split up the week before . . .

ASH: There's a pattern developing there, don't you reckon?

JAKE (laughs): Yeah, bollocks. But Kazza's up the next morning, helping one of her mates move house. Fucking hardcore. And she plays the bass like a bloke.

ASH: She'd kick you in the goolies for saying that.

JAKE: She would, but it's true. The plectrum she uses is like a fucking pound coin. She can play for four hours straight, and never complains of blisters or anything. I play my Les Paul for forty minutes and my back starts killing me. Karen's a monster. And she absolutely never, ever takes any of our shit. I made some mistakes (laughs) . . . fuck, did I cock up in the first six months . . .

Example?

ASH: The Big Mac theory.

JAKE: Aw, bloody hell. I'm still feeling the aftershocks of that one.

The theory being?

JAKE (*sighs*): We're having a pizza before this gig we did in Brighton. The waitress is, well, she's blonde and fit. What can I say? We're full-blooded males. Christ, there ain't much rocket science going on there. And of course, I say some of my usual stuff . . .

ASH: 'Fuck me, I wouldn't mind *her* getting stuck into *my* pepperoni.'

JAKE: Is that what I said?

ASH: Yeah . . . or something equally witty.

JAKE: Right (*laughs*). So Kazza jumps down my throat and demands to know what I see in this bird. And how can I explain it? It's like trying to explain why . . .

ASH: Why you like a Big Mac.

JAKE: Exactly! So that's the theory I came up with. Blonde, pretty, fit – it's like a Big Mac. Inasmuch as a man doesn't have to make any effort to appreciate it. It's obvious. Whereas, a girl like Karen . . . y'know, there are finer points to her. More subtle, but . . . no less attractive, in the end. So . . .

ASH: Sushi.

JAKE: That was it – sushi. That was the food example I used. Can't stand the stuff personally, but . . .

An acquired taste?

JAKE: Exactly. But Kazza fucking leaps on my theory and rips it to shreds. 'Why should I be any less immediately attractive than that fucking blonde tart?' – and all that.

ASH: Silly, cos –

JAKE: It *is* silly, cos the truth is –

ASH (*slightly dreamily*): Karen's beautiful.

JAKE: Absolutely. She's well fit. Gorgeous. Shit, none of us'll ever get *near* a girl like Karen. Told her so, as well, at the time. It didn't exactly calm her down, though.

Have any of you ever been interested in her?

JAKE: Oh, we've all gone through our periods of wanting to shag her. Even Russell. It's funny, it's probably one of the only even slightly disrespectful things he's ever said to me – when I joined the band, I of course immediately said something foul about her, and Russ just smiled and said, 'Yes, I think it's the first time I've ever fancied a bass player.'

ASH (*sighs*): But we got over it.

JAKE: Yeah. Or, more accurately, she beat it out of us. She's just like a bloody younger sister now, all naggy and irritating (*laughs*).

ASH: Although . . . sometimes I think maybe Russ isn't *entirely* over it.

JAKE: Y'think?

ASH: Yeeah.

JAKE: Hmm. Well. If he *isn't* . . .

ASH: Dream on.

JAKE: Yeah. Go and give the old man a tug, Russ, and forget about it.

Wandsworth 2

Another band practice. The principal difference between this and the previous one is that Jake, presumably shaken by yesterday's hunch that his position has been under review, is behaving himself. He is cooperative, diligent, cheerful, obliging (he shows up with a bag of Sainsbury's doughnuts for everyone and buys a round of teas halfway through the evening), doesn't mention a spliff or a beer until gone ten o'clock and has clearly eaten his dinner before arrival (the Brazilian chef looks devastated). This is all just as well — for the other alteration from earlier in the week is that tonight, Karen is quite impressively all over the place.

She stumbles in at twenty past seven with no word of apology, and appears to be drunk. Not a slurring, out-of-control drunk, but a buzzing, been-drinking-vodka-all-day drunk. There is also another ingredient to her oddness — a sort of wide-eyed unhingement – prompting each of the chaps at various points throughout the evening to individually enquire what the matter is (Russell's memorably simple question is, 'Why are you *like* this?'), but a satisfying answer she will not be drawn upon. She frequently vanishes – to the loo, one must assume – often for as long as ten minutes, making tonight's musical progress slow and stilted. It is Karen who this evening requires substantial sustenance from the café, ordering a stout jacket potato and beans, three-quarters of which she leaves. Her bass playing can best be described as spirited – on the dancier, more driving numbers ('Testing Ground', 'Nightclub', 'Krystal Palace') she shuts her eyes and pounds away at full pelt, in something of a trance by the end and drenched in sweat. The more subtle moments ('River Song', 'Wish', 'Cry') are less successful: her notes clunky, ill-timed and undynamic, like Sid Vicious guesting on a James Taylor song. After a couple of hours Russell quite reasonably proposes that they stick to the former breed of track, being in any case more appropriate for Sunday's festival show.

'Ahh, bollocks, Russ, you diplomatic knob-end,' Karen blurts. 'I'm playing like a dick and you know it.'

Outside in the studio yard, taking the evening air during a fag and coffee break, the boys discuss the possible reasons behind Karen's performance.

'Liquid lunch,' Jake ventures.

'Surely not,' Russell frowns. 'She's had those before and it hasn't affected her like this.'

'A big liquid lunch, then. And breakfast.'

'Naah,' Ash says, blowing a cloud of smoke away from Russell. 'I reckon drugs.'

'Pill?' Jake blinks.

'Yeah. Or coke. Possibly both.'

'But the thing is,' Russell ponders, 'she's done all of that before and been perfectly happy to admit and discuss.'

'Mmm, true,' agrees Jake, puffing daintily on his cigarette and gathering his evidence like Poirot. 'Which, my friends, would lead me to conclude that . . . it's not the *what* that we should be considering . . . it's the *who* . . .'

'How do you mean?' Russell asks, growing slightly pale.

'Ah, I get it!' Ash clicks. 'She's been out shagging!'

'Exactly,' Jake beams. 'The dishevelled appearance, the showing up late, then needing to grab food from the café . . . it all makes sense. The little hussy's been snorting coke off some lucky wanker's cock all night . . .'

'Wow, that's an image,' Ash sighs.

Russell makes a face and skulks back inside.

Two bookish-looking guys in plain black T-shirts appear from the other side of the small car park, ambling along with a bottle of wine each. Although the exact nature of their conversation can't yet be heard, they radiate musical knowledge and maturity, like a pair of trainee orchestra conductors.

'Aw, 'ere we go,' Jake calls in their direction. 'It's Rodgers and bloody Hammerstein.'

'Evening, boys,' grins the taller, slimmer one.

'Your turn to get the tea?' Jake suggests, nodding at the bottles.

'Well,' says the other (a little on the plump side, National Health specs, shaved head), 'it's a bit of a celebration, actually.'

'Oh, yeah?' laughs Jake. 'Finally written a chorus with less than fifteen chord changes?'

The two guys smile knowingly at each other for a moment, then the tall one shrugs.

'What the hell. We go back a long way, you might as well know.'

It's Ash's turn to grow pale.

'Know what?'

'Parlophone are going to sign us.'

Twenty minutes later, Ash is still no closer to calming down.

'"Eoah, Parlophone are geeoing to sign us,"' he sneers, with an uncharacteristic wad of sarcasm, as the final note of 'Petrol' dies out. 'What a bunch of arseholes.'

The band in question, Perish the Thought, have been something of a nemesis inside the minds of Russell and his group for the last few years, and not just for musical reasons. Neighbours in the same rehearsal-room complex and regular bill-mates on the usual circuit of London gigs, Perish the Thought (often shortened to PTT – or 'Prat', if Jake is talking) possess the grating habit, whether intentional or not, of perpetually going one better: slightly catchier songs, slightly more accomplished chord progressions, arrangements and rhythmic patterns. When Russell bought his functional but characterless Casio synth, Graeme from PTT showed up at the next gig with a top-of-the-range Moog; if Russell takes a recording to be mastered at the Exchange, PTT take theirs to Abbey Road; if Jake uses his falsetto voice for a chorus, Mark from PTT will use it for a whole song – and when Russell booked a five-date trip to northern England, PTT toured up and down the American East Coast for a fortnight. (To stretch this facet to historical extremes, Russell and Jake attained standard university degrees – whereas not only do both Mark and Dan from PTT have an MA under their belts, but Graeme even has a PhD in Biochemistry, surely making them one of the most educated rock bands since Queen.) This rivalry, however, became personal in early 2000 when Ash's girlfriend was effectively stolen from under his nose by PTT's drummer, a technically brilliant and annoyingly good-looking stickster by the name of Tom Weitzmann – unsurprisingly nicknamed Tom Shitesmann by Jake and Karen.

'It was at a Camden Underworld gig,' Jake later explains, as Ash retrieves a fortifying can of beer from the off-licence. 'Prat were headlining. It was the classic drummer cliché – it'd almost be funny if it weren't so bloody awful . . . The Underworld demanded all the bands share the same drum kit, so Ash lets everyone use his, Prat play last, Shitesmann comes straight offstage – having eyed up Ash's bird all night, apparently – and fucking goes for it then and there while Ash is taking his drums apart.'

'Poor Ash,' Karen comments, shakily crumbling some tobacco into a Rizla.

'And the worst thing is,' Jake continues, 'Shitesmann comes up to him in the yard here a few days later and does the whole "hail, fellow, well met, all's fair in love and war" bollocks. How Ash controlled himself I do not know. I'd have fucking decked him immediately.'

'I almost did,' Karen admits.

Ash returns. The evening's news has dramatically altered his demeanour: usually affable and difficult to agitate, his face now wears one of Russell's thunderstorms and his every move is informed with aggression. When his hi-hat stand gives him gyp, he simply slams the two cymbals together a few times until they behave.

'Remember, Ash,' Karen reassures him, 'people are *always* saying they're gonna be signed – doesn't mean it'll actually happen.'

'Yeeah,' grunts Ash, cracking open a second can of lager. 'You could be right.'

But the damage has been done. Ash barely says anything for the remainder of the rehearsal, laying into his drums with alarming ferocity at the climax of 'Drama' and wordlessly departing a few minutes before eleven o'clock. All this succeeds in diverting attention from Karen, who is no less of a mess by the end and visibly running out of steam. Finally she gives up altogether and crumples in a heap on the floor.

'Come on, party girl,' Jake chuckles, giving her a playful kick on the backside. 'Spill the beans.'

'Mind your own fucking business,' comes the mumbled response from under her black jumble of hair.

A final attempt is made to extract the coveted information. Russell, who has also been unusually, if not quite so noticeably, silent for the second half of the evening, waits until Jake has gone before making his slightly more informed observation.

'So,' he says, in what he might think is a mock-inquisitive, matey sort of tone, 'you're, um . . . wearing the same clothes as last night?'

'Oh, fuck off!' Karen replies, hoicking her bag onto her shoulder. 'What *are* you lot, my bloody parents?'

And that's the end of that.

'They probably slept together,' Russell unhappily speculates, sliding the last amp into the equipment cage. 'I knew they would. I just *knew* it.'

It now emerges that Josh phoned Russell halfway through the Alien Ant Farm gig, just as Russell was cleaning brick dust off the cistern in one of the backstage loos.

'He's getting a bit impatient,' Russell sighs, kneeling down and clicking the first of the three padlocks into place. 'He can't work out why I'm stalling.'

Doesn't he realise that it's not your decision alone?

'Not really. "You call the shots," he kept saying . . .'

He closes the last of the padlocks and rises wearily to his feet.

'. . . probably followed by "man" or "dude".'

A long-haired teenager, one of the studio employees, comes barging down the corridor with a battered Marshall speaker.

'Mind out, boss,' he says. Russell sighs again and makes off towards the exit.

At the reception desk (a rather grand term for the dirty white counter where a tattooed, bored-looking girl sits smoking and texting) Russell hands over a cheque for the week's activities and, unusually, buys himself a can of Coke.

'Might need it later,' he states, cagily. 'I'm conducting a bit of an experiment.'

He walks out to where his faithful Volkswagen is waiting, a single yellow lamp now illuminating the darkened car park. Unleashing a third and final sigh, he unlocks the car and perches on the driver seat, his Dunlop Green Flash plimsolls resting on the dirty ground.

'I kind of mentioned to Josh that the important one to convince was Karen – that if she agreed, Ash would too. Which is true, I think. Then last night Josh asked me if Karen was there at the Imperial too, so I said yes.'

Russell swings his legs into the vehicle and starts the engine.

'I reckon he tried to convince Karen by . . . you know.'

Or perhaps he just took her out, bought her a few drinks, tried to get to know her, convinced her that way. Which might ultimately make your life easier, in fact?

Russell looks dubious.

'You saw the shape she was in. "A few drinks" doesn't do

that. I may be a lamentably dull and boring teetotaller, but I know *that* much.'

He slams the door and carefully steers himself out of the yard. All things considered, it seems an odd moment for Russell to suddenly feel self-conscious about his sobriety.

RUSSELL: Band members sleeping with each other is the kiss of death. Seriously. And of course it's always booze's fault. They go out after a gig, or a rehearsal, or wherever, they chug away, and then think, 'Ooh, one little moment of indiscretion won't hurt.' But it does. They show up at the next rehearsal, and it's *weird*. Even if it hasn't been weird up until that point. What happens outside the confines of the rehearsal room is totally different to what's going on inside. The other members feel it instantly. And it messes everything up.

Why is that?

RUSSELL: The key to a successful relationship between people playing music is detachment. There's a connection, sure, but it's entirely formed by the music. If two people have colluded on something as intense as sexual intercourse, they're never going to have that detachment – even if they never end up becoming an 'item', or whatever you want to call it.

Why is this detachment so important?

RUSSELL: Because it's crucial to the selflessness of being a band. The anonymity. If that's my friend from years ago over there, playing bass, or keyboards, I might do something – anything – because I think he might find it funny, or impressive, or because it refers to something from our life as friends. Immediately, inequality raises its head within the unit. At the same time, I might *not* want to do certain things – play certain notes, make certain moves – because I'll worry that my friend will laugh at me, or think, 'Oh, Russell's behaving differently to how he normally does.' You see? The mechanics collapse. The band members are no longer able to work to their full – selfless – potentials.

Does the need for this detachment stretch beyond the actual members of the band?

RUSSELL: Oh, definitely. If the sound engineer is Jake's best friend, he's automatically going to spend more time making Jake sound good than anyone else. A manager being a friend would be an absolute *nightmare*, for every thinkable reason. The same with a producer.

But what about Morgan?

RUSSELL: What about him?

He's your friend.

RUSSELL: Well, not really. The only thing we ever do together is work. Anyway, the same theory applies to all the band's surrounding paraphernalia – being filmed, photographed, reviewed . . .

Being interviewed?

RUSSELL: Absolutely. One of the reasons that all of us – well, most of us – are able to completely open up to you, is that we didn't know you before, and you didn't know us. Selecting us at random was a masterstroke. And because of that, you really ought to end up with the most perfectly balanced piece of journalism. There's a complete singularity of purpose. You obviously have a decent understanding of these things.

It should always be the same way with band members. Justin Sullivan from New Model Army once said that bands formed of close friends don't work, because 'it's the wrong things bringing them together'. Excellently put. And the 'right' things are probably different for every group. In our case, it's simply a need to bring our sound to a wider audience and to gain the respect of our peers. Or at least, it's supposed to be. But you can imagine – if we wanted to play five-a-side football or go to the cinema with each other, those things would end up taking over from the music. Perry Farrell from Jane's Addiction said his band weren't friends – he didn't hang around with them on his days off. Again – nail on the head. The four of them get together – and there's a strong, collaborative, unified vision. On days off, they have other friends. It all makes sense. One of the reasons Jane's Addiction worked so well.

But didn't Farrell and Dave Navarro almost end up killing each other?

RUSSELL: Er, yes. Well . . . there are always limits.

But surely, people who play together in bands can become good friends?

RUSSELL: They can, but the dynamic is very, very different. It's a terrible cliché to say bands are like families, but the statement contains some truth, as . . . a lot of the *fluff* of being friends is stripped away – you say what you mean, you don't worry too much about being offensive, you may argue, but you recover from the arguments quickly. I'm an only child myself, but I'm told that's exactly how it is between siblings. And it's amazing how quickly this sort of bond forms. With Karen and me, it was there by the end of the first rehearsal. Ash very soon afterwards. But I'm quite certain that none of this would've happened if we'd been friends previously.

Jake and Ash manage to have both sorts of relationship with each other.

RUSSELL: It's true, they've become 'muckers', as Jake would put it. Obviously there's nothing you can do to stop it. But because they're the drummer and the singer, I'm not too surprised – a strong bond always forms between those two. Such huge similarities. Both of them competing to be the loudest. Both referred to as 'the driving force' at one time or another. Both seen as the most macho, attractive . . . primally connected to the music. And both of them want to *be* each other. Every singer I've met has been a frustrated drummer, and vice versa.

Why do you think that is?

RUSSELL: It's partly because the two functions are so different to each other – using your vocal cords and hitting things. So to a drummer, singing must look totally refreshing. And to a singer, drumming . . . On the other hand, I doubt there are many guitarists who want to be bassists, and so on. And then there's the limelight thing – a singer might occasionally think, 'Gosh, wouldn't it be lovely to just sit at the back and pound away, unnoticed,' but a drummer probably gets fed up with no one paying him the blindest bit of attention. So anyway – Jake and Ash being close friends has never worried me.

Until now?

RUSSELL (*flinches*): Uh, yeah. Maybe.

What about you and Jake?

RUSSELL: Uh?

Did your sibling bond form immediately?

RUSSELL: Oh . . . well . . . I suppose we're like the eldest and youngest siblings in a family of five. Not much in common, other than the fact we belong to the same group.

Has there ever been a moment over the years when you've considered Jake a friend?

RUSSELL (*looks exceedingly uncomfortable*): Um . . . well, he has a . . . like I said, it's better to keep these things at arm's length. (*Coughs, sips more coffee.*) But members going to bed with each other is absolutely the very worst.

Right.

RUSSELL: A band's workings fall flat immediately.

Right.

(*Silence.*)

There must also be the problem of lovers falling out and not wanting to be in the same band any more.

RUSSELL: Well, precisely. And cheating on each other with other members. And sleeping with other members of other bands. The whole thing is an absolute minefield.

So, have you ever done it yourself?

RUSSELL: Don't be ridiculous.

Wimbledon 2

Friday afternoon, and Russell is cross-legged on his bedsit floor, dutifully carving up four hundred or so A6 promotional flyers: an activity that normally cheers immensely, but which today doesn't lift him from a somewhat grouchy mood. Nor is he looking particularly in the pink, leaving one to ponder the precise nature of last night's 'experiment'. He scowls and grumbles as his radio churns out the usual daytime XFM fare: Coldplay, Travis, Radiohead, Stereophonics.

'They play that Groove Armada song again and I'll scream,' Russell says.

Thankfully, before Ash sank into his trench of self-pity and despair at last night's rehearsal, he managed to give Russell the details for Sunday's 'Big Joint' festival all-dayer. He even mentioned that he'd spotted an advert for said event in *M8* magazine – but which did not, as Russell was quick to establish, bother to list the band name.

'Which is half the reason for doing this type of thing in the first place,' Russell moans, guillotining an inch-thick border from a wedge of paper. 'Free publicity. Raise the profile. But mind you – I'm fairly surprised it's happening at all.'

If Russell's distrust of events booked by other members seems uncharitable, it's not completely without foundation. Shortly after Jake joined, one of Karen's contacts promised them a slot at the 'Donington Festival'. Expecting a pivotal outdoor performance on a scintillating bill of hard-rock bands, they rehearsed eight of their loudest songs and schlepped up to Nottinghamshire, only to discover this particular festival took place in the beer garden of a village pub, filled with two hundred real-ale swigging fifty-somethings ('I think our set lasted six minutes,' Russell painfully recalls, 'after they discovered we didn't know any Credence Clearwater Revival'). A disaster of similar magnitude took place in the summer of 1999, when Jake arranged for them to appear at another open-air concert, set to take place on a country estate near Downham Market, Norfolk. They piled into a Transit and roared into town, whereupon they were pointed towards a makeshift stage in a children's playground and instructed to deliver a practically unamplified ninety-minute set to a couple of old blokes and a horse.

Russell could therefore be forgiven for bypassing Ash and personally telephoning the event organiser, a friendly-sounding lady by the name of Megan. She admitted the *M8* advert had been finalised prior to their addition on the bill, but reassured Russell that their 2 p.m. slot was secure, keenly anticipated, and that they could load in from 10 a.m. She even mentioned they could arrive the night before and camp, like many others planned to do, as the sound system would already be set up and the DJs might 'spin a few tunes' in advance of the big day.

'Might be a good idea?' Russell suggested to the others. 'I have to pick up the van on Saturday afternoon anyway. And she says the site's really near the town, so we could pop into some of the local places with flyers – see if we can drum up some interest.'

The others nodded, although Jake's wink at Ash and Karen suggested distributing flyers would probably be the last thing on his mind.

Russell is working on two types of flyer. The first is fairly standard: a little photo of the foursome, the band logo, their onstage time and the 'Big Joint' emblem at the bottom. The second, a creation Russell is particularly pleased with, proudly states – in slight homage to a 1970s BBC sitcom – 'You Have Been Watching . . .' followed by the band insignia. At the footer of the sheet Russell has inserted the website URL; again, another touch he considers exemplary of his promotional nous.

'Not to sound too sanctimonious,' he sighs, 'but this stuff would *never* occur to the others.'

Debate has raged over how to circulate this latter communication, it only considered a truly effective exercise if foisted into the hands of the audience no later than the very second the band leave the stage, or preferably while they are still playing. When Jake was going out with Sarah Nuttall, she would tag along for such missions and would be happy to wander about during the set, handing out whatever she was asked to; now that she is officially out of the picture, volunteers to assist with this kind of task are few (Morgan considers such activities entirely beneath him). Various solutions have been suggested, from hurling a few handfuls into the crowd as the feedback dies out, to all four members simply jumping off the stage after the final chord and frantically dispensing the things to the hopefully cheering public. It was Ash who, with typical practicality, suggested a slight modification of this last method.

'Tell you what we do, right? It's a dance festival. So people'll be tripping and pilling their nuts off . . .'

'At two thirty in the afternoon?' Russell blinked.

'Yeeah, Russ, trust me. So anyway. We hit upon a groove, and then we extend it. We finish the set with, say . . . "M3", or "Nightclub" . . . or even "Testing Ground" . . . we pile into the last chorus, then Jakey stops playing and leaps into the crowd, but the three of us keep going, we lock into the outro and repeat it, over and over, however many times it takes. Build it up, make it like a mash-up dance ending. The freaks'll love it. Then at last Jakey bounces back up, we blast round one more time, then – bosh.'

'Wizard!' Jake hooted. 'That's brill, and I get to do the whole "conquering frontman" thing. Love it.'

'Twat,' Karen pronounced.

This is now regarded as The Plan, although a whiff of doubt still lingers within Russell.

'It's all a bit Michael Stipe at Glastonbury,' he admits, shoving a fistful of paper trimmings into his cardboard recycling box. 'I'm not really a fan of those gestures of self-adoration, until a band really deserves it.'

But hopefully it'll be just a neat way of executing the promotional task at hand, in the spirit of the event. Self-adoration mightn't come into it.

Russell smirks scornfully.

'This is Jake we're talking about. Believe me – it'll come into it.'

His phone rings.

'Hi . . . What? . . . No, I did . . . I *did* tell you . . . Rubbish, I *definitely* told you . . . Maybe . . . I'll see what I can do . . . But I definitely told you . . . OK, yeah . . . Bye . . .'

He shakes his head and grabs another pile of untrimmed flyers.

'Morgan,' he explains, gesturing at his phone. 'Claims I never told him ELO were playing the Imperial tonight. He's livid. They're one of his favourites. So now I've got to try and get him a last-minute freebie.'

The familiar intro to 'Superstylin'' by Groove Armada drifts out of Russell's radio.

'Give me strength,' he growls.

Half an hour later, Russell chops his last flyer. With impeccable timing, Karen arrives to help.

'Aw, sorry,' she says guiltily, flicking through a stack of perfectly trimmed sheets. 'I got up late.'

'Never mind,' Russell mutters, turning off the radio and settling on the edge of his mattress. 'Perhaps you can make yourself useful and put some coffee on.'

Normally this type of instruction would set Karen's overactive female-stereotyping antenna twitching, but Russell gets away with it.

'Can I have tea?' Karen asks, filling the kettle.

'Have what you like.'

Karen fixes the drinks in the little kitchenette corner of the room while Russell tinkers with his Telecaster. He's busy attempting some physiologically challenging chord shape and doesn't notice Karen pausing for a couple of seconds before dropping her used tea bag into the pedal bin; she frowns as she peers down inside, then flashes Russell a quick glance and resumes.

'No milk, by the way,' Russell murmurs.

'Don't worry, I haven't forgotten,' Karen replies, with a hint of irritation.

'No, I mean, I haven't got any milk. For your tea.'

'Aw, bollocks, really?'

'Sorry.'

'Can you ask one of the inmates for some, then? I can't stand tea without milk.'

'Oh . . . I hate asking them for things. Then you're obliged to talk to them . . .'

'All right, *I'll* go and ask.'

'No, no, I'll go,' Russell grumbles, rising. 'Don't get your hopes up, though.'

Russell mooches off with Karen's mug. Karen waits until the door swings shut before hurriedly looking inside the pedal bin again. Her words come out quickly and it's a second or two before their meaning sinks in.

'There's an empty sachet of Alka-Seltzer in there.'

She looks up, then back down again.

'*Two* empty sachets.'

Her eyes dart about the room – to the bed, to Russell's little desk, his computer, his hi-fi, his practice amp, the windowsill. Then she turns back to the bin. With a grimace she bends down and fishes about, shortly producing an empty Coke can which she sniffs.

'Can't believe I'm fucking doing this.'

She leaps across the room to Russell's little cabinet fridge and freezer, both of which she opens, neither of which contain very much.

'Christ, what does he *eat*?'

At last, sighing apologetically, she kneels down and looks under

Russell's mattress. It's during this final examination that Russell returns.

'What on earth are you doing?'

'Looking for porn, what do you think.'

'Success with the milk,' Russell says, plonking down her mug and picking up his Telecaster again. 'Except I think it might be skimmed.'

Karen sits down on Russell's folding wooden desk chair, slurps some tea, then eyes him craftily.

'So, Russ. Why've you got two empty packets of Alka-Seltzer in your bin?'

Russell tweaks one of his guitar strings and looks up.

'What?'

'Oh, God! You blokes are *ridiculous*. Do you really think anyone *ever* believes that you haven't heard when you say "what" like that?'

'Sorry, I . . . er . . .'

'Alka-Seltzer. In your bin. Two empty sachets of.'

'Oh, I . . . er . . . had a bit of a tummy ache first thing this morning.'

'Bollocks.'

'I did! I ate too much when I got home –'

'Bollocks –'

'– and I've been finding recently, every time I eat bread or pasta –'

'La la la, bullshit, bullshit, la la laaa –'

'– I suppose that I might be –'

'Russell, you don't take Alka-Seltzer when you've *just* got an upset stomach.'

'I know.'

'Then . . .'

'It was all my housemate had – I borrowed it from one of my housemates.'

'I thought you didn't like borrowing things off your housemates.'

'It was a really bad stomach ache.'

'Is it better now?'

'Yes,' Russell nods, turning back to his guitar. 'Thank you.'

'Don't mention it,' Karen smiles dubiously, sipping her tea.

No more is said for a while. Karen idly picks up Russell's copy of *NME* and leafs through. Russell seems to be playing the chords to Duran Duran's 'Is There Something I Should Know?', but this might be a coincidence.

'JJ72 are headlining the Imperial in September,' Karen notes.

'Yup,' Russell replies.

'We could see if –'

'Already asked him,' Russell states. 'Usual thing – "It'll be up to the promoter, but I'll make sure he knows you're available." Which means . . .'

'He'll do absolutely bugger all.'

'Yup,' Russell sighs, contorting his fingers into a tricky new formation.

'Mind you,' Karen points out, laying down the paper and sitting back, 'we might not be ready for a gig like that next month.'

'How do you mean?'

'Well, if we're breaking in a new singer, and stuff.'

Russell stops playing and stares at her.

'You mean Josh?'

Karen nods, then shrugs. 'Guess we've gotta do *something*.'

Russell bites his bottom lip and looks down at his feet for a minute or so. That he doesn't appear instantly pleased suggests either continuing doubts of his own, or that he regards Karen's turnaround as the only proof he needs of Josh's precise persuasion methods a few evenings ago.

'And before you fucking ask,' Karen snaps, 'this has *nothing* to do with the other night.'

Russell rather pathetically feigns ignorance. Karen is having none of it.

'You know what I'm talking about, Groom. I'm no fucking pushover. I came to this conclusion *well* on my own.'

Russell glumly returns to his riffing.

The entity known as the Electric Light Orchestra now comprises only about two of the original forty-six (or thereabouts) members, but of course no one cares and the Imperial is rammed. As expected, the most frequently visible punter is the sort of bespectacled, bearded old bloke who mutters things like: 'Of course, I saw them in '71 before Roy Wood left', or 'I was there at the fateful Hammie Odeon gig when the mothership collapsed on Bev Bevan', in between sips of their specially stocked Bathams Mild Ale. A perhaps equally predictable presence is a drove of trendy individuals who'd look more at home posing around Hoxton Square, and for whom ELO represent the latest thing to pillage. It is this second brand of observer that Russell and Karen quietly bitch about when their paths cross briefly in the first-level bar, just before the veteran rockers hit the stage.

'Bunch of arseholes,' reckons Karen. 'They probably weren't even *born* when ELO were out the first time.'

'I don't get it,' frowns Russell, sipping some water from a plastic cup. 'Why would you enjoy something ironically? I find this whole "so bad it's actually good" thing really upsetting.'

One of Karen's male colleagues, a gothy-looking mature

student with an almost palpable argumentative streak, smirks at the exchange.

'Because?' he shrugs.

'Because, Berman,' Russell replies, 'you should be able to appreciate something on its own merits, rather than according to how the current fashion perceives it, or, as in this case, twists it. And the fact is –'

'They're shite,' nods the guy.

Russell almost coughs up his drink.

'They're *genius!*' he spits. '"Mr Blue Sky"? "Shine a Little Love"?'

'"Don't Bring Me Down"?' Karen suggests.

'Exactly,' agrees Russell. 'Pop *masterpieces.*'

'Hardly Pink Floyd, is it?' smiles Berman, pouring a pint of lager for a customer.

'Thank fuck,' scoffs Karen.

'And Pink Floyd,' adds Russell, 'were *not* pop.'

'Oh, no? And who would you consider to be pop nowadays?'

Karen and Russell's replies are instant, indistinguishable.

'*We* are.'

Berman hands his customer some change and chuckles.

'Wow. You put yourselves in the same bracket as those who're really doing it, yeah?'

'*We* are really doing it!' Karen snaps.

'I suppose you have to say that, eh?'

'You'll be fucking sorry,' growls Karen, 'when we're headlining this place and you're still back here, opening cans of Red Stripe for wankers.'

'And you really believe you've got a chance. Admirable.'

'Watch it, Berman,' Karen tells him. 'I'm still your fucking Bar Leader, remember.'

'As it happens,' Russell declares, somewhat haughtily, 'we *have* got a chance. More than a chance, actually. We've got a new manager waiting in the wings – we're in pole position for a record deal. Just watch. In two years' time we'll be as big as Feeder.'

'You've already got a following, then?'

'We've got a five-hundred-strong mailing list.'

'How many of those fuckers turn up, though?'

'Enough.'

'So how are you gonna get the breaks?'

'Our manager will put our work into the right hands,' Russell enunciates, with decreasing patience, 'and those people will notice that we're brilliant.'

'Mmm . . . y'see, this is something I've always wondered,' Berman sighs, shaking his head with mock sympathy. 'Why unsigned bands are always so bloody arrogant.'

At this point, with hitherto unseen aggression, Russell bangs his fist on the bar counter and roars, with genuine fury in his eyes, 'We *have* to be! Because we're the only ones on this fucking planet fighting our corner!'

Stunned silence follows, broken only by a burst of static from Russell's radio.

'Russell Groom?' a voice says.

Russell unsnaps the black box from his combats. 'Go ahead.'

'Yeah, Russ . . . we've got a bit of trouble in level-two Gents. Get up here as soon as, and . . .' – the radio goes quiet for a moment – 'bring a mop.'

'On my way,' Russell replies gruffly, and is gone.

Karen and Berman remain silent for a few seconds.

'He's passionate,' Berman finally concedes.

Karen looks blankly around the bar, then steadies herself on the cigarette machine.

'He said "fucking",' she gapes, reaching for her mobile phone.

RUSSELL: To be part of an unsigned band is to be a true outsider, an untouchable, a walking hazard sign, a leper. You feel unclean, unwanted, disabled. It's the closest − I think, I hope − that any of us will ever feel to being a refugee in a strange land, arriving with only the clothes you're wearing, having to fight for every single thing you need in order to live. OK, I overdramatise − but there's something about the plight of the immigrant, the asylum seeker, that we can relate to.

KAREN: No one wants to know you.

RUSSELL: That's it. You exist on the margins of life.

Do you think it's like this in most entertainment industries?

RUSSELL: To a degree.

KAREN: Jake, what was that thing about Tarantino you said?

JAKE: Oh, yeah − before Tarantino made *Reservoir Dogs*, he said if you'd sent him a letter and just wrote on the envelope: 'Quentin Tarantino, The Fringes of the Movie Industry', it would have reached him.

KAREN: I love that.

RUSSELL: But it's much, *much* worse than that in the music business.

ASH: Yeah. I drummed for this guy Dave Black once −

KAREN: Oh God . . . this is painful . . .

ASH: He was like a singer-songwritery geezer . . .

RUSSELL: A lot of fuss about him in the late nineties.

ASH: Yeah. And the bloke had a publishing deal, a record deal, an agent and so on, and he was on the books of one of those whatsits . . . music PR firms . . .

RUSSELL: Bean and Gawn.

ASH: Yeah. Cool crowd, up in Camden. So, I moonlighted with 'im for, what . . . a year or so?

RUSSELL: On and off.

JAKE: We thought we'd lost you, fella.

ASH (*laughs*): Yeeah . . . it did get like that, for a bit. Never amounted to anything in the end. So anyway, we go and do this photo session with him, me and the bass player, and this dude from Bean and Gawn comes along to give us a hand, can't even remember his name now . . .

KAREN AND RUSSELL: Colin.

ASH: Yeeah, thassit. And we have this really great day, Colin's driving one of the cars, and we get on really well, go to this pub for lunch . . . have a cheeky biffta together, all of that. Saw him at one of Dave's gigs a few weeks later, same vibe. Nice guy. Swapped phone numbers, and so on. But then it all goes wrong for Dave Black – he gets dropped, falls out with his manager, ends up going to the States to work out his publishing deal on a few songs with some soul act. So that's the end of me working with him. Coupla months later, us lot have just finished another demo, what was it . . . ?

RUSSELL: *Hook-Laden.*

ASH: Yeah. So I think, what the hell, I post a copy to Colin with a little note. Don't hear anything for a month. Fair enough. Probably busy. So I call him. Nothing. Doesn't return my calls – I think I called twice, left it at that, didn't wanna be weird. Then we support one of his other acts at the Dublin Castle and I go up to him and say hello –

KAREN: So fucking rough –

ASH: – and he completely blanks me. Like, *completely*. Looks through me like I'm a fucking, I dunno, pane of glass. So I think, well, maybe he's tied up, stressed out, so I leave it . . . then later that evening after we play, he's just chilling by the bar, he can't possibly be busy or anything, so I risk it again. Same thing happens.

JAKE: Man, I don't know how you held it together.

ASH: Well, you know what I'm like . . . but to be honest, I almost didn't.

There was no other reason for his behaviour?

ASH: Nah. I've thought about it long and hard. Like, maybe Dave Black pissed him off or something. But naah. At the end of the day, when we did that photo shoot . . .

RUSSELL: You had a reason to exist in his life.

ASH: Yeah. I meant something to him. But at the Dublin, I was a . . .

KAREN: Non-entity.

ASH: Yeah.

RUSSELL: But worse than that – you were in an *unsigned band*. You were actually less than a non-entity. If you were just a random person, drinking in the pub, he'd have probably at least acknowledged your existence, even if it was just to say, 'Sorry, I think you've got the wrong guy' – or similar. But the fact was, he *did* know you, and he knew all too well where you were coming from.

ASH: But I didn't fucking wanna talk *business* with him, did I? I was just saying hello.

RUSSELL: Of course you were! But that's just it. If he spoke to you – or more importantly, if he was *seen* speaking to you – he'd have been – 'Colin, who speaks to unsigned bands'.

This all seems rather . . .

RUSSELL: Far-fetched?

Yes.

RUSSELL, JAKE AND KAREN: It's not.

★   ★   ★

Russell has grabbed a mop and bucket from his maintenance cupboard, and is now thundering down the corridor towards the level-two Gents' toilets. He takes a deep breath and bursts through the swing doors to behold a room not dissimilar to a gigantic rinsing pool in a public swimming baths after someone has run amok with a carton of apple juice, and a smell akin to a hundred packets of Scampi Fries being ripped open simultaneously and wafted about a lot.

'And he calls this,' Russell stammers, '"a bit of trouble".'

One of the runners is already here: a cheerful, long-haired skater of about seventeen by the name of Jamie Simpson, his jeans rolled up, valiantly wading about with a few towels and a broom, ineffectually slopping some of the foul liquid into a bucket.

'Yo, boss,' he beams. 'Drains are blocked, innit.'

'Thank you,' Russell replies. Beyond the stagnant echo of the lavatory walls, the venue's crowd can be heard heralding the arrival of Jeff Lynne and team, as the opening notes of 'Do Ya' are unleashed with all accompanying nostalgia. Russell sighs.

'OK. Let's do it.'

The mop-up job takes almost an hour and is, as usual, punctuated by moments of idiocy: a euphoric City banker comes bursting in, despite the doors being sealed with gaffer tape and plastered with 'Out of Order' signs, then drunkenly berates Russell and Jamie for messing up his cowboy boots; the venue manager pokes his head round the corner and asks how long it'll be before the loos can open again; Jamie, buckling under the weight of a tub of piss, answers his mobile and drops the lot.

'Satan!' he shouts.

'Yup,' Russell nods. 'He's "in da house", as you'd put it.'

Once they have averted widespread permanent damage to the

structure of the building, the two of them admit defeat and stagger out. Russell firmly chains and padlocks the doors, then the pair skirt around the back of the level-two auditorium and reconvene in Russell's little maintenance room where they assess the damage to their clothing. Wisely, Jamie has been wearing a hefty pair of army boots.

'I think dese tings a' lived through most of da damage, ya know?'

'Wish I could say the same for these,' Russell grunts, peeling off his piss-drenched Green Flashes and running them rather hopelessly under the tap.

'You got no spares?'

'No,' Russell replies. 'I mean – yes.'

Jamie frowns. 'Yes or no, boss?'

'I have no spare trainers,' Russell clarifies, realising this is no time for an English grammar lesson.

'Dat's bad news, yo,' Jamie comments, settling down in an orange plastic chair. 'Might go an' see if I can find you some, after I smoke dis.' He produces a pre-rolled joint from his tobacco tin and holds it up for Russell's approval. 'You mind?'

Russell draws a quick breath, then pauses.

'Actually . . . no.' He leans over the sink and opens the little window. 'I don't mind.'

'Schwee-*eet*,' Jamie grins, lighting up.

Over the next few minutes, as Jamie puffs away and Russell wonders aloud whether there's any point in attempting to save his shoes, the room fills with the rich, sweet aroma of cannabis resin. Perhaps it's the combination of a warm night, ELO pounding out the hits and the visit to drainage hell he's just paid, but Russell – as strange as it sounds – appears to be growing curious of the burning substance within Jamie's Rizla.

'It's funny,' Russell admits. 'The guys in my band smoke that stuff all the time, but it never smells . . . like that.'

'Probably different shit,' Jamie suggests. 'Here.'

He passes the joint over. Russell shakes his head, but remains intrigued.

'So . . . what exactly is it?'

'Maroc.'

'It smells . . . well, almost like *coffee*.'

'Yo,' Jamie improvises, 'I guess those Moroccans, dey smoke a toke while drinkin' a coffee, innit. S'all da same.'

Jamie's radio crackles. 'Jamie Simpson?'

He snaps it up. 'Go.'

'We need another few crates of Boddingtons on level three.'

'On it,' Jamie replies, jumping up. He chips the joint on the cassette box he's been using as an ashtray, then balances it on a wooden workbench. 'Mind dis for me, boss. Don't finish it all at once,' he winks, bounding out of the door.

A barefoot Russell (his socks are also entirely beyond hope) now sits alone in the little room, contemplating the familiar intro of ELO's 'Mr Blue Sky' which is now pumping out. It's a peculiar place to be stationed: so close to the action, every note loudly teeming through the thin walls, but so far removed, neither witnessing the show nor feeling any of its warmth, as if experiencing the whole thing from a private listening pod that the designers have forgotten to provide with a window. Confined to this curious lair, the scent of hash gradually receding and the stench of Scampi Fries quickly returning, Russell continues to eye Jamie's little tube of browning white paper, perhaps wondering how much more peculiar life could possibly become via its contents.

Tempted?

'No!' Russell laughs, shaking himself out of it and standing up. 'Don't be silly.'

He pretends to look busy for a few seconds, then realises there isn't much to pretend to do.

'It's an interesting thought, though,' he says, settling down again. 'How naturally "anti" I am when Jake's the one doing the offering. Never been remotely interested in it . . . . but . . .'

He seems to be just on the verge of some deep revelation when there is a violently loud banging on the door. He leaps out of his seat.

'Good *grief*!' he exclaims, unlocking the door. 'For goodness' sake, Jamie, there's no need to –'

But it is not Jamie. It is Morgan, paying his habitual mid-show visit.

'Groooom!' he howls, lifting aloft his pint of beer in one hand and – strangely – his umbrella in the other. Russell ushers him inside and closes the door.

'You expecting rain?' Russell asks grumpily.

'Nah,' Morgan bleats. 'I've brought it to shelter from the bucket-load of cowturd being hurled from the stage under the guise of classic musical entertainment.'

'No good?'

Morgan flings himself down in the orange seat. 'I s'pose it's all right, if you like cover bands. Fookin' stinks in 'ere, you been eating Scampi Fries all evening or what?'

'Long story,' Russell replies, starting to assemble some of his plastic display lettering.

'And where've your fookin' shoes and socks gone?'

'Part of the same story.'

'Funny man y'are, Groom.' Morgan swigs his drink and clocks

Russell's current activity. 'Ooh, 'ere we are, it's hangman again. Who's next?'

'Joan Armatrading.'

'Bit of a job, that. Can't you just put "Brummie Lezza"?'

'Morg, to paraphrase yourself, are you here for anything constructive or are you just going to irritate me and drink beer?'

Morgan leans back in his chair, thinking.

'Ahhm . . . I'm just gonna irritate you and drink beer.'

His eyes survey the room, settling fairly quickly on the remnants of Jamie's joint.

'Ayup,' he observes. 'Hang on. What the fook's that?'

'Don't touch it,' Russell instructs. 'It's not mine.'

'A doobie, Groom?' Morgan grins, ignoring Russell and inspecting the item. 'What the fook are you doing with a' – he gives it a quick sniff – 'if I'm not too much mistaken, a fairly good-quality jawn?'

Russell advances across the room and tries to grab it.

'Give me that thing, Morgan! Now.'

'Ah-ah,' Morgan beams, producing a lighter from his pocket. 'Not before I've had meself a free sample.'

Morgan is squashed into a corner of the little room, behind the door, holding Russell at bay with his left hand while sparking up the spliff with his right. He avails himself of a healthy drag and his eyes narrow in appreciation.

'Hmm! Not bad.'

Russell gives up and stomps back to his lettering. 'It's something called Maroc, apparently. Don't have any more, will you? It belongs to one of the runners.'

'Have you partaken?'

'Of course not.'

'Bloody puritan. Probably do you some good.'

'Not you as *well*,' Russell winces, banging an 'A' down on the other red characters he has so far assembled (JO DING).

'Why?' Morgan frowns. 'Someone been on at you?'

Russell studies his letters unhappily.

'The guy I told you about. Producer's son.'

'What, fookin' Chigwell George?'

'Josh Chigwell,' Russell corrects. 'Spoke to him on the phone the other night. He told me I needed to get "more interesting".'

'And what concern's it of his?'

'He's probably going to join the band, remember?'

'You're not still poncing about with that caper, are you?'

Russell shrugs and exhales. 'Oh, I just don't *know*, Morg. I mean, in some ways these people make a lot of sense, but . . . part of me wants to . . .'

'Tell 'em to naff off?'

'Mmm,' Russell mopes. 'Anyway, I ended up experimenting a bit.'

'How d'you mean?'

'With alcohol. How do you *drink* that stuff?'

Morgan slaps the bench and shouts with laughter. 'Haa! *You!* What did you drink?'

'Coke.'

'And?'

'I . . . er . . . I just bought the cheapest thing they had.'

'Which was?'

'Some wine stuff.'

'What wine stuff?'

'I don't know. Thunder something.'

'My *God!* Thunderbird! Hahahaa!' Morgan doubles over with mirth. 'You mixed Coke with fookin' Thunderbird! Oh, Christmas.'

164

Russell scowls around the room at the jars of screws and pots of paint. Outside, 'Shine a Little Love' begins.

'The guy in the shop said they'd go well together,' he grumbles.

'Oh, Groom. This is priceless. If you're gonna start drinking, you might as well do it fookin' proper. Did you puke?'

'Of course.'

Morgan cringes. 'Oh Christ. Takes me right back to uni. Well . . . at least you can tell Chigwell George that you've abused some alcohol.'

Russell looks up sternly from his display board.

'I'm not telling *anyone*. And neither are you.'

RUSSELL: People are always looking for some big reason for it. Like, that my dad was an alcoholic, or that it's because we lived in Malaysia, or that I drank loads in my teens and my liver can't take any more. Which is ludicrous, looking at me. But really . . . it's because I simply don't *like* the stuff. OK, maybe the occasional glass of champagne is quite pleasant. But everything else is horrible. Beer tastes like cold tea mixed with Marmite. Wine, like they tried to make grape juice and something went horribly wrong. Whisky and brandy just taste *appalling*, like medicine. Why would you drink that? Vodka doesn't have any flavour at all, so what's the point? You might as well have water.

People think you have an alcohol intolerance.

RUSSELL: To be quite honest, I started telling people that towards the end of university, if only to stop them offering me the stuff. I got so bored with hearing, 'oh, come *on* . . . just a sip . . . it'll put hairs on your chest!' – and so on. And I suppose in a way I *am* intolerant now, purely because my body isn't used to being poisoned like everyone else's. And it *is* poison. All that these people have done is built up an immunity to a poison.

Karen suspects it's because you hate the thought of not being in control.

RUSSELL: Oh, does she? Well, she's wrong. Actually I'd *love* to not be in control. I'd love to throw the reins up in the air, sit back, not care. Like everyone else. But where would that get me? Us? Who else is going to do what I do? Who else is going to write the song, get the gig, pack the car, collect the money, design the poster, send the flyer, mix the demo, phone the label?

Does it ever strike you that they might not do these things because they're certain that you'll have already done them?

RUSSELL: Well, the thought has occurred to me. But . . . I don't know. Sometimes I do wonder where we'd be now if I wasn't continually on the ball.

And where are *you now?*

(*Silence.*)

Russell has now radioed Jamie four times to check on the hunt for replacement shoes and socks, but something's gone wrong with the beer pumps on the ground floor and Jamie has been busy helping the bars manager avert a near riot. Consequently Russell hasn't moved, despite various requests for his services (seat broken on the third level, sanitary bin overflowing in first-floor Ladies, vomit on the foyer stairs, etc.). He has ignored his ringing phone twice, the first time Karen, the second time Ash, the voice-mails virtually identical ('Just checking you're OK, not too stressed out . . .'), Karen's call also followed by a text ('*dont worry R, well show that tosser ps. swearing is fun isnt it*'). Morgan has at last left him in peace, driven more by the thirst for another pint than any wish to check on Jeff Lynne's progress. 'JOAN ARMATR

DING' is now spelt out on Russell's wooden board ('I'll get the final "A" from "ORCHESTRA",' he explains). In short, Russell has very little to do, and his attention once again returns to Jamie's joint. He now allows himself to actually handle it, rolling it between his thumb and index finger, holding it up to the light, even shaking it. Finally he lifts it to his nose and inhales.

'Hmm,' he ponders. 'Herb cupboard . . . with burnt paper. And cigarettes, of course. The least appealing part.'

He scrutinises it for a few more moments. It's like watching a baby being given a brief, all-too-alluring chance to hold a much forbidden item: some car keys, a remote control, a mobile phone. One half expects Russell to go the whole hog and cram the thing into his mouth.

'Let's just say,' he mutters, 'for argument's sake . . . that . . .' but then drifts off.

Without any change in his expression, not a shrug, nor even the slightest twitch in either his eyebrows or his lips, he steps across the room, pulls open a drawer and extracts a box of matches. He lays the joint down on his display board, takes out a match, strikes it, swaps the matchbox for the joint in his left hand, then lights the end of the spliff. It momentarily flares up, then dies down. He stands there – head slightly cocked, frowning at his two burning items – for about ten seconds. The tableau looks preposterous.

Finally the match goes out and he glances up.

'What do I do now?'

Put the end that isn't burning into your mouth, and slowly inhale.

No, slowly.

Wiltshire 1

Next morning, Russell has been awoken by his phone ringing.

'At *ten thirty*!' he exclaims, frantically towelling his hair and jumping into his combats. 'I never sleep past nine, whatever's happened the night before.'

As curious as this oversleeping is, it wouldn't normally be a problem – were it not for the nature of the call which has today doubled as his alarm clock. It came from his boss at the Imperial, desperately trying to locate the keys to the maintenance room after Joan Armatrading's tour bus pulled in and the tour manager disembarked to behold the sight of 'JOAN ARMTARDIGN' unapologetically slapped across the front of the venue.

'Joan's arriving around noon,' Russell splutters, 'at which point she'll apparently go *mental*.'

Of all Russell's abilities, damage control is the one which

receives the least practice, principally because he very rarely makes mistakes. As a result, he's not coping terribly well. He cuts himself shaving – one of those vicious, diagonal cuts that doesn't stop bleeding (the suggestion that he forgo a shave on this occasion is met with incredulity) – he forgets to lock his bedsit door, has to run back upstairs, trips and almost goes hurtling into a Czech medical student's room on the floor below his, very nearly drops his car keys down a drain, kicks them out of the way at the last millisecond. Misses the turning for Wimbledon on the Savacentre one-way system, has to drive round the entire thing again. Loses, as we shall see, his temper.

'Damn!' he shouts at the dashboard, then looks rather ashamed. If one counts 'damn' as a swear word, this is the second time such a word has passed Russell's lips in the last twenty-four hours and it doesn't particularly suit him. But then, Russell could be marking the dawn of a new era in his life in which strange, unplanned things occur, such as oversleeping, misspelling the names of pop stars on the front of high-profile London venues, and forgetting to hand the maintenance keys to security before a day off.

'And before you say a word,' he spits, 'none of this has *anything* to do with me smoking a joint.'

This could be correct. The remainder of Russell's spliff episode was punctuated by all the coughing, spluttering and gasping for water you might expect, and probably didn't really introduce any further psychoactive ingredient to his bloodstream than he'd already passively inhaled via Morgan and Jamie the runner's efforts. That said, there was certainly something unusually distracted and absent about Russell towards the end of the evening – for which Russell, conveniently, has decided to blame Morgan.

'He was drunk, obviously,' Russell recounts, while speeding up and down Wimbledon Broadway looking for a parking space. 'And he kept coming up to me while I was busy.'

Jamie had eventually found Russell some replacement socks and shoes (some oversized but clean Converse All Stars) around eleven, at which point Russell had to quickly complete all the other tasks that had built up over the previous hour or so. Morgan, at the gig alone and therefore with little else to do, hung out on the mezzanine of the main stairway, a zone Russell had to hurry through on the way to and from every chore.

'Each time he saw me, he kept saying that it was all about Supertramp. "I know the answer, and it's about Supertramp," he said. I thought it was utter gobbledegook, naturally. Then he finally cornered me while I was fixing the lettering out front and told me what he'd been harping on about. By which time it was raining, and of course he had his umbrella, the fluky devil. So I was hanging off the front of the venue at ten to midnight, getting soaked, listening to this idiot down on the pavement talking about Supertramp. No wonder I messed up the spelling.'

Morgan's thesis, in a nutshell, was this: given that Russell and his two henchpersons were evidently having such a tough time summoning the gumption to give Jake his marching orders, perhaps it would be better to think of new ways to deal with the elements within and without Jake that were causing the problems, possibly enabling them to keep him on the team. 'Like that hasn't occurred to me before,' shouted Russell, from up his ladder. But Morgan had a new idea, an idea based on the 1978 actions of Roger Hodgson, formerly one of the two lead vocalists and songwriters of Supertramp. According to

Morgan, the progressive rockers had been holed up in an LA recording studio busily assembling what was to become their best-known album, *Breakfast in America*, but relations between Hodgson and his counterpart, Rick Davies, had already reached rock-bottom, to the point where they allegedly avoided being in the studio building at the same time as each other. 'It was probably all Davies being jealous, anyroad,' Morgan speculated. 'Hodgson penned all the decent tunes and had the voice everyone knew, while Davies just wrote damn-fool Steely Dan rip-offs and sounded like a busker.' Faced with choosing between an unwisely timed exit from the band and suffering in silence, Hodgson took the unusual step of airing all his grievances with Davies via the lyrics of a song, 'Child of Vision'. The master-stroke, in Morgan's view, was the pre-chorus call-and-response section, during which Davies actually sang comebacks to Hodgson's many charges – for the listening audience, presumably, to form their own judgement.

'Morgan's brilliant plan,' Russell recounts, while reversing into the Imperial's loading bay, 'is that I do the same with Jake – except in this case I get him to sing the entire song. So he's basically singing all the stuff that annoys me about him – himself. The theory is that, perhaps subconsciously, it'll force him to think, "Blimey, the bloke in this song is a bit of a moron, I'd better make sure I don't behave like that." Problem solved.'

And what do you think of this idea?

'Completely stupid, desperate, unrealistic, time-consuming, unlikely to have much effect' – Russell wrenches up his handbrake and switches off the engine – 'and probably worth a try.'

No sooner has he disembarked from his vehicle than a bald guy in an Alabama 3 T-shirt emerges from the huge loading door and nods at the car.

'Can't leave it there, Russell.'

'I know I can't, Phil. I'm not staying long.'

'Not even for a minute.'

'Sorry, I just need to alter the spelling on the front of the –'

'I know you do – but that's going to take you at least ten minutes, isn't it?'

'Look, Phil, there aren't any parking spaces and I'm running terribly –'

'Not my problem, Russell. I can't have –'

Russell slams a fist down on the bonnet of his car.

'I'll be here for *five minutes*, Phil! Just fucking *deal* with it!'

He pushes past the incredulous Phil and marches into the backstage area.

'I'll say one thing for this suddenly-swearing business,' Russell confides while waiting for the lift. 'Everyone suddenly starts listening to you.'

Once on the second floor, Russell races round to the maintenance room, grabs the ladder and the wayward letter 'A' and quickly takes his position out front. Unfortunately the next few minutes are not so straightforward. It's one thing doing this job at midnight, but a different matter on a busy Saturday shopping morning. At the very best, Russell gets some funny looks, but frequently has to endure teenagers throwing things at him, a few idiots asking him to write their own names on the white display panel ('Just for five minutes, pal. I'll give you a fiver'), a drunk bloke – clearly still enjoying the night before – who decides it will be amusing to grab the ladder and give it a few shakes ('Go on, brother, imagine yer doin' it in a thunderstorm, hah haar . . .'), and finally, least dangerously but probably most tediously, a pair from Joan Armatrading's road crew who harangue

Russell with tales of hilarious alternative interpretations of their boss's name ('That time in Hungary, when they wrote "Jo and Arms Trading" – that was *priceless*,' one of them chortles). Keen to get back to his car, Russell swiftly completes his task and grimly descends the ladder.

'Cheer up, mate,' frowns one of the chaps.

'Sorry, in a rush,' Russell brusquely replies.

'Bloody Londoners,' comments the other bloke. 'So unfriendly.'

Russell folds up his ladder and stomps off.

'Maybe I *should* have put "Brummie Lezza",' he mutters.

His stressful, foreshortened morning finally at an end, Russell's early afternoon is given to various preparatory activities for the band's trip to the West Country, and passes, much to his relief, without further upset.

'You see?' he observes, happily pumping some diesel into the rented Transit van. 'When it's just me, nothing ever goes wrong. It's only when other people are involved that things start falling apart.'

Which is presumably why Russell rejected Jake, Ash and Karen's offer to meet him at the rehearsal room so they could pack the vehicle together, and instead seems happy to do it all on his own – from hiring and filling the Transit, to picking each of the others up, even making a substantial trip to Asda in Roehampton for everyone's food and drink essentials. It is slightly baffling, then, to record three or four instances throughout the late afternoon and evening when Russell can be heard saying things like 'I always have to do everything', and 'no one else bothered to help'. When they make a stop (some five minutes' drive off the motorway) outside a large mock-Tudor abode in Camberley, from which a beaming, backpacked Jake strides, the collective desire to give Russell a thick ear is almost tangible as he leans out of the driver's window and announces, in lieu of a proper greeting, 'Jake, you'll have to put an extra fiver in for petrol, we've come *miles* out of our way to get you.'

In fact, as the M3 becomes the A303 and then Hampshire becomes Wiltshire, it's clear that something is particularly amiss with the band captain. He complains of tiredness, but refuses to let anyone else drive. He won't allow music to be played on the van's tired-looking cassette player, nor the radio. As their route snakes past Salisbury, he finally goes a step too far and requests that no one speak any more, as this is distracting him and making him nervous.

'Jesus, Russ,' Karen moans. 'We're driving to play pop music at a festival, not to bury dead bodies in a forest.'

Jake and Ash, seated behind Karen on Ash's new drum hardware 'coffin' (a fearsomely heavy black hard-plastic box, which manages to double the total weight of Ash's gear), grin at each other as if to say 'Who needs speaking?' – and spark up a large number Ash has just rolled.

'Window please, Karen,' snaps Russell.

'Aye aye, fucking sir,' she sighs.

By the time the van approaches the town nearest the festival site, it is almost nine o'clock. Megan's instructions were to pick up backstage wristbands from a pub, the Cherry Tree, 'just in case security give you trouble'. For most of the journey Russell has been worrying aloud about finding this pub – a concern which the rest of the band have been cheerfully rebuffing.

'I really don't think it's gonna be a problem, fella,' Ash

commented. 'The place doesn't exactly sound like a sprawling metropolis.'

Nonetheless, Russell's directions from the AA website have been tucked in between the dashboard and windscreen since passing Andover, and now, as the Transit rolls along the main road into the town – a town which suspiciously resembles a rather tiny village – Russell anxiously clutches the A4 sheets as he steers.

The first building of any prominence is the Cherry Tree pub itself, on the right as the main street hits the village square.

'Wow,' deadpans Jake. 'That was a fucking labyrinth, eh, Russ? Thank God you brought along your ball of string, we'd never get out again.'

Russell ignores the ensuing chuckles and pulls up a few yards down from the establishment. Karen gets out and stretches, followed by Ash, who climbs over the passenger seat and glances happily up at the pub sign.

'Ah, lovely,' he comments. 'Pint of Wadworth's while we're here, then, eh?'

'Too right,' Karen nods.

'No,' Russell states, firmly. 'We pick up the wristbands and we get going. We've got tents to construct.'

'What happened to giving out some flyers, Russell?' Jake blinks with pretend disappointment.

'We come back later and do that.'

'*Later?*' Karen frowns, gesturing around the near-lifeless Saturday-night square. 'Russell, look at this place. It's past its bedtime as it is. I don't think there's going to be any "later", do you?'

'Mmm . . . s'pose not,' Russell grumbles.

'Wahey!' whoops Jake, leaping out of the van and skipping up the street. 'Mine's a Throbbing Villager's Bowel-Basher. Diet Coke, Russ?'

Russell growls and starts locking up the vehicle.

By the time Russell pushes open the door of the pub, the others have not only ordered their drinks but have already received them, paid and sat down. This is partly because Jake wanted to get them in as quickly as possible in case Russell changed his mind about staying, and partly because Russell took ages to secure the van, but mainly because the pub is practic-ally deserted and the barman had nothing else to do. A pair of middle-aged blokes, one wearing a '6th Annual South Wiltshire Folk-A-Thon' T-shirt, are parked at the bar, a young couple are enjoying an argument by the window, and that is pretty much it. A dent in Russell's wad of flyers seems unlikely. Russell marches straight up to the bar and cuts to the chase.

'Is Megan here?'

'Whassat, mate?' smiles the rugbyish chap in charge.

'Megan.'

'Um . . . there's no Megan here, no, mate. Should there be?'

The barman looks genuinely keen to assist and this is obviously just his turn of phrase, but unfortunately Russell takes his response as indifference, scoffs, rolls his eyes and stomps off to where his bandmates sit.

'Megan's not here. Drink up, we're going.'

Jake pushes a pint of Coke across the table at him.

'Here y'are, Russ. Get that down yer.'

'I don't want it. Come on, we've got to go.'

As only she is able, Karen takes control of the situation.

'Russell, what's fucking got into you? We've just been

squashed into a van for three hours and we've only just sat down with a drink. Perhaps Megan will show up, or maybe we can ring her. We can put the tents up in the dark, we've got torches. Now for God's sake just siddown and chill the fuck out.'

'Mmm . . . OK,' Russell says, suitably scolded. 'I don't want a Coke, though.'

'Well. The bar's just there, I'm sure they'll do you a coffee if you ask them nicely.'

Sadly, it is too late for that.

'Um . . . can I have a coffee, please?' Russell meekly asks the barman, who gives him a wide, sarcastic smile.

'We don't do coffees or people called Megan after nine, I'm afraid – *sir*.'

A minute later Russell is grudgingly sipping the pint of Coke.

For the next twenty minutes the pub remains in roughly the same state. The arguing couple departs, another one arrives. A few more beery blokes appear and join the twosome already propping up the bar, where they compare notes on the latest guest ales and draw the barman's attention to the passed sell-by date of the pork scratchings. Jake, drinking at Saturday-night speed, orders himself another pint.

'Just up from London, y'see,' he banters to the barman.

'I'd never have guessed.'

'Why, do we come across as wankers?'

'Well . . . not all of you do,' the barman winks. 'Just gonna change the barrel, pal.'

'No worries.'

Back at the table, Karen is again on the warpath.

'Why are you acting so bloody strangely?' she demands in Russell's direction.

Russell exhales and checks Jake's progress at the bar. 'Had a text from *him* before we set out,' he quietly confides.

'Josh?'

'Yeah. He's *coming* tomorrow.'

Karen is silent.

'Says he's looking forward to witnessing Jake's final performance.'

Ash huffs his cheeks and swigs from his ale.

'Did you know about this?' Russell asks Karen.

'No!' she responds, angrily. 'I wish you knobs would stop picking at me about it. I had a good night on the charlie with the bloke, and that's about it.'

'Nothing else?'

'No!' she hisses.

A pause, during which Jake can be heard loudly discussing the football results.

'So what are we going to *do*?' Russell says, finally.

It is Ash who replies, with unusual vehemence.

'We are going to have a bloody good time. We are going to enjoy whatever happens tonight, and everything we do tomorrow. We are going to give the fucking performance of our lives, and so is Jake. And that's it. We come home. Anything else, we can decide about another fucking time. And no one . . .' – here he looks at Karen, then shrugs – 'sorry, Kazza – *no one* tells that posh twathead anything for now. That's it.'

'Shp!' hisses Karen as Jake returns, plonks his new pint down and starts singing – in a mock-West Country accent and at a volume he thinks only his companions can hear – The Wurzels' 'Combine Harvester' song. The blokes sitting at the bar look over and roll their eyes. Jake is unfazed.

'Aw, brilliant,' he blethers, giving Russell a fraternal shake by the shoulders. 'This is the life, eh, Russ? Getting out of the shitty city, belting down to the coun'ry and playing the yokels some rock. Makes me want to roll around in some haystacks with a wholesome lass and squirt some of my filling into her pasty. Eh, Kazza?'

Karen glares in Jake's direction.

'Just look at him,' smiles Ash. 'Like a little kid.'

'Seriously, I love it,' Jake iterates, supping his ale. 'We should do this more often.'

'Yeeah,' Ash nods. 'So I noticed you, er . . . brought along your radio-controlled aeroplane?'

'Yes, I noticed that too,' Russell frowns. 'I was wondering what it was doing in the back.'

'I've got a very special plan for that,' Jake grins.

'Like what?'

'Ah-haa. It's a surprise.'

Russell's current expression plainly illustrates how small a fan he is of surprises, but there is no chance to press Jake any further on the matter, for as if Saturday night itself were suddenly making a tardy appearance on the premises, the pub door is suddenly flung open and into the little saloon bar pours enough crusty ravers to fill an entire squat party: a mad tornado of dreadlocks, threadbare jumpers, shaved heads, beanie hats, facial jewellery, outward-bound fleeces, interestingly shaped beards with trinkets hanging off them, fluorescent clothing items, back-slapping, gurning, laughter, funky handshakes, hugs and at least three dogs. Rather than groaning and making a hasty exit, the pub's earlier occupants turn happily to greet these friendly revellers like, well, neighbours. The barman is particularly delighted to see them, and starts indiscriminately pulling pints without even receiving an order.

'Guess this is our crew, then!' Jake observes after a minute or so. 'Go on, Russ – do your thing.'

'Are you serious?' Russell splutters. 'I doubt many of them can understand English.'

'S'all right,' Ash reassures them. 'I should think Welpo'll be along in a minute.'

Trance music starts booming out of the pub's stereo as the gang gradually spread around the room. Snatches of over-heard conversation reveal that this particular crowd have just finished assembling the stage and PA system, and are rewarding themselves with a few drinks before the evening's extra-curricular activities commence. They are a universally cheerful bunch and seem endearingly excited about their upcoming event, but Russell begins to shoot worried looks at the rest of the group when phrases start to be bandied around like, 'Christ knows when things will actually kick off tomorrow' and, most ominous of all, 'I can't imagine anyone being awake for the first few bands anyway'. With still no sign of Welpo, Ash – perhaps feeling, correctly, that it's his job – decides to break the ice. He approaches a jolly chap with enormous wooden earrings and a Red Snapper T-shirt, introduces himself and meekly asks where they might find Megan.

'Megan?' he laughs. 'Well, my old mate, it's half nine now so I would imagine she's . . . ooh, just finished putting her kids to bed and she's settling down with a glass of wine before *Parky* comes on.'

'Oh, right . . . she's not coming here, then?'

'Doubt it, sunshine. But she only lives round the other side of the village. You gotta nice accent there, matey – where you from?'

'Sutton Coldfield,' Ash replies.

'Right. My missus is from Wolverhampton, y'see. Why you after Megan?'

'Ah, well . . . we were told to meet her here to pick up wristbands.'

One of those remarkably well-timed moments of silence occurs just as Ash says the word 'wristbands', and immediately everyone in the vicinity falls about with laughter. Not unkind, mocking laughter, but uproarious laughter nonetheless.

'Hahahaa!' roars Red Snapper man. 'Wristbands! Oh dear. Dear old Megan. Bless her.'

Ash frowns with slight panic at his bandmates. Predictably, Jake looks delighted, Karen worried and Russell furious.

'So, er . . .' Ash timidly insists, 'are we not getting wristbands, then?'

'Hahaa! Um, almost certainly not, my friend. Oh, Megan. She gets rather carried away, the poor love.'

Russell leaps up.

'But how are we supposed to get past security?'

'*Security!*' Everyone hoots once again.

'You might have to get past Dave Berwick's bull terrier,' quips an older guy in the corner, 'but that's about it.'

'Oh, bloody Megan,' chuckles a large girl with green leggings. 'She thinks she's at Wembley.'

The band continue to look horrified in the midst of all this mirth.

'Cheer up, my old mates!' Red Snapper man jovially instructs them. 'Don't need a wristband to have a good time, do you?'

'Guess not,' murmurs Ash, the beginnings of a smile returning to his lips.

'I just hope none of you's expecting much sleep tonight.'

'No,' Jake smiles, winking at Karen and patting one of his combat pockets, where his tin of drugs resides. 'We won't be worrying about sleep, my friend.'

Everyone in the room suddenly seems to be smiling and the atmosphere lifts, apart from the little cloud above Russell – which, as he scowls into his glass of Coke, blackens and finally breaks into a steady drizzle.

If everything Russell has been told by Megan so far proves to be riddled with errors, one area in which no inaccuracies lie is her depiction of the Big Joint's setting. 'It's a little paradise! You'll love it – beautiful gardens, nice cool woods, huge open fields, little hidey-holes, stone statues and sculptures, gorgeous trees and flowers. If the weather holds, it's going to be wonderful.' The late-August weather, mercifully, shows no sign of slipping: it's still warm enough to wear just a T-shirt, and as the Transit trundles along the dark, winding country lanes (luckily tailing the camper van belonging to Red Snapper man), the beginnings of fairy lights and illuminated bunting become visible through the thick greenery, as do some of the anticipated follies and other eye candy. Russell's bandmates, already three or four pints into their weekend, handle all the excitable reactions as Russell expressionlessly steers everyone towards their destination.

'How *cool*!' Karen gushes.

'This is going to be *legendary*,' laughs Jake.

'Too right, fella,' Ash agrees.

'They've made such an effort to make it look nice,' adds Karen. 'I really appreciate that.'

'Actually, all this stuff was put up for a wedding last weekend,' Russell tells them. 'They just decided to keep it.'

'Well – it looks lovely anyway.'

Russell mumbles something as a reply – the words 'fire risk' are just about audible.

Soon the van reaches an illuminated, grassy clearing, on the far side of which can be seen the back of a silver-hooded outdoor stage. A little wooden lodge lurks at the end of the green, with some other vans parked outside. Medium-volume chill-out music drifts from somewhere. Red Snapper man stops his vehicle and signals for Russell to pull up alongside.

'This is the backstage bit,' he shouts, 'so I'll be parking over there next to the house. But you guys wanna do your tents and all that, so you need to keep on going down that lane there.'

He points towards a pitch-black hole in the trees.

'How long for?' Russell asks.

'Until you come to the tents,' comes the reply. 'You can't miss it.'

'Thanks, geezer,' yells Jake. 'We'll see you in ten.'

'Ten,' Russell grumbles. 'When was the last time you put a tent up in the dark?'

He points the Transit at the hole and puts his foot down.

'Easy, Russ!' Ash exclaims, still holding his quarter-full pint glass from the pub.

'Sorry,' Russell replies, as they charge down the little track. 'I just thought we should get there before breakfast.'

Despite their differences, all four members are a little surprised by what they see at the other end of the lane. In a larger illuminated clearing a total of two tents have been erected, both big enough to hide a medium-sized London bus. The reason for knowing this statistic is that one such red bus is incongruously parked next to them. The two marquees are made from industrial white canvas and are presently closed to the world, but there is a glow of light from inside.

'You sure this is it, Russ?' asks Karen.

'How on earth should I know?'

'Maybe these have been here since the wedding too,' Jake sniggers.

'Perhaps you missed a turning?' Karen wonders.

'What turning? There weren't any turnings.'

'Either way,' Ash says, 'this don't seem right.'

Russell exhales angrily and slams the van into reverse. He's just about to vanish back down the hole when the 'door' to one of the marquees opens and out pops a blonde, hippyish-looking girl in a yellow dress and multicoloured cardigan.

'Oh, hello!' Jake comments.

'Don't start all that shit,' Karen glares.

'Ask her where the campsite is, Russ,' suggests Ash.

'*You* ask her!'

'*I* will!' Jake volunteers, leaping over Karen and bursting out the passenger door. 'S'cuse me!' he calls, trotting across the lawn to the girl. She turns and smiles delightedly at him. They chat for about a minute, while the others observe in silence.

'God, he's such a flirt,' Karen mutters after a while.

'Yeah . . . tip of the iceberg,' Ash smiles.

'Oh, shit,' Karen scowls, 'you're right. He's gonna be on fucking heat, isn't he? Like he always is when we're out of town. How could I forget?'

The girl gestures towards the two large tents, then to an empty area of field next to them. Jake points at one of the marquees, the girl nods enthusiastically, then the pair of them disappear inside.

'What the *fuck*?' Karen spits.

'Fuck,' Ash agrees. 'He don't waste much time, does he?'

'Come on,' Russell decides, taking off the handbrake and

spinning the van around as fast as the bumpy ground will allow. 'Jake can mess about, but I'm not waiting. Let's find the right place.'

'This might be it, though, Russ.'

'How *can* it be?'

'Oh, Russell! Just wait one bloody second!' Karen instructs. 'I don't know what you're in such a rush for anyway.'

A minute later Jake and the girl emerge again. She beams and waves at Jake, then skips off, leaving Jake to amble back towards the van. When he reaches the passenger side he winks and thrusts his hips back and forth. Karen groans.

'Get over it, weirdo.'

'So, what's the deal?' Ash asks.

'Well – this *is* the campsite! Everyone came down here in that bus, and those two tents are basically fucking massive stoner dormitories. It's brilliant! You should see it in there. It's like a huge living room, a massive fucking mong zone! Carpets, rugs on the wall, armchairs, cushions, beanbags, candles, lava lamps, a little sound system . . . man, it's my fucking dream bedroom. There's about thirty sleeping bags in there, and space for more – everyone's basically gonna get mashed and chill out all night, and I reckon we should do the same!'

Russell's reaction is instant.

'No *way*!'

'Well, you don't have to do that yourself, Russy, there's space over there for normal tents . . .'

'Look!' Russell barks. 'We have got a very important show tomorrow! I do *not* think it's a good idea for us to get into a state tonight. We need a proper good night's sleep and –'

'Oh Christ! Can't you fucking see that . . .'

Another nauseatingly circular argument ensues, eventually

terminated by Karen, who decrees that all three of their tents be erected anyway so they still have a place to crash if no sleep has been managed by, say, nine in the morning.

'If that happens,' Russell growls, 'I'm going *straight* home.'

'You do that,' Jake snaps back. 'We'll fucking hitch.'

The fussy industry of pitching tents helps briefly to calm tempers, perhaps recalling memories of slightly rosier times. Jake makes a great show of issuing cans of warm Stella from the 24-pack he has brought along ('You've gotta have a beer while putting up your tent, eh?'). Ash is sharing Jake's enormous green family tent: an impressive, Tardis-like affair which they construct within seconds; Karen's old-school pole effort isn't too far behind ('I bought it at a car boot sale in High Wycombe in 1994, it's never let me down'); Russell's tent, reportedly purchased for his 1999 trip to Glastonbury and which clearly hasn't seen daylight since, is one of those ultra-flat mountaineering jobs, allegedly built for two people but looking barely ample enough to even accommodate Russell's rucksack. Russell painstakingly lays all the poles out, stretches the tent fabric over the ground, then meticulously checks he has the correct number of pegs ('I should have done all this at home,' he sighs, 'but of course, I had too much to do'). He's one peg short, and a little put out.

'Just stick it up, Russ,' Ash advises, sipping his Stella.

'But then it won't be secure,' Russell grumbles.

'It'll be fine, Russ. Here y'are, I'll give you a hand.'

'But what if it rains?'

'Just *stick it up*, Russ.'

Ash steps in and within a minute it looks like a tent. They have a slight difference of opinion as to what poles go over which, but Ash's greater experience prevails and soon Russell's quarters are complete – apart from just one of the flysheet's loops, pegless and flapping freely.

'I find that a bit upsetting.'

'I've probably got a spare one,' Karen says.

Russell eyes Karen's cumbersome and mostly bent corrugated spikes.

'But then it won't be the same as all the others,' he complains.

'Oh, fuck it, whatever.'

Having skewered in the last of his own pegs, Jake waits barely three seconds before grabbing his sleeping bag and marching straight into the neighbouring 'stoner dormitory' (its official title remains unknown). Here he is now, already cross-legged on the carpet, skinning up while happily chatting to a pair of already-quite-spaced-looking teenage girls and a bearded bloke with a thick metal bolt through his nose.

'I'm Jake, by the way,' he smiles, holding out his hand to nose-bolt man.

'Godfrey,' the guy nods, 'and this is Emma, and Flower.'

'Flower,' Jake laughs. 'Wow. Not your real name, obviously?'

'No, it is,' confirms Godfrey, glancing at the wispy, dazed-looking female for approval. 'You were christened Flower, weren't you?'

Flower nods dreamily, but says nothing.

'And her elder brother's called Hillock,' Emma offers.

'Hillock!' Jake hoots. 'Did he survive school?'

The three of them eye Jake strangely.

'Aw, this is quite superb, isn't it?' Jake blusters, looking around the impressively furnished tent. 'All this, with one intention, and that's for people to get [Jake wiggles his fingers as if performing an elaborate drum roll] . . . *fucked*!'

His three companions frown and appear for a second like they're going to make their excuses, but then Jake passes Godfrey the mammoth joint he's just been rolling and everyone cheers up.

The Big Joint pre-party is, Karen and Ash quickly decide, wonderful. To the point where it's already difficult to imagine the day itself being anywhere near as good.

'It's that Christmas Eve feeling, innit?' Ash sighs, as they stroll along a particularly pretty flower-lined and fairy-lighted avenue, puffing on the latest 'number'.

'Yeah,' Karen laughs, 'when your mum's still in a good mood, your dad's still sober and you haven't yet discovered you've been bought all the wrong LPs.'

'Ha, yeah,' Ash chuckles. 'Kinda takes your mind off . . . you know what.'

'Aw,' Karen winces, the complexities of the Jake Situation almost visible on her furrowed brow. 'Don't.'

They reach the edge of what will be the festival's main field, a lush, paddock-like arena with a scattering of youthful folk sitting in circles or, next to the stage itself, dancing to some gentle drum and bass. Although nearing 1 a.m. it feels distinctly as if things are only just warming up; accordingly, Ash produces an Ecstasy pill from his tobacco tin and offers it to Karen.

'Cheeky half?'

'Is William Hague a wanker?' Karen winks, taking the tablet and biting it in two.

They traipse along towards the centre of the field, where a small campfire has been constructed. Smoke of various sorts rises into the air, cans of beer and cider are swigged, conversation flows, a long-haired bloke inaudibly strums a bashed-up acoustic guitar, people dance, some with energy and purpose, others aimlessly but nonetheless contentedly, the whole scene illuminated by subtle lighting from the main rig. Karen and Ash are comfortably silent for a few minute, before Karen gives a little yelp.

'Oh, shit,' she says quietly. 'Do me a favour.'

'Whassat?'

'Oh . . . guilty pleasure, I suppose.' She gestures towards a small nearby group, loosely gathered around a handsome, bare-chested guy with short dreadlocks, leaning against a unicycle.

'You like?' Ash smiles.

'Ya-ha,' Karen replies. 'You've gotta love a fit hippy.'

'Well, girl, this could be your lucky day.'

Ash starts marching quickly in the direction of said fit hippy.

'Ash, what're you *doing*?' Karen hisses.

'Welpo!'

One of the other blokes in the circle – an older, rather less obviously attractive individual with short black hair and a gaunt, stubbly face – turns and grins.

'Hey, Ashley!'

Thus, mingling is achieved and Karen is soon addressing her guilty pleasure. She offers him the spliff and they chat for a few minutes before it occurs to either of them to introduce themselves.

'Oh, I'm Karen.'

'Hillock,' comes the reply, before availing himself of a drag so deep that the joint practically halves in size.

'Nice name.'

'Thank you. My ma was looking at a hillock in Cornwall when I was conceived.'

'Oh?' Karen nods.

'Yes. My earth place.'

'Right,' she replies – then, with a slight air of mumsiness – 'Are you not cold?'

'How can I be cold,' he dreamily replies, 'with all these good vibes here to keep me warm?'

Karen considers this.

'Mmm. Is there a toilet around?'

Soon she is ambling back across the field towards a distant clutch of Portaloos.

'Space cadet,' she shrugs. 'But they're usually quite creative in the sack.'

After about ten minutes Jake appears with his new friends from the bedroom marquee (or the 'stonerdrome', as Jake has now christened it). The party notches up a gear as everyone's drugs gradually take hold, although the main stage's soundtrack, perhaps for licensing reasons, never increases much in volume. But a few characters are carrying exotic drums which they pound in time to the music, producing progressively strange outbreaks of dancing. Conversations acquire a less inhibited, slightly more peculiar edge as the majority all gravitate around the campfire, donning hooded tops and blankets as the night drops a little in temperature. Suddenly everyone knows each other – has been friends for years.

'Hillock!' Jake grins, shaking the man in question by the shoulders, now partly covered in a blanket, the other half of which is wrapped around Karen. 'Hilly, me old mucker! Aww . . . what a great name. Wish I had a name like that, instead of boring old Jake.'

'What would yours be, friend?'

'Haha! What, if I was named after the thing my old dear was gazing at while the old man did the job? Oh Christ. "Telly", I should think. "BBC2".'

'Ha!' laughs Karen. 'I'd have been "That cobweb in the corner I've been meaning to get rid of for ages".'

Meanwhile, Ash is attempting to extract speech from Hillock's sister.

'Yeeeah . . . well, like I say . . . can't wait to play tomorrow. Gonna inject a bit more dancey vibe into the tunes, y'know?'

'Ah . . .' hums Flower, staring into the fire. 'Right . . .'

'Whassort of thing do you listen to?'

'Oh . . . just . . . y'know . . . whatever's . . . mellow . . .'

Flower's sentence drifts off and she finally curls up on the floor and shuts her eyes; Ash rather sweetly drapes his hoody over her.

Three o'clock arrives from nowhere. The main stage's music has decreased to a vague dribble, and the bashed-up acoustic is being slowly passed around the circle. As usual under such circumstances no one can really hear what's being played by the various people who coyly pluck at it, until it's given to a foghorn like Jake. He shrugs as if to say, 'well, I might try to struggle through *something* . . .' – and then bellows through an uproariously loud version of The Police's 'Can't Stand Losing You', which everyone suddenly remembers the words to. Although it hardly matters, a more informed observer might notice that the chords Jake bashes out bear very little relation to what he's singing. And then, as if by magic, a more informed observer shows up.

'Hey – Russ!' Karen whoops, with genuine delight.

'Russy, my man!' shouts Jake, their earlier spat apparently forgotten. He jumps up and gives him a hug, which Russell returns stiffly. 'Where've you *been*?'

Russell has changed into sensible trousers and a khaki jacket. He has also disposed of his contact lenses, and now wears his rather geeky metal-rimmed specs. He stands there for a few seconds, rucksack on his back, smiling awkwardly at the assembled, many of whom probably wonder who this straight man is and where he's come from.

'Oh, I . . . er . . . tried to sleep. Not much luck. Then I heard your . . . um . . . rendition.'

'Aw,' Jake grins, slightly embarrassed, handing the guitar to Russell. 'A bit rubbish.'

'No, no!' Russell replies, clasping the instrument. 'Good fun. We should . . .'

'Do a tune?' Jake asks. 'Yeah! Let's do an old one!'

'Um . . . you mean . . .'

'Yeah! Like a DC song or a Nirvana one . . . y'know, like we did at school, something really looking back.' Jake shuffles aside to make space for Russell to sit, as does Ash.

Russell looks uncertain.

'Go on, Russ!' Karen yells from her cosy spot next to Hillock. Russell blinks at her for a second and then finally takes his rucksack off and sits down.

In the end they settle for 'Alive' by Pearl Jam. There's something rather incongruous about this meat-and-two-veg American grunge classic being served up to a bunch of blissed-out techno-heads, but something about the song's rolling earnestness makes sense in this setting. Perhaps it was always destined for a campfire. Not that anyone sings along, apart from some vague, bass-note murmuring from Ash – but as Jake quickly proves, it's a song he was born to sing. Russell's playing, too, is effortless – relieved as he evidently is to be at last engaged in an activity he understands. He even blusters his way through part of the guitar solo while Jake deafeningly hums the chords. When they reach the end, they are repaid with a sincere and entirely deserved round of applause.

'That was so . . . real,' Hillock comments. 'Inspiring.'

Jake does his best 'ah! it was nothing' shrug.

'OK,' Russell decides, warming up. 'One of ours.'

'Oh,' Jake frowns. 'Nah.'

'Why not?'

'Are you sure, Russ? I'm not . . . erm . . . I mean, no one will know it.'

'No one knew the last one.'

Karen, as usual, is the mediator.

'Come on, have a go, Jakey. You guys could do "Smaller Weaker" quite easily?'

Jake shakes his head. 'Aw, probably not here . . .'

'All right, "River Song",' she suggests.

'Yes, that'll work!' Russell nods.

Jake finally agrees.

The song, the tale of a riverside walk while missing a certain 'someone', begins quietly, Russell's chords pulsing away while Jake repeats the gently varying lines of the first verse (*'This was the river where we met/laughed/sang/kissed'* etc.). The pair of them build the sound nicely – another instance of their musical relationship still forming the occasional sharp negative to their personal one – and the campfire's population is plainly rapt. Unfortunately Jake doesn't seem to realise this, perceiving their silence as rigid boredom. Upon the arrival of the chorus, the temptation to somehow make their performance more outwardly exciting gets the better of Jake and he promptly leaps both an octave and ten decibels: *'Will the lock of the river hold as fast as the lock in your heart?!'* he screams, prompting all of his listeners to look up with some alarm, as if Jake's parked his hand on a burning cinder or knelt on a pine cone. The audience's attention now *does* begin to wander, and halfway through the next verse a few conversations have resumed. Jake quickly clocks this and abandons the song just before the second chorus.

'Fuck it, Russ, no one's really into it. Shall we do something else?'

Russell opens his eyes, surprised.

'Oh! They are, I think?'

'Nah. Not well-known enough.'

'Um . . .' Russell glares, 'I *really* don't think it matters. It was sounding great –'

'Yeah, it does matter. People were starting to chat –'

'– until you messed up the chorus.'

'Messed it up?! I didn't fucking mess it up, you have to do things slightly differently in this setting –'

'I'm aware of that, Jake. I just don't think you've got any confidence in our material, to be honest – you're certainly not doing it justice, and if you *think* that I'm going to . . .'

Swap the campfire for an IKEA dining table and the spliffs and cider cans for a first-course serving of *insalata tricolore*, and we could be at any squabbling couple's dinner party. The campfire kids, who have definitely stopped chatting now, look away awkwardly in the manner that English people of all ages do particularly well, as any half-decent vibes of the moment are well and truly buried by our dying musical partners.

Hillock, shouldering Karen's usual role, steps in.

'Hey . . . friends, friends! No need for this. The tunes were strong. This is a free gathering – mistakes are loved, errors are shared. No judging here. Take it easy, Russell, my brother. Can I interest you in anything?'

'Like what?'

'Oh . . . do you need some vibes? A pill, a livener?'

'No *thank* you.'

Russell grumpily lays the guitar down. Separate conversations slowly recommence. Minutes later, Godfrey addresses Jake from halfway around the campfire.

'You lot are playing tomorrow, then?'

Jake's reaction is almost apologetic.

'Er . . . well, yeah,' he replies. 'Two in the afternoon. But to be honest with you, I'd be quite surprised if we're playing by four – know what I mean?'

'What makes you say that?' Russell asks immediately.

'Aw, just look at everyone, fella! We're all fucked. It's almost four in the morning now and no one looks remotely like they're gonna be hitting the sack any time soon. Everyone'll probably sleep until midday. They're not gonna be ready for us to soundcheck until two, let alone have us play.'

'That's absurd,' Russell spits, glaring into the fire. 'What's the point of making a schedule if no one's going to keep to it?'

'Aw, Russy, it –'

'And please stop calling me "Russy".'

'Aw, I thought you liked it,' Jake mopes, looking genuinely gutted.

'It might not run that late,' Godfrey offers. 'Some of the people running this thing are pretty organised.'

'Like Megan?' Ash chuckles.

'Not Megan,' Godfrey concedes, smiling. 'But Dave Berwick's *fearsome*. He won't be letting anything lag behind.'

'Oh, him!' Jake replies. 'I met him about an hour ago, by

the stonerdrome. He was absolutely off his tits. Couldn't even form a sentence. Even his dog looked embarrassed.'

Russell growls.

'Yeah, Russy,' Jake laughs, 'that's what his dog sounded like.'

Without further comment, Russell rises and departs.

'Russ!' Karen shouts after him, but this is ignored.

'Is he all right?' Godfrey frowns.

'No,' Karen says. 'He isn't. He never is, these days.'

'A shame when people have blocked energies at this kind of thing,' Hillock remarks. 'This is meant to be the place where you discard all your stresses and troubles, y'know? Leave them at the gate.'

'Try telling that to *him*,' Jake mutters.

'Actually,' Karen says, turning to Hillock, 'if you *do* tell that to him, I'll buy you breakfast.'

'Will do,' Hillock replies. 'I'll catch up with the man later . . . give him some vibes.'

'Vibes,' Karen nods, blowing smoke towards the fire. 'If anyone's in desperate need of vibes, it's Russell.'

RUSSELL: Comparisons are always going to be made with established artists, favourably or unfavourably. So what? It's healthy – educational. I'll never forget the time we made the first Nerveswill demo. I was sixteen years old and relatively happy with it – aware of its shortcomings, of course, but Jake had decided it was rubbish virtually by the time we got home from the studio. This wasn't helped by one of his elder sisters commenting, without a shred of irony, 'Jake, this is brilliant! It sounds like Whitesnake or somebody!'

Jake's always had very fragile faith in our own recordings. He claims it's because of the comments he receives. Rather snagging forms of criticism – someone saying, 'Jake, have you got anything decent to listen to?' when he's playing one of our demos. Which I always find rather vexing – I never get anything but compliments when I play our stuff. And then the eternal excuse comes out – 'It'd be OK if we'd got someone to mix it properly.' (*Pauses, visibly irritated.*) Consequently, he's given up listening to our stuff. Claims to never put it on at all. Which is infuriating if we ever go back to an older song – 'How does this one go again?' 'Well, like it goes on the CD, Jake.' 'Aw, that's no help. I haven't heard the CD since the day we finished mixing it.'

But it also appears to be the songs themselves he's uncertain of.
(*Long pause.*)

RUSSELL: Songs. Songs are very strange, complicated things. More often than not, people judge them according to how many people know them. They are *songs*, after all – meant for singing. You get a crowd of people sitting around a guitar roaring the words to 'Yellow Submarine' because it's incredibly well known, although it's hardly a great song. But I rather like hearing a song weave its magic in a different way – noticing the subtle changes in audience reaction as the piece progresses. All of which, sadly, goes straight over Jake's head. If people aren't singing along, smiling or clapping, he interprets that as indifference.

People weren't singing along, smiling or clapping to the Pearl Jam song by the campfire, though.

RUSSELL: That's different, because Jake knows it's famous. Its worth has been proved time and time again, although I suspect 80 per cent of the people sitting around that campfire didn't know it. But that wouldn't occur to Jake, because he thinks everyone thinks the same things and feels the same way as he does – *all the time*. One of Jake's biggest problems. If he's hungry, he automatically thinks everyone's hungry. If he's thirsty, or tired, he thinks everyone else is. If he hates a song, he thinks everyone does. Even when told otherwise.

There was an early incident which made all this sort of thing very difficult. It was in Plainly Amy. We'd given a demo to this A & R man at EMI Music Publishing – he was one of the few people to get back to us, and one of the few to say he liked the band but didn't like the songs. Quite often it was the other way round. So he made us an offer. He wanted to see what we would do with a slightly better-known song, so he gave us a list of songs owned by EMI, told us to pick one and do our own version. Said that he'd pay for studio time. So this list was biked over to us – biked over, to our rehearsal room, *very* exciting when you're eighteen – and of course it had all sorts of incredible songs on there. Eventually we decided to do 'Fashion' by David Bowie. Can't remember why. So I went home that night and worked up this rather good, punky little arrangement on my Tascam – I've still got it actually, *very* cool for the time, even though I say it myself – took it into the next rehearsal, and Jake had completely gone off the idea. *Completely*. 'Oh, I don't wanna be famous for doing a cover . . . all the rest of our songs will sound useless in comparison . . . why should we spend time doing that when we can work on some of our own songs . . .' (*Old anger rising.*) Well, Jake . . . we don't have to become famous for doing a cover if we don't want to . . . as it happens, I've got enough faith in our material to believe that it *will* stand up next to the Bowie song . . . and yes, we could spend time on our own stuff, but here is an opportunity to work with someone from a major publishing company – who knows where that might lead us? But no. Flat refusal. I went ahead and sent my little demo to the guy, but of course the whole point was that he liked the band itself. He was confused and, to be honest, probably affronted that we decided not to do it. Understandably, in my view. And so died the biggest major lead we'd ever had – possibly *have* ever had.

Was that the beginning of the end?

RUSSELL: No. Not even the middle of the end.

The end of the end?

RUSSELL: Yup.

When Russell vacates his spot next to the campfire, any last whiffs of rational conversation seem to leave with him. Many present simply stare silently into the flames; others attempt the odd fractured exchange. Karen is still absorbed in vague mumblings with Hillock, and for a time Jake does a few rounds of the circle, babbling various pieces of cheery clap-trap to people (at one point he can be heard arguing, to a wholly bewildered female audience, that no *Carry On* film is complete without the presence of Sid James), but eventually, through tiredness, inebriation or otherwise, he settles back down next to Ash, who has abandoned any attempts to revive Flower and now picks absently at the acoustic.

'Ash*leeeeyyy*, you diamond,' Jake grins, wrapping his arm around the drummer. 'You diamond among diamonds.'

'Yeeeah . . . Jakey.'

'Aww . . . isn't this superb behaviour?'

'Yeeeeaah . . . shame about Russ.'

'Russy. Russy-Russy-Russy. Doesn't like being called that, apparently.'

'Naaah . . .'

'Never knew that, did he ever tell you that?'

'Never . . . erm . . . but I never call him that.'

'No? Am I the only one, then?'

'Might . . . erm . . . yeeeeah . . . might be.'

'Kazza!'

A muffled 'What?' can be heard from the region of Karen and Hillock's blanket.

'You ever call Russell "Russy"?'

'Not if I expect him to answer.'

'Aw . . . right. Well, anywa*ayyy* . . . ohh . . . whyyy . . . why's Russy always in such a wig . . . wig-wig-wiggington.'

Ash gazes into the fire, offering no conclusive answers.

'Cos he's all right, y'know . . . Ashley?'

'Yeeeahh . . .'

'He's all right, our Russy . . . troubled, but he's OK. A troubled prince . . . a fine, troubled prince . . . a hardworking, unappreciated prince . . .'

'Jakey . . . what the shit are you on about, man?'

'Oh . . . nothing. It's hard this . . . innit . . . Ashley?'

'Yeeeaaah . . . what?'

'This band stuff . . . this musical band business.'

Ash inhales, summoning some coherency from somewhere.

'Yes,' he frowns. 'It *is* hard, Jakey. Very hard.'

Jake's face acquires a concerned, slightly urgent flavour. He grabs his lighter and relights the joint in his hand.

'You must be . . .' he begins.

'Whassat?'

'Gutted,' Jake suggests. 'Y'know . . . about Prat . . . and Shitesmann. Parlophone. All of that.'

'Uh . . . yeeeaahh . . .'

'Does it . . . how does it . . . how does it make you feel . . . about all this?'

Ash sips from his beer can and deepens his gaze. It feels like five minutes until his eventual, enigmatic reply.

'Tough,' he says.

They continue to glumly stare at the fire. Both seem to be on the point of asking or telling each other something, but for whatever reason they decide not to. They look up at one point, lock eyes, and give each other a little grin. Partly the standard 'we're both stoned, isn't this hilarious?' grin – but also something else. The suggestion might be fanciful, but it looks like Ash is offering a telepathic apology for what might come – and that Jake is telepathically accepting it. Then Karen stirs and reappears from under her blanket, and the moment passes.

'Hate to disturb you loverboys,' she announces, 'but I'm gonna hit the stonerdrome.'

'Aw, ker-racking idea,' Jake replies, staggering to his feet. 'Ashley?'

'Yeeeah . . .'

'Hilly, me old man?'

'Hillock's going to look for Russ,' Karen says. 'He's worried about him.'

Hillock nods solemnly, stroking his goatee.

'Won't he just be sulking in his tent?'

'No,' Karen answers, holding up her phone for Jake to see. A text message, typical in wording, ambiguous in subject: '*Am having a wander, trying to assuage the sinking feeling that this is all a mistake.*'

'Aw . . . rather you than me, Hilly. Go for it, mate. Best of British.'

Hillock gives Jake a disarmingly lengthy hug, bumps fists

with Ash, kisses Karen on the hand (prompting none of the disgusted winces Josh's gesture did), mounts his unicycle and rides off into the woods.

'How in fuck's name does he ride that thing?' Jake mutters. 'Especially now. He must be totally numbered.'

'He says the more stoned he is, the better he rides,' Karen explains.

'Well, in that case,' Jake beams, nudging her in the ribs, 'you'd better go and check all your tent pegs are in properly.'

'Ya-ha,' responds Karen, either too knackered, drunk, stoned or secretly pleased to answer back.

Wiltshire 2

Hillock has been on the scene for less than twelve hours but he's already proved himself enigmatic, thoughtful, generally away with the fairies, but in possession of an enviable sense of physical balance, and probably, judging by Karen's quiet little smile when she eventually emerges from her tent, a demon in the sleeping bag. And to this list we must also add discreet. More than the following he will not be drawn upon.

'I found the man drifting, over by Henley's Mount, watching the dawn break . . . I took him by surprise . . . At first, his guard was up . . . I'd invaded his space, upset his equilibrium . . . but I crouched down and laid my hands on the cool, dewy grass . . . I showed him I was unarmed, defenceless . . . assured the man he had nothing to fear . . . and slowly he opened up, came to trust me a little . . .'

'Blimey,' Jake puffs, squirting some ketchup into his fried-egg sandwich. 'It's like the fucking *Horse Whisperer*. Did you manage to get your feet into one of the stirrups?'

Hillock shrugs. 'We found our neutral ground.'

'Great,' laughs Karen, pulling her hoody around her and giving Jake a wink. 'I'm sure Russell loved that.'

'And?' Jake presses. 'What the hell was the matter with the silly sod?'

'We spoke for a long time,' Hillock replies, putting the finishing touches to a copious breakfast joint. 'We explored together, laughed, told stories, shared secrets.'

Karen sleepily ruffles her hair and shoots an apologetic glance at Jake. 'Seriously. He won't budge. I've tried to get more out of him . . .'

'Using more interesting methods than me, I should think,' Jake grins, biting hugely into his sandwich. 'Ahh . . . sweet breakfast . . .'

Karen tosses a carton of juice onto the grass next to Ash, who is juggling with three pans on a single camping stove. Then she fixes Hillock with a frown.

'Can't you just tell us *something*? Like . . . is he all right? Were there any, erm . . . vibes involved?'

'Plenty of vibes,' Hillock nods, sparking up his creation.

Karen shakes her head at Jake and Ash.

'So bloody cryptic. It's pissing me off.'

Apart from basic nosiness, the main reason for this frantic probing is that it's now fifteen minutes before noon and Russell is still fast asleep. The precise time he returned to his tent remains unknown; Hillock briefly poked his head into the stoner-drome at around 7 a.m. (not that anyone remembers this) to invite Karen back to her own tent, by which time the sun had already taken a firm hold on the sky and Russell was still 'exploring'. The natural assumption by his bandmates is that drugs of some sort have been involved.

Hillock receives the towering pile of eggs, mushrooms, beans and plastic white bread Ash has been constructing for him, and strokes his goatee thoughtfully.

'Seems that no one here is content to be told that I simply helped the man,' he muses, a hint of irritation flitting across his chiselled features.

Karen and Jake's reaction is typically loud and simultaneous.

'No, no! Honestly, babe! You've done great . . .'

'Hilly, me old mate! We're over the bloody moon that you rescued our chum . . .'

'. . . you probably talked more fucking sense into him than us lot ever could . . .'

'. . . and we only want to know more because . . .'

Here Jake's explanation grinds to a halt, unsure what the precise reason really is. Karen picks it up.

'You've gotta realise, we're a band. We have to know everything about each other, or it feels weird. Plus' – at this point she gestures towards Russell's tent, still a den of inactivity, and whispers – '*this is very unusual.*'

Russell proves no keener to reveal all than Hillock, but a few telling pieces of evidence are spotted. When he bursts out of his tent at 12.05 p.m. he is still dressed as he was by the campfire, suggesting that he slept fully clothed. He drinks two litres of water in his first ten waking minutes, and refuses Ash's camping food and coffee (although he might be rather unrealistically hoping there are better versions of both to be found elsewhere). Later, in the makeshift dressing room before the band's set, he is seen to be tinkering with a full set of lyrics to a song called 'You Brought It On Yourself' ('Yes,' he admits quietly, 'it *is* the Jake song'), a composition which certainly did not exist yesterday. More than any of this, he looks, speaks, moves and smells like a man who has recently indulged in at least a small quantity of class-A drugs. Sadly, it seems to have done nothing for his equilibrium.

'Oh . . . my . . . *God!*'

– is the first thing to be heard from his tent.

'What the . . . Guys? Are you up, is anyone up?'

– is the second thing.

'It's five . . . past . . . *twelve!*'

The others giggle at each other. The tent door unzips and Russell appears.

'I can't believe it, I slept through my . . . my . . .' He glances at his empty wrist, then looks up, horrified. 'How come *you're* all up?'

'Chill, Russ,' Ash murmurs, stirring the tin of beans. 'I set my alarm.'

Russell is frantically pacing between the van and his band-mates, checking all his pockets for the keys. Hillock looks a little disturbed, perhaps wondering which drain all his hard work has gone down.

'The van's open!' Russell yells. 'Someone's broken into the van!'

'Oh *no!*' Karen shouts back. 'Broken in, and stolen all the cooking equipment! Who on earth could that have been?'

Russell stops for a second and focuses on Ash's breakfast production line: Karen buttering bread, Jake pouring tea.

'Where did you get the keys?'

'From your tent, Russ,' Ash explains.

'But . . . why didn't you . . . ?'

'You looked like you needed the sleep, fella.'

'But . . . it's five past *twelve*! We were meant to be at the soundcheck . . .'

Jake rolls his eyes. 'Oh, for the love of bollocks . . .'

'They might not let us *play*!' Russell gasps, his forehead vein starting to bulge dangerously.

Ash plonks down two of his pans with a clatter.

'It's all *right*, Russell. I strolled over there at about half eleven, the guy said to come back at quarter to one. Bacon sandwich?'

Aside from his raging, wide-eyed anxiety, Russell seems genuinely annoyed that so much has been achieved in his absence. It's quite possible that Russell promised himself an alternative version of this morning – one on which he rose at eight after a bumpy but surprisingly restful six hours' sleep, had an early stroll around the grounds, perhaps even drove to the village to pick up a newspaper and a proper cup of coffee, then became steadily incensed as ten o'clock neared and no one had surfaced – and is now furious to have been denied it, especially as its replacement is clearly so relaxed and well organised.

That said, the others are nonetheless a little ropy, having managed only three or four hours' sleep themselves. Karen claims to feel a little sick, Ash hurries to the loo more often than usual. Jake being awake at all remains something of a miracle, but he will later put this down to the strength of Ash's farts and the promise of fried food. The two stoner-dromes, even when the band depart for the backstage area at about 12.40, are ominously devoid of any stirring activity, at last giving Russell something genuinely worth complaining about.

'That's our audience, asleep, in there,' he moans, starting the van. 'I'd be astonished if anyone watches us. What a worth-while experience this has been.'

No one bothers to respond.

But at the other end of the lane the backstage area is a hive of activity, exceeding even the most optimistic expectations. Three or four extremely jaunty technicians bustle about, up and down the wooden gangplank to the stage, carrying amps, turntables and crates of water; Dave Berwick, a bearded six-foot-sixer with life-threatening tattoos and the aforementioned brown-and-white bull terrier (whose name appears to be Oi!), is as fearsome as has been described, presiding over the scene with almost military discipline, an alarming contrast to the state he was reportedly in last night.

'Right! Park the van over there by the lodge, between the two white lines. Your dressing room's in the backstage tent over there, and I want you lot out of there no later than thirty minutes after you leave that stage, so off you go, look lively . . .'

All that is missing, as Russell repeats with maddening frequency, is someone to watch the band's set. The DJs apparently started at eleven, probably just as the most hardened punters were finishing their yesterday. They proceeded to spin tunes for the next hour or so, largely to amuse themselves, occasionally producing outbreaks of insomniac frugging in the area immediately before the stage, after which those responsible either sloped off or collapsed. Now nearing 1.30 p.m., the current DJ, a baby-faced character in a parka, alternately sips an energy drink and a can of Stella while gazing out at the deserted paddock. Brian Eno once said he knew it was time to leave Roxy Music when he caught himself thinking about his laundry onstage, and it's easy to imagine the parka-clad DJ having similarly domestic thoughts just now. Ash, having already set up his drums on a wheeled riser, stands next to the poor guy for a minute or two, taking in the empty site with an unsteady mixture of amusement and mild panic. A couple of trestle tables sit to the left of the stage under a hand-painted sign declaring 'BAR', but there are no drinks to be seen. Very occasionally, a figure in a blanket or hoody is spotted wandering about at the far end of the field; even rarer is the flash of a pale face as it turns this way to give the main stage a moment's attention.

The DJ turns to Ash and smiles cheerfully.

'Don't worry about it, mate!' he hollers above the din from his turntable. 'They'll all come. The main entrance is next to the breakfast tent, just the other side of that clump of trees. As soon as you guys start playing, they'll drift down.'

'Why aren't they drifting now?' Ash asks, unconvinced.

'Cos I'm just a fucking DJ, innit,' he beams.

Back in the dressing room – an unimpressive area of tent augmented by a couple of plastic chairs, a half-hearted bowl of fruit and four cans of Tesco lager, one of which Jake has already finished – Russell isn't remotely comforted by this piece of optimism.

'We will play,' he grunts, 'to the bar staff. That's it.'

Karen, busily tuning her bass, looks up crossly.

'Russell,' she hisses, 'I swear, if you carry on fucking moaning someone's going to finally lump you one, quite possibly me.'

'You don't understand,' he murmurs.

Jake is chatting to the neighbouring band, a pleasant New Age three-piece from Rotterdam named Day of Krud, who have just installed themselves in their own corner of the large tent.

'Aw,' Jake observes, 'I bet you Dutch hate coming over here and having to smoke our substandard shite.'

The Dutch boys smile politely.

'It isn't so bad as drinking your beer,' one admits.

'What are you saying?' Jake quips, opening another can. 'This is Tesco's finest! A quality brew, handmade from quality chemicals in some factory near Stevenage. Better than your Amstel.'

'No one drinks Amstel in Netherlands,' comes the deadpan reply.

Talk turns to their respective careers.

'We're nowhere,' Jake happily announces. 'We've been at it for three years now, and we couldn't get arrested.'

'But you enjoy playing your music?'

'Aw, yeah! Of course. That's the main thing, innit? We all love it. Apart from Russell over there, he prefers doing the hoovering.'

Day of Krud, it is revealed, have just released a double album on their own label.

'How awesome is that!' Jake comments. 'To release your own double album. I wish we had enough decent material to fill even a single album.'

Russell rolls his eyes, but carries on studying his new lyrics. Perhaps anticipating a row, Ash wanders outside.

'Most of our album is improvised stuff,' explains Day of Krud's bassist, extracting a six-stringed bass from its hard case. 'It's meant to be just put on, chilled out.'

'Glorious,' Jake replies. 'You're gonna go down a storm here, then, eh? Plenty of chilling to be done this morning.'

'It's afternoon,' Russell points out.

'Yes, I know it is, Russell. Feels like morning, though. Must do especially for you, eh?'

Russell inhales deeply, his forehead visibly throbbing.

'Although,' Jake ponders, glugging more beer, 'I dunno if I'd want to release a double album, actually. I've always been a fan of the short, sharp shock of a record, y'know? Call it the pop fan in me. Forty minutes, I think, is the perfect length.'

'Wow,' Russell says quietly, opening another bottle of water. 'Finally something we agree on.'

'It happens from time to time, eh, Russy?' Jake replies over his shoulder. 'That'll save us a couple of hours one day.'

Ash reappears, clutching his lower abdomen.

'I've got incomparable arse problems,' he announces, to a disgusted groan from Karen. As if it will help matters, Ash opens a can of lager. He only manages one sip before Dave Berwick crams his hulk into the room.

'OK, lads and lasses,' he booms. 'We're just about ready onstage, so if we can get you on five minutes early, we will.'

'Ah,' Russell frowns, 'we'd prefer not, if you don't mind. People know we're playing at two, so –'

'We've got a tight schedule today, son, so any extra time we generate is going to be more than welcome at the other end of the day.'

'But no one's in the arena yet,' Russell persists. 'At least if we come on at the proper time, it'll give them a chance to –'

'Don't you fret, my boy, as soon as you start playing they'll all appear.'

'Yes, but we don't particularly want to start playing to an empty field. If we wait until two, there'll be –'

Dave Berwick points a giant finger at Russell. His dog suddenly looks extra threatening.

'I'm not going to argue with you, young man. You'll take to the stage when we tell you to, and that's that. You're not Massive Attack yet, you know.'

He turns sharply away and walks over to greet Day of Krud.

Russell mumbles something and sips his water, then realises his band are all glaring at him.

'What?'

'Fuckin'ell, Russ,' Ash snaps, 'can you try to not fall out with the fucking stage manager directly before we go on?'

'Yes, but –'

'But nothing, Russ! Stop bloody arguing! You're always fuckin' arguing! I'm sick of it! Just button it!'

Russell buttons it.

It is therefore a silent and somewhat grouchy bunch who drift onstage (at one minute to two, after all that), watched by the still-empty field. Jake vanished from the dressing room a few minutes ago – his standard pre-show loo visit, it is assumed – but when Ash, Karen and Russell reach the top of the gangplank, Jake is up there waiting for them.

'Thought you were in the toilet, fella,' Ash says.

'S'OK,' Jake smiles, a wicked glint in his eye. 'Just sorting something out.'

They assume their regular positions – Jake stage centre, Karen left, Russell right, Ash's kit parked behind Karen but slanted slightly towards Jake. Faced with the unusual (some might say non-existent) audience conditions, they decided to amend their set list half an hour ago to open with 'Krystal Palace' – the theory being that the crowd can drift into the arena during the quieter, metronomic section of the song, and then be awestruck by the rock attack of the final quarter. It's a great theory. Whether it works in practice is soon to be discovered.

The DJ powers down his final record as Russell fires up the synth. An electronic beat pumps out, carrying two repeating bass notes in the kick drum. Russell clips his guitar and a chunky, abrasive sound reverberates around the field. All is as it should be. Jake steps up to the microphone.

'*Since I came to your Krystal Palace I've had this ache . . . A nagging pain that's hard for me to take . . . It seems that all my life I've been asleep . . . Until you woke me . . . Until you woke me . . .*'

Ash joins the synthetic beat with a tight rhythm of his own. Karen takes a final drag on her cigarette, tosses away the stub and begins her bass pattern quietly.

'*Your congregation worship in your church . . . Your military men begin their search . . .*'

Russell is leaning over the synth, softly prodding the song's distinctive melody into the keyboard's higher register. He looks across the stage at the rest of his band and nods his approval. Then, and only then, he risks looking out over the paddock to see if the famed 'drifting' has started to occur.

Apparently not. All that can be seen, as Russell acknowledges with a gasp, is Josh.

He's standing right at the back of the arena, dead in the centre of the gap in the trees. He's wearing something fairly nondescript – a black shirt and combats – but his expression, even from this distance, says it all. He's even managed to locate a bottle of Beck's from somewhere. Russell's eyes dart over to Jake, who appears to be staring straight at Josh. The next words to leave Jake's mouth do so with an unmistakable barb of malice.

'*And they say I'll never have you . . . And they say that I'm beneath you . . . And they say I'll never get to put my hands around your pretty throat and squeeze . . . and squeeze . . . and squeeze . . .*'

Josh smirks, sips his drink and ambles forward. Onstage, Jake turns to Russell, who has become rather pale, his face plainly stricken with concern for what might happen next. Jake takes a few steps towards him, stops . . . then turns away again to prepare his guitar. Russell practically deflates with relief. He leaves his post behind the synth, moves forward to the lip of the big stage and starts to chug away on the octave chord which runs throughout the third-verse build-up. Jake approaches the mic to sing again, and as he does: a miracle.

First a pair of girls wrapped in a blanket, drowsily shuffling along, both holding cans of Red Bull. Then an eccentric-looking character in a trilby hat and a trench coat. Another group of punky girls, dressed up to the nines, who look unlikely to have spent the night in a tent. The crew from the campfire – not before bloody time, you might think – Godfrey, Emma, Flower and, lurching to and fro on his ever-present unicycle, Hillock. Then a large herd of the standard crusty-raver type which filled the village pub last night, a bunch of normal-looking kids carrying drinks in paper pint cups, yet more exceedingly groggy-looking stoners wrapped in an unruly combination of blankets, hoodies, hats, vintage jackets and fake-fur coats. More and more, from heaven knows where, all trudging through the gap in the trees, surrounding Josh, who sniffily takes a few steps to the side. It's a dance festival's take on the coming-over-the-hill scene in *Zulu*, a recreational-drug cavalry. By the time the third verse has reached its climax, the field, while far from full, has stopped looking like an empty field and started to look like an audience. Galvanised by this astonishing turnaround, Jake turns and winks at Ash, then issues the crowd with the most heartfelt, carefully worded call to arms he can muster.

'Morning, you fucking hippies – let's rock!'

The world stands still for a nanosecond, in which everything could go horrifically, embarrassingly wrong again. It's left to Ash to take off the pause button with his trio of drum flams – at such a juncture they are so powerful as to appear nigh on apocalyptic – then the entire band leap a good five feet into the air and rip into the rock assault of the song's final quarter. Memories of spinning bowls filled with brownie and ice cream are a mercifully long way away. Karen spanks her bass with such ferocity one wonders how her fingers remain attached to her hand, Russell and Jake attack their guitars with all the violence and aggression they might at times wish to inflict on each other, Ash seems to punish his drums for their very existence. The sound is fat, fast, brutal. Some of the audience are merrily bemused – but most of them are dizzily hooked.

From this point onwards, it's a textbook festival gig. They're hardly the liveliest crowd in the world, many of them sitting around on the grass in sleepy huddles, but what they lack in animation they make up for in attention span. Each song – the driving groove of 'M3', the punky-dance spree of 'Petrol', even the more standard pop-rock of 'Smaller Weaker' and 'Ghost of Pop' (with restored original lyrics) – is rewarded with a fervent ovation. The gap in the trees filters a steady flow of one-way traffic into the arena; by the set's three-quarter mark there must be close to two hundred people in the field. Finally, as the penultimate song ('Warning') begins its Zeppelin-esque, riff-driven, four-to-the-floor stomp, about ten ravers are throwing energetic and eccentric dance shapes down at the front. Jake, in his element, takes this development as all the encouragement he needs for what is to come. When he removes his guitar for the final song ('Testing Ground', with extended outro), he surreptitiously retrieves a device of some sort from the back of his amp, which he stuffs into the lower-leg pocket of his combats. It looks like a walkie-talkie, similar to the one Russell uses at the Imperial, but – as we are about to discover – it isn't.

The band zip through the principal portion of the song, its infectious bass line and chorus drawing another five or so revellers into the dancing circle: a major achievement, remembering what the arena looked like thirty-five minutes ago, but still not exactly a moshpit worthy of a stage-diving frontman. Nor does it look like Jake will comfortably get away with the sort of heroic, run-around flyer-distribution antics planned for this moment in the band's schedule, and Russell, judging by the concerned expression creeping onto his face as the end of the song approaches, knows it. The good news is that Jake has a different plan. The bad news is something else. At the point Jake is expected to jump off the stage he simply turns round, extracts the black box from his trousers, pulls out an aerial and points it towards the back of the stage. Charging along between Ash's rightmost cymbal stand and Jake's amp, before the astonished eyes of Russell and Karen, is Jake's model Spitfire aeroplane, a little plastic basket firmly gaffer-taped to its fuselage, in which sits an enormous pile of 'You Have Been Watching . . .' flyers. The little plane speeds its way to the lip of the stage – and is airborne. It zooms over the gaping audience's heads, steadily gaining altitude as it flies towards the rear of the field, then banks round and sails back in the direction of the stage. Jake, his face steeled with concentration, zigzags the Spitfire around the paddock until it reaches a height roughly level with the stage's grey plastic canopy. Then he flicks his wrist and deftly flips the plane over.

In a parallel universe, this stunt would have worked. A gust of wind would have caught the loosely assembled pile of flyers as they fell out of the basket, scattering them far and wide, enabling them to flutter down impressively on the crowd of happy punters – the unsigned-band equivalent of a New York ticker-tape parade. This is not what happens. There is no gust of wind. The pile of flyers, until recently clenched together by one of Russell's industrial-strength rubber bands, hardly separates at all – instead it drops like a stone and clunks embarrassingly to the ground, landing on a bare patch of grass next to an indifferent middle-aged hippy who is idly flicking through his festival programme. To round things off, a nearby Jack Russell terrier races over to investigate, eagerly sniffs the sudden descendant from the sky, and lifts his leg.

JAKE: You've got to try new stuff. What's the point of always doing things in such a boring, predictable way? Surely the whole point of all this rock'n'roll nonsense is to have fun. Theatricals! Big ways of saying stuff and doing stuff. Not being so bloody po-faced about it all. So I occasionally attempt something new without warning the others. And d'you know why? Because nine times out of ten if I suggest doing one of these things beforehand, the idea'll get shot down by you-know-who. 'No, Jake – I'm sorry. The margin for error is unacceptably wide and the likelihood of the whole thing teetering into comedy unavoidably high.' And maybe it is, sometimes. But so what? What would rock music be like if all big, dumb ideas got pooh-poohed at the start?

There's a time and a place for some of these things, perhaps.

JAKE: But how do you *know*? These things have gotta start *sometime*, haven't they? A band like . . . I dunno . . . Iron Maiden. The first time they had their fucking monster Eddie onstage, eyes lighting up, mouth squirting fuck-knows-what at the audience – what would have happened if someone held up their hand and said (*adopts military officer voice*), 'Ah, hold on a tick, chaps. This might not be such a splendid idea after all. Harvey Goldsmith's coming to see us tonight.'

But you're very different to Iron Maiden, wouldn't you say? The whole point of Iron Maiden is that they're big, dumb and theatrical . . .

JAKE: And bloody brilliant, yes.

Sure. Whereas your band is more cerebral, introverted . . .

JAKE: And fucking dull. Right. But I didn't set out to be this dull. That was never the plan. The advert I answered didn't say – 'cerebrally dull vocalist wanted for fucking boring introverted rock band'. It's become this way because . . .

Because of Russell?

(*Long pause.*)

JAKE: Your words, not mine.

In the grand scheme of things, such as it is, Jake's plane experiment is of very little consequence. Most of the audience expected their day to be filled with various laptop-and-turntable-wielding dance collectives (as the remainder of it largely will be) and were pleasantly perplexed in the first place to be returned to daytime consciousness by the tunes of this funny little guitar band; that their singer chose to have some fun with his model aeroplane during the final song hardly mattered. Indeed, for some of the more hardened danceheads it was by far the most entertaining part. At any rate, the very last thing on anyone's mind, with the yawning exception of Russell, is whether or not the incident managed to hurl the band from atop the slick, professional mountain they had climbed over the course of their forty-minute slot, down to the depths of the amateur valley below.

Not that Russell makes any comment. He seems too scared of the newly assertive Ash to open his mouth. Besides, as soon as he leaves the stage he retires to a quiet corner of the backstage clearing, where he can soon be seen vomiting.

'I felt worse and worse throughout the show,' he explains afterwards. 'Various reasons, I suppose. Caffeine withdrawal, for one thing . . . plus I think I ate a Pot Noodle before I went to bed last night – er, this morning.'

You *think* you ate one?

'Ah, er . . . yes. It was very late. Uh – early. I was very tired, not thinking straight. I think I had it with cold water.'

That must have been lovely.

'Erm, yes. Old university trick, for when the electricity money ran out. Right, better go and find Josh.'

While the rest of the band decide to make the most of their final fifteen minutes in the dressing room, where they are soon engulfed by a cloud of smoke, Russell stalks around the little fence cordoning off the backstage area and enters the main arena itself (a security guard, as with everywhere else, is deemed excess to requirements – 'I'd like to meet this Megan before we leave,' Russell grunts). Josh can be seen hovering near the bar, sucking on his beer bottle, engaged in conversation with a wispy-looking girl in a Laura Ashley-ish dress. Russell steers himself in this direction – but takes a surprisingly long time to get there.

'Nice set, mate,' someone says as he passes.

'I'm sorry?'

'Nice set,' repeats the guy, sitting on the grass nearby, a Sunday paper spread between him and his girlfriend. 'Wicked tunes.'

'Oh! Er . . . thank you,' Russell smiles. 'Glad you enjoyed it.'

A little further on, another well-wisher.

'That was brilliant!' enthuses a girl with dyed-black hair and a large nose-ring. 'Not normally my cuppa tea, that kinda thing, but it was perfect for this time of day . . . your singer is hilarious!'

'Ah – right! Thanks!'

More nods and grins as Russell traipses along.

'Good songs, man . . .'

'Dude, your band fucking *rocks* . . . what's the name of that last song?'

'Mate, that one about petrol, fucking mosh-central, man . . .'

'Sweet beats, mate. Not exactly your sort of festie, though, is it? Shouldn't you be at Reading?'

Russell thinks for a moment.

'Yes,' he nods, finally. 'Yes, you're right! We should.'

'You got any CDs on sale?'

Russell winces, appalled at his own oversight.

'Ahh! Yes, but not on me now . . . give me ten minutes, I'll get some . . .'

By the time he reaches Josh, Russell is practically walking on air. Exactly what he is expecting Josh to say is unclear; anything along the lines of 'You know what? I was wrong . . . Jake's great, keep him . . . I'll co-manage you instead' would of course be fanciful in the extreme, but at the very least one anticipates something slightly more congratulatory than what actually emerges from his mouth.

'Yep,' he breezes, turning briefly to Russell. 'That's *that* out of the way at last. Now do the fucking deed and let's get on with it.'

Without waiting for Russell's reply he turns briskly back to the girl, who predictably enough is very attractive. Russell is left standing there, looking more or less stupid.

KAREN: Poor Russell. He does sometimes go around with the weight of the world on his shoulders. He's really sensitive, actually. For someone so apparently confident of his own abilities, it doesn't take much to knock him. I think that's why he needs his life to be so ordered – everything's got to be presented in precisely the right way, or he gets paranoid that the good bits won't shine through. But like I've said, I can't help wondering what he'd achieve if he'd just . . . y'know. Chill a bit. Take his foot off the gas, just a little.

Do you think Jake seems similarly paranoid, on occasion?

KAREN: Yeah . . . sort of . . . but Jake's only paranoid because he's a complete fuckwit. And cos he smokes too much. Whereas, with Russ . . . I sometimes think he's genuinely got a problem.

Of the psychological variety?

KAREN: Yeah. Like, I dunno, that compulsive disorder thing. You sometimes find him tying himself in knots over the most bloody ridiculous . . . like, trying to find that pub in the village. Crazy. I mean, no amount of us saying 'it'll be all *right*, Russ . . . it'll only be a small place . . . and if we really can't find it we'll just ask someone' would've made him relax and stop worrying. And there's worse examples. A couple of years ago he became obsessed with the fact that he'd run out of money. Like, for about a week, he was totally inconsolable about it. He was in credit, mind, but down to his last two hundred quid – a bloody miracle in my bank account (*laughs*) – and he was behaving like one of his family was dying. So we do the usual thing: 'Don't worry so much about it, Russ', or 'It doesn't matter if you go a *little* bit overdrawn' – which we got absolutely nowhere with, as you can imagine – and then at the end of the week, when we've all had it up to here with the fucker and we're finally ready to lop his head off, he sighs and says, 'Well, there's nothing for it. I'm gonna have to break into my savings.' What the *fuck*? Savings! Who in fuck's name has *savings*? Turns out he's got a couple of grand in some bloody Post Office account that he just so happened not to mention. I mean, Christ!

But do you think that sometimes Russell simply enjoys a good moan?

KAREN: Oh, definitely. I think it goes a little deeper than that, though. It's like there's some sort of mental . . . itch, that he can't get rid of, that he's constantly scratching. Moaning is maybe one way of scratching. Working as hard as Russell does is another, and I'm not necessarily talking about composing and playing, but more the menial stuff, chopping up flyers and that. And arguing, of course. Like that stage-time argument at the festival – I mean, who was *really* going to give a shit if we went on five minutes early? But Russell has to scratch. Morgan reckons Russ suffers from mild persecution complex – and I'd be inclined to agree. Russell's convinced there's some greater force in the world actively conspiring against him being a successful rock musician. It's like he's already admitted defeat, at the hand of this greater power, but he carries on doing what he's doing because otherwise the itch would drive him barmy. I don't honestly think he expects anything that he's doing will *solve* his problems, but –

Really?

KAREN (*drags on cigarette*): Yeah. I think it's got to the point now where he's just blindly scratching, and he'll keep on scratching until something drags him away. And it'll have to be something pretty dramatic. God knows. We'll see.

Russell storms into the backstage tent. His three bandmates, plus Hillock, Godfrey, Flower and the three members of Day of Krud, are all doubled over with laughter, swigging glasses of red wine they've found from somewhere, puffing on numerous joints and showing no signs whatsoever of vacating the space any time soon. Even more unexpected is the sight of Dave Berwick, on all fours in the centre of the scene, apparently doing impersonations of a cow.

'Uh-oh,' he gruffs, spotting the new arrival. 'Here comes trouble . . .'

'There you are, Russ!' Karen hoots.

'Russy!' Jake yells, holding aloft his wine glass. 'How's it going, fella? Great show, eh? What did you think?'

Russell grabs his khaki jacket from a chair, the only personal item of his in the room, and makes his announcement brief and to the point.

'I'm leaving in fifteen minutes. Anyone who isn't ready can find some other way of getting home.'

He marches out again.

'Ooooh!' laughs Dave Berwick. '*Someone* got out their tent the wrong side this morning, didn't they?'

'Christ, what the fuck's wrong with him *now*?' Jake groans.

Ash rises, hands one of the joints to Hillock and goes into his usual, practical mode.

'I'll go and sort him out.'

'No,' Karen says, stopping him. 'I will.'

She hurries out. Russell is by the van, angrily dismantling Ash's drums and hurling them into the back. Karen approaches him gingerly and says nothing for the time being, letting him fume. Her strategy works. After a minute or so, Russell stops what he's doing and looks at her with knackered eyes.

'Josh,' he says.

'Ah,' Karen nods. 'Cock?'

'Yup.'

Karen lights a cigarette while Russell packs down the keyboard stand.

'Sorry,' she says.

'What are *you* sorry about?'

'Oh . . . nothing, really. But I think it's . . .'

'What?'

'Well . . . kind of my fault that he's down here.'

Russell grunts. 'I suppose he's *into* you, then.'

Karen rolls her eyes and takes a drag.

'Well, I wouldn't worry,' Russell advises, laying the synth inside its box. 'Looks like he's already lining up his next conquest.'

'Russell, how many fucking times, I was *not* a conquest.'

More packing and smoking.

'It was a good show,' Karen comments after a while.

Russell leans a flight case against the van door and gives a nasty laugh.

'Karen . . . we've been playing good shows for *three years*. What difference does it make?'

'I know, I know . . .'

She smokes silently as Russell winds up a few cables.

'Did Hillock enjoy it?' he asks.

'The show? Er . . . yeah, of course! Why?'

'No reason.'

Russell grabs the handle of Ash's drum coffin and yanks it

a few feet towards the van door. Karen parks her cigarette in her mouth, takes hold of the other handle and together they lift it into the back. The van's rear drops a good few inches as the huge box clunks down. Karen blows a lungful of smoke at it.

'Running off won't make any of this easier, Russ.'

'It'll make it easier for *me*,' he mutters.

Karen waits a minute longer, then sighs and ambles back to the backstage tent. Russell gathers the remaining pieces of band paraphernalia and reverses the van out of the space. He is just about to drive off when he spots a plump, cheery-looking lady, with a floor-length cardigan and long, greying hair, standing over by the little wooden lodge, smiling and waving. He winds down his window.

'Russell?' beams this apparition, advancing towards him.

'Yes?'

'Hello, we spoke on the phone! I'm Megan!'

'Oh . . . right!'

'Sorry we've not met before. How's it going? Lovely site, eh? Get a good night's kip?'

'Er . . . yes, not bad . . .'

'Good, good, that's what I like to hear! Ha ha! So – what time are you playing?'

Russell's complexion veers through about eight different shades before he manages to reply. Megan's response is sweetly, ramblingly apologetic, but her punchline makes everything worth it.

'Well! If you've already played, you'll want to be paid! Eh?'

'Paid?' Russell blinks.

'Of course! Four hundred, I think it was, plus petrol and meal allowance. There's four of you, yes?'

'Oh. Er . . . yes! Four.'

'Follow me, sweetness,' Megan chuckles, turning back towards the lodge.

Russell gives his arm a quick pinch, then slams the van door and hurries after her.

Back in the dressing room, Ash and Jake have eagerly agreed to an offer Hillock and Godfrey have just made: to stay for the rest of the day's bash, then to travel back with everyone in the bus tomorrow. After not much persuasion, Karen agrees to the same.

'Brilliant,' Jake says, exhaling. 'We get shit-faced for another whole night, without knobhead being around to spoil it.'

Next on the agenda, they all quickly resolve, is food. Wishing Day of Krud good luck for their set, they gather their belongings and mooch off into the now bustling main arena, where their route to the other end of the field is peppered with similar positive encounters to those Russell enjoyed. The lion's share of the compliments are received by Jake; Karen and Ash, hanging back slightly, shoot guilty looks at each other.

'Oh, *awesome*,' Jake gushes, once they round the corner and are greeted by the sight of some hearty-looking food stalls. 'I bet they've got some crazy fucking farmer shit here, sausages and pies and what have you.'

He is not wrong. Hillock, Godfrey and the three bandmates (Flower has retired for a well-earned lie-down) hit the stalls and stock up on starchy grub, then carry their meals back into the main space where they all naturally decide to wash their lunch down with a drink. Approaching the busy bar, Jake dives in to get the pints while the rest turn their attention to the stage, from which a strange noise has begun to emanate: a mixture of yodelling, classical guitar and what sounds like a didgeridoo being played underwater. Day of Krud's set has begun.

'Bollocks,' Karen mutters. Hillock turns to her, surprised.

'Give it a chance, sister.'

'No, no,' she says. 'I've just seen someone I don't wanna see.'

Josh and his wispy companion are standing on the far side of the bar's trestle tables, and have briefly halted their discussion while they check out the musical entertainment on offer. It doesn't take Josh long to turn to his female friend with a sardonic grin and utter some presumably disparaging remark. Karen yelps and turns to give Hillock an overenthusiastic hug.

'Peace,' Hillock responds, wrapping his tanned arm around her and squeezing his eyes shut. When Karen sneaks another glance, Josh is looking over in her direction. By now Ash has spotted him too.

'Oh gawd,' Ash says, spinning round to check on Jake's progress. Jake is five or six heads deep in the throng, loudly ordering five pints of pear cider from one of the bar girls.

'What's the vibe?' Hillock asks.

Karen puffs and leans in.

'That guy over there in the black . . . he's . . .'

Hillock looks over.

'*Don't* look over,' Karen snaps, pulling him round. 'He's . . . oh, Russell probably told you about him last night?'

'Him?'

'Yeah . . . didn't Russ mention . . . a singer . . . ?'

'No singer,' Hillock murmurs. 'I heard a lot of things from the man, but he didn't mention any singer.'

'What about a manager?' Ash suggests.

'No . . .'

Karen frowns and her voice returns to normal volume.

'Then what the hell *did* you talk about?'

'Shh!' Ash hisses.

Josh is approaching.

'Oh, mother of fuck . . .'

Josh weaves his way through the crowd, smiling smarmily, nursing another full Beck's. Where he is keeping his secret hoard of bottled beer is anyone's guess – perhaps stashed in one of the hedges.

'Karen,' he begins, kissing her on the cheek. He ignores Hillock but nods at Ash.

'Fella,' Ash grunts.

'You made it,' Karen comments, with a desperate lack of enthusiasm.

'Ya,' he replies. 'Shot down here in the convertible. The A30's a delight. Nice set, by the way, kids. Best yet. Thought I was gonna be your audience for a minute there.'

'Us too,' Ash admits.

Josh's female companion catches up and stands next to him, but she is not introduced. It's awkward, but about to get worse. Jake bowls up with a cardboard tray full of drinks and smiles sarcastically at Josh.

'Aw, here we go, it's Henley fuckin' Regatta. Where's yer top hat, fella?'

'Left it in the car, man.'

'Christ. Enjoy the gig, then? Unsigned enough for you? Unfinished, unpolished and thoroughly un-fucking-marketable?'

'Leaps and bounds, actually, dude.'

'Oh, yeah? Gonna tell that to Bazza the Bulldog, then?'

Josh chuckles and sips his drink. Jake distributes the pints, takes his food back from Ash and bites into an organic steak-and-kidney pie.

'Nice plane, chief,' Josh offers.

'Uh?' grunts Jake, through his mouthful of pie.

'Nice model plane. Spitfire Mark II 60, yeah?'

'Possibly.'

'Had one of those myself back in the eighties. Great model. Superb handling. But of course,' he adds, winking at Karen, 'it doesn't perform so well with a great tub of paper stuck on top.'

'Whatever,' Jake gruffs, gulping his cider now.

'I was in the Avon county flying team,' Josh continues, looking casually over towards the stage. 'Your control was all over the place. I think you need to work on your wrist action.'

Karen and Ash look warily at each other. Jake swallows his cider.

'You think I need to work on my wrist action?' Jake repeats, dangerously.

'Yah.'

'Yaahh. OK, *yaahh*. I'll go and work on my fucking wrist action. Something I wouldn't have thought you needed any practice at, you fucking frantic wanker.'

Karen and Ash close their eyes painfully. Josh spins back to Jake.

'Frantic wanker, pal? I'm not the one who's going to be out of a fucking job as soon as he gets back to the smoke.'

'*What* did you fucking say?'

The voices are rising, nearby onlookers are turning round. Hillock holds up both his hands, calling for calm.

'Friends, friends – '

'Ain't no fucking friends here, hippy boy,' Josh snarls.

'Hey, brother, I don't think you should be —'

'Stay out of this, Hilly,' Jake instructs, manoeuvring him to the side, then advancing on Josh. 'What *was* that you fucking said?'

'I said,' Josh leers, 'you are fucking *history*.'

As is customary with these incidents, the precise order of the next thirty seconds is a little sketchy. Jake throws the first punch, for some reason neglecting to let go of his organic pie, showering pastry, steak, kidney and potato over Josh and at least four people in the immediate vicinity. Josh retaliates, but is attacked at the same time by a suddenly non-pacifist Hillock. The three men collapse on each other, tumbling to the ground, knocking over another bloke and a girl, whose drinks go flying. Karen dives in, mainly trying to pull Josh off the other two, but in doing so falls to the floor herself. Cider, mashed potato and yet more pie fly everywhere, and everyone within ten yards appears to be shouting, pulling or kicking, with the conspicuous exception of Ash, who stays out of it entirely, instead puffing sadly on the remnants of his joint. For a moment it looks like the worst is over, but then Hillock leaps up and tries to headbutt Josh, who is yanked out of the way at the last nanosecond by Godfrey (still vainly flying the pacifist flag), causing Hillock to topple over again. Many, many indecipherable and unrepeatable things are said/shouted/screamed, mostly by Jake and Josh, but when Jake finally finds his feet he hollers his one audible, near-coherent line.

'Fucking . . . if you *think* that you and your fucking little pit bull are going to manage anything within shitting distance of our fucking band, you can fuck off back to your lah-di-dah Chelsea twathole and shove foie gras up your fucking rectum.'

'Manage!' laughs Josh — silence suddenly, and chillingly,

filling the entire field (even Day of Krud seem to hang poised over their rain sticks). Josh wipes a piece of kidney off his eyebrow and shakes his head. 'You haven't got a clue, have you, you fucking rock-school monkey. You don't really think I've come all the way down to this fucking haystack because I want to fucking *manage* you? I ain't no fucking below-stairs admin crap merchant. I'm centre stage, fool. I'm the fucking main attraction. I'm gonna be where you were – emphasis on the "were" – except a hundred times better, fitter and on the right side of a six-figure record deal. Hear it and weep, cuntsmith.'

Understandably, the precise gist of this outburst is slightly lost on Jake. He does not, however, need to do much more than glance at the pallid, shame-ridden faces of Ash and Karen for the true meaning to reveal itself in all its treacherous glory.

'Ash?' Jake gasps.

'Fella . . .'

'Kazza? What the fuck's going on?'

'Jakey . . . nothing's been agreed . . .'

Jake blinks back sudden tears. 'Nothing . . . nothing's been agreed? Then he . . . *him*?'

'Yeah,' Josh sneers, 'they fucking want me, dole-boy –'

'Josh, shut the fuck *up*!' Karen screams.

'– and we'd be at it right now if your songwriter wasn't such a fucking pussy.'

Ash has had his eyes screwed shut for the best part of the last three minutes, steeling himself for a fulsome smack in the face, but he now opens his eyes to see Jake dashing away through the crowd, his head bobbing along towards the backstage area.

'Oh, *shit*!' Karen yells, tearing after him.

Ash puffs his cheeks and follows at a more measured, grudging pace, while Josh brushes himself off and turns to Hillock.

'Sorry about that, dude. You kinda got caught in the middle there. Can I interest you in a bottle of Beck's?'

Hillock bites his lip and for a moment looks like he's going to headbutt Josh again. Thankfully, Godfrey puts his arm around his friend and frogmarches him off.

'Rock'n'roll,' Josh announces to the world in general, wiping the last bit of gravy off his chin.

JAKE: People probably don't realise how difficult it is, being me. They don't! You may laugh, but it's true. I'm seen as being this constantly 'up' person – but, you know, I think about stuff quite deeply. And to be honest, there aren't many people who see this part of me. Sarah's one of them, and I suppose that's why I still like seeing her so much.

What about Russell? He's known you for years.

JAKE: It's totally different with Russell. I used to be closer to him, in a friendly way, back when we were in Plainly Amy and Nerveswill. But him chucking me out ruined most of that.

What did you do in the interim years?

JAKE: A lot of selling. Hardly did any music at all, apart from the odd cover gig, karaoke and so on. I didn't think I was ever gonna do it seriously again, until I had a . . . what's the word . . . when there's this pacific moment when everything turns around?

An epiphany?

JAKE: Epiphany, that's it. It was while watching The Verve in 1997, at Earls Court, they were supporting Oasis. Something about them almost reduced me to tears. During that song 'The Drugs Don't Work', my girlfriend at the time heard this weird noise coming from me. Said it was sort of a cross between a growl and a yelp. Wasn't even aware I'd made it. I made it two or three times, so I'm told. It was basically me yearning . . . yearning to make music again. The very next morning I started searching for a band. Went to loads of auditions, all of them pretty rubbish. I'd almost given up again by the time I met Ash and Karen.

Y'see, I do love it, all of this, but there is a limit. And Russell pushes me closer to that limit every day. He's a talented guy, but he doesn't realise how hard he makes it for everyone. Bit by bit, it becomes less fun, more like just a fucking normal job, with irritating co-workers you have to tolerate. If it all just ended, I'm not sure I'd be totally devastated. To be honest, there are more important things in life.

By the time Russell completes his business with Megan and emerges from the lodge happily slurping the last of a cup of Fairtrade coffee, Jake has transformed Russell's bottle-green Telecaster from an item which might fetch upwards of £700 on eBay to a collection of items which might fetch £1.50 as part of a bag of firewood. Watched, but in no way interrupted by Ash and Karen, Jake has also used the guitar to visit considerable cosmetic damage on both the Transit van, which has been left at a rather jaunty angle awaiting Russell's return, and a nearby conker tree. Dave Berwick and his henchmen, for whom this particular band are proving more entertaining by the minute, sit on the gangplank with cans of beer waiting for the next instalment of the soap opera.

But this time, there are no words.

Russell trots lightly down the steps of the lodge, and looks up as he hears an ominous 'DUK!' sound.

This is the sound of the bottle-green body slamming into the tree trunk.

It is the sound of three years' hard – if erratic – work, coming to a violent end.

It is the sound of a twelve-year on-and-off, up-and-down, troubled and complex partnership, gasping its last.

It is the last straw, the frustration of never being able to quite reach each other, the final reflection on why they are not yet world-famous rock musicians.

Russell freezes, horrified at the sight of his ruined instrument, bewildered that this is happening right now – but somehow understanding why.

Jake holds aloft the unrecognisable tangle of wood, wire and metal, pauses for a moment, then tosses it onto the grass.

He locks eyes with Russell for one last time, and then slowly walks off to . . . well, anywhere.

Russell Groom sinks to the ground and buries his face in his hands.

Part Two

'Of course it makes a difference, man! A record contract is your fuel card, your fucking badge of authenticity, and the certificate which says to the whole planet that you've got some top wad and a bunch of useless lackeys running around after your every whim. You ain't putting your hand in your pocket for nothing, and the only pieces of paper you touch are either to sign autographs on, or to roll up for a fat line of charlie. Yeah, boy, there *might* be bands out there who can do it without being signed, but I wouldn't know cos I wouldn't glance twice at the sorry fuckers. They must be *insane*.'

JOSH

Waterloo

Two days have passed. Ash, sensing that things can hardly disintegrate further, has bravely decided to confront at least one of his demons.

'Can't feel much worse is what I reckon,' he explains, 'so I might as well get this over with while I can.'

Wearing a paisley charity-shop shirt and the flared vintage jeans he saves for special occasions, he trots down the steps from Waterloo Bridge to the South Bank and walks purposefully to the outdoor seats by the National Film Theatre bar. Not his usual type of haunt, but then he is not here to meet his usual type of acquaintance. He scans the early-evening drinkers for a face he recognises. Over in a far corner, a blonde, tanned girl in a black business suit stands and waves. Ash waves back, exhales and wanders over.

'Ashley,' she smiles, combining genuine warmth with a slight tinge of pity, the tone of all triumphant exes.

'Hullo, Sam,' Ash grins, and they hug. 'You've, er . . . got a drink, I see . . .'

'Certainly,' Sam replies in her Australian lilt, rising and grabbing her handbag. 'Let me get you one.'

'Nah, s'all right . . . I'll go . . .'

'No, sit. My pleasure. Bitter?'

'Yeah . . . you know me well.'

'I heard, by the way.'

'You heard?'

'About Jake.'

Ash frowns. 'Who from?'

'Sarah Nuttall of course. She emailed. She seemed bloody delighted, to be honest. But never mind – you can tell me yourself as well, if you want.'

She smiles again and hurries inside.

Although there have been numerous phone conversations, few of them particularly pleasant, Sam and Ash haven't actually seen each other since the fateful Underworld gig more than a year ago when Sam was 'stolen' by Perish the Thought's Tom Weitzmann. As well as simply wanting to see her again, Ash has formed a tenuous parallel between Sam's romantic situation back then and his own musical position right now, and is convinced that tonight will reveal what he needs to do. Unfortunately, due to nerves or otherwise, one of the first things Ash does is blurt out this ulterior motive and its basis.

'Good to see you haven't changed a bit,' Sam says, shaking her head into her glass of white wine. 'Still a dreamer.'

'Is it *kind* of similar, though?'

'How? Let's list the differences. One – Tom's not a wanker,

and from what you're saying this Josh character most certainly is. Two – I had to put up with you salivating at that bass bitch's backside for eighteen months, while from what I can gather Jake's been pretty faithful to you. And three – you *can't* bloody compare being in a group with someone to being in a relationship. You always tried to, but you can't. And to be frank, mate, if you'd realised that . . . maybe we . . .'

She trails off. Ash gulps his pint and scowls around the tables for a minute.

'So Tom's lot really are getting signed?'

'Uh-huh.'

'Parlophone?'

'Yep.'

'Really happening? Or just "firm interest"?'

'Really happening. Deal with the lawyers right now. Agents, publishing, press, support tours . . . it's all being discussed. It's the real thing, Ash.'

'Good.'

'You don't mean that.'

'Yeah,' Ash nods, 'I do. Shows that it can really happen sometimes.'

He bites his bottom lip and continues nodding to himself, as if a final decision had just been made. Sam clocks this and is having none of it.

'But don't you start getting carried away, Ashley. Tom's is a very different set-up to your little hotchpotch. They all love each other like brothers. They can spend a week in a recording studio without so much as a cross word between them, and their manager is this great guy who they trust, *implicitly*. I mean, he was bloody best man to two of them. Your Barry bloke sounds like you wouldn't trust him with a fiver to pay for your parking, and the day you lot get through a rehearsal without a row, we'll be seeing a flying pig.'

Ash considers Sam's points, studying his pint gloomily.

'Jake's not talking to you, then?' Sam asks.

'What d'you think?'

'You had any contact with him at all?'

'Sent him an apologetic text last night.'

'Any reply?'

Ash is silent for a second, takes a breath, then smiles and looks away.

'Ashley? What did it say?' Sam frowns.

'Nah. You don't wanna know.'

'Ashley!' she commands.

Ash extracts his mobile from his pocket, presses a few buttons and holds it up for Sam's inspection.

'"*Hope . . .*" – aw, the cheeky fucker! – "*Hope Shitesmann becomes the new Roger Taylor*"!'

'Told you you wouldn't want to know.'

Sam's frown breaks into a resigned smile.

'OK, you got me,' she shrugs.

They chuckle for a second, then sadness washes over Ash's face again.

'How's work?' he asks at last.

'Miserable,' Sam replies, knocking back her wine. 'Had to make three people redundant today.'

'Ah,' sighs Ash. 'So . . . another?'

'Too fucking right. It's the Chilean Sauvignon. A large, if you don't mind.'

Ash stands and turns to go, but Sam suddenly grabs his hand.

'Ashley, listen to me. You don't wanna go with these pricks.

They sound horrendous. And I bet I know who's gunning for this. Listen to your instincts, not to bloody Russell.'

Ash bites his lip and saunters off to the bar. Funnily enough, he will later follow this last piece of Sam's advice to the letter, but not quite in the way she envisaged.

It's nearly eleven thirty and Russell has just finished taking down the name of tonight's outgoing attraction at the Imperial (Gary Moore) and putting up the name of the incoming one (Sandra Bernhard – 'Tricky swap,' he comments, 'hardly any common letters'). He is just about to unsnap his radio from his belt and switch it off when there is a stab of static and the voice of Will Gibson, the venue manager, emerges.

'Russell Groom?'

'What *now*?' Russell mutters, glancing at his watch and pressing the 'talk' button. 'Go ahead?'

'Er . . . yeah, Russ, can you, er . . . come and have a word in my office?'

Russell sighs and sets off through the various corridors. Will's voice always sounds fairly devoid of enthusiasm or conviction, so this 'word' seems unlikely to consist of anything more diverting than cleaning inside one of the dressing-room microwaves, or repainting a door frame. This is wrong.

'Just had JJ72's manager on the blower,' Will says lazily, his feet up on the desk, a bottle of Rolling Rock in his hand.

'Er . . . yes?'

'Sounds like he's had a visit from your fairy fuckin' gigmother. Next month, Tuesday 25th? You're opening for 'em.'

'What . . . er . . . *how*?'

'Their usual support's gonna be elsewhere, promoter's not

fussed, so your lot can do it. But make sure you're fuckin' good, all right?'

Russell's face does a decent job of hiding what is certainly a torrent of instant concerns, not least among them the small question of how on earth they are supposed to fulfil such an engagement without a singer.

'Will, that's . . . amazing! How did you manage to . . . ?'

'I didn't do nuffin, mate. Didn't even mention it. Manager asked for ya. Must be someone else tooting your trumpet somewhere.'

Seconds later, Russell is on the phone to Karen.

'Have you left yet? . . . OK, stay there . . . need to talk *right* now.'

Karen is pacing up and down the alleyway by the stage door when Russell comes bursting out.

'Have you mentioned JJ72 to Josh?' he blurts.

'What about them?'

'Have you mentioned them? Playing here?'

Karen frowns. 'Might have done. Why?'

Russell tells her the news.

'But Russ, that's . . . wicked!'

'Is it?'

Karen lights a cigarette and thinks for a moment.

'Uh – no. Probably not.'

'Right,' Russell nods.

They stand in silence for a minute, pondering the various complexities of this formidable piece of career blackmail.

'When is it?' Karen asks.

'Twenty-fifth of September.'

'Almost a whole month away,' she mutters.

'Meaning what?'

'Nothing, Russ. I'm just saying, it's almost an entire month away.'

A couple of Karen's bar colleagues tumble out of the stage door, say goodnight and disappear up the alley. Karen looks back at Russ, smiles awkwardly and feigns some wide-eyed optimism.

'Um . . . it might not have been Josh and Barry? Who got us the gig?'

'Oh, come on. Of *course* it was.'

'Yeah,' she concedes. 'Of course it was.'

Deciding this is a situation which requires immediate action, but it being too late at night for a band meeting, the two of them repair to the residential street behind the venue where they position themselves on a wall and attempt a rather messy makeshift conference call using Russell's mobile. Ash has just returned from the South Bank and sounds a little the worse for wear; Karen is appalled to hear what he has been up to, Sam's ill feelings towards Karen clearly mutual.

'Lovely to see her then, was it?' she growls. 'Aussie bint.'

'Yeah . . .' comes Ash's crackly voice over the phone's loudspeaker. 'It was all right, really. Quite useful.'

'Oh, yeah? She give your confidence another well-intentioned fist-fucking?'

'Easy, Kazza. I'm all right with it . . . maybe you should be too. Found out all about Shitesmann's lot, as it happens.'

Russell and Karen listen bitterly as Ash elaborates. When he gets to the bit about supporting other bands (Sam later revealed that Perish the Thought are in the running to open for Weezer on an upcoming European tour), Karen launches into the true nature of their call.

'Let's do it,' Ash replies, without hesitation.

'How?' Russell gapes.

'With Josh.'

'He's a prick!' Russell spits, to amused surprise from Karen's direction.

'I know he is,' Ash says. 'But what the hell have we got to lose? How else are we gonna play a fucking great gig like this?'

'It's not *that* great,' Russell replies, to some more of Karen's surprise, this time not of the amused variety. 'It's only JJ72 –'

'*Only* JJ72? Fuck, Russ, you've changed your tune a bit –'

'– and I'm not sure that much good can come of it –'

'Russell!' Karen snaps. 'Don't start talking bollocks. We all know Josh and Barry are twats, but we've *always* believed that supporting someone big is the fucking gateway to –'

'I've *never* really believed that.'

'Oh, that's such *crap!*'

'Oi, oi, you two,' drones Ash's tinny voice. 'Chill out. This is like being on speakerphone to my bloody parents. Russ, mate, listen to me. I've been thinking about this. We've been through such a lot of shit with that Jake stuff, and I don't know about you guys but I've never felt lower in my fucking life [Karen nods at this] . . . and I know it sounds weird, but . . . having done what we've done, it'd be bloody criminal if nothing came of it. Know what I mean? And I can't face auditioning people again – but Russ, you said Josh was pretty good, yeah?'

'Adequate,' Russell mumbles.

'Well, OK. But the key – and hear me out, right? – the key to this is a trial period. We give Josh and Barry a trial period. All right? We don't sign anything – or if we do, we sign something really short-term. We see how it goes, see what they can do. Particularly Barry.'

'Good idea,' Karen comments.

'Hmm . . . none of this is reassuring me –'

'Russell! Have you got a better plan?'

'Kazza,' Ash moans, 'please stop yelling, I can't hear a fucking word anyone says.'

'Sorry.'

Russell shifts uncomfortably on the wall.

'There's something really unsettling about this. The way the gig has been . . . acquired for us, without us even being consulted.'

'Agreed. It's typical Josh,' Karen shrugs. 'He's the sort of arse-hole who probably sends girls anonymous drinks from the other side of restaurants, then appears twenty minutes later. "Eeoh, hi! I'm Josh. Did someone by any chance bring you a cosmopolitan just now?" It definitely sucks, Russ, there's no doubt about that. He'll text me tomorrow, I bet . . . asking me whether anything unusual has happened . . . but . . .'

'Yeah, but,' Ash continues, 'we've gotta see it for what it is. An opportunity, and the best bloody thing we've got going for us right now – the *only* thing, actually. And it's a big gig, man! I mean, yeah, the JJs aren't Radiohead, but they're fucking popular, heaps of people to see us, old Bazza can invite some of his knobs down, pretty impressive . . . and above all, man, it's the fucking Imperial! What a fucking stage! Don't tell me you guys haven't stood up on that stage at the end of a night slopping shit, and thought, "Fuck, if only I could be up here *playing* . . ." '

'That's true, Russ,' smiles Karen. 'You have, I've seen you do it . . .'

'Have you?'

'Yeah. Air guitar.'

'Ah,' Russell gruffs. 'Right.'

'Seriously, Russ,' Ash's voice intones. 'Short-term experiment. Nothing to lose.'

'Well, there *are* a few things to lose, actually. Our reputation, everything we've built up this far —'

'Oh, wake up, Russell!' Karen groans, attempting to keep her voice down. 'What *have* we built up?'

'And,' Ash adds, 'our reputation won't bloody matter, cos to be honest with you, if *this* doesn't work . . . I'm not sure how much fight I've got inside me to dive in again.'

Karen inhales, possibly to say 'me neither', but thinks better of it. Russell, meanwhile, has not given up.

'There's one thing you organisational wizards haven't considered.'

'Whassat?'

'How on earth are we going to break Josh in, so we're good enough to support a major band, in less than a month's time?'

'That's up to him, innit.'

'What do you mean?'

'Well, if he's so impatient to get going, we can put the onus on him, fella. He's gonna need the courage of his convictions, hunker down, get learning. In fact —'

'Oh my God!' Karen exclaims. 'We're meant to be playing the Barfly next Tuesday!'

'That's exactly what I was gonna say,' Ash says, evidently enjoying his new-found role as second in command. 'You haven't cancelled it, Russ?'

'Erm . . . no . . .'

'Cool. So we *still do* the Barfly gig next week. Put some fucking pressure on the cocky wanker. We basically say, "OK, poshie, if you're so up for it — here ya go, learn these seven songs by next week."'

'Ash, *Ash*!' Russell cries. 'Have you taken leave of your senses? That just isn't possible!'

'Like I say – that's up to him.'

'No, *no*! It's not just him learning the stuff! We – or, let's be frank, *I* – I'm the one who'll have to rearrange the entire set for his vocals –'

'Not necessarily. He can fit in with us. If he's so damn keen –'

'Ash, I'm liking this plan,' Karen admits, lighting another cigarette.

'– then he can do some of the fucking donkey work. That's the thing about this whole business – yes, we're gonna be throwing a bit of the ol' caution to the wind, but to an extent, *we're* gonna be the ones calling the shots.'

'Well, actually,' states Russell, 'part of the point of having a manager is that *he* calls the shots.'

'I said "to an extent", Russ. You don't have to patronise me, man. I'm not Jake.'

'Aw,' Karen mopes. 'Jake.'

Mention of Jake's name saddens the conversation. Russell looks particularly downcast. The phone call is wrapped up, the general conclusion being to sleep on the decision – but hooking up with the gruesome twosome is pencilled in for tomorrow evening. Just as Karen and Russell are about to go their separate ways, Karen's phone beeps.

'Oh, cock,' she says, reading the text message with distaste. 'There y'are, Russ. What did I tell you?'

Russell looks.

'*I trust you kids have asked for the night of the 25th off? Speak 2moro. Jx*'

'Ugh,' Russell pronounces, his distaste still lingering as he unlocks his bike and meanders home. Tomorrow, he will claim to have had a nightmare in which the band plays in front of an empty Wimbledon Imperial.

RUSSELL: Supporting other, much larger bands is always seen as some sort of holy grail. You hear utterly absurd rumours about it – bands being charged huge amounts of money to be the opening act on a big tour. One particular band paying twenty thousand pounds to support the Foo Fighters at a *one-off gig*. Whether that's true or not, I don't know. But it gives you some idea of the kind of emphasis that's placed on it. Obviously for an unsigned band, paying any amount of money whatsoever is out of the question, so the likes of us have to sit around and wait for someone to ask us.

Would it be worth it?

RUSSELL: Well, like all of these things, it's only worthwhile if you've got some promotional backup. You could support U2 at Wembley Stadium and go down an absolute storm, but everyone will have forgotten your name within five minutes if they haven't got a flyer or something to take home.

But it's presumably good experience as well.

RUSSELL: Good experience, yeah. Whatever that counts for.

Chinatown

Josh pours everyone a glass of wine (even Russell, who regards it strangely for the duration of the meal), then lays his hands flat on the table. A visual metaphor, if ever there was one.

'The first thing I need to do for you cats,' he begins humbly, 'is offer a couple of apologies. First up – rancid behaviour there at the country hoedown. Frustrated, I guess. And also, I'd stopped at a Little Chef near Salisbury for a piss and a line of charlie – affected me badly, as it sometimes does before sundown. Was . . . not . . . good. Won't . . . happen . . . again. Karry, sis, I came on a little strange. I realise this. No contest. Apols, yeah? Russla, dude – if I ignore you like that once more you've got my full 'mission to sail one into the gob.'

Russell says nothing.

'He's considering it,' Barry deadpans.

'Least I deserve, Bazza,' Josh nods. 'Least I deserve. But secondly – I know that Jakey was offended by some of the things we said after the acoustic show. Didn't mean no harm, please tell him that. I know how special he is to you kids. Ashy, you gonna be seeing him?'

'I hope so,' Ash replies, sipping his wine.

'Me too, chap.'

'Right,' Karen announces. 'One thing before we go any further. Russell is called Russ or Russell, Ash is called Ash, or maybe Ashley if you're taking the piss. I am known as Kaz, Karen or Kazza, nothing else. Not babe, not darling, not sis, and *certainly* not Karry. OK?'

'You got it, Karen,' Josh winks. 'And I am known as Josh – and you can call Barry whatever you bloody like.'

'True,' Barry nods, extracting a notebook from his bag and opening it up. 'And I want everyone to know that I'm not fuckin' apologising for anything.'

Muted laughter circulates, then a waiter arrives with the spring rolls.

The meeting lasts a couple of hours and bears few surprises. Barry is his tedious and hostile self but throws just enough nuggets into the pot to keep the attention bubbling (support slots with both The Cooper Temple Clause and Gay Dad are mentioned, interested A & R men referred to by name, a drum endorsement deal with Premier already on the cards for Ash). Josh retains his air of apologetic deference but fails to stick to the approved list of Karen monikers ('honey' is heard on more than one occasion, Karen responding with firm kicks under the table) – and Ash drinks a little too much. Where the proceedings differ from those previous is that Russell, for some reason, hardly utters a syllable.

'Something about Josh completely takes the wind out of my sails,' he admits to Karen and Ash later. 'I find him so . . . odious. I can hardly operate my own vocal cords.'

'That's all right, though, Russ,' smiles Ash. 'Gives me a chance to say a few words for a change.'

Naturally the acquisition of a recording contract is an underlying, if not directly discussed theme – that is, until the meeting's conclusion when Karen poses a very simple question, but one which not many unsigned musicians might ask for fear of looking unattractively naive.

'What actually happens,' she asks, fixing Barry with a firm gaze, 'when a band gets signed?'

'Depends,' Josh answers.

'Wasn't asking you,' Karen says, not taking her eyes off Barry.

'Well,' Barry begins, sipping some sparkling water, 'it *does* depend. Depends on the size of the label, the age and the taste of the A & R bloke, how much money they're gonna invest, the length of the deal, what sort of band you are, what sort of following you got, what your –'

'Barry,' Karen insists, '*what happens* when you get signed?'

'All right, I'm your A & R man. You got signed yesterday. With you lot, I'm pretty much gonna start from scratch. You need everything. Some of the songs are there, but you need more singles. Aw, thank fuck – I can say that now whatsisface ain't here to bite my fuckin' head off. Anyway, your recordings are completely fuckin' unusable.'

'Because of Jake?'

'Nah . . . well, yeah, partly, but . . . they ain't nowhere near commercial quality, right? So we slot you in with a decent producer, he gets a real product going. You've got no following, so I'm gonna send you round the country in a splitter – supporting, headlining, whatevering, buildin' up a live show, gettin' your name around . . .'

'That's another thing,' Josh interjects.

'Yeah,' Barry nods, 'that *is* another thing. They'll immediately wanna change your name.'

'What's wrong with our name?' Karen blinks.

'What's fuckin' right with it, love? Anyway, it don't matter, ninety per cent get their names changed by the record company as soon as they sign –'

'Blur, Radiohead,' Josh recites.

'Thassit,' Barry nods. 'They'll probably sit you down with some fuckin' awful list that you're all gonna hate, but it don't matter . . . these labels usually know what looks good on the side of a CD case.'

'Usually,' Josh sniggers.

'Anyway. You do all that, photo shoots, all that bollocks, and then sometime towards the middle of next year they might release one of your records, if you're very lucky.'

'And we'll get an advance?' Karen suggests.

'You'll get an advance,' Barry confirms, leaning back on his chair and stretching, 'but I warn ya – with you guys it ain't gonna be big. It's gonna be all about striking while the iron's hot, getting it wrapped up as soon as poss, so it can all get started. Otherwise it ain't never gonna happen. There ain't gonna be no bidding war. So hold on to yer day jobs for the time being,' he concludes, smirking at Josh.

Russell spends most of this explanation fingering his wine glass and shifting awkwardly in his seat, as if suffering from a particularly nasty crop of piles. There are several moments when he looks like he is going to say something – following the casual declaration that their recordings are 'unusable' he turns a bright shade of crimson and practically levitates – but never manages to get any words out. He could also be adjusting to a new kind of meeting where he isn't simply required to present a lot of ideas that only he will end up carrying out. But it's not too apparent that he likes it. At the very end of the meal (during which he has quietly managed to drink a whole thimbleful of his wine), Russell asks Barry in a very small voice whether he is still 'allowed' to do his pre-gig phone-around.

'Your what?'

'My, er . . . my pre-gig phone-around. It's when I go through a list of all the people we've sent demos to, call them and ask if they're coming to the gig.'

'Do what you like, mate,' grunts Barry. 'I fuckin' won't be doing that kinda shit. Can't do no harm, though . . . pack 'em in . . . only, best show me that list tomorrer so you don't ring my lot. That'd be a bit fuckin' embarrassing, know what I mean . . . ?'

To his credit, Josh leaps upon next week's Barfly gig as a golden opportunity for what he refers to as a 'preview' as if it were some new West End show; the real 'opening night' considered to be the hotly anticipated JJ72 support slot next month at the Imperial. Josh offers to spend a large part of tomorrow going over the songs at Russell's, in addition to the three full-band rehearsals scheduled between today and next Tuesday. When talking about the actual playing of music Josh appears genuinely, boyishly enthusiastic, his preposterous lingo even taking a turn for the better. For this reason more than any other, Karen and Ash are suitably cheered as they amble back to the Tube station.

'The only thing I really didn't like,' Karen reflects, 'was

when they were talking about our appearances, and vibe, and all that.'

'Yeeah,' Ash agrees. 'Can't believe they want me to dye my hair blond.'

'Sweetheart, don't do a damn thing unless you really want to.'

'Are you going to try and look more innocent, then?'

'Am I fuck,' Karen snaps. 'If they want some demure fucking damsel they can hire one.'

They go their separate ways, Ash down to the Piccadilly Line and Russell to where he has parked his car in Holborn. Karen, however, is heading off for a late-night date, commonly assumed to be Hillock, although for some reason she doesn't confirm this.

'Gotta stay discreet,' she chuckles, turning back up Charing Cross Road. 'We'll have the gossip columns to worry about next.'

Russell watches her go, sighs and marches back along Long Acre, looking as unsure of the future as he's ever been.

Chalk Farm Road

KAREN: Getting a new member is *weird*. It's exciting, but at the same time it's so odd. I keep looking up and expecting to see Jake . . . and then I see Josh.

ASH: And it makes the songs sound completely different, even if we're basically playing them the same way.

Have you had to do much reconstruction?

KAREN: Not really. What we've found is that certain songs simply don't suit Josh, so we haven't even tried to change them. The ones which do work –

ASH: 'Petrol', 'Warning', 'Testing Ground' –

KAREN: Yeah, and that new one, 'You Brought It On Yourself' – so fucking good, that's *totally* gonna be a single –

ASH: Fucking right.

KAREN: Anyway, when the songs *do* work, they're fantastic. There have been some strange ones, though –

ASH: 'Smaller Weaker' –

KAREN: Oh God, yeah. I never thought we'd ever do a gig without that one, but there you go. It's just not Josh's sort of song. I suppose it needs to be sung by a sort of geeky bloke for it to really make sense, but (*laughs nervously*) . . .

What about Josh's guitar work?

ASH: He's pretty good . . .

KAREN: Oh, he's great. I don't wanna be getting into the Jake comparisons, but –

ASH: He's much better –

KAREN: He's much fucking better. Russell can basically leave him to it, can't you, Russ? While you get on with the synth, and all that.

And personally? Ash, you must miss Jake?

ASH: Oh, I miss him, of course. Big time. But, y'know . . . there was always something . . . *wrong* about Jake. Too much fun, all the time. With Josh, I mean, I don't know him very well, but we tend to just . . . get on with it more. And he's got quite a commanding nature, which I think we appreciate.

KAREN: Stops us fucking around.

ASH: Yeah. Makes us more of a band.

That must please you, Russell?

RUSSELL (*after a pause*): Yes, it does.

So, all in all – a good decision?

KAREN: Yeah.

ASH: Yeah!

Russell?

ASH: He's not counting his chickens.

RUSSELL (*stony-faced*): I never count my chickens.

KAREN: You should know that about him by now (*laughs*).

* * *

Russell is sitting in his Passat outside the locked door of the Barfly. It's half past four – the official load-in time – but no sound engineer is anywhere to be seen. Russell is finding this familiarly inefficient situation oddly comforting.

'Some things,' he smiles quietly, 'never change.'

He sips his coffee and hums to himself. It's been a funny week. Josh appeared, as arranged, at Russell's bedsit on Thursday morning, but by lunchtime claimed to have become so acutely depressed by the dingy environs ('What would happen if you brought a chick back here, dude?' he asked – a question Russell couldn't fully answer) that he suggested they transfer operations to his own Chelsea flat ('A palace of vulgarity' is Russell's only comment). While rehearsals – both those between the two of them, and those with the full band – have gone smoothly, Russell's usual cloud of dissatisfaction hovers.

'He's got a very irreverent attitude towards my lyrics,' Russell complains. 'If he doesn't like a line, he'll just change it. Without asking me. I work long and hard on those words, ensuring they scan and make sense . . .'

The most serious and telling example of this is a line in 'Drama'.

'*What can I do when I dream when I'm sleeping with you,*' Josh sang, to frantic waving of arms from Russell's corner of the rehearsal room. Ash stopped drumming and the band fell silent.

'Sorry, Josh, the line is "*What can I do when I dream* that *I'm sleeping with you.*"'

'Sure, chief. Got it.'

The music hurtled forth once more.

'*What can I do when I dream when I'm sleeping with you . . .*'

Russell chopped his guitar crossly and the song skidded to a halt again.

'Josh . . .'

'I know, I know . . .'

'Just think – "*that*", not "*when*".'

'Sure, sure, it's locked in . . .'

Music.

'*What can I do that I dream when I'm sleeping* –'

'No, no!' Russell howled. 'The first word is "*when*", the second is "*that*".'

'It doesn't make as much sense, though.'

'What do you mean?'

'Dude, you dream *when* you sleep, not *that* you sleep.'

Russell frowned incredulously.

'You're dreaming *that* you're sleeping with her! As in, you're *not* sleeping with her at the moment, but you're trying to.'

'But why wouldn't I be?'

Karen rolled her eyes and lit a cigarette. 'For God's sake, Josh.'

'No, honestly, I don't understand.'

'It's not bloody quantum physics here,' Karen said irritably. 'You're trying to get the girl. You haven't got her yet, but you want to. That cannot be a concept you're totally unfamiliar with.'

But apparently it was, and twenty minutes later 'Drama' was duly eliminated from the band's set.

Russell attempted, on both Thursday and Friday, to do his pre-gig phone-around – the kind of ordered task which anchors him to some semblance of sanity – but this didn't prove as satisfying as it normally does. Even after Barry had edited around twelve names from the list, a disappointing number of Russell's contacts responded to his radio-DJ opening line ('Hi! My name's Russell Groom, and you may remember I called earlier this month telling you about a show we were playing at Putney's Half Moon . . .') with something along the lines of 'Oh yeah – you're Barry's new lot, ain't ya?'

Remembering Barry's words about the band name, it also seemed fairly pointless to continue with any promotional activity. Russell's guillotine has lain dormant in the corner of his room for almost two weeks, as have his reams of A4 paper and, largely, his computer. The only activity that has really enthused him, predictably enough, has been the purchase of a new guitar – but even this had its downside.

'It's nice,' he says of the slick black instrument which now sits in the flight case behind him, 'but the old one was a Japanese import from 1983, hand-lacquered by the man who owned it before me . . . completely unique . . . now I have to settle for one of the new ones, which are all made in Mexico . . . *and* it had to come out of my high-interest account . . .'

Now, still waiting outside the deserted, blackened corner pub that is the Barfly, Russell's week isn't about to become any more pleasing. A text message arrives from Karen.

'*Sound geezer not getting there til 5, we r all in wetherspoons. Come!*'

'Oh, for the love of . . .' Russell begins, sighing and looking back at his packed carful of equipment. Usually all communication with any venue staff is done exclusively via Russell; yet another new thing to get used to.

'Well, I won't,' he decides, flicking on Radio 4 and folding his arms defiantly. 'I won't come.'

Bearing in mind that this is a Tuesday evening and a cancellation gig – therefore not subject to the hysterical mass-mailing activity Russell usually undertakes – the turnout tonight is surprisingly good. Almost exclusively friends, of course: friends of Karen's and Ash's who aren't also friends of Jake's, and who are eager to see this famed new recruit, and friends of Josh's who are eager to see *his* famed new recruits.

And Morgan.

'Which one is Bazza the Blockhead, then, Groom?'

'He's over there in the checked shirt.' Russell points across the darkened bar. 'You've seen him before, though, in Holland Park?'

'Can't remember that, can I?' Morgan scowls. 'I was still smarting from my run-in with fookin' Chigwell George.'

'I do wish you would call these people by their correct names.'

Morgan shrugs and swigs from a can of Red Bull, as a tiny, jet-black-haired girl in an Easyworld T-shirt hovers nervously near Russell.

'Uh . . . Russell!' she stammers.

'Yes?' he snaps, spinning round.

'Miki from *Zinehead*.'

'Gosh! Sorry!' Russell exclaims, jumping to his feet. 'Dark in here, didn't recognise you.'

'Oh, no problem!'

'How are you? Is Clem here?'

'Um . . . no.' Miki holds up her enormous camera. 'I'm here on my own to, um, take some photos.'

'Well, I'm sure you'll do it very well,' Russell smiles. 'But it might be an odd one tonight . . .'

'Yes, I was told . . . you have a new singer?'

'Ah,' Russell nods. 'News travels fast.'

'Well, if you don't mind . . . I would like to take his photograph.'

Ten minutes later, Karen smokes and watches with increasing frustration as Russell stomps around the drum-filled store cupboard that masquerades as the Barfly's dressing room.

'What on earth does she want to take *his* picture for?'

Russell moans. 'Why him? What the hell does he have to do with anything?'

'Russ, for God's sake . . . just let it go a little, will you?'

'Why not the rest of us?'

'*I* don't know, do I? It happens occasionally. Josh is new, *Zinehead* have probably got plenty of shots of the rest of us already . . . and he's the frontman now, so he represents the whole band, y'know?'

'But he shouldn't be representing us! What does *he* have to do with the history of the band?'

'What does it matter, Russell? As far as they're concerned, the history of the band starts *today*.'

Russell growls. 'God, it irritates me that you and Ash perpetually take his side, particularly *you* –'

Karen rounds on him furiously.

'Don't you dare start that shit. Fucking pull yourself out of this, Russell, for fuck's sake! We made this decision, and he is our fucking singer for now whether you like it or not. Christ! You astonish me! Things are finally moving, and you're still bloody pissed off!'

Ash barges in and beams at the pair of them.

'Happy days, eh?'

Russell mumbles something into his can of Coke and starts tuning his guitar.

Morgan spends most of the actual set in his usual position at the back of the gig room, gazing over the heads of the audience, trying to imagine what anyone might see in his friend's band. If that sounds uncharitable, it is only what Russell himself instructs Morgan to do.

'"Find a reason to love us," he always says,' Morgan explains.

'That unique, magical thing which will make some fookin' teenager in Bridlington want to pay twelve quid for their album when he only gets a tenner a week. If I spot whatever it is – Karen's tits, Russell's sideburns, fookin' Ash's nostril hair – I'm to let him know so they can accentuate it. And I've never spotted a damn thing.'

He takes another sip of Red Bull.

'Until tonight.'

Which is?

'Credit where it's due,' Morgan sighs. 'Chigwell George is a bit of a fookin' rock god.'

This is an exaggeration, but only a slight one. Even the most cynical music follower – and Morgan isn't a long way from fitting this description – would have to concede that Josh is a natural. Shorter than Jake by a good five inches, he also looks far, far more comfortable with an electric guitar around his neck (he plays a Fireglo Rickenbacker 330) and slips seamlessly into the band's front line-up – slightly shorter than Russell, slightly taller than Karen, rather than towering over the pair of them like Jake did. He wears a black, tight-fitting sleeveless T-shirt and grey combats, and his hair flops coolly in the heat of the packed little venue. More than any of this, though, is his voice: cutting at the same time as smooth, distinctive as well as versatile. On the two or three occasions in the set when Karen provides the backing vocals – particularly during 'You Brought It On Yourself' – their voices blend deliciously in a way that almost makes Morgan's hair stand on end.

'Fook me,' he observes. 'Game over.'

For Russell the gig is not so great. His tuner pedal's battery runs out halfway through the outro to 'Krystal Palace', producing a deafening roar of static which he only just turns into an effect by stomping on his delay pedal. The rest of the band don't seem too unhappy with this sudden stab of Rage Against the Machine-style noise pollution during an already very chaotic part of the song; what they have more of a problem with is that by the final number, Russell's guitar is noticeably out of tune.

'Dude,' Josh winces, as they shift the gear offstage to make way for the next band. 'You *have* to make sure you've got spare batteries, man . . .'

Russell seethes with frustration.

'I *do* have spare batteries!'

'Well, then . . .'

'Normally! I mean, I *always* have spares! Karen, don't I always have spares?'

'He always has spares,' Karen confirms, unplugging her bass.

'But I can't *believe* I didn't have my spare tonight! Tonight, of all nights . . . it's because I've had too much on my mind, too much to *do* . . .'

Karen rolls her eyes.

'Russ, man,' Josh smiles magnanimously. 'It's no biggy. Just make sure you have a spare next time. Yeah?'

For this first gig, Barry has allegedly invited only a few from his vast contact pool ('just in case it's completely fuckin' shite,' he reasons), but a healthy flock of industry observers are nonetheless present, haranguing Barry excitedly in the downstairs bar afterwards. Some light eavesdropping reveals that the twin front-line attractions of Josh and Karen, as Morgan hinted, are much of this excitement's source.

Josh and Russell's paths briefly cross on the stairs – Josh going upstairs with a drink, Russell coming downstairs with Karen's bass amp.

'Bazza wants a quick debrief,' Josh tells him.

'When?'

'Five mins, outside, just a quickie – but he's going off to Manchester for a few days tomorrow and he's got things to say, apparently . . .'

'Um, well, I've just got to take this stuff . . .'

'I know you've got stuff to carry, dude, but seriously, five mins, because' – and here Josh leans in and whispers in Russell's ear – '*someone wants to fucking sign us already!*'

He giggles and playfully pokes Russell in the tummy, then spots one of his friends at the top of the stairs and runs up to greet them.

The next five minutes for Russell are so complicated that he simply hasn't a chance to feel any enthusiasm for what Josh has just told him; partly because, as usual, the rest of the band have vanished, but mainly due to the crazy way the venue has been designed. The dressing room, where the band's gear has been stashed, is halfway down the rear 'Staff Only' stairs. To transfer equipment to the outside world, one must take it back up the staff stairs, through a Yale-locked door at the top which frequently slams shut, through the crowded gig room itself, and then back down the regular stairs. Russell optimisti-cally leaves his Passat across the street on double yellow lines with his hazard lights blinking, and gets started. It takes a total of six trips back and forth to the dressing room to deliver all the equipment to the car; on his final descent of the stairs, pushing through a bunch of drinkers, Russell sees a Camden parking-control vehicle next to his car.

'No! Wait!' he shouts, plonking down whatever he's carrying and racing out onto the street. The parking attendant glares at him.

'Move it,' he growls.

Russell drives round the block, makes sure the parking vehicle has moved well away, and dumps the car in exactly the same place. He sticks his hazards back on, locks the car, hoists his ever-present rucksack onto his shoulder, exhales heavily and crosses the street. Only now does he see Karen and Ash calmly having a fag by the door.

'Need a hand with the gear, fella?' Ash enquires. Russell merely growls at him.

Barry and Josh appear and they all move round the corner of the building for the short debrief. Barry, typically, downplays the recent bit of good news.

'Yeah,' he winces, scratching the back of his head, 'but don't get yer knickers in a twist over it. Someone always says that at a first gig like this, but they never end up being the one you actually sign with. It's useful, though, cos if one cunt says it, they usually all start to.'

'A buzz,' Josh translates, sucking his beer bottle.

'So who was this interested person?' Russell asks.

'Prefer not to tell ya, mate,' Barry replies, but grunts affirmatively when Josh mumbles quietly into his ear, 'It was Lawrence, wasn't it?'

'Wow,' Karen puffs, glancing at Ash. 'It all happens pretty quickly when it happens, doesn't it?'

'Now, look,' Barry tells them, 'like I said, you're not to start gettin' all worked up – you've still got a fuckin' long way to go, and a lot needs to change. Karen, the BVs worked great, and I'd like to see you doin' that in every song. Drummer boy, you need to sort your hair out asap – three times I heard someone say, "The drummer looks a bit old."'

'Oh,' Ash responds glumly. 'Right.'

'Biggest problem we got, though,' Barry scowls, 'is *you*.'

Russell, who has been trying to angle himself so he can see his car, jumps to surprised attention.

'*Me?*'

'Yeah, mate. *You*. Two things. Firstly – don't ever, *ever* sip from a fuckin' Coke can onstage. There's only two things a band like you ought to be drinkin' onstage, one's a bottle of Evian, and the other's a bottle of beer. I reckon you go for the beer, because you look fuckin' squeaky clean enough as it is.'

'But, I –'

'Yeah, I *know* you don't drink, mate, so either fuckin' learn quick or work out a good way of faking it. And the other thing' – Russell shoots a helpless look at Karen, who shrugs back at him – 'is you've got too much goin' on up there. Half the time you're boffing away with your keyboard and then grabbing your guitar to play a bit, and then twiddling about with more knobs –'

'Er . . . *yesss* . . . because all those things need to be done!'

'Yeah, but it looks shit, mate. You look like a fuckin' . . . lab experimenterer, or whatever. You wanna get a sequencer or something to do all the fiddly shit, then you can concentrate on performing.'

'That would be *very* tricky to arrange.'

'Well, you gotta do something, mate, cos it ain't working.'

Josh attempts some diplomacy.

'Russ, dude, don't take it personally – when you do perform, you look *great*' – Karen and Ash nod frantically, Barry has started to text someone – 'it's just that we probably need to investigate a long-term solution for the electronics.'

Russell frowns and shakes his head perplexedly. The discussion moves on to other topics and soon Russell makes his excuses and goes to check on his car.

'It's odd,' Karen muses, once Russell is out of earshot, 'hearing someone criticise Russell.'

'It's all for the best,' Josh shrugs.

'Yeah, I know – it's just weird, though, hearing this stuff from a completely new angle.'

'Bazza never pulls his punches,' Josh smiles. 'Make no mistake, kids – he used to say the *worst* things about me. But Russell's got nothing to fret about, he's a handsome lad and that's half the battle.'

'Yeah,' Barry winces, looking up from his text. 'But Phillip fuckin' Schofield's handsome, innee, and you wouldn't buy one of his fuckin' records.'

The business of the evening completed, Josh suggests a foray into Soho for some additional drinking antics, to which Karen and Ash eagerly agree. Russell returns one last time to sign off with everyone, then looks more than a little downcast when he hears of this plan.

'S'all right, Russ,' Karen beams. 'If you learn to drink like Barry says, you can come on one of these jaunts too!'

Russell grumbles something, smiles awkwardly and heads off. He lets himself into his car and pulls away from the kerb, slowly driving down the quiet street to the north of the venue. When he can no longer be seen by his colleagues, he stops the car again, gets out his phone and squeezes one of his speed dials.

'Morg, it's Russell . . . Yeah, I know it is . . . Are you still there? . . . OK . . . Listen, are you busy tomorrow? . . . No? . . . Are you in the mood for something slightly unusual? . . . No, not *that* unusual . . . OK, listen . . . I need you to do me a favour . .'

Raynes Park 2

Jake mentioned having a musical epiphany. Have you ever experienced one?

KAREN: Oh, there've been several moments in my life when I've thought, 'Yes! This is it . . .' Some of them cooler than others, really . . .

Such as?

KAREN: Oh . . . er . . . well, my first gig was Roachford at the Hammersmith Odeon, I was only twelve so that fairly blew my mind at the time . . . Blur at Mile End . . . saw The Who the other year, that was pretty jaw-dropping . . . Bowie at Glastonbury . . . then a different kind of epiphany I s'pose when I got backstage with The Bluetones at Shepherd's Bush Empire – that definitely made me realise what life I wanted to live, if you know what I mean . . . But to be totally honest with you, the closest thing I've had to a specific moment when everything suddenly just clicked – and I know this is gonna sound a bit gay – but it was meeting Russ. Not meeting him, but playing with him – hearing his songs. I'd never met anyone like him – he just kind of inhabits the songs he plays, especially the ones he's written. I told him so. After about three rehearsals, probably – he might have found it a bit weird if I'd started spouting that sort of crap before that.

What did you say to him?

KAREN: I'd had a few drinks, I suppose. Me and Ash decided to venture out to the off-licence which was something we'd never dared do before. I dunno why, we just thought Russ wouldn't approve. Which he doesn't, of course. Anyway, we bought a bottle of wine or something and started to consume it through the second half of the rehearsal . . . Then Russell played us his new song, which turned out to be a really early version of 'Smaller Weaker' . . . and I dunno why, I got all teary-eyed and I just *knew* . . . like, in the way you just know when you first see a bloke you're gonna end up shagging . . . I just knew that if I ever made it in music, it'd be with Russ. So I think I said something utterly appalling to him like (*adopts tearful voice*) 'You're the person I've been looking for all my life . . .' or something equally vomit-inducing.

You don't think there's the slightest chance he got the wrong end of the stick?

KAREN: What do you mean? Of course not.

In the end, Morgan decides they should just go to his nearest pub.

'Thing is, Groom,' he explains, as they cross the road from his flat, 'you can't just trundle into an offie and buy twenty different types of booze. Well, you can, but it'll cost you an arm and leg. Better to come t' pub, then it's all laid out for you. And there's the ol' camaraderie, y'know, we can play a bit of pool later, and maybe get into a punch-up if we're really lucky.'

'Later?' Russell frowns. 'I'm not planning on staying long, you know. Should be able to get this done in half an hour at the most . . .'

Morgan shakes his head and pushes open the pub door.

'Funny man, y'are, Groom.'

It being three in the afternoon, the pub is practically deserted. An old bloke drinks Guinness by the window, reading the *Daily Express*. A couple of young guys with heavily gelled hair nurse energy drinks near the dartboard ('Probably conducting some sort of drug deal,' Morgan estimates). That's it. The early-twenty-something girl behind the bar looks up from her copy of *Heat*, sighs and ambles over. It's hardly the sort of convivial, 'what a swell party this is' atmosphere needed to effectively indoctrinate Russell into the merry world of boozing, but it'll have to do. And Morgan doesn't look like he's going to let it bother him. He settles himself on a bar stool, gestures to Russell to do the same and nods at the barmaid.

'OK. We'd like a pint and a half of Bombardier to kick off with.'

'What's Bombardier?' Russell asks.

'Ale, Groom. Don't you worry.'

Russell looks like a small child in the doctor's waiting room. He gazes around the pub unhappily and then fishes about in his rucksack for something.

'What do you keep in that bloody bag?' Morgan frowns.

'In my rucksack?' Russell blinks. 'All the things I need.'

Morgan sniggers and the drinks appear.

'Ta,' Morgan mutters, handing over a note.

'Do you come here often, then?' Russell enquires. Morgan plonks the half-pint down in front of him.

'There y'are,' he says. 'Get that down yer, and stop trying to chat me up.'

Morgan clinks his glass against Russell's and takes a gulp. He swallows, sighs with satisfaction, puts his glass down then notices Russell is just staring at him.

'What yer watchin' me for?'

Russell looks back at his half-pint.

'Why so much froth?' he frowns.

'You know when you get froth on a cappuccino? It's like that.'

'I don't drink cappuccino.'

Morgan rolls his eyes and takes another gulp. 'Blimey. Afternoon drinking. You'll be the death of me, Groom.'

Russell is still staring at his drink.

'It's not gonna get any tastier by looking at it, y'know. Go on, just try it.'

Russell lifts the glass to his lips, then to his nose.

'Eurgh.'

'Oh, Christmas. Look, it may not end up being your drink, but we'll never find out if you don't . . .'

Russell is finally drinking. He takes about three gulps, then bangs down the glass with a grimace and wipes his mouth.

'Absolutely repulsive. OK, next.'

KAREN: The only thing I've ever known about it is that he's incredibly fussy. On a couple of occasions we've been killing time somewhere – between soundcheck and gig, that old no-man's-land – and I've tried to coax him into giving me some clues, just out of interest, really. You know, we're sat outside a pub or something, and girls have walked past and I've said, 'What about her, Russ? And her? How about that one?' And there'd always be something wrong. 'No, too short', or 'No, too tall'. 'Don't like blondes.' 'Don't like redheads.' 'Something funny about her nose.' And so on. Never once did he say, 'Yeah, she's nice.' At first it was a nice contrast to Ash and Jake, who'd basically be sitting there with their tongues out at any girl who walked past, going, 'Aw, fuck me, she looks like she could suck whatever through a golf hole' – or however those bloody expressions go. But after a while I did start to wonder – what *does* Russell like?

It's understandable, then, that you thought he might be gay.

KAREN: I bloody *never* thought he might be gay! That's just the boys shit-stirring. Twats. I'm not stupid. All I said was you can never completely rule it out. Because it's difficult to say anything about Russ when you've got so little to go on. Most blokes are so readable. I mean – with Ash for example, I could see after about an hour in his company that he likes large-ish blonde girls who'll dominate him (*laughs*), knock him about a bit. I'm serious! And Jake'll basically fuck anyone who'll have him. Pretty much the only thing I know about Russell's love life is that he had a childhood sweetheart in Malaysia.

Before he moved to Britain?

KAREN: Yeah. He's got a little picture of her.

But he can't have been more than . . .

KAREN: Six, yeah. This is what I mean! That's the only thing I've got. Oh, and Morgan once told me there was a girl at university – but Morgan being Morgan, he couldn't tell me a single thing about her. So I've no idea. As far as I'm concerned, the guy's *asexual.*

Do you think that, consequently, you behave differently towards him than you do to other male friends, or colleagues, of yours?

KAREN (*frowns*): I don't think so. No. What sort of thing d'you have in mind?

Thinking that it might be a good palate cleanser, Morgan's next idea is a vodka and tonic. He only orders one, presuming that it will meet with a similar reception from Russell. He tastes it first, just to check the barmaid hasn't learned her drink-mixing skills in Moscow, and then hands it to Russell, who appears momentarily hypnotised by the fruit machine.

'Not bad,' Morgan judges. 'Groom. Here. Bit o' voddie for you. Drink it slowly.'

Russell sighs at the little glass – the Smirnoff emblem on the side, a green drinking straw poking out – and lifts it up. To Morgan's horror, he then puts the straw in his mouth.

'Don't use the straw!' Morgan yells, snatching the glass away.

'Why not?'

'You're not meant to drink it from the fookin' straw, Groom.'

'Then why is the straw there?'

'It just *is*. But yer not meant to actually use it.'

Russell scoffs. 'Preposterous.'

'It's like when Englishmen have umbrellas. They carry them about, but they're not meant to actually put them up. Unless they're sheltering a bird.'

'Where on *earth* did you get that from?'

'Established fact.'

'You and your established facts,' Russell comments, finally putting the drink to his lips. He sips, and then winces so violently it's as if he's been electrocuted.

'Oh *God*!' he spits, causing the barmaid to look over. 'It's like battery acid! How the hell does anyone drink that and actually *like* it?'

Morgan grabs the glass again and takes a swig. 'Sorry,' he smiles at the barmaid. 'Nothing wrong with it. Just me friend here, he's . . . erm . . . a Methodist.'

The barmaid frowns and returns to her magazine.

'Groom,' Morgan whispers, 'you're gonna have to find a way of doing this without us getting barred.'

'Well, then, you're going to have to order some drinks which don't taste like they'd start cars.'

Morgan casts his eyes over the spirits on offer, then nods to himself.

'OK. I think I've got it.'

KAREN: I'm not sure I agree. I mean, it's definitely true that I relax the rules slightly more with Russell than I do with Ash and Jake . . .

And Josh now.

KAREN: Yeah. But I don't think that I . . . I dunno. I suppose it's just never occurred to me that he'd find anything I do attractive. It's also that thing of being in a band. The old cliché – you're an instant sibling. And I'd strip off in front of my brother. Give him a hug, sometimes even a kiss, whatever.

You said once that Russell had been very supportive towards you when you'd split up with a boyfriend.

KAREN: Oh yeah! He was a total godsend. Kept coming round, checking I was all right, took me out for meals, all sorts. And one night he . . . um . . . Nah. Never mind.

Perhaps finally cottoning on to the experiment that's being conducted, the barmaid places the small, creamy glass in front of Russell and gives him a little smile.

'Enjoy,' she says.

'Right,' Morgan instructs. 'Have this one slowly. There's no mixer, remember? So it'll be a little stronger, but not much. The ice'll melt as well.'

Russell stares down at the glass.

'Go on, Groom. You're gonna enjoy this one. Promise.'

'Why?'

'Just taste it.'

Russell takes a sip, his eyes not leaving Morgan's. He does not wince, nor instantly expectorate the contents of his mouth.

'OK,' he concedes. 'Creamy. Quite . . . erm . . . smooth. I can understand someone liking it. But there's always that weird twang you get, which ruins it.'

'That's the alcohol,' Morgan sighs.

'And what did you say this was?'

'Baileys.'

'Baileys,' Russell repeats. 'OK. Baileys. I can stomach that. Can we go now?'

'Hang on, hang on. That's one drink. You need more than that.'

'But why?'

Morgan rolls his eyes. 'Because you're not always gonna find Baileys everywhere you go, are yer? And anyway, it's not gonna solve your problems. Bazza the Blockhead'll have six fookin' fits if you rock up onstage with a tumbler o' Baileys.'

Russell crossly dumps the drink to the left of him, where it joins the little collection of glasses in front of Morgan.

'Then why on earth did you make me drink the damn thing?'

'Just to get fookin' ball rolling, Groom,' Morgan snaps, finishing the glass of vodka and tonic with one gulp. 'OK. Time to stop gadding about. Let's hit the hard stuff.'

★　★　★

KAREN: Oh God. I'm full of fucking paranoia about this now. You're right . . . I guess it's because, in some ways, he's so confident, and because of how he looks . . . he comes across as more experienced than he probably is. But . . . ah. (*Pauses, thinking hard.*) I dunno, it still felt completely natural. He came round, kind of late afternoon, and we were gonna just have a walk and get some food in, then go home, cook and watch a video. Kind of classic 'quiet night in' stuff. Without the booze, of course (*laughs*). So we do all that, we're chatting away . . . and this is only a week after that twat dumped me so I suppose I'm still in a bit of a state. We watch a film – I think it was *Life Is Beautiful* – and when that's over we're a bit all over the place cos it's bloody sad at the end, so we decide to cheer ourselves up by watching something totally silly, *Austin Powers* probably. And we're watching it in my room so we don't get anyone barging in and talking, so consequently we're on my bed. And when the film finished we just stayed there, on the bed, talking. And it was so nice. Talking about everything, y'know, mainly music, but all sorts. And I'm returning to my old subject every so often, and he's being really great, talking it through with me . . . and before I knew it, we're both kind of nodding off . . . probably about 1 a.m. by this point. Then I wake up about half an hour later with the light still on, and . . . we're both really groggy, he just grunts, 'Can I stay over?' and I'm like, 'Yeah, whatever.' I go and clean my teeth, get my cacks off and jump into bed. He comes back from the toilet and settles down on the floor, so I'm like, 'Don't be silly, just get in the other side,' and I'm asleep within seconds. 6 a.m. I wake up . . . and I'm in his arms.

Naked?

KAREN: Nah, we've still got clothes on. He's got, I dunno, vest and pants, and I'm in a long T-shirt. But still.

Have you any idea who moved over?

KAREN (*puffs and ruffles her hair*): I think it was probably me. Christ, I mean – a week previously, I've been sleeping with the same bloke for two years, basically every night. How could I help it? I swear, not even a single thought went through my mind. As soon as I realised, I moved back over again.

Was Russell asleep?

KAREN: I think so. I'm . . . 99 per cent sure he was.

Did he have his arms around you, or was he just lying flat?

KAREN: He . . . um . . . well. He had moved slightly, I think, like he was *sort* of holding me. But . . . oh . . . I guess that's just the natural thing your arms *do*, when someone . . .

Cuddles up to you?

KAREN: Look. This wasn't a biggy. Honestly. It was totally cool in the morning. No awkwardness or anything. He woke up before I did, made us both tea, we chatted for another ten minutes or so and then he went home. Completely fine. Met that evening at the rehearsal – business as usual. It's left my mind completely, until now.

But you must have thought about it a little.

KAREN (*drags on cigarette, glances around the room*): Well, yeah. Of course.

Why did he feel the need to stay at all?

KAREN: He didn't come over in his car for some reason, and by the time the film finished he'd already missed the last train, so I guess it just made sense to kip over.

He doesn't live very far away from you, though. Walking distance.

KAREN: Ah, but I wasn't living in Southfields back then – this was when I was over in Gipsy Hill, just near . . . um . . .

Near?

(*Long pause.*)

KAREN: Crystal Palace.

Like the song?

(*Silence.*)

'I'm not desperate!'

Morgan knocks back Russell's untouched glass of Jägermeister and slams it down, again alerting the attention of the barmaid.

'You *are* fookin' desperate.'

'I'm not!' Russell insists.

'You *must* be,' Morgan drawls. 'It's not like you to change something about yerself like this, Groom. I fookin' *know* you, lad.'

'But –'

'I've known you fookin' donkey's years, and you've not changed fook all about yerself the whole time, particularly not after someone's told you to.'

'Honestly, it just seemed like the right time –'

'Balls. Desperation has set in. You're fookin' stressed to the max, man. And if I didn't know you so well, I'd also say there was summat else to it . . . like you're trying to *impress* someone.'

He eyes Russell knowingly. If this gesture was calculated to infuriate Russell, it succeeds.

'Ahp . . . right, Morgan! Just cut this *out*,' he splutters, 'cut it out *now*!' Russell looks around for the barmaid, who has conveniently disappeared. 'I'm not willing to sit here and listen to this nonsense while drinking these . . . *chemicals*. I need a drink . . . a *real* drink.'

'Which is what – everyone else's idea of a *pretend* drink?'

'Yup, just that,' Russell snaps, glaring at the collection of half-filled glasses that now litter the bar counter. 'All this . . . *medicine* can go to hell.'

'Fookin' gratitude, I tell yer,' Morgan spits. 'I take you out, I buy you a score's worth o' booze –'

'*I'll* pay, then,' Russell replies, crossly reaching into his rucksack.

'And I give up my valuable time to come 'ere and think about what alcohol you'd like to try –'

'Well, thank you very much, I appreciate it. Now for Christ's sake, get me a coffee.'

'– and I reckon this was a fairly well-balanced selection –'

Russell grabs one of the glasses – a clear liquid with a coffee bean lurking at the bottom – and holds it angrily in Morgan's face.

'Well balanced? Look at this! Look at that poor little bean, surrounded by this . . . *poison*! And I'm meant to consume, and savour, and be *refreshed* by this?'

'All right, clever-arse. *You* fookin' pick something to drink. You wanted to try some booze – imagine I was busy, or just told yer to fook off, which frankly I'm tempted to do right now. What would you have done? What would *you* have picked?'

Morgan glugs down the glass of sambuca, swallows, and then gobs the coffee bean in Russell's direction. Russell breathes in and out for a few seconds, then when sufficiently calm, glances up and down the bar. The barmaid hovers worriedly at the far end, probably wondering whether or not to call the landlord.

Russell's selection criteria are a mystery. He has zero pleasurable taste memories with which he can associate the fridges full of bottles, so it's possible that he is just going on the colour of the liquids, and perhaps the shape of the containers. But being a wordy sort of chap, it's likely he's paying a lot of attention to the names. Contrary to his earlier denials he certainly seems a little stressed out, so it would have to be something . . . tranquil, smooth, fresh, pure, natural . . . organic? Yes. Like nature's very own spring showers, or droplets of . . . dew? Yes. Organic dew. An ocean of calm washes over him, as he imagines warm sunshine breaking through the clouds while he snoozes on the grass, the sweet smell of flowers and the buzzing of the bees . . . hmm . . . flowers and bees . . . honey . . . mmm . . . honey . . . organic . . . honey . . . dew . . .

'Organic Honey Dew,' Russell announces, extending his finger towards a brown bottle in a distant fridge.

'Yer what?'

'Organic Honey Dew,' he repeats. 'I want that.'

'That's beer,' Morgan points out.

'I want it.'

Morgan shrugs and calls the barmaid over.

'Er . . . bottle o' the Organic Honey Dew, please, love.'

The barmaid wordlessly fetches the drink and parks it in front of Russell, who regards it with thirsty eyes.

'You need a glass?' she asks.

'Nah – think we'll be all right,' Morgan replies.

Russell holds up the bottle and wipes off some of the condensation. For some reason he's regarding it with the sort of reverence he usually reserves for an espresso cup. Perhaps he is method acting: if he puts this much ritualisation into the act, he *will* enjoy it as much as he enjoys a coffee. He puts the bottle to his lips, and drinks.

Morgan waits with trepidation.

'*And* . . . ?'

Russell swallows, then nods.

'Yup. It'll do.'

Pease Pottage

Despite Barry's built-in nonchalance and warnings of prematurely twisted knickers, even he has to concede by the end of the week that things are going pretty well. News of the band's promising Barfly show has spread throughout Barry's contacts, and then filtered down through *their* contacts, until four record companies – two of them apparently 'majors' – are reportedly on the verge of contacting their legal departments and producing chequebooks.

'What did I tell you cats,' beams Josh at Thursday's rehearsal. 'Barry's a *demon*.'

'Demon he might be,' Russell hisses to the others when Josh nips out to the loo, 'but I overheard Josh talking to him on the phone earlier – and you know who one of these companies is?'

'Who?' Karen asks.

'Eluxor!' Russell scoffs. 'They were our contact in the first place! So much for brand-new leads.'

In addition to this record-label action, a prominent music publisher has also pricked up its ears, as has renowned music PR firm Bean and Gawn, employer of Ash's infamous unsigned-musician-ignoring friend.

'The irony,' Russell winces, 'is almost unbearable.'

Much to Russell's disappointment, Ash has next to no enthusiasm for finding out whether Colin still works there, much less for texting the two-faced so-and-so with some arch comment.

'Nah, s'all right,' Ash frowns. 'We'll bump into him eventually.'

'Yes,' nods Russell eagerly. 'Then you can watch him squirm.'

The obvious missing piece in the proceedings right now, however, is a recording of the band in their current incarnation.

'That's fine,' says Russell. 'We can knock something up at Morgan's this weekend.'

'No, dude,' Josh replies. 'We need something better than that.'

'But . . . his equipment's unbelievable! And it'll be free, if we allow him to produce it?'

'Man, those previous demos are unlistenable.'

'Yes, because of Jake.'

'Not just because of Jake. The mixing's *frightful*, chap.'

Russell groans, clearly exasperated that this same argument has returned to haunt him.

'Ash, Karen? You're OK about using Morg again?'

'Um,' Karen begins, thinning her lips, 'I've gotta be honest – I wouldn't mind trying something different.'

'Ash?'

'Yeeah . . . sorry, fella. Me too.'

'Maybe go somewhere' – Karen lowers her head, clearly fearful of Russell's reaction – 'proper?'

'Well,' shrugs Russell, 'we'll have to *pay* something proper, then.'

'Not if we use my old man,' Josh winks. 'And I think he's free at the weekend.'

If there is the creeping sense that Russell's dominion is weakening, this is reinforced by a phone call he receives late Friday night as he is engaged in a few last-minute bits of equipment maintenance in preparation for Saturday's recording session.

'Hello? . . . Speaking . . . Who? . . . Oh! . . . Oh, right! . . . Um, yeah? . . . fine, but who's . . . sorry, yes, Colliers Wood, but who's . . . Er, 34 Grove Road, but who's . . . 9 a.m., right, no problem . . . But . . . OK, bye.'

He puts his phone down on his desk and looks aimlessly around the room for a few moments.

'I'm being picked up tomorrow. By a roadie.'

He twiddles the lead which connects his guitar to his amp and looks, for the briefest of seconds, like he's going to cry. Then:

'But who's *paying* for this?'

The question is no closer to being answered as three loud bursts of a car horn are heard the following morning at 8.58, but once onboard, Russell doesn't waste much time in asking. Josh, black hair escaping all over a large pair of wraparound Gucci sunglasses, lights a cigarette and nods at Russell sleepily.

'My old man's treat,' he drawls. 'Enjoy it while it's non-recoupable, kids.'

He settles back in his seat and blows a few smoke rings.

The van, far from being a regular Transit in which members must rattle around seatless in the back, is a relatively posh Mercedes splitter with leather seats and a video player. Russell is sitting up front with the roadie and driver, an affable long-curly-haired character by the name of Bing ('Long story, very long story,' he laughs). While Ash and Josh snooze and Karen listens to her Discman, Bing fills Russell in on the plan.

'Josh and me go back years, years and years,' he explains, as the van trundles southwards. 'I tour-managed him in Hypotenuse and The Eclectic, and it was always fun, lots of fun. Now I'm working for people, various people . . . but I still do bits an' pieces, pieces an' bits for Lenny, that's his dad, Josh's dad. So we're gonna show up there, show up at the studio . . . we'll have a tea, cup of tea, and then we'll set it all up, set up the gear and get going. You're a songwriter, one of the song-writers, yeah?'

Russell blinks at him for a second.

'I'm *the* songwriter.'

'Yeah, that's what I'm saying, what I'm saying, yeah.'

Later, Russell debates this point frantically as he and Karen take a short stroll around the studio's pleasant grounds.

'I know,' Russell reasons, 'that other people in this band have occasionally written songs. I also know that Bing, charming chap though he is, has a rather strange way of talking.'

'A stammer,' Karen defines.

'Well, it's not a stammer, really, is it?'

'Yes, it is.'

'No, it's not. A stammer is when you repeat the c-c-c-consonants at the beginning of w-w-w-words. This is more like a sentence stammer.'

'Yeah, exactly. A stammer.'

Russell stops walking and screws up his face. 'But . . . you can't really call it a stammer.'

'*Russell!* All right, it's not a fucking stammer! Get on with it!'

'OK. Whatever's slightly wrong with the way he talks, in this instance he *added* the words "one of". It wasn't just an idle, meaningless part of his impediment. It *meant* something.'

'And? You *are* one of the songwriters.'

'Um . . . well, I'm not really. I'm *the* songwriter . . . but sometimes other people write songs too.'

Karen trots up some steps to a paved area, next to the main house.

'Well, that sounds to *me* . . . like you're *one* of the songwriters.'

'Er . . . I don't think it's quite as –'

'That's the logic behind this kind of statistic, Russ. If you had written every single song we'd ever played, you would certainly not be "one of" the songwriters. But unfortunately, as soon as one other person in this band writes a song which this band starts playing – I'm sorry – but you become *one* of the songwriters.'

'But what if you apply the same logic to vocalists? Damon Albarn, for example, is *the* singer in Blur, although both Alex James and Graham Coxon have on occasion recorded lead vocals. But you'd never describe Damon Albarn as "one of the lead singers in Blur", would you?'

Karen stops walking and turns abruptly.

'That's *completely* different, Russell.'

'Is it?'

'Yes!' Karen yells triumphantly. 'It is. Because "lead singer" is a role in a band that remains basically constant – unless you're in some weird constantly-swapping-instruments set-up like, I dunno, Gomez or somebody. But *anyone* can write a song for a band. The drummer, the backing vocalist, even the bloody manager. Fuck, a band could theoretically never play any songs that anyone who is actually *in* the band has written.'

Russell must realise Karen has whipped his backside because, sensibly, he keeps quiet for a moment. Karen walks on for a while, then turns and eyes her colleague.

'What's this really about, anyway, Russell? Now Jakey's gone, the only other person who's written stuff is me. And I'm not planning to tread on your toes. You know that. So . . . what is it?'

Russell folds his arms, sighs and looks up at the sky.

'I think Josh might be telling people he's written some of the stuff. If he changes a lyric — like, one word, or one line — or if he plays a chord slightly differently . . . or something like that . . . I'm worried that he's going to start considering that a co-write.'

'Oh. I don't think he would.'

'He might!'

'Nah, really?'

'He might. Why else would Bing have said that? Why on earth would he have thought anyone else was writing stuff? I mean, no offence, but your songs haven't really . . .'

'I know, they haven't made their mark, don't worry about it. But —'

'He must have been *told* that Josh writes some of the stuff —'

'Oh, Russell, I think you're being a bit —'

'— unless he's under the impression that this is some all caring-sharing collaborative effort, which — peace and love aside — I don't want people to think!'

They are standing next to a large hedge, on the other side

of which is a lawn. The main part of the studio looks out onto that lawn. Karen stops walking and, realising how close they are to the others, puts her fingers to Russell's lips.

'Shh, Russ. For God's sake,' she whispers, 'simmer down. The bloke probably just heard that you write songs. Which you do. That could mean you're the only songwriter – or that could mean you're one of thirty songwriters. How the fuck does he know? He drives the van and carries the gear.'

'Hmm . . . I'm still not –'

'Listen. Have a word with Josh when the session's over. It's probably the sort of thing we need to discuss anyway – how all this is split. Don't worry about it for now, though. We've got a recording to make.'

Russell, at last, is silent. The pair of them round the corner, and are greeted by the reassuring sound of Ash whacking his snare drum.

The famous Lenny Chigwell is not at all as expected. When Bing zoomed off the M23 at Pease Pottage and swung the van down a narrow country lane-cum-gravel drive, two men were seen drinking mugs of tea by the front door of the complex's main building (a pretty, timber-framed farmhouse) – one an elegant, grey-haired man with a tan and well-fitting dark clothes, the other a much smaller, wiry guy in a dirty navy-blue fleece and jeans, his shoulder-length blondy-grey hair held back by a battered pair of mirror shades. When Josh tumbled out of the van, it was this second man he staggered up to and manfully embraced.

'Pater!'

'There y'are, son,' Chigwell senior grinned, wrapping a firm arm around his taller offspring and kissing him on the head. 'Looking the part, I see? Come to visit the ol' homestead, 'ave ya? And who's all this, then, eh?'

('East End, circa 1955,' Russell comments later of his accent, to a not-particularly-interested Ash.)

After a cursory introduction for the boys, Josh got down on one knee and blew a pretend trumpet fanfare for Karen as she daintily disembarked from the vehicle. Karen rolled her eyes and stepped forwards, fluttering her eyelids and smiling sweetly with such contrived charm that steam could almost be seen spurting from both Russell's ears.

'Aha!' hooted Lenny, with a throaty laugh. 'Now I see what all the fuss is about! Heard a lot about you, my darlin'.'

'You too,' Karen chirruped.

After this, the grey-haired man was presented as 'Francis, who will be organising your session today' – and with that, Lenny climbed into an ancient Vauxhall Cavalier and sped off, 'to get some provisions'.

'What's going on?' Russell managed to hiss in Karen's ear as they started carrying the gear inside. 'Is he producing us, or what?'

'Shh!' was Karen's only response.

Matters became slightly less confusing once Francis had taken everyone through the residential part of the house (messy, but not without mod cons) and into the studio area itself: a rabbit warren of carpeted live rooms, vocal booths and control rooms, all partitioned by breathtakingly heavy steel and glass doors, its most impressive and unique feature being the huge, wooden-floored space which gazes through enormous windows onto the sunny lawn, and further into the green Sussex valley beyond. After a few excited noises from Karen and Ash (Russell was more circumspect in his appreciation), the marathon setting-up process began, the majority of time as usual devoted to Ash's drums, at which point Karen and Russell headed out for their songwriting debate.

Now, upon their return, Chigwell senior is still nowhere to be seen, and his son seems to have disappeared too. Russell, rather perturbed, corners Bing in the kitchen area where he has been sent to conjure yet another round of teas.

'Lenny? Oh, he's gone up to Crawley, where he's gone,' Bing explains, filling the kettle. 'To the supermarket, gone to supermarket.'

'Oh,' Russell grunts. 'Are we going to wait for him?'

'Er . . . no, what's the, why, whassat for?'

'Isn't he producing the session?'

'Nah, no, it's Francis gonna do the session, produce the session.'

'I see. Does, er . . . does Lenny *ever* produce stuff?'

Bing snaps on the kettle and frowns around the room.

'Ah, er . . . yeah, yeah, I think, er . . . sometimes, yeah. But . . . not often, not very often.'

'Hmm,' Russell thinks. 'And have you seen Josh recently?'

'Yeah, he'll be upstairs, gone upstairs.'

'How come?'

'Probably a jacuzzi, to have a jacuzzi.'

Russell gapes at Bing for a second.

'To have a *jacuzzi*?'

'Yeah,' Bing confirms. 'He always has one when he's home, when he comes home.'

Russell shakes his head in astonishment and stomps back to the control room. He is further alarmed to see, a few minutes later, Bing extracting Josh's equipment from its various bags and cases, and plugging it all in.

'That's what a roadie is for, Russ,' shrugs Ash, after Russell has declared his dismay.

'Yes, but why's he only doing stuff for Josh?'

'Have you asked him to do anything for you?'

'No, but . . .'

'Well, there you go,' Ash says, pointing at his cymbal stands. 'You see all those? Bing set 'em all up for me. You've only gotta ask, Russ.'

Russell studies his shoes glumly for a moment.

'But what about the jacuzzi?'

'Oh, I dunno, Russ, do I? It's his home too, don't forget. Surely there's one or two things you do when you go back to your folks?'

Russell stamps his feet in sheer frustration.

'Yes, but this is meant to be a *recording session!*'

After all this, the good news is that the session proves to be in safe hands, Lenny or no Lenny. Francis knows precisely what he is doing (he has apparently been the studio's in-house engineer for more than twenty years) and a crisp, powerful drum sound is soon cannoning out of the speakers. Josh reappears ('Sorry, punks, had a bit of family business to take care of upstairs') and the day proceeds with little drama. As seven o'clock approaches, the smell of a barbecue wafts its way into the studio; Russell glances out of the window to see Lenny himself poking the charcoal.

'He's just the studio dogsbody,' he murmurs, within the vague earshot of Karen. 'He's not a producer at all!'

Karen growls and heads back towards the control room. Russell, with mounting suspicion, takes out his phone and starts to text someone.

ASH: You do meet a lot of bullshit artists. After a while you get a kind of sixth sense for it. I mean, we all exaggerate stuff sometimes – like, an A & R geezer promises to come down to a gig, so you start telling people you've got 'record company interest', even if you've no idea whether he'll eventually turn up or not. Russell always says we've got five hundred people on our mailing list, although I helped him do the mailout for the gig before last and there was only three hundred-odd, and no *way* have two hundred people signed up since then. But that's all right, y'know? The music industry probably floats along on that sort of overblowing. But there really are some genuine bullshit merchants. Promoters who make you pay to play – that's a good one. 'Pay a deposit of fifty quid, you'll get it back as soon as fifty punters walk through the door.' Sod off. Then there's people who promise to do certain things but never do, or who claim to have connections. 'Oh, yeah – my cousin cuts Paul McCartney's hair. Give us a CD, I'll make sure she passes it on.' Right. For starters, she probably doesn't cut Paul McCartney's hair, but even if she did, she's not gonna wanna randomly hand Macca a CD after she's finished chopping his barnet, is she? It ain't gonna happen. I remember one night I was pissed in my local, and there was this mouthy American lass there who was talking to everyone, and when she found out I was in a band she was like, 'ooh, I've got heaps of contacts in the music industry' – so I grilled her a bit on it, and whittled it down and whittled it down, and by the end it turned out she had a cousin who played piano. That was the sum total of her industry contacts.

Do you think Barry might be a bit of a bullshit artist?

ASH: Well, yeah, he's a mouthy fucker, and I'm sure at least 25 per cent of what he says is bollocks. But it doesn't matter, because the results speak for themselves. Support slot with JJ72 and four interested record companies in less than two weeks?

And you're sure it's all true?

ASH: Yeah. You just know. Like I said, sixth sense. And the JJ72 thing *can't* be bullshit if Russ's boss told him, so that earns Bazza a bit of trust for the other stuff.

What about Josh?

ASH: Again, the results speak volumes – the bloke can sing like a fuckin' dream. Looks good, plays well, and he's brought along a manager who's shaking things up – at the end of the day, he could be lying about all sorts of things, but you can't fake that other stuff.

Do you think Russell trusts them?

ASH (*screws up his face for a second*): Y'know . . . Russell's got to start believing.

At eight o'clock, Lenny Chigwell comes barging into the studio dressed in a chef's hat and an oversized white T-shirt declaring '*I Like The Pope, The Pope Smokes Dope*', complete with convincing spoof photo of the poor old pontiff, puffing on a number.

'Aw, *Pater*,' Josh winces. 'Must you?'

Lenny leans on the sound desk, beaming around at the assembled.

'Thought you'd like to see one of the ol' favourites, son.'

'Where'd you get it?'

'Tidying out some of yer old drawers.'

'Stylish, Josh,' Karen chuckles.

'I never used to wear that,' Josh insists.

'Anyway,' says Lenny. 'How are we getting on, Francis? Anyone in the mood for some nosh?'

Whether he was once a world-famous producer or not, there's something rather endearing about Lenny. He's got a smile and a joke for everyone as he bustles about, handing round paper plates and napkins, flipping burgers and guiding his guests in the direction of the buns, condiments and salad. Even Russell warms to him. If Josh has inherited his supercilious air from either of his parents, it's certainly not from his father. As the last of the daylight fades, the four band members, plus Lenny, Bing and Francis, seat themselves around a garden table, at which point Josh asks what Karen and Ash must also have been wondering.

'Erm, Pater . . . you got any beers?'

Lenny leaps out of his seat again – 'Ooh, blimey! What an omission, eh?' – and scampers off.

Russell, who has conveniently sat himself next to Francis, asks as surreptitiously as he can what they might expect from the remainder of the evening.

'We've done well today, haven't we?' Francis reflects. 'You all work fairly quickly – I personally don't believe in pushing it, if we don't need to. Perhaps we should just finish Josh's guitar overdubs tonight, then we can start refreshed tomorrow? What d'you reckon, Josh? You ready for some guitar heroics later?'

'I was *born* ready, Frankie.'

Russell nods, smiles at Francis and quietly slips away. Lenny returns with a cool box, which he bangs down on the floor next to Josh.

'There y'are, son. You can be mother.'

'I'd rather not be mother,' Josh winks, parking a spliff in his mouth and taking a huge drag, 'cos then I wouldn't be able to do this.'

Lenny chuckles at his son and opens the cooler to reveal a couple of dozen chilling beer bottles. He and Josh pass them around the table.

'Ah, no need for one here,' Karen says, pointing to Russell's place.

'*Teetotaller*,' Josh stage-whispers. Lenny nods thoughtfully.

It is of considerable surprise, then, when Russell reappears a minute or two later bearing a large bottle of Organic Honey Dew. Ash is the first to notice.

'What the hell's *that*, Russ?' he practically yells across the table. Everyone turns.

'Uh,' Russell shrugs, meekly sitting down, 'I tried some of this the other day, and I, er . . . quite liked it.'

This development provokes a reaction akin to a former satanist announcing they've finally seen the error of their ways. The others immediately clink their bottles cheerily against Russell's, and even though Russell probably has no more than four sips for the duration of the meal, the difference in atmosphere is dramatic. Ash and Karen, knowing Russell as well as they do, are slightly more measured in their excitement, but Josh in particular starts yapping away at Russell like never before.

'Fuck me, the stuff is sounding schwee-*eet*! Don't you reckon, chief? What did I tell you, man? Ahh . . . to think, only a few weeks ago we were sitting in that Soho queenhouse, sipping late-night coffees, bashing this very idea about . . . and now *here we are* at my old man's yard, necking the beers after a day's musical toil! Who'da thought it, dude?'

'It is amazing, yes,' Russell replies, rather uneasily.

'And I had this wicked idea, chap . . . you know what ol' Bazza was chatting about, trying to relieve some o' your commitments onstage? Yeah? Well – what if we got Frankie to bounce down the synth tracks onto a stereo pair, slam it on a DAT, link it up to a click for Ashley, and then we can just play along to it live?'

'What, and then . . .'

'You got it, dude! You just play your guitar and perform yo' *ass* off, man! Frankie, you could do that in secs, right?'

'Don't see why not,' replies Francis, forking salad into his mouth.

Karen looks at Russell hopefully.

'That sounds like a good solution, Russ.'

'Erm . . . it wouldn't really be *live*, then, would it . . . ?'

'That don't matter,' Josh reasons. 'Everyone does a bit o' this kinda thing, man.'

Ash nods. Russell takes the third of his four sips.

'Hmm . . . I'll *think* about it.'

Thankfully, Karen changes the subject.

'Oh my God, Russell – I am *so* not going to get used to you with a *beer* . . .'

They continue to drink and scoff burgers for another half an hour, the meal acquiring an unusually Mediterranean feel in the mild early-September night after Lenny snaps on outdoor lights that coil around the farmhouse's many bushes and creepers. Francis eventually lays down the law and insists they get back to work. Josh, who for some reason has put his sunglasses back on, carries the cool box back inside and cracks open another bottle on one of the studio door handles.

The rest of the evening, until Francis admits defeat just before midnight, is given alternately to recording Josh's guitar (he manages to deliver some semi-decent takes amid his increasingly beer-and-spliff-fuelled rockular antics) and sitting around chatting about the usual indiscriminate rubbish that tends to be unearthed via the combination of alcohol, cannabis and musicians. Russell, contributing to these rambling discussions for perhaps the first officially recognised time, gradually speeds up his drinking, progressing to his third bottle by eleven o'clock.

'How many of those things did you bring, fella?' Ash laughs.

'Oh,' Russell replies with a slight belch, 'just a few.'

Ash grins and shakes his head in disbelief. 'After all these years,' he mutters.

Once Josh has recorded his parts, the control room is shut down for the night and the party transfers to the games room, complete with a pool table and permanently credited Wurlitzer jukebox.

'This'll be interesting,' Karen announces, turning to Josh. 'Russ says pool's the only thing he can enjoy in a bar, and then he thrashes us cos he's sober and we're all pissed. Now he'll get to play it like it's *meant* to be played . . .'

Fuelled by his new-found beverage, Russell still summarily beats each of his bandmates, plus Francis and Bing. Finally, with a crafty smile, Lenny picks up the cue, breaks and slaughters Russell within three minutes.

'You're a pro!' Russell hollers.

'No – it's just my table! It's a warped old thing and I know all the little quirks . . .'

'Plus,' Karen grins, 'I think Mr Groom there might be getting a little drunk . . . eh, Russ?'

She gives him a few playful prods on the arm and winks.

'Oh . . . no. No! Not at all,' he blusters.

The opposite, of course, is almost certainly true. By 1 a.m. Russell is on his fourth half-litre bottle, a skinful by most drinkers' standards. While Josh, Karen and Ash play table football in another part of the room, Russell steadies himself at the jukebox and tries to focus on some appropriate records. Francis and Lenny having now turned in for the night, Bing ambles over to assist.

'Nice tunes, lot of tunes in there.'

'Yeah,' Russell drawls. 'The Jam, eh? Love it.'

'Oh, yeah?' Bing nods. 'Underground, the "Going Under-ground" one.'

'Oooh,' Russell thinks, 'I'm more of a "Town Called Malice" man myself.'

'Oh, right, yeah, it's good, it's good that one, yeah.'

Both tunes are soon pounding out.

'Isn't it funny?' Russell mumbles. 'Those punk-pop people. So many of them start out playing punk, punky rock, and so on. Sting, Weller . . . must be more of them . . . then in the eighties they all grew up, and they all suddenly started playing jazz and soul.'

'Yeah, the Byrne, the talking Byrne guy, him too. Talking Heads.'

Russell widens his eyes and nods with unexpected respect at Bing.

'David Byrne! Absolutely, you're completely right. But it never happens the other way round, does it? You never get some jazz virtuoso, like, I dunno . . . André Previn or Harry Connick Jr . . . you never get them deciding in later life that they wanna play punk.'

'Er . . .'

'You never hear about Miles Davis going through his Sex Pistols era. Why's that, d'you think?'

'Um . . . I'm not, I dunno, I'm not sure myself . . . er . . .'

Karen wanders over.

'What are you pair of drunkards talking about?'

Russell tells her.

'Fascinating. Starting to slur a bit, there, Russ . . .'

'I'm . . . I'm not, I don't think? Am I?'

'Are you feeling all right?' Karen grins, clearly loving every incongruous minute of it.

'Er . . . yeah! It's . . . erm . . .'

'You wanna get some air?' she asks, touching him lightly on the shoulder.

Russell looks at her sternly for a second, then:

'Yes. Yes, OK.'

RUSSELL: An epiphany? Was that Jake's word, by any chance? It's just the sort of thing he'd say. He likes these sort of vacuum-packed moments in life, does Jake. 'That was the moment when *everything* suddenly made sense.' I don't really think I go in for that sort of moment.

Not at all?

RUSSELL: Well . . . I suppose coming to Bracknell from Malaysia was certainly a moment of *some* description. I'm not sure it meant anything in musical terms, though. It was just arriving from what I thought was a tremendously exciting, colourful, nature-filled place with incredibly warm and friendly people, to this dull commuter hellhole where I couldn't even walk down my street without some kid throwing a rock at me. So yes, I started to play music, but I don't think there was any one moment when it all turned around. I'd been playing the guitar for a year or more before I could honestly say I was enjoying it.

Why did you continue?

RUSSELL: Because I'd told myself I was going to learn it, and . . . I'm not the sort of person who gives things up easily. As you might have noticed.

Josh and Ash have transferred to one of the games room's ample, squashy sofas, where they sip a whisky nightcap.

'Always feel kinda sorry for my old man when I come here.'

'He never remarried, then?' Ash asks.

'Nah. He's had a few chicks over the years, but . . .'

'What about your mum?'

'Yeah,' sighs Josh. 'She remarried. Less said about that the better, though.'

They both look up at the sound of the sliding patio doors opening. Karen comes stumbling in, not a picture of happiness. She squints at the two boys and ruffles her hair.

'Y'all right, Kaz?' asks Ash.

'Tired,' she replies. 'Bit pissed. Time to hit the hay.'

'What did you do with Russ?'

Ash means this neutrally but Karen is instantly on the back foot.

'Nothing. Nothing at all. Why?'

'Having one of his wanders, is he?'

'Yeah. Something like that. Josh, can you . . . ?'

'Uh-huh,' Josh says, pulling himself up from the sofa. 'Let me show you to your quarters.'

'What about Russ?' Ash reminds them. Josh looks at Karen, who shrugs.

'All right,' Josh decides, necking the last of his whisky. 'Wait here.'

He saunters out through the doors. The outside lights have been turned off so it's not immediately obvious where Russell is, but he can eventually be recognised on the far terrace, looking out over the darkened valley. It's plain that all is not well.

'Russ, man.'

No reply.

'Russ. Y'OK, dude?'

Finally, a muffled response.

'Yup.'

'Just wanted to say, man . . . the bedrooms are on the second floor, you can crash in the first one on the left . . .'

'OK, thanks.'

Josh waits for a second, then turns to go.

'Josh?'

'Yo,' Josh replies, spinning round again.

Russell's face is vague in the murky light. He looks at Josh for what seems like a whole minute, as if considering a multitude of questions. Finally, he settles for:

'Where's the bathroom?'

'Same floor, all the way to the end. G'night, dude.'

Josh crosses the lawn quickly and disappears inside the house.

Russell remains where he is for a good few minutes. He sways slightly, certainly the worse for wear, a completely alien sensation. He murmurs something, various phrases, disparate words, sometimes what simply sounds like moaning. Eventually one of the more regularly repeated words – 'sorry' – can be deciphered, followed by another phrase – 'not like that' – and then another word, which sounds initially like 'cowpat', but after a couple of repeats seems more likely to be 'cowbag'. At last, two sentences, repeated louder and clearer, with an unavoidable edge of despair to both: 'Everything I've ever wanted, on a plate, for the taking' followed by 'You brought it on yourself'.

This strange trance in the silence of the country night is broken by a familiar pair of electronic beeps. A text message. Russell pulls his phone out of his pocket.

'Bloody Morgan,' Russell mutters. He opens up the message. '*Done some research. 2 long 2 text. Check yr email.*'

Russell stares at the phone for a moment.

'Check email, how on earth am I meant to check email?'

Then he laughs softly.

'I'm speaking like Bing now.'

He replaces his phone and wends his unsteady way back to the house.

ASH: I suppose I've had many epiphanies. Sort of stages you go through, y'know. The first time I realised I was gonna play the drums. Aged four, I was, in my parents' back garden in Sutton Coldfield, my sister and my cousin and me decided to form a pop group and I was put on drums, which were actually orange cushions from my parents' sofa. Funny the stuff you remember. Anyway, that must have been an epiphany of some sort because I never looked back, never even considered another instrument.

But then there've been others, y'know . . . the first gig I played, the first time I made a recording, all of that. But to be honest with you . . . the epiphany I'm thinking of right now is recently, getting Josh on board and the band reforming like it has. It's never been better – makes me kind of wonder what we were up to before.

How do you get along with Josh?

ASH: Well . . . he's a weird kid, innee? Mixed up, I should think. And it can't be easy trying to prove himself in music, with his dad being who he is. But he's nicer than I thought he'd be, on the whole.

Russell shuts the patio door and flops down on the sofa for a few minutes, before wincing and leaning forward. It looks like he's going to be sick, but then he stands up and paces around.

Eventually he stops, and utters the name of the one substance he believes will help him.

'Coffee.'

He wanders out of the games room and into the residential section of the house: a dark, wood-panelled hallway lit by a dim light from upstairs, and with the vaguest scent of cigars. Russell pads down the corridor and pushes open a white wooden door. He snaps on the light and finds himself in a very male kitchen – tidy but far from spotlessly clean, brown colour scheme, white-tiled floor, ashtrays, no cookbooks. He manages to quickly and quietly find the instant coffee and get the kettle on. Waiting for it to boil, he spots another little corridor leading away from the kitchen, and investigates. A utility room on the left, and on the right, a small office stuffed with papers, files, books, records. There is a desk. And a computer.

'*Check yr email.*'

He switches on the lamp next to the desk and eyes the computer. There are two speakers on either side of the monitor, both of which he turns to zero. He turns the computer on.

'God,' he breathes. 'What am I doing?'

He dashes to the kitchen as the machine boots up and quickly makes his coffee. Taking a scalding, much needed sip, he marches back to the office. The screensaver is a live photo of glam-era David Bowie, colourful enough to obscure the icons on the far left of the screen. Already suffering from booze-impaired vision, Russell struggles, but finally finds Internet Explorer.

Ten seconds later Russell is logging on to his email account, where the following is waiting for him:

DEATH OF AN UNSIGNED BAND

From: X MORGAN
            (MORGAN@MORGANX.freeserve.co.uk)
Sent: 9 September 2001 01:34:02
To: russellcgroom@yahoo.co.uk
Subject: your text

Groom

OK, don't ever say I don't do you any favours. I've done some thorough poking about and while I haven't uncovered anything exactly earth-shattering here are a couple of choice nuggets for your delectation.

First off there's absolutely bugger all about Lenny Chigwell being a producer anywhere. Been through about thirty google pages with a toothcomb and nothing, crossreferenced his name with the brotherhood of man and sad cafe and sheena easton and hazel o'witch project and all those other cretins you mentioned and diddly-squat. But his name came up with beverley craven's a few times, so fuck, maybe he did manage her for a bit. Crack open the lambrusco.

So I reckon he just owns the studio and Chigwell George is a right bullshit artist. But if you're now wondering how the hell his dad afforded it in the first place when he was only a fuckin dustman or whatever . . . look no further.

On my travels I discovered one Chigwell entry on a website called lordship.com which is like this massive family tree of lords and earls and posh twats. Turns out this little entry is his ex-wife, and just as chigwell george told you she's the niece of lord Elmuir . . . BUT she's also the daughter of lady Elizabeth froedean who was married to Lord haydew. So Lenny's ex-wife, Chigwell george's mam, is actually lady Stephanie haydew. Sounds like a fuckin oscar wilde play don't it.

So she is a lady, right, more money than Barclays, her old dears own enough land to swallow half of Switzerland including – TA DAA!! – the bit of farmland in Sussex where the studio is. So this young lady arsedew married this poor penniless sod Chigwell in 1969, I expect she was a pretty young toffee-nosed thing charmed by this swingin eastend hipster who probably pumped her full of LSD and christ knows what. My guess is her posh parents didn't approve so they thought fuck, better put the useless git on his feet quick, let's give him some wedge so he can turn that rundown shitheap of a farmhouse into a studio. They divorced in 1980 according to this site so he's probably been surviving on handouts and what little money the studio makes since then.

BUT THAT'S NOT ALL GROOM so keep fuckin reading. Lady Chigwell is now married to MARTIN STEINWOOD and if you ain't heard of him, well you should have done because he's an absolute MEDIA GIANT, major shareholder and board chairman and what have you for a proper empire of companies, a lot of them in the music biz so if your lot are getting heaps of interest already it's likely because of him rather than the skills of bazza the blockhead.

As for Chigwell george himself, I did a search on The Eclectic and managed to find a band called Limpet featuring one of his ex-bandmates. So I dropped their info email a line saying I'd just auditioned Chigwell george and wanted to know what he's like and that. So let's see what they come back with.

Anyway groom, it's all a right messy old pile of shite. But the fact remains that his voice is grand and it's getting you somewhere. So fuck knows what you're gonna do about it.

Love Morg

Russell stares at the email for a few more seconds, then glances sadly around the dimly lit room. He staggers to his feet and notices a few of the items adorning the wall: a teenage picture of Josh, fresher-of-face but otherwise very much the same; a smiling picture of Lenny himself with a much younger Francis; a few framed *Giles* and *Far Side* cartoons; last year's Pirelli calendar, still stuck on June; even a Health & Safety certificate (made out to 'Leonard Chigwell'). But there is nothing else, no postcards from recent clients, no photos of Lenny with Sheena Easton or Beverley Craven, and certainly no gold discs.

'Poor old bastard,' Russell mutters.

Russell is just about to sleepily shuffle off when he remembers to cover his tracks. He deletes his email account from the computer, shuts it down, kills the light and, clutching the remnants of his coffee like a security blanket, finally heads upstairs.

Camden Town

Next morning Russell wakes, with a surprisingly light hang-over, at eight o'clock on the dot. He trudges around the studio's estate, drinks coffee, reads yesterday's papers. Last night's revelations, however, prevent him from being at all content.

'I've no idea why someone would lie about something like this. I've never cared what people thought my father did for a living. He's a construction manager. Why would I pretend he's an architect?'

You might do – if you wanted to convince someone to let you design a building.

'Only if I was rubbish at it. And Josh isn't rubbish, is he? So it's a bit confusing. Karen says that he's insecure. That's how a lot of upper-class people are, she reckons . . . which may be true . . . I dunno.'

It appears to be just a deliberate, calculated scheme to get people to play with him.

'Yeah, maybe. I knew people like him at school. They'd say things like, "Come round my house on the weekend, I've got a Technical Lego Car Chassis!" And then you'd get round there and find they had nothing of the kind. They'd have the tractor, if you were *very* lucky.'

So . . . what are you going to do about it?

Russell sips his coffee and stares out at the dew-covered Sussex valley for what seems like ten minutes.

'Nothing,' he shrugs, finally.

Francis appears at nine and the pair of them start work (more guitar overdubs, synth, preliminary mixing – 'by far the most enjoyable part of the whole weekend,' Russell confesses). The rest of the band gradually drifting downstairs by eleven. There's an expected awkward atmosphere between Russell and Karen following whatever mysteriously happened between them last night: they simply don't seem to communicate at all, only acknowledging one another's existence by mid-afternoon when the closest thing the session has to a real artistic argument rears its head.

'Right,' says Francis. 'Backing vocals.'

'Yup,' agrees Russell. 'Who first, Karen or me?'

'Er, dude,' begins Josh, 'I was thinking it should *just* be Karen?'

'What? Um . . .'

'Since all the industry peeps seemed to be waxing about how sweet the two of us sounded together . . .'

'Yes, but there'll have to be *some* male backing vocals?'

'Sure . . . was planning to do 'em myself, chap . . .'

Russell's 'Jake vein' – having had a well-earned rest of late – reappears.

'But . . . I do the backing vocals *live*, so –'

'Yeah,' Josh nods. 'That's a live solution. It may not be the best-sounding solution for recorded work, though.'

Russell looks around the room for support. Francis is staring impassively at the glass in front of the mixing desk, Ash is leafing through August's edition of *Modern Drummer*. Karen blinks at Russell: it could be neutrality, it could be concurrence with Josh.

As Russell gazes back at her, a look crosses his face, a look never before associated with Russell. It is a look which seems to say one word, and that word is 'whatever'. His 'Jake vein' recedes, he waves a flippant hand in the air, crosses the control room and flops down on the sofa.

But then, backing vocals are a long way from Russell's primary concern. They're far from the thing which keeps him perpetually imprisoned in this strange world of making music. They're miles from the subject which – he has confessed – often interrupts his sleep. They're a long way from that all-important sentence which he's imagined being written at the bottom of his album credits since he was eleven years old, the line which will help him command that earnest respect from his peers of which he has always dreamed. And that line is:

All music and lyrics by Russell Groom

or possibly, the absolute worst-case scenario:

All music and lyrics by Russell Groom (except★)

The asterisk will refer to a strict maximum of two tracks per album, and on both of these he will have earned a hefty co-writing credit ('Karen's song, for example, "Thameslink", which I practically glued together for her').

Backing vocals are in no way as crucial as this. They are, after all, only backing vocals.

The weekend finishes, and the completed DAT is taken away by Josh for Monday-morning delivery to Barry. They have committed three previously unrecorded songs to tape: 'Testing Ground', 'Ghost of Pop' and 'You Brought It On Yourself' – plus 'Warning', originally included on last year's *Demo*, but considered sufficiently current and single-esque to necessitate a Josh version. Josh is ecstatic with the finished recording; Karen and Ash are amazed that it's the work of a line-up who have effectively been together only a week and a half. Russell mumbles a few things about it sounding 'undeveloped', but Josh reminds him, as they board the van for home, that it is still 'only a demo'; the intention will be to eventually re-record these songs at a more leisurely, studious and creative pace, with a record company picking up the tab. Wearing his all-new 'whatever' face, Russell nods vacantly and settles back into his seat.

Barry receives the demo and begins frantically chucking it about, but the world screeches to an unprecedented halt on the Tuesday: 11 September 2001. For a good few days, the assorted machinations of the music business resemble the dribblings and toy-throwings of small children, but Barry nonetheless kicks back into gear by the end of the week, even commenting, with all the charm of a government spin doctor, that the catastrophe 'could buy us a bit of buzz time'.

For the whole of the next week, Russell drifts about in something of a daze. He confesses to feeling 'powerless – powerless to argue, complain, confide or, worst of all, forget'. Another more surprising feature of their newly elevated position is also far from lost on him.

'There isn't much to do!' he shrugs. 'We're closer, I suppose, than we've ever been, and all I've done this whole week is rehearse a few times, speak to Morgan about synching the synth sounds to a click, write a few songs and endlessly watch BBC News 24. No making flyers, no mailouts, no calling venues or record companies, no website maintenance, nothing.'

He pulls the lid off a bottle of Honey Dew and sighs.

'Frankly, I'm bored.'

The following Wednesday, however, Russell is promptly shaken out of his boredom and to the very foundations of his being. A week to go until the JJ72 show and Barry deems it time to discuss the battle plan. For this important occasion he selects what he considers to be an auspicious venue: the Good Mixer in Camden Town.

'Shit pub,' he spits, settling into a corner table with a bottle of Corona, 'but it might be a good omen.'

Both Ash and Russell have been quietly excited about this meeting due to the two major things they have altered about themselves. Ash bowls into the pub with a newly bleached and trimmed head of hair, which, while making it far less obvious that he is succumbing to male-pattern baldness, bears a rather unfortunate resemblance to the style sported by Joe Pesci in *Lethal Weapon 3* (it was supposed to make Ash look like Larry Mullen, Jr). After he is greeted at the bar with great amusement by Josh and Karen, Ash strides up to the table where Barry sits, texting away. Ash stands there grinning for a few seconds before Barry glances up.

'What?' he grunts, and resumes his message. This is the nearest Barry comes to commenting on Ash's hairstyle.

Between eleven and twelve minutes after the meeting's scheduled start time, Russell comes marching into the pub ('Signal trouble at Goodge Street! Didn't anyone else have that problem?') and then proudly approaches the bar.

'Bottle of Organic Honey Dew, please.'

The girl serving (bright red pigtails, Hundred Reasons T-shirt) shakes her head.

'Don't have it, mate.'

Russell frowns at her, clearly under the impression that all pubs sell all the same things.

'What do you mean, you don't have it?'

'I mean . . . we don't have it!'

'What *do* you have?'

The girl looks to her left and right, then shrugs.

'All them drinks there, and there, and in the fridges.'

'What's the closest thing you have to Organic Honey Dew?'

'Organic what?'

Russell huffs.

'Oh, never mind, I'll just have a pint of lime and soda.'

Russell looks devastated as he shuffles back to the table.

'Hi . . . Look, Barry, I *know* I haven't got a beer, but . . . look, it's really annoying, I found this one beer that I like, which is this stuff called Organic Honey Dew, and it's quite decent, and I'll have some of it at the Imperial gig, but this stupid pub doesn't have any of it, which is why I've got this.'

Barry blinks at Russell for a few moments.

'Fine,' he mumbles. 'Whatever.'

The meeting proceeds and is full of the usual promises,

rumours, whiffs of interest and pockets of utter nonsense. A total of seven record companies have now promised to come to next Tuesday's big Imperial show ('Four indies and three majors,' Barry explains, 'but a few of them'll probably drop out of the race after the gig'). One of the indies has even gone so far as to furnish Barry with a preliminary draft record contract ('It's all right,' he reports, 'but it could be a lot fuckin' better'). In addition to all this frenzied activity, a couple of publishers, a booking agent and the aforementioned music PR firm also require their names to be added to the guest list.

'For the booking agent in particular,' Barry says, with his usual weary drone, 'you lot are gonna have to be *jaw-dropping*.'

'I was thinking,' Josh muses, apropos not very much at all, 'that you kids should all perhaps have slightly more fashionable trainers. Karen, yours are OK, but your laces are a bit last year.'

Karen dispenses with this comment quickly and fiercely. Josh moves onto his next victim.

'And, Russ, man . . .'

'Yes . . . ?'

'D'you think you could get rid of that rucksack of yours?'

'My rucksack?'

'That's right, dude . . . it's gonna look *shit*, you rocking up to gigs with that on your back . . . couldn't you exchange it for one of those vintage leather airline shoulder bags?'

'Er . . .'

'They're schwee-*eet*, man, and they only sell 'em round the corner, I could take you round there now to pick one up if you want . . .'

Barry thankfully brings this particular avenue to an abrupt end.

'I don't think that's the fuckin' priority here, Josh.'

The priority is closing up a few gaps in the inter-band administration, an essential before any external agreement is embarked upon. Top of the list – and the item which truly kicks Russell out of his recent daze of apathy – is the song-writing credits. Barry initially mentions this in an offhand tone, as if it's a mere formality.

'Josh told me,' he breezes, scribbling something in his note-book, 'that you guys are gonna be fine with splittin' the song-writing four ways, and I'm really fuckin' pleased to hear that.'

Josh nods around the table of astonished faces.

'It's going to make life so much easier,' he says.

At first Russell is so flabbergasted he can't even move his jaw; a vague groaning drifts out of his mouth. Karen and Ash sense a thunderstorm brewing and keep quiet. Russell fortifies himself with a gulp of his drink, and movement returns to his facial muscles.

'Um . . . we haven't agreed to that, no,' Russell begins. 'Why would we?'

Josh turns to Barry, who growls and puts his pen down.

'Christ. I should keep a fuckin' diagram of this somewhere so I don't have to keep explaining it. OK, I'll give you two scenarios, right? One. You have ten songs . . . one of them's written by, I dunno, the drummer . . . wha's yer name again?'

'Ash.'

'Ash, right,' Barry nods, turning back to Russell. 'So Ash writes one, the other nine are written by you. So you go off on tour, playing those ten songs every night. Everywhere you go, people are buying the record. Meanwhile, the songs are gettin' radio play, used in adverts, on TV, all that. You come home off tour. You ain't getting much money from touring, cos it's early days, right? So you get home, a royalty statement's

on the doorstep. You open yours – nine hundred quid. Ash
opens his – one hundred quid.'

'Yes, but –'

'Ash's been out playing those same songs every night. You
can go and pay your rent, your leccy bill and, I dunno, stock
up yer fuckin' fridge. Ash can't even pay his leccy bill. Then
two months later, you go off on tour again – same songs. Ash
is already pissed off cos he's had his leccy cut off and he's had
to borrow money off his folks to pay his rent, but then you
rock up wearing a new pair of fuckin' trainers. So that next
tour's got a shit atmosphere, then you all come back . . . Ash's
got another hundred quid, you another nine hundred –'

'Yes, yes, I know what you're saying, Barry. But –'

'Scenario two. You and Ash split all the songwriting two
ways. You both come back off tour to find five hundred quid
waiting for ya – OK, not great, but you're both in the same
fuckin' boat.'

'I get it! I understand! But –'

'Ninety per cent of all band break-ups,' Josh interjects, 'have
been over this sort o' thing, dude. Financial inequality. Unease
over –'

'Yes, Josh – I read those music magazines too. OK? But the
point you're both missing is that . . . this *isn't* about the money.'

Barry blinks at Russell.

'Well, what in fuck's name is it about, then?'

'I wrote these songs,' Russell states, with a subtle but unavoidable pride, 'and I want people to *know* that I wrote them.'

Barry sneers and looks away. Josh shrugs.

'But they *will* know that, dude.'

'How?'

'You can tell 'em.'

'No, I mean – people, as in, people all over the place.'

'Uh-oh,' Barry mumbles, with a nasty chuckle. 'Ego alert.'

'It's not ego,' Russell continues, blushing very slightly. 'It's just that . . . I wrote them. No one else did. I want . . . recognition for that. The money's not the problem. We can split the money four ways – fine. No arguments from me. But if I wrote a song, I want it known that I did.'

'You can tell 'em,' Josh repeats.

'We've just been through this.'

'No, dude, I mean you can tell 'em in interviews and so on.'

'But so can you!' Russell says, his frustration rising. 'If the song is credited to all of us, any of you could go around telling people you've written it. But you haven't.'

'We wouldn't do that, though, Russ,' Karen frowns.

Russell pauses for a second. This is possibly the first complete sentence Karen has said to him in more than a week.

'But you *could.*'

'Tell yer what,' Barry grins. 'We'll make you a T-shirt with "I WROTE THE SONGS" written on it.'

A very small chuckle circulates. Russell looks down at his lime and soda, once again like he's on the verge of blubbing into it. He speaks slowly, his voice soft with emotion.

'Look, please . . . don't belittle this. I've put everything I've got into these songs. This is the one part of all this I really care about, when it all boils down. I understand your point about the money, and . . . honestly, I'd be fine with twenty-five . . . I'd take less than twenty-five per cent if it came to it, I don't care! But I'm *not* having these songs attributed to someone else when . . . it's me. Surely there must be a way of crediting the songs to me, but then splitting the money?'

'Not without a fuckload of extra work,' Barry grimaces.

'Well,' Russell says, attempting a helpful smile, '*I* wouldn't mind doing the extra work. To make up for it. Seriously, I'd probably enjoy it.'

'Nah, mate. Whattabout when you're on tour?'

'Well, I'd –'

'Come on, Russ, dude,' Josh blethers. 'You're not going to want to sit in your hotel room doing accountancy when there are a hundred screaming chick-a-teenies on the pavement outside.'

'You'd be surprised,' Russell mumbles.

'Not gonna happen, mate,' Barry continues. 'And how do we know you won't be diddling?'

'Well, I never would,' Russell replies, visibly hurt at the suggestion. 'OK, another idea. What about I pay you' – he says to Barry – 'the extra cost of doing the admin?'

'Oh, fuckin' come on, mate. This is all getting a bit too fuckin' complicated. Listen, it's fuckin' simple. I've been managing bands for years, and the four-way split always works. The one-way credit ends in huge fuckin' rows and the band splitting.'

'Well,' Russell responds, 'I don't know what we're going to do, then.'

Amid the stalemated silence, Josh looks over at Barry, who is studying his phone as if it will provide the answer.

'Bazza . . .'

'What?'

'I was thinking . . . what about the Blur solution?'

'Aw, bloody hell. I was hopin to fuckin' avoid that.'

'What,' enquires Karen, leaning forward, 'is the Blur solution?'

'*I* know what the Blur solution is,' Russell responds. 'The credit is "Songs by Albarn – Music by Albarn, Coxon, James, Rowntree." So Albarn gets fifty per cent, I imagine, for originally writing the melody, chords and lyrics. Then the band all split the other fifty for adding their own parts.'

'It's a fuckin' headache,' Barry grumbles.

'Sounds fair,' Ash offers.

'It probably is,' Russell nods, 'for Blur. But it wouldn't work for us.'

Barry looks up from his phone and scowls.

'Aw, for fuck's sake, why fuckin' not?'

'Well, for a start, I would still end up getting far more money than anyone else, and as I've already said, I don't want it to be like that.'

'Bloody communist,' mutters Barry, to an unimpressed stare from Karen.

'And secondly . . . sorry, but when I say I've written a song, I *mean* I've written a song. All of it. I compose the guitar parts, and the bass line, and the drum pattern. I do it.'

'Occasionally I change a lyric, though, dude . . .'

Russell regards Josh coldly.

'Well, I don't *want* you to change a lyric. That's the whole point. Nor do I want you going around saying you've co-written something if you've just changed part of a line.'

Round and round it goes. Eventually Russell plays his final card, before sinking back into his apathetic trance.

'Listen – here's my only solution. Credit the songs to me, and I *swear* I will split the money four ways. I'll sit down in front of a lawyer and sign a contract stating this. I'll do all the admin – I don't care. But just let me have my credit. It's all I want.'

Barry looks around the table of sullen faces, and then leers back at Russell.

'I think the fuckin' answer is no, mate.'

★   ★   ★

The meeting finishes on an uncomfortable note, the question of songwriting splits an unexploded time bomb. Russell departs before anyone else, still seething as he rides the Northern Line back towards Colliers Wood.

'This is worse than I feared,' he mutters. 'God. This is terrible. Ugh! The way Josh had *obviously* told Barry we'd agreed to it already! It's . . . *criminal!*'

But when he gets back to his little room, his email inbox is full of exciting things. A message from JJ72's tour manager, with technical information and stage times. Another from the gig's promoter, with security information, who to acquire triple A passes from, and a request for dietary requirements (as the official support band for the night, they have been included in the tour's catering rider). And then a couple of things from Barry: details of a photo shoot to take place in a few weeks' time, and of the potential tour with The Cooper Temple Clause.

Russell reads it all, then finds himself pacing frantically round his room, repeating a now much used, much pondered phrase.

'Everything I've ever wanted . . . but at a price.'

He grabs his acoustic guitar, sits and bangs out some savage chords for a few minutes – it sounds like The Vapors' 'Turning Japanese', but with Russell's own alteration after the chorus – then jumps back up and strides over to his computer.

'That's it,' he decides, sitting down and cracking his knuckles. 'I'm gonna give that yob a piece of my mind.'

He opens up his email page but then stops. A new message has just arrived.

'Ah,' Russell says. 'That name rings a bell . . .'

The email is short, but manages to effortlessly hoist Russell from the abyss.

DEATH OF AN UNSIGNED BAND

From: Miki Hayashi (miki@zinehead.co.uk)
Sent: 18 September 2001 22:18:45
To: russellcgroom@yahoo.co.uk
Subject: Portraits

Hello Russell

Miki from Zinehead here. I really enjoyed the Barfly show.

I hope you don't mind but Clem gave me your email address. I'd very much like to take your picture for a series of portraits I'm working on. I'm aiming to feature six songwriters, some established, some up-and-coming. So far I have taken shots of Matt Hales from the 45s and Gruff Rhys from the Super Furry Animals. I am in Paris right now but I will be back in time for your JJ72 gig, which I'll be coming along to. Perhaps we can find some minutes earlier that day to do it? I very much hope so.

Let me know whether this will work for you.

Best
Miki x

Russell reads it three times, his laughter increasing with each read. By the end, it borders on the maniacal. He skips across to the other side of the room and cracks open a new jar of Nescafé to celebrate.

Whitechapel

The day before the big Wimbledon gig: an unexpected occurrence.

A call from Jake.

'I know I've been ignoring your voicemails, fella. I haven't been in the mood to talk to anyone, to be honest with you. Needed a while to think and calm down. But I woke up yesterday morning with a blinding hangover and realised I've got things to say.'

It is now almost a month since Jake's dramatic exit from the band. He has not, reportedly, been in contact with any of them (apart from the occasional acerbic text message to Ash), but seems nonetheless well informed of their progress.

'Big show tomorrow night, so I've heard . . . moving pretty swiftly without the ol' ball and chain, then, eh? I've half a mind to buy myself a ticket, but I've got other things to do, thank fuck.'

Tonight he is attending a friend's gig at the Rhythm Factory, despite the previous inclusion of the club within his 'all those trendy wankholes' bracket. He suggests a drink beforehand. It is pouring with rain upon arrival in Whitechapel and the pub Jake has selected is small and very crowded. Black-clad, minus his summer beer paunch and oddly businesslike (even his hair has received something of a chop), he offers a curt, smile-free greeting and then insists on taking our drinks outside to a dripping alleyway, where he lights a roll-up and gets straight to the point.

'They know I'm hurt and furious – all of them – but probably none of them know pacifically *why*.'

Which is?

'Not cos they booted me out, and not cos they went behind my back . . . although all of that was fucking shitty. But I just can't *believe* they've chosen to replace me with such a fucking . . . useless prick. They've bloody ruined any chances of the band being really, truly great by settling for some half-arsed hooray knobhead. Who they can't've had any idea was any good or not.'

That's not completely true.

'Oh, what, maybe they'd listened to his *demo*? So they boot me out and get him in, on the strength of a fucking demo? That's it. Jake's out. After three years, Jake's out because they found someone with a famous dad and an OK demo. And I can just guess what he's like. Slick, capable, but square as fucking Sunbury. Characterless. Am I right?'

Not exactly.

'Soulless,' he continues. 'Voice like a Gillette commercial. No spontaneity. All planned, scripted – right up Russell's street. No emotion. And the fucking thing is – although it'd never occur to Russell in a million years – the precise thing Russell's songs *need* is emotion. They're supposed to be about . . . well, love and loss, right? Most of 'em. The best ones, anyway. Unrequited love. For you-know-bloody-well-who.'

Ah. You've noticed too.

'Course I've bloody noticed. He's *besotted* with the girl. Or at least – he thinks he is. The fact that him and Kazza would make about as perfect a couple as bloody Charles and Di is totally lost on him.'

It never appeared that you'd realised.

'No, I suppose it didn't. I'm actually quite discreet, did you know that? Diplomatic. I am capable of being discreet and diplomatic, despite what you probably think after Russell got his fangs into you.'

He takes a large gulp of his drink and gazes up the alley towards the main road, where a couple of buses fizz past. The rain continues to bucket down.

'You know . . . I was dead against this whole business of you following us around and taking notes.'

Yes.

'I just thought it'd be yet more bullshit. But then I figured out it might be useful.'

Because?

'Because someone from the outside world, someone none of us knew, would be able to come in and see for themselves . . . and I was *sure* that you'd notice what a pillock Russell was being.'

But the intention has never been to judge anyone's behaviour.

'I know that. But I thought you'd notice anyway. And instead . . .'

Instead?

'Well, you've hardly remained neutral, have you?'

I don't think that –

'I mean, you knew all about them giving me the bloody push, and never said a damn thing to me . . . Whatever. I just can't help feeling fucking shafted. By all of you.'

He stares down at an empty fast-food container lying in the sodden gutter for a few minutes.

'You see, the bloody problem with Russell is he's always treated me, and spoken about me, like I'm some total moron. An insensitive, uncultured moron. He thinks I don't understand . . . things. But I do! I know the way the world works. All right, so I drink and smoke too much, I'm lazy and I've got no willpower. But since when has that stopped someone from getting somewhere in the bloody *music* industry, for God's sake? If you ask me, I'm *far* more suited to a career in rock'n'roll than fucking Russell is. You know what the hoity-toity idiot said to me once? When he was on one of his bloody martyr missions? "I feel like I've committed myself to a career in an industry I neither like nor understand." What's the bloody point, then? *He's* the one fooling himself, if you ask me. Taking himself for a ride, right down the fucking . . .'

He trails off as two blokes in sopping rain jackets troop down the alleyway. Jake blows smoke at them as they push past, then quickly turns round and continues.

'And I *am* cultured. I know my music and my films. I know all about postmodernism. I like a bit of Van Gogh. I know my Renoirs from my . . . Impressionists. And classical music, which Russell also likes to think he's got a monopoly on. But I love a bit of Mozart. And anyway, Russell's not that bloody cultured himself. You've probably noticed, he hardly has any CDs. Never goes to the cinema. And he reckons just cycling up to the Tate Modern on a Sunday to hang out makes him at one with fucking art. But it's all bollocks.'

He looks at his watch hurriedly and exhales.

'Anyway, look, none of this is what I wanted to say. I'm just gutted, that's all. Gutted for Ash, gutted for Karen . . . gutted for me, of course. That it's all come to nothing. I said to Kaz – oh, ages ago, when we were pissed – if Russell ever decides to give me the push again, just make sure, for your own sake, that you don't settle for someone shit. But they have.'

He's actually –

'Well, whatever, even if he's fucking technically all right, I mean he's shit for *them*. Shit personality, shit attitude. Shit twat-head of a manager.'

This sounds a little like . . .

'Sour grapes? Sour fucking grapes? Go on, say it. Well, you're wrong. Being out of the band doesn't bother me. I should have left on my own . . . Sarah was right. I'm cool with it. I'm chilling. I've got plans. I'm actually thinking about going into business. You watch. I might open up a venue. S'what I've always wanted to do, really, you know that? Run a little venue, not in London, somewhere nice, deck it out, get on the tour circuit, invite some wicked bands down, have a few spliffs and beers with them and put on some cool nights. It might happen now. So I'm gonna be *well* fine, mate. No . . . I'm just gutted, because it's another great band down the drain. They could've at least got someone *better* than me. Isn't that the whole point? I'd have been fine with it. In the end. But we had something, y'know? The main concern should be to make the band as good as possible. And that's still important to me . . . whether I'm a member or not.'

That's laudable, but . . .

'But what?'

From an observer's point of view, it wasn't immediately apparent that . . .

'Spit it out.'

Making the band as good as possible didn't appear to be a particular concern of yours when you were *in* the band. Let alone now.

'Bullshit. What the hell gave you that idea?'

Some of your actions.

'Which ones?'

Oh, come on.

'What single fucking thing did I do that halted the progress of the band?'

Well, there —

'Nothing. I was just behaving like a normal, everyday guy in a rock band should. Having a laugh. Fucking about. Getting stoned and pissed. Rocking hard, playing hard. How could we've ever done a gig as good as the Big Joint if I was buggering everything up? And it was a *great* gig. The last great gig they'll ever do. But none of it's ever good enough for Russell, who thinks he's got the fucking "Becoming A Successful Pop Group" thermometer in his back pocket, and stupid Jake always pushes it right into the red. That's what drives me fucking insane! It's all being measured against bloody Russell's standards — and people believe him, trust him! Ash, Karen, and obviously *you* now as well! But fucking listen to me. This is fucking *crucial* for your final article, or whatever the fuck it is you're writing. I'll say it nice and slow, so that you can get it all down, OK? *Russell . . . hasn't . . . got . . . a . . . clue*! He hasn't! I could run off a list of twenty successful bands, right now, whose behaviour Russell would without a fucking doubt consider "*inappropriate*" and "*detrimental*". But it's all in his head! And he *poisons* people's minds with it, you know that? And *that's* why I destroyed his fucking guitar. Because he poisons people into believing stuff that he's basically made up to suit his own tight-fucking-fisted personality.'

Jake glares back up the alleyway one last time.

'Rock'n'roll's a messy fucking business, all sorts of ridiculous and crazy shit happens all the time – rows, fights, riots, overdoses, suicides – that's how it keeps going, if you ask me. But I'll say it again – Russell does not understand *any* of this! In Russell's world, absolutely nothing is messy, unplanned, spontaneous . . . and because of that, it's fucking *totally* lacking in passion. And so is *he*.'

Jake downs the last of his pint, parks the glass on a drainpipe, and marches back up the alleyway and out onto the rainy street. It's not too difficult to calculate that he does not wish to be followed, and that the conversation is over.

Wimbledon 3

JOSH: Man, I can't wait to get back on the road. I miss it so bad . . .

Did you do a lot of touring with your previous bands?

JOSH: Shit, yeah. In Hypotenuse we were on the road solidly for eighteen months.

Eighteen months? That's . . . a very long time.

JOSH: Yeah, dude.

So you must have toured a lot in other countries.

JOSH: Nah, man . . . we only went abroady just the once, did a big festie in the south of France, headlined the fucker . . .

Which one was that?

JOSH: St Tropez. Massive stadium there. Beachside. Twenty thousand peeps digging it as the sun went down.

So you were quite big in France.

JOSH: Yeah, boy. Top five. All over the radio like a fucking garden sprinkler.

Russell Groom turns left onto Wimbledon Broadway and marches along in the direction of the venue. It is half past four. He's not scheduled to arrive until half past five, but there's time for a bit of flouncing about, accidentally-on-purpose bumping into a few colleagues, rubbing it in. Plus he's still awaiting a text from Miki, the *Zinehead* photographer, to see what time she can do the photo shoot. ('What a nice text to be waiting for,' he sighs. 'This is how it *should* be . . .') He's already been to his favourite music shop (Gig Sounds on Mitcham Road) for plectrums and spare guitar strings – a performance-day ritual, whether he needs the items or not – and has also picked up a spare battery for his tuner pedal ('A spare-spare, actually – I'm never making *that* mistake again'). Now he strides along the busy street, his new Air France shoulder bag bouncing off his hips ('Not as many useful pockets,' he sighs, 'but Karen said it looked nice'), and soon the pavement widens slightly to make way for the elaborate old music hall which now calls itself the Wimbledon Imperial. Russell pauses, regarding with pride the large red letters declaring 'JJ72' (he put them up there himself, but never mind), quietly lamenting the fact Will Gibson didn't let him stick his own band's name underneath, and toys with the idea of snapping a quick photo. He eventually decides this would spoil the image of his nonchalant arrival somewhat, and continues round the corner of the alleyway to the stage door.

'Ahh!' smiles Harry, tonight's stage-door security guard. 'There he is!'

'Evening, Harry,' Russell smiles proudly. 'Any of my lot here yet?'

'Yeah, I think your tour manager is here . . .'

'Tour manager?'

'Yeah,' Harry replied, looking down the list of names. 'Bing, is it? Talks funny. He's out the back.'

'Ah, right! Thanks.' Russell turns towards the backstage area.

'Oh, and Russ, when you get a sec, a light bulb needs changing on –'

'Ha, you're funny, Harry . . . very funny . . .'

'Best of luck, my friend.'

Russell beams back at him and bounces off down the corridor.

The backstage area of the Imperial – a high-ceilinged, stone-floored, hangar-like space festooned with equipment, lights, ladders, ropes, pulley systems, enormous bits of scenery and endless flight cases – is the exclusive lair of Phil Preston, stage manager. Phil doesn't like Russell. It's probably because he views Russell as a competitor for the crown of most anal person working at the venue, although his dislike increased after the Great Joan Armatrading Name Misspelling Incident a few weeks ago, when Russell swore at him in the heat of the parking moment. Phil is here now, Damned T-shirt and newly shaved head, studying poor Bing with distrust as he fights with Ash's broken hi-hat stand: a very flimsy, amateur-looking item in the midst of all this grown-up steel, concrete and industrial black plastic.

'Hello, Phil!' Russell hoots, with unnatural enthusiasm.

'Hmm,' Phil responds. 'Just been chatting to your man here.'

'Oh yes? Hello, Bing, by the way.'

'Yeah, yeah, hi, Russ, hi . . .'

'He says he's your only crew member,' Phil states.

'Er . . . well, yes, he is.'

'I see. Well, I want no messing around after your set finishes. You're to get straight back onstage to take your gear off, OK? I don't care who you think you are.'

'Right,' Russell replies, unzipping Ash's cymbal bag. 'Well, thanks for that, Phil.'

'And remember – you still work here.'

'Yes, I remember that, Phil.'

'So if something needs doing over the course of the evening, and you're free, I still expect you to do it.'

Russell frowns at this.

'Er, probably not, Phil. Isn't Jamie doing my job tonight?'

'He's called in sick.'

'OK . . . well, I'm not really working tonight, y'see, so –'

'I know you're not, Russell. I'm just saying, if I'm in a spot and you're about, I might ask you.'

Russell's expression flattens.

'And I might say no.'

Phil narrows his gaze and flares his nostrils, then stalks off, straightening some boxes on a passing shelf.

Bing looks up at Russell with droopy eyes.

'He's er . . . he's not, er, not really welcoming, not welcoming, is he?'

'Nope,' Russell agrees, sliding a cymbal onto one of Ash's stands. 'Trouble is, he's kind of my senior here. I've never really worked out the precise relationship, but –'

'Russell,' Bing says, his speech for once free from excess baggage. 'Tonight, you are a rock star.'

Russell stops, nods and grins.

'Yes!' he says. 'Yes, I am.'

★   ★   ★

JOSH: Well, y'know . . . I *say* eighteen months . . . I mean, there were bucketloads of gigs stuffed into an eighteen-month period. I wasn't actually *physically* on the road for eighteen months! That would've been mentalist.

And the St Tropez stadium? I don't remember there being a stadium there.

JOSH: It's not a stadium exactly. It's like, y'know . . . the place where the holidaying peeps go to . . .

Go to?

JOSH: All right, what d'you want, dude? The fucking entertainment stage next to the holiday camp. Fuck it, though. The sun *was* going down, people were digging it, it *felt* like a fucking stadium. And you've gotta exaggerate a little in this game.

Of course.

Karen and Josh find Russell sitting in the dressing room – the tiny one on the top floor of the venue, but a dressing room nonetheless. Russell has had enough flouncing around the venue. It wasn't as much fun as he thought it was going to be.

'Everyone's too busy to comment, really,' he reports, staring out the window at a grey-skied view of the Wimbledon rooftops.

'I'm not surprised,' Karen replies, pulling open a bag of crisps from the little pile of refreshments that have been laid out for them. 'Honestly, if some twat came up to me while I was getting the bar ready and said "Hullo! I'm playing here tonight", I can't imagine even giving him four seconds.'

Josh sniggers and sparks up a cigarette. A tacit truce has prevailed between him and Russell over last week's songwriting argument. Still, Josh has continued his creeping alterations to the lyrics – Russell noticed at last night's rehearsal that the lyrics to 'You Brought It On Yourself' now feature the line:

'*Words that make you mad don't mean a thing*', instead of the original: '*Words that make us laugh don't mean a thing*', but was too busy helping Ash control his new click track to do anything about it.

'Nice bag, chap,' Josh comments, indicating Russell's new purchase.

'Thank you.'

'You might wanna scuff it up a bit, though – make it look like it ain't just come from the shop.'

Russell ignores Josh and extracts three bottles of Honey Dew from the item in question, then opens the little dressing-room fridge and frowns. No light has come on. He feels one of the bottles already inside.

'Isn't it working?' Karen asks.

'No,' Russell replies. 'I'm sure I changed the fuse in this one last week.'

'Ah, man . . .' Josh grimaces. 'Gotta have cold beer, dude.'

'Mmm,' Russell thinks. 'Maybe we should tell Will Gibson.'

'But Russ,' Karen reminds him, 'you know where the fuses are.'

'I do,' Russell nods. 'But . . .'

He pauses. Karen and Josh stare back at him.

'Josh,' Russell begins, 'perhaps *you* could go and ask Will Gibson?'

'Who is Will Gibson?' Josh asks distastefully, his voice going up a posh notch.

'The venue manager.'

'Your employer.'

'Well, yes . . . normally . . . but tonight . . .'

'Tonight what?'

'Well, I'm not really here, am I?'

Karen rolls her eyes.

'Russ, come *on*. You know exactly where the fuses are, it'd only take you five minutes –'

'I know, but that's not the point! I'm not here to –'

'– as opposed to Josh going to find Will, who he doesn't know, so he'd have to ask someone, and then they'd have to find him, and you know how hard that is sometimes, and then Will would in all probability come straight to find you and ask you to do it anyway.'

Russell growls and slams the fridge door.

'All right, fine, but this is the last damn thing of this nature I'm prepared to do.'

He huffs and leaves the room.

'Didn't you hear?' Josh deadpans to Karen. 'Damn is the new fuck.'

Karen smiles and brushes a lock of Josh's hair away from his eyes.

Russell lets himself into his little maintenance room and is fishing about for some fuses when his phone beeps. He whips it from his pocket and a little smile appears on his lips.

'My photo shoot,' he grins. 'She can only do it at seven thirty . . . might be a bit tight, we're on at eight thirty . . . ah well, never mind, should be OK . . .'

He finds the fuse and locks the little room again, hurrying back across the level-two auditorium as JJ72 finish their sound-check. He hurtles down the back steps to the stage door, hands the keys to Harry ('Oh, Russ! Loos are blocked on level three, haha . . .') and jumps into the lift to take him back up to the top floor, back to his dressing room and – most importantly – back into character. Just as the lift doors are closing, Mark

Greaney, JJ72's singer, embarks. Russell holds his breath. The doors are about to shut again when Will Gibson barges in. Finally the doors close and the rickety lift begins its ascent.

Russell's eyes dart about, his mouth alternately tightening and loosening. The lift reaches level one – if he's going to say something, he's only got about five seconds left to do so. Just before the level-two light comes on, he inhales and turns to the vocalist.

'Er . . . hi, I'm –'

'Aw, Russ,' Will Gibson suddenly says, 'remember to come and hoover my office later, will ya? Haha.'

The doors open and the other two get out, leaving Russell standing there with his mouth open.

JOSH: Oh, it was all circumstantial, of course. We were *hot*. The Eclectic – the U2 that never was. Hypotenuse – The Verve can go swivel, pal. We had the tricks, the hooks, the looks. But what can you do? The industry is the industry.

Did your label drop all their bands?

JOSH: What?

Did your label clear their entire roster?

JOSH: 'Course not.

So why do you think they dropped you and not others?

JOSH: Hey – do you think I know how these pillocks work? It's arbitrary, man.

So you're more confident of your chances this time?

JOSH: You watch, mate. The time has never been righter.

Barry strolls around the stage sipping a Red Bull. He eyes the pair of Honey Dew bottles lined up on top of Russell's amp and shrugs with moderate satisfaction, then turns his attention to the band's set-up. JJ72's equipment has been left in place, so Ash has squeezed his drum kit over to the far right while Russell's gear is over to the far left, and Barry is not certain he likes it.

'It's a bit fuckin' flat,' he moans. 'You're all in one long line along the front, like a fuckin' folk band.'

Russell stops tuning his guitar and examines the scene. Ash is indeed a very long way away from him; worrying, particularly as this is the first show with the artificially generated synth.

Josh turns from his mic and points.

'Russ, man, why don't you go over there?'

'What, *there*?' Russell replies, indicating a small space next to JJ72's drums, directly behind Josh.

'Yeah, chap. Might break it up a bit.'

'But . . . that'll look ridiculous! No one'll be able to see me.'

'Here we go,' Barry mutters under his breath. 'The ego has landed.'

'It's nothing to do with my ego,' Russell snaps. 'It'll just look terrible!'

'Nah, dude,' Josh signals, 'what about if I move along here a bit? Then you'll be between me and Karen, but slightly further back. Give it a bit of dynamism, man.'

Karen concurs. 'You'll be nearer to Ash too.'

Russell grumbles something about having never been positioned in this way during rehearsals, but looks at the clock (it is 6.40 p.m.) and, realising he is likely to be outvoted, starts shifting his equipment.

In the end, as is the traditional fate of the support band, they only have time to soundcheck one song ('Warning'). Bing takes longer than desired to familiarise himself with the monitor desk and Ash's click track initially misbehaves, but the eventual sound is crisp, fat and bowel-shakingly loud. The bad news is that Russell looks desperately awkward in his new place, and knows it.

'It looks fine, Russ,' Ash tells him, tightening the legs of his floor tom.

'How do you know?' Russell growls. 'You can't tell from where you're sitting.'

Russell jumps off the stage and trots a few metres back, then turns round to look.

'It's going to look *rubbish*,' he decides.

Karen and Josh have already wandered off, and Barry is also nowhere to be seen.

'I've a good mind to change it back.'

Ash rolls his eyes. 'Don't, Russ.'

'I'm going to!' Russell confirms, climbing back onto the stage.

'Russell, *don't*. Barry'll go mad.'

'Barry'll go *mad*?' Russell spits. 'Since when was Barry the authority here?'

'He's the manager,' Ash points out.

'He might currently be the manager, but he's not the *boss*, is he? I'm sick and tired of everyone thinking they have to do exactly as he says, as if he's the oracle! He's not *that* experienced!'

'Russ . . .'

'He's also a complete idiot!'

'For God's sake, man. It'd do you good to trust someone else's opinion occasionally.'

'Ash, I find it *so* annoying how subservient you can be some-times . . .'

Ash throws both his drumsticks at his snare drum, which responds with a clatter loud enough to make the bar staff turn to see what's going on.

'Yeah, go on, Russell. Ruin *this* one with an argument as well, just like at the Big Joint.'

Ash stomps off.

Russell looks up and realises where he is. He gazes around at the venue's grand interior, the lights, the ornate tiers, the painted ceiling and the rows of dark red seats on the upper levels – then sighs sadly, glances back at the stage, and wanders off without altering anything.

JOSH: You know what it's like, man. You're in a band with some dudes for what, two, three years, gigging your face off, spending half the time locked in a room trying to come up with the next 'Live Forever'. When that all comes toppling over onto its arse, it's difficult to start again with the same mob. You wanna clean slate, new faces, fresh blood. So no, I won't play with them again. But I get on fine with 'em. The old drummist came to see that show I did at the Monarch, or whatever the shit they call it now.

And what did he think?

JOSH: Same thing everyone thinks. The tunes are sweet and the bass player's schwee-*eet*.

Did you find your previous bands' personnel in the same way as this one?

JOSH: What, rocking up to a show and going with the flow? Yeah. Best way, man. Fucking about with adverts? It's beyond depressing.

But doesn't the 'showing up at a gig' method always necessitate firing someone?

JOSH (*grins, exhales smoke*): 'Fraid so, boss.

Doesn't that make you feel a bit of a . . . ?

JOSH: Parasite? Go on, say it. I'm a big boy. I can take the heat. I've had that shit levelled at me before. And you know what? No. Truth is, son, any band playing at the Half Moon, or the King's Head in fucking Fulham, or the Bull and fucking Gate, or any of them squareholes – they've gotta have something wrong with 'em in the first place. So I show up. I see them do their thing, and spot that loose screw – or in Jake's case, that major design fault – and see if it can be cranked. And usually, ninety-five clicks of the time, it's some turkey of a frontman who they'd need to send to Scunthorpe anyway. So all I really do is speed the process.

And this has happened three times now?

JOSH: Totally. And that's not counting the times when I've rocked up, dropped the bomb and then *not* ended up joining. Simply told 'em what they probably knew themselves anyway.

And none of this makes you feel particularly bad?

JOSH: No way, boss. Those turkeys were born to die.

Russell and Bing are sitting at a long table in the backstage bar, eating a plate of pasta. On the neighbouring table are two of the three members of JJ72 plus some of their crew, also chomping away. At the far end of the room some serving dishes are laid out, behind which a pair of cheerful caterers beaver away.

'It's funny,' Russell observes quietly. 'Before Josh joined, we had this singer called Jake, and if he was here now the first thing he'd do would be to bowl straight up to the other band and say hello.'

'Right, yeah, right,' Bing nods.

'And he'd probably end up chatting to them for ages, get invited to the after-show party, probably even get their phone numbers.'

'Is it . . . yeah, yeah.'

'But I can't do that sort of thing. I get all nervous . . . wouldn't know what to say.'

Bing considers this point while chewing a piece of garlic bread. Karen, Josh and Ash waltz into the room, survey the scene and amble straight up to JJ72's table.

'Hi . . . Mark, isn't it? . . . Like to introduce myself . . . Josh Chigwell . . . Karen . . . Ash . . . big fan . . . can't wait for to-night . . . thanks for having us along . . .'

Russell sighs and looks at his watch.

'Seven thirty,' he smiles, rising and pulling out his phone. 'At last.'

Russell reaches the edge of the pavement and sees Miki waiting across the street. She gives a little wave, which he returns, then signals that he'll come over to join her. After waiting for a 93 bus to trundle past, he crosses.

Miki is dressed in a Mercury Rev T-shirt and a little denim jacket. Her jet-black hair is tied in two bunches and she has surrounded her big brown eyes with some glittery make-up. A grey equipment bag is slung to one side of her. She grins at Russell as he approaches.

'Hello,' she says, holding out her hand in greeting.

'Hello, you,' Russell says – then must decide this is far too flirtatious, as he shakes her hand rather stiffly. Not that it appears to faze her. 'So . . . where would you like to do it?'

'Well, I normally try and take some natural snaps while we chat . . . nothing posed, just doing something that you feel comfortable doing? Having a drink, a coffee?'

'A coffee,' Russell laughs. 'Now you're talking my language.'

They decide to go to Russell's usual café, just a few doors down. There is nothing trendy nor remotely distinctive about it, so Russell knows it will be empty. Russell orders his usual, and a herbal tea for Miki, then puts his phone on 'silent' and positions himself where his face benefits from the light of the street windows.

'I've never really done this before,' he confesses. 'Not by myself, anyway.'

'Well, don't worry!' Miki chuckles, adjusting a few settings on her camera. 'It will be nothing . . . complicated. Just behave as if the camera isn't here.'

This well-intentioned comment has the predictable effect of clamming Russell up completely. Miki laughs and tries an ice-breaker.

'So . . . how long have you guys known about *Zinehead*?'

'Oh, a long time [*click!*] . . . Marko and Clem approached Karen when we [*click!*] . . . did a gig at the Spitz [*click!*] in . . . erm . . . '99 I think?'

'Right! Before my time.'

'I see . . . you've [*click!*] . . . not been with them long then?'

'Just a year.'

'Ah! Just a year! It's a very good [*click!*] fanzine.'

'Thank you,' Miki says. 'I like it. Not too pretentious.'

A transatlantic edge to her voice comes and goes; the result, Russell later discovers, of a year spent studying in San Francisco.

'You're looking so serious!' she grins.

'Am I?' Russell frowns, sitting up straight.

'Yes,' she nods, lowering her camera. 'And now you've made it much worse. Relax. Sit back, like you would if you were here on your own.'

'Oh . . . well, I'm sorry . . . I suppose I'm not that relaxed a person.'

'Come on,' Miki smiles. 'Talk about something . . . nice. Tell me about some music.'

'Music?'

'Yes, you know – that stuff that you play sometimes. Tell me . . . your favourite bits in some pop songs.'

'My favourite bits,' he repeats.

'The bits which make your spine tingle.'

This works. Russell sips his drink and thinks, then his answer emerges in a veritable torrent of pop.

'Um . . . well . . . ah . . . the chord progression in the chorus of "Shake the Disease" by Depeche Mode [*click!*]. The four drum flams before the loud bit of "Come As You Are" by Nirvana. The choppy acoustic rhythm guitar on "Mrs Robinson" – *The Graduate* soundtrack version [*click!*]. McCartney's bass frills on "Paperback Writer". The pre-chorus of "Rush Hour" by Jane Wiedlin [*click!*], possibly the best pre-chorus ever. The extended outro of "Like A Prayer" by Madonna. The drum part on "The Swing of Things" by a-ha. The percussion in the early section of "Paranoid [*click!*] Android" by Radiohead. Everything Radiohead ever do, really. The piano part on "Summer Night City" by Abba [*click!*]. The chorus of "Take the Long Way Home" by Supertramp. The synth [*click!*] loop on "Girls & Boys" by Blur. The way the chorus of Elliott Smith's "Sweet Adeline" only occurs [*click!*] once. The way Beck's voice cracks in the second verse of "Deadweight". The guitar solo on "Alive" by Pearl Jam. The [*click!*] outro to "Cave" by Muse. The hand-claps on "The Cedar Room" by Doves. The drum sound on "Race for the Prize" by The Flaming [*click!*] Lips. "True Colours" by Cyndi Lauper – the whole song [*click!*]. Is that enough?'

'Wow,' Miki murmurs. 'That's one way of using half a roll of film.'

'Any common ground?'

'Elliott Smith,' she replies, fishing around in her bag. 'OK. So just for fun . . . tell me about your *least* favourite bits. The bits that make your spine shiver.'

'OK,' Russell grins, leaning back. 'Let's think . . . bands who completely alter the way they perform songs live, to the point where you can't even recognise the [*click!*] melody of the chorus. The drumming on all White Stripes records. Middle eights that sound like they're just there for the sake of it. Songwriters who [*click!*] recycle their own chord progressions. Pointless chord changes, particularly the change to "B" in the chorus of "Light My Fire" by The [*click!*] Doors . . . ugh! The horn part on "The Lady In My Life" by Michael Jackson. Any song which [*click!*] actually mentions the name of the band singing it, especially "Joyride" by Roxette.'

'Hmm . . . interesting.'

'Sorry. Probably going on far too long.'

'No, no! I was just thinking . . . it's interesting how your face looked much happier when you were talking about the things you didn't like.'

'Oh. Does that make me seem terribly negative?'

'No, it's nice to be a little opinionated. Especially when you know what you're talking about. Some people never have anything interesting to say.'

Miki plays with some of her camera's controls for a moment while Russell gazes out of the window.

'How was Josh, then?' Russell enquires.

'Josh?'

'Our, um . . . singer. As a photo . . . erm . . . subject. At the Barfly.'

'He was fine.'

'Nice-looking guy, I should think.'

'Uh, yes,' Miki confirms, a strange expression crossing her face.

'Was he . . . interesting?'

Miki puts on some black-rimmed glasses and scribbles in her notebook, but doesn't answer.

'Sorry,' Russell says, returning to his straightened-up position. 'Shouldn't pry.'

'No,' Miki nods, looking up and smiling sweetly at Russell. 'Perhaps you shouldn't.'

JOSH: No, I haven't got another job. And if I had, it'd be something real, as opposed to these rent-paying pieces of shit the others are saddled with. I mean, come *on*, man! Spending thirty hours a week, or whatever it is, in a fucking *call centre*? Give me the fucking gas pipe now, dude.

What would you do, then?

JOSH: Well, something in the bloody music industry, for a start. I mean, isn't that a no-brainer? I've been in this industry longer than most of the twerps working at the labels as it is – I'd be able to spin plates around the dozy pricks.

A job like that isn't necessarily easy to come by.

JOSH: For who? I'd have *no* problem, pal. I've already been offered jobs! Fucking industry's crying out for peeps who know their shit, who've seen it from the other side of the mixing desk. Why the others don't go for this kinda slot is beyond me, man.

Some would argue that to work in the same industry as where their ultimate dream lies might be too close for comfort.

JOSH: Nah, fuck that. Depends how you rock it, dude.

Karen and Russell seem to find it tricky, on occasion.

JOSH: Huh? Karen and Russell don't work in the fucking

music industry, man! Gimme a break. That's like saying someone who hoovers the floor at J.P. Morgan is a merchant banker. I mean, Christ . . . I'm not surprised they find it fucking depressing, arsing around below stairs in this pile of rotten bricks, while utter Normans like Badly Drawn Boy peddle their shite. Good God. You know what Russell said was one of his fondest memories, working here? Being told a joke by Mark King from Level 42 while he was emptying his dressing-room *bin*. Jesus wept. I'd go straight home and neck an entire packet of painkillers. So, the answer's fucking no, man. None of these fucking monkey day jobs for me, thanks very much.

So how do you support yourself?

JOSH: That's a bit of a fucking personal question, isn't it? I thought this was meant to be a music interview.

Miki plonks her camera on the table and looks Russell straight in the eye.

'OK,' she winces, 'let's put professionalism aside . . . he was *horrible*. He was creepy, he kept calling me babe. And he had *nothing* to say for himself.'

The faintest smile appears on Russell's face as he sips from his cup. 'You don't say.'

'And he knew nothing about your band! I mean, I know he's only been with you, how long?'

'Three weeks,' Russell puffs, scratching his head.

'But he knew nothing! He barely knew your drummer's *name*! You'd always find out a little about the people you're gonna play with, wouldn't you?'

'Well, I'd have thought so. But . . . oh, Josh, he's not terribly interested in other people. Maybe that's the mark of a good frontman, though? Complete self-absorption?'

'I don't know. Sorry, but he didn't seem very interesting. I asked him a question, the standard *Zinehead* question which I ask everyone to try and relax them – and he could *not* answer.'

'What's the question?'

'"What does it all mean?"'

Russell sniggers into his coffee.

Miki shrugs. 'It's not very good, I know, but it usually provokes some interesting facial expressions. But Josh . . . Josh just . . . laughed at it. Not even charmingly, just, well . . . mockingly.'

Russell stops sniggering.

'What would you have said?' Miki asks.

Russell blinks at her. 'What would *I* have said?'

'Yes.'

'Is that you actually asking me the question, or you asking me what I would have said?'

Miki giggles. 'Is there a difference?'

Russell glances around the cafe for a moment and then grins.

'Yes, there is a difference. Ask me again.'

'OK,' she mutters, picking up her camera once more. 'What would you have said?'

Russell leans back and puts on a pompous rock-star voice.

'Well, Miki, I would have said that . . . what it all means is . . . breaking down the barriers between the audience and the band, becoming one with the music, opening your mind to the myth-ical majesty of [*click!*] rock'n'roll, peace and love, feed the world.'

'Fabulous,' Miki smiles.

'And the real question?'

'Right,' she replies, adopting a mock-serious expression and pretending to use her teaspoon as a microphone. 'Russell Groom. Songwriter. Guitarist. Multi-instrumentalist. What does it all *mean*?'

Russell gathers himself, takes a deep breath to answer, then exhales sadly.

'I don't have the slightest idea.'

Karen strides into the dressing room at five to eight, so sure of who will already be in there that she doesn't even look up.

'Ahh . . . such nice guys. You should have come and chatted to 'em with us, Russ. They've invited us all to the after-show. They're so fucking young, though, it makes me . . .' – but she finds herself speaking to an empty room. 'Russ? Are you in the loo?'

Silence.

'How bloody peculiar.'

Ash is next through the door.

'Christ, she's fit,' he mutters – presumably concerning JJ72's own female bass player.

'Aw, go and have a cold shower, cockhead.'

'Where's Russ?'

'Just thinking the same thing,' Karen replies. Ash settles down with a beer and a roll-up while Karen presses her mobile to her ear. 'Russ, it's Kaz . . . it's almost eight o'clock, dunno where you are . . . hope you ain't got yourself caught up in some work bollocks . . . we're all here . . . well, not Josh, he's still got his head up Hilary Woods's arse, but . . . anyway, see you soon . . .'

Barry mooches into the room, also glued to his phone.

'Yeah . . . Well, not tonight, mate, obviously, but . . . Just come an' see what the potential is . . . Yeah, needs a lot a' work . . .' – Karen shoots an irritated glance at Ash; now Josh saunters in, quickly catches the drift of Barry's conversation and listens attentively – 'Yeah, my boy's fine . . . Drummer's OK . . . Yeah, female bassist . . . Yeah, mate, workable . . . but the guitarist still looks like he's on fuckin' *Play School*, d'you know what I mean? . . . Nothing that a four-month tour with Mogwai couldn't sort out . . .'

'Speaking of Russell . . .' Josh says, turning to Karen.

'S'OK,' she tells him. 'Just called him. He won't be far.' She nods in Barry's direction and hisses. 'Who's he talking to?'

'Booking agent,' Josh replies.

'Nah,' Barry continues. 'Not my cup of tea, but that ain't important . . . Yeah, well, they'd probably sign my auntie banging a few saucepan lids together right now, so . . . Cool, I'll stick you on the list, and try to get here for the start, I've made 'em play the couple of half-decent ones up front, so you don't have to bother with the other shite . . .'

'Does he realise we're actually in the room?' Karen asks Josh, quite loudly.

'Shh . . . he's just doing his thing,' Josh smiles.

Barry hangs up and helps himself to a beer.

'Where's the other one?' he grunts.

'What,' Karen scowls, 'Russell . . . Russell Groom, the guitarist and songwriter of this band? Composer of the "other shite"?'

'Aw, don't worry about all that, love, I'm just talkin' to 'em like they're used to.'

'Charming.'

'Anyway, where is the silly bleeder? Only half an hour to go.'

'Dunno,' Karen thinks, extracting her phone again and starting to text. 'It's unusual.'

Five minutes later Karen has yet to hear back from the elusive songwriter. Barry, who has spent the meantime stretched out on the dressing-room sofa enjoying one of Ash's joints, swings his feet back onto the lino floor and looks at his watch.

'OK, guys, it's five past and I've gotta get down to start

licking arses, so . . . I wanted to say a coupla things beforehand . . . Christ knows where that tit's got to but I ain't fuckin' repeating all this so you'll have to tell him for me.'

'I'm calling him again,' Karen says.

'Nah, don't worry, sweetheart, he'll turn up, he's probably researching songwriting percentages or something [Josh chuckles, Karen and Ash do not]. Anyway – you've gotta forget about the fact you're supporting JJ72. Just go out there and act like it's yer own fuckin' show. I don't want any reference to 'em whatsoever. Try an' speed up the gaps between songs. You won't have to fuck around with the synth, so that should help. Josh ain't gonna say a fuckin' word, so just bang through it. And I don't want any of that fuckin' jumping up and down . . . that's all a bit sixth form for the kinda knobs I've got here tonight. You gotta be a bit more fuckin' dignified, d'you know what I mean . . . and at the end of the set – and this is really fuckin' important, all right? – your gear is brought off by Bing and the local crew. Bing's already asked 'em about this. I don't want *any* of you guys goin' back onstage. That lot'll bring it all off. Got it?'

A mumble of agreement.

'OK. I'm gone. Laters.'

Barry leaves the room. Karen smiles sarcastically at her bandmates.

'Oh, and by the way – best of luck, everyone! Have fun! Hope you enjoy it!'

Amid the subdued laughter, Karen dials Russell's number once more.

JOSH: You've gotta play these cocks at their own game. There's no point whatsoever in being nice. To anyone. You can be sweet

to you and yours, obviously – within the ol' fraternal band
circle, that is, and perhaps to your manager . . . although thankfully Bazza's such a blunt bastard that you don't need to bother
– but otherwise, they're all just potential employees, man. That's
the first hole Russell and that lot fall down. They talk to an
A & R, or whoever, like they're conversing with some sort of
hallowed being – whereas they should just be viewing them
like someone who they'll eventually sack. When a band gets
signed, they do *not* become employed by the record company.
They don't get a pay packet at the end of the month. They
get a chunk of cash to do what the fuck they like with, and
the record company had better work its *pants* off to ensure they
make back every penny. So they need to be told who they're
dealing with from day one. And that includes everyone – road
crew, press agents, promoters, journos. They're just all useless
dicks who need to be shouted at, or absolutely nothing gets
done.

One of the saddest fucking stories I've had the displeasure
to be told since joining this band is the drummist's tale of woe
about Colin Cosgrove from Bean and Gawn . . .

Yes, Ash mentioned that.

JOSH: He did, right? Did you not, like, immediately get out
your violin and then throw up all over it? Give me fucking
strength, dude. I mean, I like Ashy, he's a gent, but that story
exemplifies everything that's been wrong with this band in the
past. You know what Ashy shoulda done? Or more accurately,
what he should *not* have done? Number one – contact the
prick in the first place. I mean, what the fuck was he expecting?
Friendship? Number two – gone up to him at the Dublin
Castle show. Let these fools come to *you*, man! Number three
– oh, the fucking desperate, cardinal, please-please-like-me sin

of all fucking sins – *gone up to him again*. Dear oh lor. Having made those three major mistakes, and with us now getting a bit of our own love from B 'n' G, I would now sit Barry down, tell him to email the company, saying that if they wanna come within a line of coke's distance of any trade with us, they'd better make darn sure Cosgrove instantly loses his fucking job for having the *nerve* to ignore one of our members at a gig.

Do you think they'd do it?

JOSH: 'Course not, but that doesn't matter. It'd tell 'em we mean business, that Ashy ain't a pushover, and it'd put B 'n' G in a nicely awkward position where they'd have to negotiate. For one thing, it'll ensure they never stick Cosgrove on a fucking job with us.

Did you suggest this to Ash?

JOSH: Too fucking right I did, but of course he said no. So now he'll have to feel like an utter goon when Cosgrove eventually comes up to him, or works with him . . . like he's been socially anal-fisted, just because some coked-up Norman can't be arsed with being civil. See? Being nice doesn't ever fucking work.

It's now ten past eight and Karen is racing down the back steps of the venue while Russell's phone rings and rings.

'OK . . . it's me again. Now I'm beginning to worry. I don't know what the fuck's going on, but . . . try and let us know *something* . . . like, if you're having a panic attack or something, or if you're pissed off, or whatever . . . just phone me so we can talk it through. Remember, this is our chance tonight. The thing we've been going on about for years. Don't let's fuck it up. I know Josh gets on your tits and that you hate Barry, he's hardly my favourite human being either, but . . .'

By this point she has reached the backstage area, yet another zone conspicuously free from Russell. Bing skulks around, shaking his unruly brown locks, sucking on the same bent roll-up he seems to have had for hours.

'Anyway, call me back, or just get your arse back here.' She hangs up. 'Bing. You seen Russ?'

'No, for a while, not for a while, no. Dinner, not since dinner.'

'You had dinner with him?'

'Yeah, pasta, plate of pasta. Said he had a photo shoot, had to go for a photo shoot.'

Karen blinks at Bing.

'A *photo shoot*?'

A further ten minutes pass before Russell, finally reminded of the time, looks at his phone and is rudely awoken from his pleasant conversational dream.

'Twenty past eight! Good *God*! Twelve missed calls!'

Russell phones Karen back as he and Miki rush out of the café and wait to cross to the Imperial side of the street. His tone of distinct nonchalance must be driving Karen mad at the other end.

'Yup . . . Yes, I know it is . . . No, it's OK . . . No, it's fine! I'm just coming! . . . Oh, nothing, just popped out . . . Photo shoot? Well, yeah, if you must know . . . Miki from *Zinehead* . . . No, not for the magazine, personal project . . . Well, because I didn't . . . Sorry . . . You all looked pretty wrapped up talking to JJ72 before, so I didn't bother to interrupt . . . Yeah, be there soon.'

He shrugs back at Miki.

'Better get my skates on.'

They cross the road.

'Well, it was nice!' Russell comments.

'Yes! It was fun.'

'You've got a pass?'

'Sure have,' Miki replies, showing her press laminate. They march straight up to the busy front of the venue – the security guard recognises Russell and lets them both through – then they stop inside the bustling foyer.

'Well, I hope you enjoy the show,' Russell says, 'and, um . . .'

Miki raises her eyebrows and cocks her head slightly to one side.

'Ah . . . um . . . well, there's probably going to be quite a few interesting things ahead for us, potentially, um, getting signed and so on, so maybe you'd like to do this again sometime . . . perhaps another, more detailed shoot? Possibly with the, um . . . others?'

'That sounds fabulous,' Miki replies.

'Right!' Russell smiles. 'Great!'

'I'm going to Berlin tomorrow, back on Sunday, so maybe gimme a call after that?'

'You're going to Berlin? Wow . . . Paris, London, Berlin . . . didn't quite realise *Zinehead*'s budget was so . . . um . . .'

'Oh, no,' Miki laughs. 'I'm not going with *Zinehead*. It's for my proper job, for Amnesty?'

'Ah,' Russell nods. 'Right. That must be . . . um . . . interesting?'

'Yes, very. Actually,' she frowns, 'that was another thing Josh couldn't understand. He kept asking me what I *wanted* to do, as if Amnesty was some rent-paying admin job that I obviously couldn't wait to get rid of . . . he didn't seem to register that someone might want to do something of non-direct profit to themselves . . .'

'Hmm,' Russell thinks. 'Well, I think we're all a bit guilty of that . . .'

His phone rings again.

'Listen, I have to . . .'

'Yes, you do. Go on – good luck!'

They shake hands again, a slightly unsure look crossing Russell's face.

'Sayonara,' he mutters. Miki's face instantly lights up.

'Sayonara!' she beams.

Russell smiles back and dashes through a little door next to the box office.

It is only now – now that he fiddles around with the code lock which lets him into the main auditorium – that it hits Russell how finely he is cutting it.

'Damn, damn!' he shouts, mucking up the code for the second time. 'Stupid thing, what a stupid . . .'

He strikes the correct code and pushes the door, which leads into a fire-escape stairwell, then flings open a second door on the opposite side and finds himself at the rear of the ground floor. And it is packed. And hot. Punters fill the room right to the very back – drinking, smoking, chatting loudly, while the new Eels album bubbles from the PA. As forcefully as Russell can without pushing people over, he squeezes his way through the crowd until he reaches some steps which lead past the toilets and on to a staff corridor, taking him straight to the backstage area. He leaps up the steps, skirts around the small queue forming outside the Ladies' loo, winks at the female security guard who stands by the 'Staff Only' door ('Break a leg, Russell,' she says), and bursts through to the other side.

And here . . . is Phil Preston.

Russell's arch-rival.

Marching along the corridor, flaring nostrils to the fore.

And behind him . . . a girl in a motorised wheelchair.

'Ah, Russell, there you are. Been looking for you. This young lady needs to use the accessible toilet, so please take her along if you'd be so kind.'

'I can't, Phil – I'm meant to be onstage!'

'Well, that's all right, Russell, because I'm meant to be giving the signal for the house lights to go down, so I need to be there before you do.'

'Phil, I –'

'Russell, please don't let's have an argument about who takes this lady to the accessible toilet. She's sitting right here and you'll embarrass all of us, particularly her.'

'Phil! I am not w—'

'Russell, if we weren't standing here arguing you'd have done it by now, wouldn't you? So there's a good man –'

'I'm *not* bloody *working* tonight, Phil!'

The girl looks up at Russell, and smiles affably. 'I'll be quick, I promise.'

Russell's phone rings again. He looks at Phil, who is almost smiling. Then he looks at his flashing phone: *Karen*, of course. Finally, he looks back at the girl, whose affable smile is understandably receding.

'OK, OK! Let's go.'

The accessible toilet is back through the 'Staff Only' door ('Ain't you meant to be onstage now?' frowns the female security guard as Russell reappears), past the loos and out yet another door leading to a little anteroom, containing the ice machine. Russell holds the door and watches the girl wheel herself through, then leaps across the anteroom and pounds another combination code into the little keypad next to the accessible toilet's entrance. It unlocks, he pulls it open, the girl enters. And now, for lack of anything else to do, Russell waits.

And waits.

And waits.

A volley of just-made ice comes cannoning out of the machine.

Russell waits.

The strip lighting buzzes. More ice materialises.

Then Russell's phone rings again. *Josh*, this time. He considers answering, but must realise there is nothing to say. Nothing that could be understood, anyway. The clock on the corner of the screen says 20:32.

He rubs his face with both hands and hums softly to himself – it sounds like 'Onward, Christian Soldiers' – then listens breathlessly as the loo flushes on the other side of the door.

Then, on the opposite side of a different door, the unmistakable sound of applause from the Imperial's audience.

'No,' Russell gasps. 'They can't!'

The machine coughs out some more ice and his phone rings again. *Morgan*. Russell snaps it up.

'What?'

His phone does that peculiar thing of replicating the exact sound heard on the other side of the wall – plus Morgan's voice, shouting: *'Where the fook are ya, Groom? They're comin' on, but you ain't there!'*

'I know, I'm . . . delayed . . .'

Well, what else is there to say?

'Delayed? What d'ya fookin' mean, delayed?'

Not a conversation worth continuing, Russell hangs up, then – at last – the toilet door unlocks.

'Sorry,' grins the girl. 'Wasn't too long, was I?'

'No,' Russell squeaks. 'You were fine. Let's go.'

Back through the door to the toilet corridor, back past the security guard, just as the DAT-generated synth intro to 'You Brought It On Yourself' rings out across the venue. Russell thumps open another door on the left, leading to the viewing platform, and holds it open for the girl. He shuts his eyes as she wheels herself past, knowing that the view of the stage from this angle would be almost unbearable. But then he stops. Perhaps he realises there's no point in running on once the song has already started, or maybe he's been gripped by a warped desire to confront the sight before him. So he looks. Not only does he look, but he actually lets the door swing shut behind him and shuffles even further onto the platform, deeper into the darkened theatre. He casts his eyes over the three people now standing before him onstage, in perfect formation, spookily lit up by the venue's lights as though their presence is solely for his benefit. Karen, shiny black shirt, knee-high boots, cranking out a hefty sound from her bass guitar as her eyes close in concentration. Ash, in perfect sync with his bass counterpart, whacking out the simple beat to the first verse, while Josh – rich of throat and lustrous of hair – enunciates the words which wrap themselves around the delicately constructed melody.

A Russell Groom melody.

And this is Russell Groom's band.

But Russell Groom is not onstage.

Nor, for some unfathomable reason, does he seem of a mind to be.

As the packed theatre listens, there is an emptiness to the music – no, a sparseness, nothing throwaway, nothing missing, everything in its correct place, and as the pre-chorus swells up the audience appears to swell with it, until finally the three musicians rip their way into the chords and lyrics of the chorus, and the sound rolls all the way to the back of the Wimbledon Imperial.

> *What makes you think you're fooling us*
> *Cos we can see straight through it*
> *So just drag it out another year*
> *Convince yourself you like it*
> *Don't look around the room for someone to blame*
> *because*
> *You brought it on yourself*
> *yeah*
> *You brought it on yourself.*

Russell watches, transfixed, for a minute longer, before tearing his gaze away from the stage.

'Now that's what I *call* an epiphany,' he mutters, turning around to dash back through the door.

Just over thirty minutes later, the post-mortem in the dressing room presents a new scene from a familiar angle. Russell, for once almost totally in the wrong, shields himself from unanimous admonishment by reverting to his very own stereotype: total mule-headedness, complete refusal to accept he was at fault whatsoever, and the resolve to argue until the sun comes up, if necessary.

'I think you're all making far too big a deal out of this,' he breezes, his feet up on the dressing-room sofa, sipping from one of his bottles. 'The show was a success, right?'

'Only fuckin' just,' Barry grumbles.

'And how many bands play the occasional song where a certain member isn't needed? It happens all the time.'

'Oh, that's so *convenient*, Russell,' Karen remarks angrily.

'But what could I have done? Tell me that.'

'I know what I'd have fuckin' done,' Barry mutters.

So far Josh has been busy holding his beer bottle, still not chilled to his requirements, up to the element of the fridge's freezer compartment, but now weighs in.

'The thing that killed me, dude, was the expression on your face as you walked on! You were *smiling*, man!'

'From ear to fuckin' ear,' adds Barry.

'Well, what would you have preferred me to do? Come onstage scowling? The way I did it, it looked like it was meant to happen. "Ah, there's the second guitarist, who doesn't play during the first song."'

'Two of my fuckin' most valuable contacts,' Barry sneers, 'turned straight round to me and said, "Who the fuck's that, where the fuck's he come from, and why the fuck wasn't he there during the first song?" It was a fuckin' shambles. I'm amazed they all stayed 'til the end.'

'But they did.'

'Yeah, mate, they did – to see you do the two precise things I fuckin' told everyone not to do.'

(Russell, slightly dismayed that Josh hadn't uttered a single word to the audience, took matters into his own hands as the band left the stage and offered his own sign-off: 'Thanks for watching, everyone, and cheers to JJ72 for having us along.' He then completed his trio of errors by returning to carry off his own amp.)

'Well, I wasn't here when you told everyone not to do them.'

'I fuckin' know you weren't, mate.'

'Perhaps if you had something as important as that to say, you should have said it sooner.'

Barry's face twists into his standard expression of astonished contempt, but he decides not to rise to the bait.

Karen turns to Russell and shakes her head disapprovingly.

'This is just so unlike you, Russ,' she moans. 'I can't believe it. Not tonight. I mean, *tonight*, Russell.'

Russell glares back at her, then quickly gets up from the sofa to deliver his Miki-inspired uppercut.

'Well, I personally think this is indicative that the whole lot of you are all losing sight of reality, to be frank. We went down well, we played brilliantly, but you're so wrapped up getting somewhere in this crazy industry that you can't see that people are sometimes required to do something of non-direct profit to themselves.'

The room erupts with screams of ferocious indignation, Karen's by far the loudest.

'Oh, just listen to yourself, Russell! If the you of six weeks ago could hear you talking now, he'd be horrified. He'd puke! He'd call a fucking psychiatrist!'

'Well, perhaps it was the me of six weeks ago who needed the psychiatrist.'

As usual, it is down to Ash to make the sanest, most concise observation on the fiasco.

'Either way, mate, I've gotta say – I really think you could've been more on the case from the word go tonight. I mean, come on, fella – still being photographed? In a café, across the road – *five minutes* before our onstage time?'

'Ten minutes.'

'Well, ten minutes, even – at a gig of this importance? You *know* you'd go potty at one of us if we'd done that.'

'And you'd have bloody crucified Jake,' leers Karen, unable to resist.

Gradually the frenzy of rapprochement subsides. Barry sits on the edge of the sofa and informs them, via his usual snooze-inducing drone, that the interested parties have now reduced from seven to two in number, but that the two in question have both promised to put something 'on the table' by Friday afternoon at the latest.

'Wow,' Karen comments. 'So fast?'

'Yeah,' Barry nods. 'It's partly cos of what happened earlier in the month [one presumes he is talking about September the Eleventh] . . . a lot of the A & Rs wanna get their deals sealed as fast as they can before the budgets get pulled. And I suggest we follow suit.'

'Any clues as to who it is?' Ash enquires.

'One major and one indie,' Barry divulges.

'Eluxor?' asks Russell. Barry ignores him and continues his monologue.

'So . . . otherwise . . . I thought the DAT worked all right . . . you all looked fine, the sound was adequate, and apart from the obvious total fuck-ups' – he pauses here, takes a sip of beer and winks at Josh – 'the performances were good. Anything else, we can talk about another time. Now, for fuck's sake, let's go and get pissed.'

Russell maintains his aloof expression as Karen, Ash, Josh and Barry gather their drinks and head for the level-one bar, but drops his guard as soon as the door closes. He casts a dejected eye around the room, sighs, opens the fridge and extracts another bottle of Honey Dew. Then his phone beeps with the arrival of a text message, which succeeds in making him smile, but then sad again.

'It's from Miki.'

Congratulatory?

'Well, no . . . apologetic. *"Sorry if I made you late — you were supposed to be gone for that first song, right?"* And an "X". Whoop-de-doo.'

He sits for a second, then hears the faint, muffled sound of the audience cheering.

'Come on,' he sighs. 'Better go and see what the fuss is all about.'

For the remainder of the evening Russell cuts a lonely, bemused figure as he wanders around the venue. He stands watching JJ72 in his usual place – to the right of the stage by an emergency exit, next to one of the friendlier members of security – and for a while seems to enjoy the Irish trio's sprint through their recent album and a few new tracks, but then gets bored and mooches off.

'I was trying to see what it is about them,' he confides. 'The "thing", the "it" factor. But I don't know what that is any more. All the songs sound the same anyway.'

Eventually he makes an appearance in the level-one bar, filled with industry types and others who have perhaps also found JJ72's repertoire a little monotonous. Russell is ignored by most of his busily schmoozing band, but finds Ash in a far corner, surreptitiously rolling a joint. Ash moves along the seat a little, indicating for Russell to sit.

'Sorry, Ash,' Russell begins.

Ash looks up. 'Really?'

'Yes, of course. That was a catastrophe.'

'Well,' Ash shrugs, 'it's all right, fella. We was all a bit stressed, I guess.'

Russell fixes his drummer with a serious look and finds himself, for the second time, repeating some of Miki's words from earlier.

'What does it all mean, Ash?'

'Whassat?'

'I mean, we've been doing this for years, and now it's looking like it's all going to happen. But what does it all really mean?'

Ash sniggers, a little stoned now. 'Fella. Wasn't expecting to have such an exist . . . existen . . .'

'Existentialist.'

'Yeeah, one of them . . . at this point in the evening.'

'I know. But . . .'

'It's all music, Russ. You gotta remember that. We're gonna be playing music whatever goes on. And, y'know, we all get caught up in the whole ambition thing . . . even me. I surprised myself with all that Tom Shitesmann stuff . . . but if none of this ends up happening, for whatever reason . . . or if none of it ever *did* happen in the first place . . . I'd still be playing it. And so would you, mate . . .'

'Yes, I would,' Russell concedes.

'Although . . . sometimes I think you forget . . . you forget that's what we're here for. I mean . . . I dunno whether you, um . . . but I've always played music with a couple of other mates on the weekend, for a laugh, just bashing about in the guitarist's front room, never any intention of getting anywhere . . .'

'Yes, I don't know how you do that.'

Ash takes a drag of his roll-up and laughs.

'Russ, mate, you crack me up. You don't know how I do it?'

'No. Playing music with . . . no purpose.'

'Fella. There's all the purpose in the world. We're the

fuckin' stars of that front room, man. You should come along and watch. By the end of the afternoon we're knackered.'

'But,' Russell blinks, 'say you've had a really exceptional session one week. Doesn't anyone ever say . . . "We could try getting somewhere with this"?'

Ash chuckles. 'Naah. The moment one of us says something like that, we'll know it's time to knock it on the head.'

Russell shakes his head slowly, somewhat dazed.

'I can't imagine that,' he murmurs.

'But think about it, Russ. How did you start?'

'How . . . how did I start? The guitar?'

'Yeeah.'

'I just . . . told myself I wanted to start, and I . . . started.'

'Why?'

Russell thinks for a minute.

'Because it was there.'

'The guitar?'

'Yes. When we unpacked all the stuff from Malaysia, I discovered my dad had a guitar.'

'Right . . . so . . .'

'I decided I wanted to play it.'

'But there must have been something about it you liked, fella. Otherwise, what . . . if your dad produced a tennis racket, would you have started playing tennis?'

'No. I don't like tennis.'

'Well, there you go, so there must have been something about the guitar you liked *more* . . . more than . . .'

'My dad played it.'

'The guitar?'

Russell nods. 'Yes. He played it and sang in front of me, and I liked it.'

'What did he play?'

Russell thinks.

'"Johnny B. Goode".'

'There you are. And you liked it.'

'Yes,' Russell confirms. 'The sound, the chords, the song. I loved it.'

'Well, that's it, then, Russ,' Ash smiles, sealing up his joint and rising. 'That's your answer. That's what it all means. Music. You love it.'

Ash tousles Russ's hair.

'See you in a bit, fella.'

He wanders over to the others by the bar.

'I love it,' Russell murmurs, and remains seated in the darkened corner for a bit, sipping the last of a bottle. But then, realising he is no longer required, and for once having no gear to shift or car to drive, he decides the rest of the night can get along without him. After-show drink be damned. He can make friends with JJ72 another time. He silently leaves the bar, grabs his jacket and his shoulder bag from the dressing room and wanders out, down the stairs, down the familiar corridors, automatically pausing by the stage door to sign out with security.

'You don't need to sign out tonight, Russ,' Harry laughs.

'Oh,' Russell smiles. 'Of course I don't.'

'Old habits die hard, eh?'

Russell nods. 'They certainly do.'

A steady rain now falls outside; Russell dons his jacket and trudges along, occasionally repeating Ash's phrase – 'I love it' – with varying quantities of uncertainty. It's not completely clear whether he's aware he's speaking out loud, he appears so troubled. As Wimbledon Broadway rounds its way into Merton

Road, Russell strengthens his enunciation of the phrase, anticipating further reflections.

'I love it,' he says finally, *'but . . .'*

But what?

'But in what other situation do you have to . . .' – he pauses, shaking his head while locating the correct expression – 'do so much damage, for something you love?'

Well . . . maybe to be successful in any field, a certain amount of ruthlessness is required.

'I know, but . . . with music . . . it seems wrong. Look at Ash. Look how much he adores music. And he's right. Music is such a . . . wonderful thing, a joyful thing, a peaceful, inclusive, natural thing . . . why does all this . . . *drive* for success have to come along and ruin it? And it *is* ruining it,' he nods, waiting for a car to halt at a zebra crossing. 'Look at me. I'm making terrible mistakes. I'm running onstage late. I'm . . . drinking, something I said I'd *never* do. I've hurt, upset and probably spoilt the life of a man who – oh, a bit of professional irritation aside – has never really lifted a finger to hurt me in his life. And I've ruined a friendship with a girl who . . . who . . . fuck, let's be finally honest here, a girl who I once . . . who I once . . .'

He stands still for a second as the wind blows a particularly bitter blast of rain into his eyes.

'I'm *swearing*. I'm taking *drugs!*'

In return for . . .

'For nothing! I'm dividing my songwriting credits to make life easier for a man I detest! I'm handing over half of what I do to a DAT machine! I've squeezed myself into a position where I actually consider myself useless, superfluous and not . . . *belonging*. That's it! I should have said this to Ash. That's the other reason I started to do all of this – well, started to do it seriously, anyway – I wanted to belong. And now I don't belong! I don't. That's the irony. I've been doing all that stuff to fit in, and the more I do, the less I fit! *I'm* the odd one out. They were fantastic tonight . . . without me. Before I hit that stage, they were great. I came on . . . and I added nothing. It's me. I'm the reason. *I'm* the weakest link. I'm the reason. All along, I've been the reason.'

Disagreeing with Russell on this seems pointless, so he is left to wander off unhappily in the direction of Colliers Wood, plainly caught in a spiral of negativity, but one which is unlikely to be so acute tomorrow.

At least, that's what one would imagine. But a quick check of his emails when he awakes the next morning reveals something which plummets his state of mind back down towards new, record-breaking depths.

From: X MORGAN
              (MORGAN@MORGANX.freeserve.co.uk)
Sent: 25 September 2001 22:52:09
To: russellcgroom@yahoo.co.uk
Subject: Fwd: Re: Josh Chigwell

Groom
This won't fill you with happiness but I thought you should see it anyway.
You were grand tonight especially the first song (joke).
Morg

> From: "Limpet" <info@limpet.co.uk>
> Sent: 25 September 2001 16:02:37

> To: "X MORGAN"
>   <MORGAN@MORGANX.freeserve.co.uk>
> Subject: Re: Josh Chigwell
>

> Mate
> Sorry not replied sooner, just got back from tour.
> Do not touch Josh Chigwell with a bargepole. I
spent two miserable years in his company. He starts
out OK but soon reveals himself to be the two-faced,
lying little cunt that he is.
> If you want a laugh before you tell him to piss off,
ask him to show you his dad's name on some
records.
> But if you do end up working with him, my only
advice is for fuck's sake hang onto your songwriting
credits.
> Good luck
> Chris
>
>
>

Southfields

Russell spends the next ten days hiding in his bedsit: 'Hiding from life,' as he describes it. He decided, with Will Gibson's blessing, to take a holiday from the Imperial, having not done so in some three years, and with nothing in the band's diary – everything apparently placed on hold while they wait for the deal to be struck – no one seems remotely fussed about rehearsing.

'The stupidity continues,' he mopes. 'The further we get, the less we do.'

In the end, to Russell's continued bewilderment, Barry and Josh have elected to go with Eluxor, who turn out to have the best understanding of the band's music, the most appropriate financial package (while certainly not the largest advance) and the best ideas for the campaign ahead. They have also moved the fastest. First label to get the deal on the table, very few quibbles with Barry's lawyer, and eager to sign as soon as possible.

'Apparently,' Russell comments. 'Because our involvement has been practically non-existent. We were given a cursory opportunity to contribute to this decision via email, but Ash and Karen never make even the most passing contribution to electronic discussion.'

And yourself?

'I couldn't bring myself to hit the "reply" button,' he frowns, flicking his television from *Neighbours* to *Home and Away*. 'I *want* to care . . . but every time I engage my mind in the details or mechanics of the whole thing, I instantly start to feel sick, like I'm going to pass out.'

At one point over the last week, Russell phoned Ash.

'I rang him up and told him how I felt. He couldn't talk for long, though . . . he was at work. He told me to have one of my beers and chill out.'

Did you?

'I opened one,' Russell says, 'but it started to make me feel positive so I knew something was wrong. I poured it down the sink and made myself an espresso.'

Did you tell Ash about the email from Limpet?

'No,' Russell admits. 'I'm scared to. I don't know how he'll react. Ash can be surprisingly fiery sometimes. He might accuse me of trying to jinx everything. Or if he gets genuinely mad at Josh and threatens to blow the lid, then the whole thing could be over. Which . . . I suppose I don't want to happen.'

The deal signing is set for the following Monday, and Russell finds himself hurtling towards the fate with a momentum he seems curiously powerless to stop. 'Perhaps I'm like a spacecraft being attracted by a planet's gravity,' he muses. 'The length of time I've been trying to get signed is equal to the gravity, and now I'm being sucked in, although every bone in my body is telling me I'm making a mistake.'

This quandary is also reflected in Russell's appearance. It turns out that his insistence on daily shaving has always been triggered by his venturing outdoors; consequently he is now sporting a rather bum-fluffy beard. In addition, his unwaxed hair has acquired a rather unfortunate helmet shape, and it is some days since he has worn his contact lenses. Midway through Tuesday morning on the way back from the lavatory, Russell bumps into one of his co-residents, who grumpily asks him whose house guest he is.

It is Morgan who eventually breaks through the barrier, and steers his old friend onto a slightly different gravitational course – even if it initially steers him only as far as Southfields. He rings on the Wednesday, and asks Russell why on earth he hasn't shown up for any of their writing sessions.

'I've been afraid to leave the house,' Russell confesses, without being completely melodramatic. Morgan advises him that he get his arse over to the studio fairly promptly, or he will delete Russell's favourite reverb plug-in from his hard drive.

'Delete it,' Russell says. 'It's too late for reverb now.'

The one thing Morgan does manage to do, wisely thinking it will hold an additional draw for Russell, is suggest that he talk to Karen.

'He said for me to print out the Limpet message and go round there,' Russell says.

Are you going to?

Russell stares at his floor, now littered with dirty plates and pizza boxes.

'Maybe,' Russell shrugs, tossing his phone onto his bed. 'But

I'm not sure. Morgan thinks that I've gone barmy, of course. Perhaps I have. But it's impossible to explain to people.'

He finally pulls himself together on the Sunday afternoon, the eve of the feted signing. He might have left it this long out of sheer lethargy; a more likely explanation is that it's now rather too late for Karen to comfortably do anything about it. He prints out the email, has two double espressos in a row and half a bottle of Honey Dew, and marches, wide-eyed and breathing rapidly, over to Karen's flat.

'Jesus,' Karen gasps, opening her front door and blinking at his appearance. 'It's Robinson fucking Crusoe.'

'Sorry,' Russell says. 'I've been . . . um . . . experimenting.'

'I see,' Karen nods. 'Are you all right?'

'Kind of.'

They stand there for a moment, Russell tapping one of his feet on Karen's doorstep. Karen, it must be said, doesn't look a picture of vitality herself – dark rings under her eyes and the possibility that she's been crying. She seems reluctant to let Russell in. He looks past her for any evidence of a visitor – a unicycle, perhaps, propped up in her hallway; as he walked up Karen's street, he kept an eye out for Josh's convertible.

'Don't you think,' Russell begins, 'that this is *weird*? I mean . . . tomorrow we're signing a record deal. We're about to achieve the thing we've been trying to achieve for over three years. And we haven't seen each other in almost two weeks.'

Karen leans against her door frame and sighs.

'Yeah . . . but I guess I've just seen it as the calm before the storm. We're going to be seeing each other every day for the next . . . well, who knows.'

'Mmm,' Russell replies, fingering the piece of folded-up paper in his pocket. 'I still think it's very odd. You, er . . . heard from Josh?'

'No . . . he's been seeing his mum.'

'Ah. So you have heard from him.'

'Only to tell me that.'

'Right.'

Finally, perhaps realising this isn't necessarily going to be a quick visit, Karen stands aside and ushers Russell in. They sit on opposing armchairs in Karen's lounge, VH1 dribbling forth at a low volume.

'Do you wanna coffee?'

'No,' Russell winces, 'I'd better not.'

'That's a first.'

'Mmm.'

Russell extracts the piece of paper from his pocket and takes a deep breath. Then they say each other's names at the same time.

'Karen, I . . .'

'Russ?'

'Sorry,' Russell says. 'You go ahead.'

'No, you,' Karen insists, lighting a cigarette.

Russell unfolds his piece of paper.

'You've written a speech?'

'No . . . this is just . . .'

He quickly scans the email.

'What is it?' Karen mutters.

VH1 starts playing 'Goddess On A Hiway' by Mercury Rev, which Russell gapes at.

'Russ . . . are you sure you don't need a coffee or something?'

Still Russell says nothing. Finally, after about half the song, he hands the email to Karen. She scans it for a second, then makes a face and flicks the email printout onto the carpet.

'Ugh. He told me about that lot. Bunch of cocks. Blamed Josh for the fact they got dropped, then refused to allow Josh to take any of his songs with him.'

'*His* songs?'

'His songs,' Karen nods.

'But Josh doesn't write songs.'

'Oh, Russ, don't start all that shit again. He may not have written any songs for us yet, but that doesn't mean –'

'No, no – he *told* me, the first time we ever met, he's never been much of a songwriter.'

'And? Maybe he isn't. He'd have to *try* writing songs to know that, though, wouldn't he?'

'Yeah, but . . .'

They stare at the TV for a further minute. Mercury Rev has given way to an unlovable Papa Roach video.

'What about the other stuff?' Russell asks.

'It's all hearsay, isn't it?'

'Well . . . not really. I mean, his dad's either a producer, or he isn't.'

'Russell, the early seventies was chocka with records that weren't credited properly.'

Russell giggles.

'What?'

'Sorry, Karen. But that's a direct quote from Josh. "Chocka". I mean, really . . .'

'No, it fucking isn't!'

'Yes, it is. And I'm sorry, but also – how would you know that, anyway? The early seventies isn't exactly your era, is it?'

'Russell, sometimes I fucking –'

'I mean, I know you're biased –'

'And what the fuck do you mean by that?'

More silence, while the Papa Roach guy eats his microphone. Soon a hiveful of insects starts to exit his mouth.

'Sorry, that's doing my head in,' Karen shudders, flicking the telly off. She stubs out her cigarette and immediately lights a new one. Russell continues to stare at the switched-off television.

'Look,' Karen sighs, 'if it makes any of this any better, I'm sorry about what happened in Sussex. OK?'

Russell bites his thumb.

'Like I said at the time, I can be a total cowbag sometimes. I shouldn't have . . . oh, led you on, whatever you want to call it.'

'Mmm,' Russell responds. 'It's all right.'

'No, Russ, it's not all right. I shouldn't have put you in that position. I'm . . . oh . . . I dunno. Confused.'

'Uh.'

Karen rises and walks over to the window, then exhales a plume of smoke across the room.

'But that doesn't mean you can start ripping all of this apart. I mean, what are you trying to achieve by coming over here and showing me this email? What do you want me to do?'

'Nothing, I just thought you should —'

'It's like you actually want me to turn round and say, "Oh, OK, fuck it, the bloke's a dick, let's ditch him and start all over again." Is that it, Russ? Don't forget — it was *you* who started all this —'

'I know.'

'— it was *you* who got me and Ash together and suggested —'

'I know! But since . . .'

'Since?' Karen glares.

Russell sighs. 'Since the Imperial I've started to wonder whether it isn't *me* we should have chucked out.'

Karen winces. 'What *are* you talking about?'

Russell's eyes dart about the room nervously.

'Well . . . it's me now, isn't it . . . making the mistakes. Doing the . . . unprofessional things.'

'But –'

'Disagreeing with the . . . signed element.'

'Oh Christ, Russell. That was *one night*, wasn't it? It was unfortunate, but –'

'A very important night.'

'– it's not going to happen again, is it?'

'Probably not, no,' Russell says quietly, almost to himself.

'And don't worry about bloody Barry. He may have contacts leaking from his backside, but that doesn't stop me and Ash thinking he's an arsehole.'

Russell looks up at her dubiously.

'What's that look for?' she snaps.

'Ash and you agree with everything he says.'

'We don't!'

'Well, that's the way it seems. Or is it that you just agree with Josh?'

'Russell . . .'

'And what are those lyrics about?'

'What lyrics?'

'Josh has changed my lyrics in "You Brought It On Yourself". "*What makes you think you're fooling us, Cos we can see straight through it*"? What's that all about? It seems to be about me now.'

Karen shakes her head with utter confusion. 'Russ, are you out of your mind? Have you finally lost it?'

Russell looks down at the carpet unhappily. Karen, still chain-smoking like a lifer, kneels down and absent-mindedly tidies some of the videotapes.

'And what about his stepdad?' Russell suddenly blurts.

'What about him?'

'Josh's stepdad is some huge player in the music industry . . .'

'Yes, Russell. What problem are you going to have with that, then?'

'Well, he's probably been . . .'

'. . . putting in a good word for us here and there? Probably.'

'But also, he . . .'

'. . . is paying for Bing and Barry at the moment, yes.'

'*Paying?*' Russell gasps. 'For Bing and Barry?'

'Yes, Russell. Satisfied? Both of them are on retainers. Part of Josh's mum and stepdad's plan to get Josh to do something with his life.'

'. . . Uh?'

'Partly that, and partly to make up for how badly they treated Josh as a teenager.'

Russell looks agog. Karen smiles thinly at him.

'There you go. You see? You learn a few things occasionally when you go on drug binges with people.'

'You've known since *then*?'

'Yes, Russell. And no, I didn't bother telling you, cos I knew you'd react just like you're reacting now. But for God's sake . . . isn't this all bloody getting us somewhere? At last?'

Russell screws up his face and plays with his unusually messy hair. 'But . . . it's so . . .'

'So what?'

'. . . contrived!'

'Why? Come on. How d'you think anyone gets anywhere in the music business? The Famous Dad theory? So isn't it our bloody turn now?'

'No, no . . . not like this . . . Karen, really . . . it doesn't feel right . . . it's . . . dishonest.'

'*How* is it dishonest?'

'Just in the same way that . . . Josh hijacking my songs is dishonest . . .'

Karen sits back down on her armchair again.

'Look, I realise that's bothering you, and I know the guy ain't perfect. He can be a little underhand. He's a messed-up boy and he's got his problems. But we'll sort it out. We'll see to it that you, me and Ash are always in the driving seat.'

Russell scoffs at her and takes a breath to retort, but then turns his head away again. His eyes settle on the poster above Karen's mantelpiece: a well-known 1982 photograph of The Clash, engaged in a frantic pre-gig huddle before taking to the stage at New York's Shea Stadium in support of The Who. Although the picture manages to conceal the problems The Clash themselves were experiencing at the time (long-time drummer Topper Headon recently fired, friction between Joe Strummer and Mick Jones), it is pretty obvious what Russell is thinking as, mouth wide open, he studies it.

Later, he will confirm this, and also admit to feeling something he never believed he would feel.

'The thing is, I've always hated The Clash. Never knew what the fuss was about. A silly mixture of styles, weird production, strange rants rather than lyrics, no discernible melodies. But there they were in front of me . . . the four of them, an unbreakable unit, that almost insane look of collective concentration, about to tear into I suppose the biggest gig of their career . . . and they looked like a gang, a clan, a pack of wild animals. We'll *never* look like that. Here we are, about to close the deal – whatever that means – and we're as unified as a recently divorced couple. And suddenly I understood what Barry was blabbing about swagger . . . as frightful as he is, he's got a point. The Clash have enough swagger in that photo to power an aeroplane.'

But . . .

'But what?'

But you've *got* the record deal.

'Oh, come *on*! I've had enough of this devil's advocate business. You've been around long enough to see the truth. It's obvious. We're dead. We're as dead as a headless chicken. We might run around for a while, but we'll collapse within . . . I don't know, months. And I know it sounds funny – but for the first time, I just sat there in Karen's dingy little lounge, looking over at her knackered face, breathing in her smoke, and I really did think . . . it's actually all right. I don't need to keep pushing, arguing. I don't need it. It's not me any more. I've been fighting something within myself for too long . . . years. And none of it means anything. I knew just then what I needed to do. She probably thinks I've gone insane. But on the contrary . . . I think that for the first time in ages, my mind is actually working properly.'

Back in her lounge, Karen attempts to wrap up the argument with a cheerful, stirring rejoinder.

'And at the end of the day . . . think of it like this, Russ. It's you and me and Ash, winning at the game we've been struggling at for ages. When we walk out of that office tomorrow afternoon, and go and have that little celebratory drink, we'll have finally won. And we'll have done it *our* way. Just imagine – telling Raz at the rehearsal room, or those knobs from PTT, or even Morgan, that we've done it. We're *signed*.'

She enunciates the word, and in the carpeted quiet of her front room it seems to acquire a new quality. She intends it to sound like the promised land, of course. But as it vanishes into the threadbare sofas and electric heater of her rented flat, into the pile of CDs on the mantelpiece, into the numerous ashtrays, dirty teacups and empty wine glasses, the word sounds like a sentence.

Russell grabs the creased sheet of paper from the floor, quickly rises and – to Karen's total astonishment – makes his excuses and heads for the door.

'Russ?' Karen yelps, a definite hint of desperation now colouring her speech. 'I'll see you tomorrow, yeah? Corner of Regent's Park Road and Gloucester Avenue?'

'Yeah,' Russell grunts, letting himself out.

He shuts the door. Not turning to Karen's pale face as it stares at him through the lounge window, he shuffles down the little path, then marches to the end of Karen's street, his steps becoming more confident by the second. He rips the email printout into four pieces, discards them in a nearby litter bin, then continues home.

Primrose Hill

The day is bright and clear, but with a slight October chill. Russell, dressed in some slightly battered jeans, a Radiohead T-shirt and a charcoal-grey suit jacket, ambles along Regent's Park Road, breathing deeply as he glances into shop windows and looks at his watch. Although visibly nervous, there is something relaxed about his bearing – a certain lightness. His hair, left uncut for the longest time since that day in 1994 when he chopped his grunge-era locks, escapes over his forehead and looks unwashed, but somehow matches his ensemble. He has, at last, shaved. The final touch, strange to no one but the people who know Russell best, is his glasses. His metal-rimmed specs, which he hardly ever wears outside. Until today.

Today is the day Russell's band sign their record deal.

Today – Monday, 8 October 2001. Russell has, of course,

worked it out. Three years, four months and twenty-three days since the day Jake joined the band, and therefore the day it all officially began. Not bad going, really. Quicker than Pulp, slower than Menswear. And now here he is, in Primrose Hill, celebrity playground. Bobby Gillespie meanders past, humming something to himself, and turns left into the post office. Even rock stars need to send letters occasionally.

Russell heads up to the northern end of the street and comes to a halt outside an office on the left, where the historic signing is to take place. He stops, and looks at his watch. Two o'clock. One hour until lift-off.

He crosses the street, slips through the line of expensively parked cars, and strides into the pub by the railway bridge. The Pembroke Castle. A fortifying drink. Jake always used to have fortifying drinks, didn't he? A little something to take the edge off. Russell never used to understand this. Now he does. He phoned ahead, to check they serve his favourite drink. Some pubs don't. Some pubs, apparently, don't like to bother with it. Russell can't think why.

He wanders up to the bar and smiles at the barman.

'A black coffee, please.'

'Sure.'

The barman busies himself making the drink for a minute or two, then turns back to Russell.

'Milk?'

Russell can't help laughing.

'The clue was in the word black,' he says.

The barman rolls his eyes.

'Duh, sorry. Going deaf.'

Russell takes his cup to the elevated back area of the pub, which looks out over the railway lines as they trundle towards

King's Cross. Flickers of sunlight drift through the windows, and Russell is for a moment simply, quietly content. A moment later, he feels the presence of a small young lady next to him. He turns.

'Miki.'

'Hi! Sorry, I'm a little late . . .'

'No, you're not. Can I get you a drink?'

'I should really be getting you one,' she smiles. 'To celebrate.'

'That's sweet of you, but don't worry,' Russell says, rising. 'You see – I have some news for you.'

'News?' Miki blinks, putting down her bag and taking off her denim jacket. 'Even *more* news?'

'Yes,' laughs Russell. 'But I'd better get your drink, though.'

'Why?' Miki giggles, putting her camera on the table and flicking her hair back. 'Am I going to need it?'

Russell laughs again and glances nervously around the pub.

Minutes later, Miki is clutching her glass of rum and Coke, regarding Russell with rather worried eyes. She hasn't known him very long, and might start to believe she's in the company of a raving nutter. Russell hasn't much time.

'I know,' he says, 'that this is going to seem irrational, crazy. But honestly, I have my reasons.'

'You're going to have to tell me them, then,' Miki says.

'I will,' nods Russell. 'But first, I have a favour to ask of you.'

'What's that?'

'Could you take a couple more photos?'

'Sure,' Miki chuckles, nodding at her camera. 'What do you think I brought this along for?'

'No . . . not of me. I mean, band photos.'

'Band photos?' she frowns. 'Now?'

Russell bites his bottom lip, then sips his coffee and looks back out of the window.

ASH: We've got what we wanted. Well, what I think we wanted. It's going to take a while for it all to sink in. Obviously I'm confused and upset about Russell, but at the end of the day, there was something wrong, and he did what was right for him. He went about it a pretty shitty way, but that's Russell – he doesn't do things by halves. If he's efficient, he's incredibly efficient. If he's selfish and unthinking, he's just that – thoughtless, beyond belief. Always with this constant thing that his way is the right way. And if he couldn't have the dream his own way, he didn't want any of the dream. He's unable to bend – he just breaks.

Miki shuffles uneasily in her seat.

'I'm feeling . . . more than a little responsible.'

'Why?' Russell blinks.

'I feel like I've sent you on a downward spiral with Josh.'

'No . . .'

'I shouldn't have told you that stuff. It was so unprofessional of me.'

'It was off the record. Wasn't it?'

'But still.'

'And honestly,' Russell smiles, 'it didn't make that much difference. I already knew those things. You haven't made *that* much of an impact on me.'

'Oh, shucks,' Miki replies, with mock disappointment.

'Well, no,' Russell laughs, 'even that's not quite true. In fact, this is all your fault.'

'Now you *are* winding me up.'

'Kind of. But I have to admit . . . in the end, it came down to that one question, "What does it all mean?"'

Miki hides behind her drink, covered with embarrassment. 'Oh no! *That!*'

'Really. If you can't find meaning in what you do, there's no point in doing it. And that's really all that matters.'

Miki shrugs and looks around uncomfortably.

'So . . . what now?'

'More music. Of course. But . . . done in a way that I don't feel is strangling me, and messing up other people's lives. We'll see.'

'No, I mean, literally – what now? You're just going to sit here?'

'No . . . I'm . . . going over there. We have a meeting. I can't stand them up. I'm meeting them on the corner at three, then I'll walk over there with them, and bring my own viewpoint to the table.'

Miki gapes back at him.

'My own unique viewpoint,' he elaborates.

'But . . . aren't they going to rip your limbs off?'

Russell takes almost a minute to stop laughing. When he finally does, it's pretty obvious that he is absolutely terrified of this very outcome.

KAREN: When Russell first started to get really frustrated – and it was around the same time as I split up with that boyfriend, so we were seeing quite a lot of each other, as you remember – he told me about this story in a book he had when he was a kid in Malaysia. There was a little boy, a really naughty little boy, who spent all his time driving his parents mad cos he was so naughty, so mischievous. And one day this witch showed up in his back garden, on her broomstick (*laughs*) – bear with me – and the witch goes to him, 'Hello, little boy. I can see you're a really naughty little tyke. Well, some other witches and I run a school, for naughty boys, to make them even naughtier. I think you'd like it.' So the little boy's like 'Great!' – and he runs off and tells his parents. His folks come out to the garden and see this witch, and the witch tells them all about the school, and they think about it and after a while decide it'd be best for the little boy to go along to the school. So he says goodbye to his folks, gets on the broomstick with the witch and they fly off. (*Rolls her eyes.*) Yeah, I know . . . So he gets to the school – but it's terrible, because all the boys there are even naughtier! Plus, they're not only, um . . . *conventionally* naughty, they're putting spells on each other, turning the teachers into plant pots, murdering cats, the works. And our little boy hasn't got a *hope* of being anywhere near as naughty as the other kids, they're all so fucked up. He does a few really wet things like kicking a door down or, I dunno, tipping a desk out the window or something, but it's no use. So the witches have a meeting with the little boy and decide it's probably better if he goes home again, he's so hopeless.

Well of course, Russ used to use this little tale as a bit of a rubbish analogy of himself trying to get somewhere in the music industry. He is good at music . . . actually he's *great* at music . . . and in his own little pond – whether it's at school, or uni, or the unsigned circuit, or in our band, particularly when Jake was still with us – he's the fucking *man*. He's naughtier than anyone. He knows more than anyone, he writes better songs than anyone, he plays better than anyone. But he's always had this enormous complex. And he found it difficult to admit to this – Jake didn't, Russell did. On the grand stage, in the music business at large, he wasn't quite good enough. Or rather, he wasn't *bad* enough. He tried doing bad things, but it just plainly wasn't his style. And I think it started affecting him terribly, and he just couldn't go on.

But the analogy doesn't quite work, does it?

KAREN: How come?

Because in the end . . . he was *getting somewhere.*

KAREN: But not on his own terms. Far, far from his own terms. Going back on promises he'd made to himself, surrendering control of things most close to his heart. Booting Jake out affected Russell much, much more than it did Ash and me. And I think, in the end, nothing made sense any more. Ash and me have . . . crossed over, if you like. Russell didn't. In his mind, the old band was well and truly dead, and he didn't like the band we became. So, no – ultimately I don't think it was really that hard a decision to make.

Oh, yeah – and you know what happened at the end of Russell's kids' story? The little boy arrives home, and his folks are really pleased to see him, and guess what? From that moment onwards, he's not naughty any more.

Miki looks up at the clock – one minute to three – then out of the pub's front window, where Karen and Josh can now be seen hanging about.

'Don't look,' says Russell, finishing the last of his coffee.

'They're crossing the street –'

'I said don't look!' Russell smiles.

Miki looks back at the clock, checks a few settings on her camera, inhales, then looks up at the clock again.

'Stop looking at the clock,' Russell instructs, grinning and staring straight at Miki's face. 'It's making me nervous.'

'Are you . . . are you sure about all this?'

'Yes,' Russell replies, turning his head slightly and drinking in the view of the now overcast but still bright sky over the railway line. 'I'm sure. Probably surer than I've ever been of anything.'

Outside, Ash has just appeared next to the others – as usual, looking hot and sweaty from the Tube station.

'OK,' Russell mutters, putting on his suit jacket and gathering up his bag, for the long walk across the road. 'It's time. Are you ready?'

Miki nods, then takes his hand and gives it a squeeze. Russell gives her a sad but grateful smile and turns, without a word, towards the door. He soon appears on the pavement, his band-mates eyeing him strangely as he crosses over (possibly wondering why he's just emerged from a pub). As soon as Russell joins the others, the four of them turn away and start strolling up the street. Miki grabs her camera and rushes out of the pub.

The previously clear sky has started to darken and a brisk breeze swirls about. As quickly and inconspicuously as she can, Miki scampers across the road and positions herself behind a tree, where she fiddles with her zoom, then darts out and takes a few snaps. But her subject is presently just a clutch of random, disparate people walking away from her, not even in an inter-esting formation – it could be anybody. She waits for a moment; perhaps they will naturally realign themselves. Then Ash pauses and turns round; Miki leaps back behind the tree. Ash relights his roll-up, cupping his hand against the wind. When he turns back the four members fall into a perfect line, symmetrically spaced across the pavement. Miki tiptoes up behind them and crouches down, firing off half a dozen exposures, the wind concealing the sound of her shutter. Now there might be something usable. She leaps back into hiding and gets her breath back. But she is still not satisfied. There is a particular image in her head, conjured up by Russell's brief, and she hasn't yet caught it.

The band are ambling over the road to their destination, weaving between parked cars and slow-moving vehicles. Miki waits until they are all on the other side, then scuttles out, almost crashing straight into a cyclist who shouts some kind of rebuke as he races past. Russell obviously hears this and shoots a worried glance back towards Miki, who shrugs, then dives down between a motorbike and a blue Volkswagen Beetle. She hurriedly adjusts her equipment and peeks out, then squeezes in five or six shots before the scene changes; among them, as they say, is the 'money shot':

Above an erratic, autumn-leaf-strewn London pavement, four people stand by an unmarked white door in a smart parade of shops. A cool-looking guy – perhaps the most 'rock star'-looking character, with black combats, a three-quarter-length leather coat, floppy black hair and wraparound shades – drags on a cigarette with one hand and buzzes the intercom with the other. Watching next to him is a girl, rather whimsically dressed in purple flares and a battered sheepskin jacket. To the left of her, a short bloke with blond locks and noticeable brown roots, facing the other way, but in front of whom can be seen a fog of smoke. Finally, unsteadily hovering at the edge of the frame, a taller man, the only face to be pointing towards the camera, a face full of concern. Concern for what? a viewer might wonder. For the immediate future: for the highfalutin gathering that awaits inside, for an announcement he might be about to make – or beyond all that, the consequences of the meeting, the path it may set them on for the next six months, year, two years? Or perhaps concern for something completely different – the people along the way he has managed to upset, has argued with, distanced himself from. But behind his un-fashionable but oddly appropriate spectacles, there is perhaps a glint of optimism. Optimism for a life with, at last, different possibilities. Above the four figures, the sky continues to darken and seems to reflect the general air of unease and ambiguity, as the entire frame suggests the unsteady beginning of something – but also, unavoidably, the end.

Epilogue

Miki Hayashi's photo, entitled 'Death of an Unsigned Band', appeared, with a small accompanying article, in the December 2001 issue of *Zinehead*, and has become something of an underground classic in the field of rock photography. Hayashi has subsequently been offered numerous photographic assignments for the mainstream rock press, which she combines with her work for Amnesty International. She still works for *Zinehead*.

An original print of the photograph hangs behind the upstairs bar of the Hawley Arms in Camden Town.

After almost a month's renegotiation, Josh, Karen and Ash's contract with Eluxor was finally signed at the end of November 2001. Upon sealing the deal, they were presented with a list of band names, among them Doreen, The Willow Wheys and The Method, eventually settling for The Fixture. With the exception of 'Krystal Palace' and 'River Song', Russell Groom allowed the band to continue to use his songs, on the proviso that his name be removed from all credits and press releases, and from the band biography.

The Fixture spent the remainder of 2001 and the early part of the new year recording, firstly for an EP, and then for what was intended to be their debut album, also playing sporadic gigs around London and the UK. Their debut release, *Fleece EP*, came out in April 2002 and was largely ignored by the music press. A second EP, *Thameslink*, was released in July, described by *NME* as 'music for people who have no curiosity about the future'. In September, having suffered months of financial woes, Eluxor went into administration, leaving The Fixture with a completed album but no record deal.

Karen Frost and Ash Williams left the band in October, jointly citing 'emotional and financial exhaustion'. They are currently working on a new musical project (described by Karen as 'folk-core') together with Ash's former collaborator Dave Black, and are expected to tour in 2003 under the name Quirkafleeg.

Josh Chigwell retained the rights to the Fixture name, and to the unreleased album. He is presently attempting to recruit new musicians.

Jake Wilcox and Sarah Nuttall reunited ('for good, this time') in the spring of 2002. Nearing the end of her teaching quali-fication, Sarah began to look for teaching jobs, eventually finding a suitable position in Lymington, Hampshire, where the couple moved in July. Jake, securing a business mortgage with the as-sistance of his parents, purchased a run-down pub in the town and converted it into a small rock club, which opened in the autumn. The venue's first few months have boasted a pair of well-attended shows by rapidly ascending rockers The Darkness.

Morgan, whose first name remains unknown, has continued to write and record pop songs, on his own and with Russell Groom. In early 2002 Morgan began to post finished demos on various file-sharing Internet sites – 'It's the only way forward,' he commented.

In October he reported that a number of these songs were being considered by Russian pop act t.A.T.u. – this, however, could not be verified.

Russell Groom and Miki Hayashi became a couple during the late autumn of 2001. With Miki's encouragement, Russell applied for various voluntary jobs in the developing world, via such organisations as the British Council and the VSO. In the spring of 2002 he was offered a six-month music teaching post in Ethiopia, which began in June. He and Miki travelled there together, where they currently reside.

He remains philosophical about his former ambition, but reflects that the hardest thing to stomach has been the death of his songs:

'When you spend so much time perfecting them, dreaming of them being danced to, blaring from car stereos, lyrics roared out at concerts – it's fairly difficult to accept that they won't be. That particular dream has died, and the only thing occupying that space in my head is a sort of numb disappointment. But I have fewer regrets than you'd imagine. It did all get pretty frantic. I truly can look back at some of it now and laugh.'

He is still largely teetotal, but admits to a weakness for the occasional glass of *Tej*, a strong Ethiopian honey wine.

ACKNOWLEDGEMENTS

For invaluable contributions, professional expertise, peripheral support and, in certain cases, deliverance from the gnashing jaws of insanity, the author would like to thank the following: Crestina, Guy Whittaker, Jannik Tai Mosholt, Dr Nick Coates, Andy 'Stickman' Harrower, Jonathan Lucas, Alex Ling, Jonathan Goldstein, Katherine Mengardon, Heledd Williams, Fin Greenall, Samar Mohebbi, Marcus and Bex Karenin, Sumit Bothra, the Library, the Parlour and Ryan's on Church Street, the Nobody Inn, the Gate and Trattoria Sapori on Newington Green, Cafe 101 on Brick Lane, the Backstage in Amsterdam, the Inn at Lincoln Park in Chicago, the Bayview Boulevard in Sydney, Georgina, Nico and Chiara (for small-hours inspiration), Damian Samuels, Robin Rimbaud, Matt Broughton and team, Dan Franklin and all at J. Cape, Matthew Hamilton, my agent at Aitken Alexander, Adrian Weston – and lastly Alex Bowler, for an editing job of heroic proportions.